HOMEBODIES

HOME BODIES

A NOVEL

Tembe Denton-Hurst

HARPER

An Imprint of HarperCollins*Publishers*

This is a work of fiction. Names, characters, places, and incidents are products of the author's imagination or are used fictitiously and are not to be construed as real. Any resemblance to actual events, locales, organizations, or persons, living or dead, is entirely coincidental.

HarperCollins books may be purchased for educational, business, or sales promotional use. For information, please email the Special Markets Department at SPsales@harpercollins.com.

FIRST EDITION

Library of Congress Cataloging-in-Publication Data has been applied for.

ISBN 978-0-06-327428-0

23 24 25 26 27 LBC 5 4 3 2 1

For the girls who look and love like me.

We work.
Lord do black girls and black women work.

—Tressie McMillan Cottom, *Thick*

HOMEBODIES

ONE

The day that everything changes tends to feel like any other, at least at first—which is why Mickey hadn't suspected anything when Chelsea Cooke asked her if she was going to that beauty event after work. The event was being thrown by a fancy fragrance brand known for peddling genderless perfumes that, to Mickey, smelled mostly like musky men's deodorant with occasional hints of gardenia or jasmine or rose. She expected to slog through it like all the other events she attended, trading niceties with the other writers and editors until it was time for her to go home. She didn't expect to find out that her job, the one she'd been doing for just shy of a year, was in jeopardy. This she would learn, over mixed drinks in a glass-walled penthouse overlooking the West Side Highway, from the very same Chelsea who had spoken to her all day as if she wasn't harboring this kind of life-altering news.

Mickey should've known something was up when, an hour into the event, Chelsea pulled her to the side and said, "So I want to tell you something, but you can literally never tell anyone that it came from me." But still, Mickey hadn't suspected anything. Chelsea and Mickey had never been friends, never leaned into the Black girl camaraderie that she'd hoped for. Outside of the occasional knowing look during an All Hands meeting, which sometimes resulted in Mickey gawking at Chelsea and her impressively sleek silk press, they rarely spoke. Chelsea was closer with the girls on her team, fashion-types who, in a past life, were

Midwest Christian-types born-again in fuzzy pink cardigans and Dries boots. But that didn't stop people from thinking they were closer than they were or (admittedly, rarely) mistaking one for another. Mickey had hoped the tides were turning, that perception had somehow morphed its way into the truth. She thought the next words out of Chelsea's mouth would be office tea: that someone was pregnant, or that their parent company, Bevy, was acquiring another digital property they had no business owning. Mickey nodded enthusiastically about keeping things secret and smiled conspiratorially, ignorant of her own demise. She'd even leaned in closer, so Chelsea wouldn't have to speak so loudly.

"A friend, and I can't tell you who," Chelsea began, taking a sip of her freshly mixed drink and plucking a convenient-to-eat cone of ceviche from a cater-waiter with shimmering bronze skin, "told me that Nina reached out and mentioned that there would be an opening on your team in a few months." She brought the cone to her mouth, and bit down. "For your role."

Mickey's chest seized violently at the news, but she held her face still, allowed a small "Oh" to escape from her lips. Chelsea continued to chew, staring at Mickey with an unreadable expression. It dawned on her that this wasn't an act of friendship, but one of duty. She was looking out, and Mickey was grateful. It's what she would do if the roles were reversed.

Now that Chelsea had gotten the big part out, the rest came easier. "My friend ignored her at first, but then Nina reached out again and asked for a meeting."

Mickey's mouth hung slightly open, and she felt the tears pressing at the back of her throat. They were tears of embarrassment, of incredulity, but she knew how they would read: as tears of despair. But she couldn't cry here, in an apartment she could never afford with people she saw no less than three times a week. It would be the talk of post-event wrap-ups between PR girls dressed in tasteful black: that Mickey had cried into a lobster ceviche and they all had to turn the other cheek. The other writers and editors would talk, too, waiting until the next beauty event to place a gentle hand on her forearm and ask if everything was okay. Mickey refused to give them the satisfaction. This isn't what she would be remembered for.

"Wow" was all she said. Twice, and then twice more, her voice thicker each time. She was surprised, given that just a few hours earlier, Nina had asked her to present a vision for the site's beauty and culture vertical. It was due in a few days, and Mickey had believed there was a small chance she was getting a promotion. That maybe everything she'd been through thus far was a sort of test to see if Mickey could handle more.

"I know. It's crazy. And my friend doesn't want it because she's happy where she is, but I just wanted to let you know so, you know," Chelsea sprinkled the debris from her hands into a napkin and stuffed it in her drained drink, the garnish stuck to the bottom with the leftover ice.

"Yeah, I know."

"I know this sucks."

"It does, but are we surprised? Nina's fucking incompetent and she never liked me anyway. You know she made me write a story twice, only to bury it with the help of her senior editor? And she didn't even tell me. The senior editor felt bad and let me know."

"They don't like us, period," Chelsea said with a nod of the head. Mickey hesitated to agree with that, because they very much liked Chelsea, who was a senior beauty editor at one of their sister sites. Although the two seemed worlds away online (Chelsea's publication catered to white, middle-aged women with bank accounts that didn't need checking and Mickey's was aimed squarely at the daughters with whom they had strained relationships), they only sat three rows apart. But she nodded anyway, because *us* was the shorthand for Black women in general, which Mickey would say was accurate. At least most of the time. They took synchronized sips of their endlessly refillable mixed drinks and traded gossip before calling Ubers home, but the air remained heavy, the unease encasing every word.

"How far away is yours?" Chelsea asked, her face illuminated by the blue light of her phone. The sun had plunged into the Hudson River hours ago, and now they were all burdened by their glassed reflections, the shimmering lights of New Jersey blinking back at them.

Mickey stopped her frantic texting to check. She'd fired off an SOS text to her industry group chat, composed of interns turned editors, friendships forged by fire. "Two minutes, you?" She checked her messages and frowned at the thick blue block of text staring back at her. No reply.

"Same, let's walk out."

Mickey gathered her things—a branded tote bag she carried all her work stuff in and even more totes filled with all the random products she'd received over the past few days—single-word brands that stood out with curved, pointed fonts and bright, punchy hues. Mickey's arm was a kaleidoscope of color. She headed for the door, and the bags sagged as she walked, weighing down her shoulder and cutting into her skin—a physical reminder that this was what she had asked for: the excess, the access, the burden.

"Hi ladies, did you enjoy the event?" a voice asked as they approached the exit. Mickey looked up from her phone to give the woman a once-over. She had a face she vaguely recognized and a name she was sure popped into her inbox at least once a day. Rows of identical, small black bags lined the floor behind her, continuing for what seemed like miles.

"Of course!" Chelsea gushed, and Mickey was reminded why Chelsea was beloved. She put in the effort to learn every PR person's name and the brands they represented, took every deskside meeting and went to all the events, bringing in business for the company and flitting from one thing to the next with the kind of unflappable enthusiasm Mickey reserved for weekends spent in bed. Mickey was a writer, full stop, something she reminded people of when they asked why they rarely saw her at events like these, rubbing shoulders with other writers and editors rather than trying to get ahead on her work. Between her overflowing inbox (five hundred new messages since the morning), brainstorming her next big idea (the fumes from her last viral article had died down over a year ago and another would prove she wasn't a fluke), and managing an untenable workload of three to four stories *a day*, she simply didn't have the time. *Had Chelsea only asked her to come because she wanted to tell Mickey she was being pushed out?* Mickey felt a prickle at the back of her neck. Something didn't feel quite right.

The voice produced two identical black bags, held outstretched and pinched between her well-manicured fingers. Mickey wondered briefly at the shade of pink dotting her hands, knowing they didn't make such a pink for her skin tone. She stared down at her own hands, critical of the bare half-moons jutting out from the base of her nail beds. She was due for a fill.

"It was so good to see you, Malinda!" Chelsea said as she pulled Mickey toward the elevator, which only had two stops: this apartment, and the bottom floor.

"Yes, we should do lunch!" Malinda called back, with Chelsea nodding enthusiastically until they were hidden by steel and plummeting gently but swiftly toward the ground, Mickey slightly nauseous by the time they stepped out.

"It's going to be okay girl," Chelsea said before squeezing a handful of Mickey's shoulder. Mickey tried not to cringe. The only thing she hated more than the implied pity of a shoulder squeeze was the pat pat of a sympathetic hug. "We've all been through some bullshit. And you're still so early in your career and so talented. You're going to be fine."

"I just don't get it," Mickey said, dividing her attention between Chelsea and her driver, Vijay, who was supposedly parked at the end of the street. Or was it the other corner? She couldn't be sure. All she knew was that the finality of Chelsea's statement was unnerving. "She asked me to present a whole creative vision board for her like two days ago. I thought she was going to give me more to do. Not like I'm not drowning already but I just thought . . ."

Chelsea cut in. "Have you never seen *Succession*? That's what the fuck they do. Bleed you dry and then cut you loose."

Mickey nodded, rocking back onto her heels before pressing her feet firmly into the ground. She turned to face Chelsea. "Can you tell me who?"

Chelsea smiled a strange smile and adjusted the small black bag hanging delicately from her fingertips. "Sorry, I can't. My friend made me promise not to say."

Mickey resisted the urge to roll her eyes. She didn't understand what difference it would make. "Okay," she allowed. "Is she?" Mickey ran her finger over the back of her hand.

"She is," Chelsea confirmed.

"Of course," Mickey said. "Thanks for looking out, girl."

"You know I got you, sis," Chelsea replied in a tone that surprised Mickey. She'd never pegged Chelsea as a code-switcher, that her voice could drop half an octave at will and get syrupy with a shared knowing. *Sis?* Mickey thought. *Interesting.*

Mickey couldn't tell if this was the beginning of something or the end. She thought of her potential replacement and cringed at the fact that she'd been so out of the loop, that she'd been caught so unaware. Then, that this new girl, Black like her, would likely meet a similar fate. She almost felt sorry for her, knowing what she was walking into: a once-cool and edgy publication now wholly dependent on clicks, chasing virality and relevancy rather than figuring out what they had to say. But the name still held weight. It had been weighty enough to keep Mickey transfixed, wanting, badly, for things to work out. The tears pressed at the back of her throat, more insistent this time, and Mickey swallowed them, hard.

She looked at Chelsea with new eyes, took in her sleek hair (today wound up into a perfectly messy bun), and the fluff of her sweater. Examined the height of her heel, and the curve of her jaw. Before this very moment, Mickey had admired her, been jealous even. Now, she wanted to kick her back to the white women she prayed to.

She checked her phone again. Still nothing from the group chat.

A black Toyota Camry pulled up in front of the building.

"Smart," Mickey commented. "I should've had him pull around."

Chelsea pulled open the door and ducked her head inside. "Roberto? Okay great." She looked back at Mickey as she eased into the car and waved. "Bye! Love you!"

Mickey forced herself to wave but she couldn't force herself to say love you, too. She did not love Chelsea, not even a little bit, and hated that the word had become a platitude.

As soon as Mickey shut the door of the Uber, the tears came. She cried all the way back to Astoria, grateful Vijay hadn't looked into the rearview mirror to ask if she was okay or turned up the music louder to drown out her sobbing. She knew she looked pathetic, but didn't even bother to wipe her face clean, tears marking her cheeks.

It wasn't long before they pulled up to her apartment building, a boxy taupe-colored structure with a brick façade and very little curb appeal. It was populated with a mix of families who had lived there for over a decade and people like Mickey, who had snapped up the newly renovated units at a premium price. She tried to gather herself before getting out of the Uber, and then remembered she had arrived at the one place she didn't have to perform.

She thanked her driver and took a moment to let the last bite of spring chill cool her skin. *She would be okay either way.* This is what she told herself as she stepped into the elevator, trying to talk herself down as she inched closer to her apartment. She reached the fifth floor, took a deep breath, and was nearly composed by the time she turned the key in apartment 504.

Mickey opened the door and found her partner, Lex, on the other side. She didn't turn her head toward Mickey—she was in her own world, her headphones plugged into her ears, the music so loud that Mickey could hear the tinny bassline from across the room. She was dancing while she cooked dinner, moving her smooth, thin limbs in time to the beat. Mickey wanted to keep crying and wallowing, but she was distracted by her woman and the ease with which she moved. It was clear that Lex was not having a terrible day. She was having the kind of day that allowed her to shake her hips and glide across their hardwood floor.

Mickey took her in: Lex was in her house clothes—a T-shirt and a pair of bright red mesh shorts—which were covered by an apron cinched at the waist, stained from her many colorful concoctions, yellow-green curries and sauces that refused to come out in the wash. It was evidence of her alchemy, her ability to turn raw materials into something more. Her curly brown hair, kinks smoothed by smears of gel and a mixed Jamaican heritage, was tied back into a bun, showing off her features. Her high cheekbones pointed toward her slanted, almond eyes, which were framed by dark lashes longer than they had any business being, even without mascara, which she never wore. Her hands, delicate but strong, gripped a pair of metal tongs, the small veins pulsing with effort.

She twisted her wrist, twirling something unseen in the pot. From the smell of it, Mickey guessed pasta—something buttery and garlicky and fresh.

When she noticed Mickey, her shoulders hopped up to her ears in surprise. Then a smile, which reached her eyes. Lex paused her cooking and wiped her hands on a nearby dish towel, then she crossed the room to greet Mickey at the door, their cat, Mango, at her heels.

Her girls.

Mickey inhaled deep. The sight of her family was enough to make her come undone. Tears gathered at the side of her eyes now, and she couldn't tell if she wanted to cry because of the day's happenings or the fact that Lex had cleaned up while Mickey was gone, disappearing the random pile of clean, unfolded laundry from the morning into the closet and hiding Mickey's overflowing piles of product samples from view. Lex had even vacuumed the massive rug that covered most of their living room, a checkered brown and cream Moroccan rug that Mickey had seen on Chelsea's Instagram story. It had cost too much money, but Mickey liked the feel of it in between her toes. Her credit card liked how much interest it accrued.

The bookshelf, crammed with books by Black women and theoretical texts she hadn't cracked open since college, had been dusted and tidied, the plants misted, and the vinyl collection rejiggered, the previous display of Earth, Wind & Fire; Peter Tosh; and Rihanna's *Anti* swapped out for Cleo Sol, SZA, and EarthGang.

The overhead lights were off in favor of the orb lamps that Mickey had dotted throughout the house, their apartment awash in a warm, low-wattage glow. It was hard to see at times, but it was a *vibe*. Jill Scott crooned through the speakers, serenading them about how good loving had the power to transform even the most basic routine. Jill was moaning the word *griiiits* when Mickey let the tears spill.

She almost forgot why she was crying but the heavy tote bags cutting into her shoulder reminded her: her life as she knew it was coming to an end and she was powerless to stop it. Mickey's shoulders drooped dramatically, the tote bags sliding from her body and onto the floor with a jumbled thump. Mickey winced at the sound, sure that at least one of the items in her many bags was glass.

* * *

"Aw baby," Lex said to what Mickey was sure was a pitiful sight, her face twisted in anguish, body slumped. This wasn't the first time Mickey had met Lex at the door like this, defeated by her day, worried she'd be fired. A few weeks ago, Mickey had only posted two stories instead of three, and Nina made sure to check in on her progress multiple times a day, avoiding Mickey in person and only communicating with her via Slack. Then she'd been left off an important meeting invite, and she became certain that it was the end for her. She had sounded every alarm bell: calling her best friend Scottie, texting the group chat, putting out soft feelers to other publications. But that had been an accident—a new assistant who was typing too quickly. Or maybe it wasn't an accident but a warning sign. Unless this was just another false alarm?

Lex pulled her close, standing on her tiptoes to kiss her on the forehead and cheeks, her mouth slick with olive oil and lemon.

"Why do they have my baby crying on a school night?" she asked, running the pads of her thumbs over Mickey's full, soft cheeks, attempting to remove the streaks. She ran a hand over Mickey's braids and brought her face close before sticking out her little pink tongue and licking Mickey's cheek. "Salty." This is what Lex always did, fixed Mickey's messes without making her feel bad for fucking things up in the first place. She spoiled her rotten, so rotten that after half a decade together it had become their dynamic—Mickey announcing her pain or her needs or her struggles and Lex doing everything in her power to make it all all right.

Mickey pushed Lex's face away and laughed. "Stop licking me."

"Oh please, you like it," Lex countered, giving the other cheek a lick for good measure and kissing her there, too. "But what's up? Did Nina pull some bullshit in the pitch meeting again?" Lex fished her phone from her apron. "You didn't text me, right? I was cooking dinner."

Mickey was tempted to fall into the routine of their evening—the kisses upon greeting followed by dinner and a show (they were on season four of *Downton Abbey*), which they half-watched while scrolling and futilely attempting to catch up on the following day's emails—but something else was pressing. She could feel the weight of Chelsea's admission on the tip of her tongue, fighting its way from her lips.

"I didn't," Mickey confirmed. "They're going to fire me." She announced it with a heaving sigh, disappointed to find Lex's mouth twisting into a sort of wry smile.

"You say that every week."

"Well, this week's different."

"How?" Lex asked, turning her back to Mickey and migrating to the kitchen, as if some internal timer cued her to the pasta.

Mickey toed off her sneakers before continuing inside, peeling off her coat and hanging her keys on the small hook in the entry. She slumped onto the couch and Mango immediately hopped into her lap, stretching her small body backward before settling into the shape of a burrito, all four paws tucked underneath her fluffy orange body.

"I brought you perfume from the event, it smells really good," Mickey called out, even though there was no need. Thanks to the construction of their boxy, awkwardly configured apartment, the kitchen was still the living room. There was an island separating the space, a wood structure they'd purchased at IKEA almost immediately after moving in two years ago. It was clear there used to be a wall where the island sat now, the scents once so fragrant the walls were necessary to soak some of that up. The new developers did away with all that, the open concept floor plan assuming that anyone willing to spend upward of two thousand dollars a month for a mail room, white subway tile, and stainless-steel appliances must not be cooking anything that couldn't be eliminated with the flicker of a scented candle. Lex sometimes cooked like that, Jamaican curry or fried dumplings or saltfish scenting the room and slipping under the door and into the hallway. Mickey's concoctions, on the other hand, rarely involved fire.

Mickey picked up her phone to check the group chat. She reread her message, a frantic missive asking if anyone had heard about Bevy hiring new writers, tossing in that there'd been murmurings about another round of layoffs. She was intentionally vague, obscuring her real fears with emojis, exclamation points, and lowercase letters. It dawned on her that Chelsea was in this chat, too. That she had seen Mickey's text while she took her own Uber home. Had possibly shook her head at the message, realizing that Mickey was both spooked and distrustful of the information Chelsea had slipped to her. That Mickey had failed to act cool. It was an unspoken breach of their tenuous sisterhood, and Mickey was unsurprised that whatever they'd built just a few hours ago was already falling apart. Their relationship was fraught, tinged with an undercurrent of fear and envy. They were as jealous as they were admiring. As dismissive as they were close. It was a balancing act, and Mickey found herself complaining about Chelsea and wanting to be her in equal measure.

She should've just texted her best friends. Mickey pressed her lips into a thin line and though she knew it to be impossible, googled how to unsend a text.

"Hello?" Lex asked between stirs of a wooden ladle, frowning her disapproval at Mickey's head buried deep in her phone. "Are you going to tell me or am I going to have to text you to get a response?" she asked before turning back to the cooking.

Mickey looked up, the beginnings of frustration blooming in her hands. She hated when Lex used that half-joking tone to communicate her needs, sarcastic and verging on scolding. It made Mickey feel like a kid who did a bad thing.

"Sorry," she said offhandedly, deciding now was not a good time to pick a fight. Not when her dinner was in Lex's hands and what she wanted more than anything else was to feel her girlfriend's fingers raking across her scalp. "I got distracted. Nina sent me an email." This was a lie, but a plausible one.

Lex made a show of checking the time and shook her head, exposing a flash of her neck. Mickey loved that neck, which was sturdy and sure. Her mane of brown curly whirly hair was often tied back into a quick ponytail, hiding the shaved underside and a tiny tattoo they'd both agreed was a bad decision: her full name, Lennox, in delicate, typewriter script. People often spoke of having a good head on one's shoulders, but Lex had a good neck. A sniffable neck that always smelled of vanilla almond body wash, a whisper of cologne, and a skin scent she couldn't name but wished could be bottled up. She wanted to be buried in that neck right now, but there was the matter of what Chelsea had said.

"Chelsea basically told me so at the event," Mickey began, pressing her head into the back of the couch. "She said Nina is going around saying the role will be open in a few months."

Lex stopped stirring and Mickey knew the shock had registered. "Wait, what?" She turned to face Mickey. "That's OD."

"Now you see why I cried all the way home." Mickey rubbed Mango harder now, waiting for the temperamental cat to spring from her lap and onto the floor. It didn't take long for the cat to take her leave, digging her claws into Mickey's thighs on the way down.

"The fact that she's making you do that dumbass presentation makes it worse."

"Exactly," Mickey said. She picked up her phone before putting it down. Still nothing.

"So, what exactly did Chelsea say?"

Mickey did her best to relay things in clearheaded detail, but the conversation felt foggy and just beyond her reach even though she'd been with Chelsea an hour ago. She painted their conversation in broad strokes, emphasizing that Chelsea had refused to say who was being courted, which Lex pointed out was strange.

"Aren't y'all supposed to look out for each other? What's the point of all the Black girl magic kumbaya shit if she won't give you the details?"

Mickey nodded in agreement. "I'm saying! Like why be all weird and just tell me half the story. I guess it doesn't matter *who* the girl is, but now it makes me suspicious of everybody." Mickey remembered the group chat and her empty stomach lurched.

"But then I kind of fucked up."

"What you do?" Lex asked. She turned off the stove's flame and drained some of the water into a separate pot, leaving the pasta noodles quivering while she whipped up a sauce to drown them in. A basic alfredo became something more refined, as Lex sautéed some minced garlic and butter before adding in a few sun-dried tomatoes, a handful of fresh Parmigiano-Reggiano, a dash of oregano, and a few shakes of salt and pepper. Lex always had a way of making the ordinary a little more interesting, taking what she had and fine-tuning it to suit her needs.

"I asked the group chat if they knew anything."

"The big one with all the Black girls?" Lex asked. "Isn't Chelsea in that one?"

Mickey nodded before burying her head in her hands, her elbows digging into her doughy thighs.

"Damn, babe. I mean that's not that serious though," Lex replied. "Everybody mutes their group chats anyway."

"It is that serious!" Mickey insisted. "Now it looks like I'm trying to figure out who the girl is or like I'm pressed."

"Okay, I could see that."

"You think they're talking shit about me?" Mickey asked.

"Definitely not," Lex replied, and she sounded sure. So sure that Mickey *nearly* believed her, or maybe it was the aroma of the pasta and her gurgling stomach distracting her from the dilemma at hand. But even a signature Lex home-cooked meal couldn't make her forget that unemployment was hurtling toward her at full speed.

"I should've known when she fired Jordan three months ago," Mickey said, pulling herself from the couch and relocating to their kitchen. She leaned up against the island. "It was only a matter of time before they got me, too." Mickey thought back to when they'd packed up Jordan's desk. She was the social manager for *Wave,* making sure their Instagram had a distinctive *voice* and *energy.* She reposted celebrities looking attractive or being relatable or acting out with captions that made the reader nod or laugh at its absurdity. She was in charge of making their readers feel *seen.*

They fired Jordan the day after a pitch meeting, but Mickey had been too rattled to notice. Nina had responded to her three pitches (two of which were profiles of white ingénues Mickey *knew* Nina was obsessed with) with a grimace and a single word—"Interesting"—uttered in the kind of dismissive tone that Mickey had come to recognize as a no. It was subtle, but Mickey had picked up on it quickly. Her own high school had been populated with primitive Ninas—white girls who wielded their indifference like a superpower, breaking down their subjects with flat tones and bemused sighs.

That day, Mickey had been faced with her failure to—yet again—pitch something that would elicit Nina's approval, the disappointment so severe that she barely noticed when Jordan's stuff was carefully packed into a box. She didn't even register Jordan's absence until many days later, when she turned to ask her a question ("What was your braider's name again?") and was met with dead space. She was ashamed, but she'd gone right back to work. It hadn't occurred to her to reach out or check in, which she still felt guilty about. Mickey wondered how long it would take for people to notice she was gone.

"You'd think they'd keep at least one Black person on the team, if only for the optics," Mickey said with a laugh, reflexively looking at the brown of her skin, wondering if this time it would save her.

Lex wordlessly responded by pouring a glass of white wine and handing it to her by the stem. "I got this one at work," she said. Mickey reached for a metallic gold coaster and placed the glass atop its corrugated surface.

"Ooh," Mickey said after taking a languid sip, the wine sweet on her tongue. "It's good."

"I know, some brand sent a case to Davis and she started handing it out to everyone," Lex explained without turning around. "Something about her making Forbes 30 under 30. She almost poured it down the drain because she didn't want to be seen sipping anything other than Something Else." She looked to Mickey for dramatic effect. "I started passing it out before she could get rid of it and then she started acting like it was her idea. Acting like we was supposed to be grateful when she owes us real money. She's acting like that last fundraising round didn't happen, but I've seen the receipts. She's taking a Suburban everywhere and we can't even expense an Uber home."

Mickey grinned, grateful for the predictable change of pace. "You're the one who turned down that cushy corporate job for the start-up."

"I'm sorry I wanted to work somewhere where I don't need to go through three different marketing teams before posting one Instagram story."

Mickey took another sip. "Fair." She liked talking about Lex's job— social media manager at Something Else, a low-alcohol aperitif company (*low* being the operative word here), which was *geared toward the sober-curious and alcohol-sensitive, but designed with everyone in mind*, whatever that meant. It was anticlimactic in comparison to hers. The main villain of Lex's work stories was her CEO, Davis, who had defected from the world of editorial and started her own thing. Davis was the kind of woman people wrote odes to on the internet and called their

Woman Crush Wednesday, with her silky blowout, petite features, and delicate solid gold nameplate necklace. Although her name was Lena she only went by Davis (except on socials, where she was lenabobena) because it was her way of pushing back against the gender normativity of names that end with *A*. She listed her pronouns in her Instagram bio and turned her profile picture Blue for Sudan, and then left it that way long after everyone had changed it back. She was woke with a capital *W* and bitchy with a big *B*, her well-worn activism cloaking the fact that she was basically a mediocre white man in Net-a-Porter digs. She was also the main source of Lex's frustration, thanks to her helicopter CEO style that required her to be everywhere always but rarely actually present, flitting from one meeting to the next in puff-sleeved Ganni dresses that made her look approachable and expensive.

There, Lex was underpaid but beloved—in addition to her talents, Mickey suspected it was because everyone at work had a crush on her. It was hard not to be in love with her curly mane of hair, and the easy-fly style inspired by the dope boys of the early aughts and the sharply dressed uncles she grew up with. She was all cardigans and button-downs and pleated slacks and expensive sneakers that prompted looks of curiosity and approval almost everywhere she went.

And then there was the warmth. Lex was sunshine. The kind that tanned your hands while driving and kissed your face on a lazy Sunday afternoon. Subtle, but unmissable. Warm.

"Okay, dinner's done." Lex looked down at the ground, where Mango sat waiting dutifully at her feet. Lex scooped some sauce onto a small spoon and brought it to Mango's waiting mouth, who lapped it up like she was seeing if it was any good. Lex looked at Mickey with a smile. "Might be some of my best work yet."

"I hope so."

"It's going to work out. Just trust yourself and the process," Lex said as she plated, using her tongs to scoop heaping servings onto the plate. It was just the two of them, but she always cooked like they were expecting one more guest.

"The 'process,'" Mickey paused to make scare quotes with her fingers, "is bullshit. It's abuse," she declared, tipping more wine down her throat.

15

"No argument there. But tell me, where is it better?"

"I wouldn't know."

"Maybe this will be your opportunity to find out."

"This isn't helping."

"What would?"

"Pass me the food."

Lex handed Mickey the steaming plates, and Mickey set them down at their small, circular lilac dining table. Mickey had found it at a vintage store that sold items exclusively through Instagram. It was the first thing they'd bought together—an investment in their future—stored in Mickey's fourth-floor walkup well before they signed a lease. It had represented possibility, then resentment, and now it was functional, holding their meals and laptops and occasionally, their cat.

Mickey inelegantly scooped pasta into her mouth. "This is good," she said with an enthusiastic nod of the head, which she knew was bordering on condescending. It was, in fact, good, but Mickey felt the added salt drying out her tongue.

"Do you really like it?" Lex asked. "Or are you doing that thing where you won't tell me what's wrong with it because you think it's going to hurt my feelings?"

"It's good!" Mickey insisted. "I would tell you if it wasn't."

"It's not a little too salty?"

Mickey pinched her fingers together to indicate that it was, but just a smidge.

"I don't know why you don't just tell me."

"Because it *is* good."

"But honesty is better."

Mickey threw up her hands. "I am being honest! I—" She was raring to explain herself when her phone dinged, her attention immediately on the glowing screen. She looked down at the phone and was reminded all over again. Nothing from the group chat, just a text from Scottie asking what moisturizer to buy. Despite being a fancy publicist whose job was to know everything and anyone at all times, she never knew what to do with her skin. That's where Mickey came in. The text was anything but urgent, but Mickey picked up the phone anyway, tapping out a message telling her to *wait*. She was sure she had something Scottie could use for free.

When she put her phone down and glanced back up, Lex looked annoyed.

"What?" Mickey asked, feigning innocence.

Lex sighed one of her big sighs. "Nothing." Then, one side of her mouth tugged upward, pasta sauce dotting the tip of her smile.

"So, tell me," Lex began, and Mickey already knew where this was going. In the past few weeks, Lex had become obsessed with talking about weddings. Davis was recently engaged and had turned her nuptials into an office-wide project.

But they'd been discussing marriage since their first year together, the hypothetical wedding a not-so-distant future event that both saw coming and neither was running away from. But recently things had taken a turn for the specific, which both terrified and thrilled Mickey. Marriage was the making of her own family, the kind of decision she had to get right. Lex had all the signs of being the one: she loved Mickey fiercely and took care of her in ways that were too boring to name. She kept her sane, laughing, fed. Sure, she had her issues, but she was a good person. That much, Mickey knew.

But that level of commitment scared her, calling up old fears about what happens when things don't work out. She had been the collateral damage of two people who loved each other until they didn't and then did an inelegant job of managing the fallout. The divorce hadn't been nasty, just totalizing, leaving Mickey—who at the time was just sixteen—with one less parent and a father who treated her like she'd left him too. For years she fed herself the narrative that it had only made her stronger, more self-sufficient. In truth, she had become increasingly desperate for a stable, sure kind of love. This love.

Now they discussed the minutiae—the music, the food, the invitations. Today:

"Thoughts on dried flowers?" Lex asked, and Mickey rolled her eyes.

"Have you been on Davis's Pinterest board or something?" Mickey asked. "Out of the question. She's the one who got engaged at Burning Man, not us."

Mickey felt flowers should be alive, vibrant, verdant. Filled with possibilities and poised to bloom. But all of this was make-believe. Despite telling everyone (and themselves) that the only thing stopping them from walking down the aisle was money and opportunity, Mickey knew it was deeper than that. Something more rooted that pushed this idea firmly into the realm of fantasy.

Lex laughed and Mickey continued, her fingers tapping against the delicate stem of her empty wineglass. The tinny click-click of her acrylics was why she kept up with them in the first place. She looked around their apartment, which they'd turned, year after year, into a home. If nothing else, this was real. She refocused on Lex's face and smirked. "Her theme is the New Mexico sand dunes, like what the fuck does that even mean?"

"Knowing Davis, something basic as hell," Lex said with a grin. "I thought the dried ones looked kind of cool though. Artsy."

Mickey's mouth spread, exposing her top row of teeth. "Still a no."

"As long as I get to marry you, I can't say that I care either way," Lex said.

She leaned across the table for a kiss and Mickey obliged, their mouths pressing together in a short, familiar rhythm, two quick kisses, followed by one they held for just a moment longer.

Mickey leaned into her warmth, placing her face in Lex's neck. Her shoulders dropped the moment she took in Lex's familiar scent, and she curled her body inward, defeated.

"I don't want to lose my job," Mickey whispered.

Lex smoothed a hand over Mickey's braids and pressed a kiss to her forehead.

"Seriously, it's going to be okay," Lex promised. "You're so fucking talented, and you know that. Nina is an idiot," she said, punctuating "idiot" with another kiss.

At the mention of Nina, Mickey found it impossible not to start crying again. Her tears dampened the soft cotton of Lex's black T-shirt.

"But what if I'm not?" Mickey asked. "What if I'm just okay?"

"You're extraordinary," she said, taking Mickey's jaw into her hands and forcing her eyes to meet hers. "Don't let this low-key racist white woman convince you that you don't have it. You do."

"But what even is it, and who gets to decide? Nina barely knows what she's doing."

"So why are you looking to her for approval? Isn't it better to get away from her then? Even if it isn't your choice?"

Mickey sighed and wiped her face. Lex had a point. "You're right."

Lex feigned shock. "Can you say that again? This time into the microphone." She picked up her phone and angled it toward Mickey's mouth.

A smile, a quick one. "Don't get used to that."

"Oh, once a year is more than enough for me," Lex said before planting a quick kiss on her forehead and then her nose. Lex pulled back to take Mickey in. "You're too pretty to be crying like this."

Mickey rolled her eyes. She didn't quite believe Lex. Her looks had never granted her access, had never saved her. She could only think of times when it held her back. Stopped her from squeezing into a quick outfit at the mall or being dressed by a designer for a show. Mickey felt frustrated, then, at all the things she didn't have, and all the things slipping through her fingers. She looked at Lex, whose eyes remained trained on her face, trying to puzzle out what emotion Mickey would cough up next.

"So, what kind of flowers would *you* want?" Mickey asked, refocusing Lex's attention and her own. After a childhood spent crying over any little thing, even the big things felt like a waste of tears.

"I don't know," Lex said with a laugh, widening the gap between them and returning to her food. "I just want it to look nice and for you to be in a sexy-ass dress. You can handle the rest."

"The rest?" Mickey asked, pointedly. "Even the guest list?"

Lex's warm brown eyes turned steely and rolled toward the ceiling. This was a well-trodden road, one that always led to the same place— the two of them at odds, questioning why they wanted to do this in the first place.

Mickey thought of herself in a fluffy, white gown, something that would cover her pudgy stomach and thick arms, something that would make her feel beautiful but not big. She imagined them standing underneath an arch next, hands clasped and gazing out into a crowd of tearful faces. She ventured to imagine the faces staring back at her. Her mother and father, reunited solely for her benefit. Lex's mom. The thought of Elda's eyes on her tugged at the already-taut threads of insecurity, but she pressed on, skipping over those dark orbs to the faces of their friends. Her stomach flipped then, too, remembering that those were technically Lex's people. *Could they be taken away, too?*

"What?" Mickey asked, feigning indignation. She didn't know if it was the stress of her career hanging in the balance or the fact that she'd never wanted to marry Lex for real more than she did right now, but she couldn't stop herself from digging in, reopening unhealed wounds with a flick of her tongue.

"Nothing," Lex replied, taking her hair out of its ponytail and tying it up again. Mickey sipped from her wine and let an arm fall across her middle. She cocked her head to one side and examined the woman she called the love of her life. Lex's mouth was drawn thin, and she looked weary. Mickey wondered, briefly, if she was the source of that exhaustion. When Lex met Mickey's eyes, she looked less than impressed.

"It's not nothing," Mickey insisted. "Say how you feel."

"You know what you're doing."

"What am I doing?" Mickey asked, fighting the smirk threatening the corners of her mouth. She reached for the bottle of wine, uncorked and breathing, and tipped a healthy serving into her glass.

She didn't enjoy this, the poking and prodding, but it felt like the only power she had in this space, where she was victim to Lex's mother's whims. Elda had intervened before in their relationship, and Mickey was sure she wouldn't hesitate to do so again, whether it was setting Lex up with one of her coworkers' sons or pretending Mickey was just a friend. And there Lex would be, her Lex, cowering before Elda, prostrated and scolded like a child.

"You're going to turn this into a conversation about my family," Lex began, and Mickey rolled her eyes. Lex reached for her hand and Mickey forced herself not to pull away. All the resentment she'd buried under the life they'd built—tucked into their foundation like an old letter— threatened to unfurl. She stroked Lex's hand, tracing the outlines of her veins before pinching the skin between her acrylics and letting it go. She mustered up a smile, but she knew it looked put on.

Lex tensed, clocking her expression. "Don't do that," she instructed. "I get it, they're not great, but is it wrong for me to hope that they'll get their shit together and show up?"

"There's a difference between hope and delusion," Mickey said, and at that moment she knew she'd gone too far. She should've pivoted to their friends like she always did, reminded Lex that they had a chosen family, and that that was more than good enough. But she couldn't conjure them up now. All she could think about was the expression on Elda's face when Lex told her that Mickey was unemployed—fodder for her endless disapproval.

"That's petty." Lex stood and crossed the few steps into the kitchen, tossing the plate into the sink. It hit the bottom with a sharp clack and Mickey jumped at the sound. "I know you're upset about your work shit, but that's fucking petty."

Mickey let the words hang in the air, and for a moment, it felt like it might crush them both.

"I'm going to get in the shower," Lex announced when she realized Mickey wasn't going to respond. She started toward the back of the apartment and shut the bathroom door.

Mickey sat and stared at her wine glass before picking it up and draining it of its contents. She didn't feel bad, not even a little bit. It was the truth.

Mickey sighed and went back to her phone, checking for any response. There was one, from Daphne Ortega, a young editor who had risen through the ranks at her site with impressive speed.

"Girl, you work there. You tell us! Y'all hiring?"

The "haha" reactions poured in.

Mickey scraped the rest of her food into the trash, no longer hungry, and ran water over their plates before scrubbing those, and the pots and pans, clean.

Mickey heard the sounds of Lex's shower winding down almost a half hour later, the water sloshing in sheets onto the tub's floor and then not at all. Mickey had found her way to their bedroom, changing into her nightclothes and settling herself in bed. She picked up the book she was rereading, a well-worn edition of *Their Eyes Were Watching God*. Normally, Janie held her attention but today it sat as an open prop, flaccidly flapping in her lap. The water clicked off and Mickey braced herself for what would greet her once Lex entered their room. Mickey hated fighting in front of all their shared possessions. Lex's toes cracked as she walked into the room, towel cinched around her chest. Mickey looked up. She could tell Lex had been crying in the shower.

"I did the dishes," Mickey offered, half-hoping the word *sorry* wouldn't have to come from her mouth.

"Thanks," Lex responded in that clipped tone that meant she wanted and required more.

"How was your shower?" she asked before flipping her laptop open, tapping away at emails that could definitely wait until the next day.

"Good. The water's still hot if you wanted to get in."

Mickey didn't look up from the screen. "That's okay, I'll take one in the morning."

She watched Lex out of the corner of her eye, her hands white with lotion and gliding over her arms, thighs, and ankles. She'd repeat the process, this time with a vanilla-scented oil that made her skin glisten. Lex grabbed a shirt from the dresser next, an oversized one that said "Conservatory Volleyball" in a big, blocky font. It was Mickey's, but Lex had commandeered it a long time ago, around the same time they'd decided there was no way out of this thing they'd built, when they'd decided two would be one, for better or worse, past death and eternity. It was said in the nights spent in each other's arms but made real in their routine. Where one went, the other followed. It had always been Mickey and Lex, Lex and Mickey.

Eventually Lex slid into their queen-sized bed, oiled and supple, her legs weaving through Mickey's. Fighting or not, they'd lay like this for the past three years and tonight would be no different. Mickey pressed her head against the tufted green velvet headboard and exhaled. She said nothing in the hopes that Lex would speak first. When that didn't happen, she continued to work.

Eventually, she asked, "Do you have anything else you want to say?"

Homebodies

There was no response, just slow, measured breaths. Mickey pressed her head deeper into the headboard, which looked expensive but wasn't and had no give. The harder she pressed, the more it pushed back, reminding her that a couple hundred more dollars would've afforded her the ability to sulk in luxury.

TWO

The next morning, Mickey found herself standing on the corner of Park Avenue South and Twenty-Third Street, sweat gathering at the back of her neck even though it was a cold day in May. She had been up half the night working on the presentation. Despite feeling like her efforts were futile, she'd plugged away, copying and pasting and dragging and dropping until her eyes pressed closed from exhaustion.

Mickey had spent a few hours sourcing images from deep archives, reference material that would show her range. She pulled from early aughts fashion shows alongside obscure punk performances in London, picking two nonwhite subjects for every one. *This was diversity!* she exclaimed in the cavern of her mind somewhere around the three a.m. mark, when a pointy green mohawk poked at the sky, accusing her of using their image to further her career aims and resisting her attempts to drag and drop it into a slide. Something told her the green mohawk wouldn't change what had already been decided, that a presentation, no matter how good, would do little but contribute to *Wave*'s bottom line and seal her fate. Now, she was late to work. She had three minutes to be at her desk, which was approximately five minutes speed walking, four if she ran.

"Oh, thank god you're finally here," Evie had chatted once Mickey plopped into her seat, her name popping up on the side of her screen even though they sat directly across from each other, computer monitors back to back, nearly touching. It was two minutes past nine. "Nina was wondering where you were."

"The elevator was slow," she wrote back, knowing a message from Nina was soon to follow. She glanced down the row of six-foot desks, and saw Nina at the very end, brow furrowed, headphones clamped around her head. She was typing quickly and furiously.

Mickey heard Slack's pinging sound before the message popped into view. "Hi Mickey! So glad you're in. When you get a sec, can you pop over so we can chat?"

"Of course!" she wrote back, wondering if one exclamation point was enough. She decided it wasn't, but she couldn't go back now, the damage was done. Evie's electric green bob peeked out from behind her screen.

"How was last night?" she shout-whispered, her eyes widening in curiosity.

Mickey mimicked typing in midair to let her know she wasn't able to do the small talk thing out loud. The same question popped up in Slack a few moments later.

It was good!!! she wrote, adding three exclamation points for emphasis even though it was anything but.

"Ready?" Nina asked in Slack, even though she could see that Mickey hadn't taken off her coat. She stood up without replying, peeling off her color-blocked fleece and draping it over the back of her ergonomic office chair. "Popping over" meant walking the ten feet from her desk to Nina's.

Nina pulled her headphones off her head with both hands and smoothed a hand over her messy low bun, her short nails painted a shocking shade of red. "Hi! Okay, so, I just wanted to quickly talk about getting to work on time." She crossed and uncrossed her legs, motioning for Mickey to sit down.

There were no seats, so Mickey perched awkwardly on the end of her desk, decorated with items to make her seem human. A photo of her cat, a half-eaten Luna Bar, and the card they'd signed for her birthday on display. A few stalks of pampas grass stood tall in a chubby translu-cent vase, arcing toward the ceiling and brushing Mickey's back. Nina blinked up at her expectantly.

"Yeah, about today." Mickey crossed her arms and then pulled them apart. "My train was delayed, so I was a few minutes late getting in."

"Yeah no, I totally get that." She folded her thin lips into her mouth and pushed them back out again before making a clicking sound with her tongue. "But, you know, that's what Slack is for. I would just really appreciate if you'd send a quick note if you're running behind just so I'm aware of what you're doing and everyone isn't wondering where you've been."

"Sure, yeah. Makes sense."

"And I get it, two minutes isn't like a huge thing, but when we need to get pieces up by ten thirty, it can be kind of tight, especially because, as I've mentioned, it takes you some time to get settled in and every-thing . . ."

"Yeah, no, I get it."

"Okay, amazing. I also wanted to talk about the IT Girl issue—I'd actually love for you to brainstorm ideas about how to tie beauty back to some of the big pop culture moments happening right now."

Mickey wished she'd brought a notebook to write this down. She nodded along instead. "Okay, amazing," she repeated. Everything was amazing, everything was okay. "I was, and I mean this is just a rough sketch obviously, thinking that I could sort of expand the queer beauty coverage on the site. Especially since we're light on Pride coverage so far."

At that, Nina pursed her lips. Mickey continued. "I feel like we don't really dig into it as much as we could. It's pretty much an unexplored space and I'd love to take that on, especially because we're starting to see a big shift in the way teens see gender even, and there's so much to be said about the industry's response." She took a breath to make sure Nina was still following and saw that her eyes had gone dim. She was nodding with a finger to her mouth and a wrinkle in her brow. "There's so much to be said about intersectionality in that space, too, I mean, how often are we considering the interconnectivity of the politics of beauty along-side race and gender?"

Nina blinked at her slowly and sucked in air like a fish. Her brow furrowed deeper, looking for the correct thing to say. "Yes, totally. But we're sort of moving away from identity here, and toward trend and nostalgia. So, if you could focus on that," Nina's eyes drifted back to her computer, "that'd be great."

She slid her headphones back on her head and looked up at Mickey with a closed-mouth smile. "Thanks, Mickey!" She didn't ask about the presentation.

Evie's bob had yet to settle into place when Mickey sat down, still swinging from peering over to see what was said. Mickey's phone vibrated against the desk. She didn't turn it over, staring instead into the glare of her computer and crawling Instagram and Twitter for news.

Before the acquisition, that would've been the kind of story that landed her a three-page spread in the magazine, complete with models of every gender in avant-garde glittery eyes and gems stuck to every available surface of skin. But things were different now, Nina was different.

She'd been brought in to replace *Wave*'s former editor in chief, Lily Markham, who was everything Mickey had longed for in a boss: feminist, accomplished, hands off.

Lily had hired Mickey to *do her thing*, which she'd deciphered to mean write about Black issues, and she preferred that to what she was doing now, which didn't feel much like writing at all. Instead of reporting on the goings-on of Black life, she was making listicles about the best lipsticks for every skin tone and scrolling through Twitter hoping one of Nina's favorite celebrities decided to show a little bit of skin. Lily was the first to go following the merger with Bevy, with plans to start her own publication, though she ended up just boomeranging to a previous magazine instead.

Three hours, one story, and a cup of scalding chamomile later, Frankie bounced in, bundled up and bespectacled with a paper bag dangling delicately between her fingers. Frankie and Mickey supposedly had the same job, or at least that's what it said on paper and in their Instagram bios. This, however, was different in practice. Frankie went to twice the events and did half the work while Mickey had taken to wearing blue-light filtering glasses full-time, brought on by the many uninterrupted hours of screen time broken up by quick trips to the bathroom and a thirty-minute lunch break that she often spent at her desk. Mickey was expected to be at work by nine, while Frankie bounced in, sauntered in, and filtered in at whatever time suited her best.

"Hi hi!" she said to no one in particular. Frankie often spoke in doubles, but the emphasis never made it any more meaningful, the second time often negating the first. Love *love*. So *so*. Great *great*. She tossed her coat onto the desk separating her and Nina, once occupied by Jordan. Now, Jordan's old desk had become a catchall for packages, possessions, and things that needed temporary housing, and Jordan's old role had been sucked up into Blah Blah Bevy, a hub of employees who handled social across the entirety of the company. Today, the desk held Frankie's belongings and Nina's lunch, delivered via freight and losing temperature in its logoed brown paper bag.

"Hiiiii," Nina sang, removing her headphones and placing them to the side. "Did you stop by that preview this morning?"

"Yes, Susan is a genius," Frankie said breathlessly, bringing a frothy drink to her lips. "But you knew that."

"Did you see Margo?"

Mickey could only see the back of Frankie's golden blond head and one of Nina's eyes, but she imagined Frankie's small features furrowed, carefully deciding what to say next. She could hear Frankie's deep breaths, more intentional and louder than anyone else's thanks to her frequent breathwork classes, which held space on their shared edit calendar every Wednesday at eleven a.m.

"I did," she said, finally. Nina's one muddy brown eye went wide. She slid closer to Frankie, closing the great divide between the six-foot desk that separated them.

"Is she, like, okay?" Okay meant functioning enough to give up the juicy details of her failed engagement to Teddy Rhodes, the son of a financier who'd found some success DJ'ing for the children of his parents' rich friends. Before he and Margo, an associate editor at a legacy publication with a fancy editor in chief, it was Teddy and Nina, who at one time had also posted photos curled up in the Hamptons or doing sun salutations at one of his family's many properties, which dotted well-manicured enclaves around the US.

"She's fine, but honestly," she leaned in conspiratorially, her bony shoulder blades threatening to meet, "I don't think she's taking it well."

Mickey shut off the volume in her earbuds so she could eavesdrop, leaning closer without moving the wheels of her chair or craning her neck. She willed her ears to work harder. They were whispering now, Mickey only catching bits and pieces of a conversation laden with insider jokes and unproductivity. Meanwhile, her second story of the day glared back at her, a three-hundred-word write-up about a young actress she barely knew and the much older man she was rumored to be dating. Mickey was meant to make this sound interesting and worthy of the clicks they were so desperately chasing—these stories the only thing keeping the vaulted, exposed ceiling from collapsing on their heads.

"You think she'd want to come over here?" Mickey couldn't tell whether that came from Frankie's or Nina's mouth, their voices slightly different versions of a nasal, transplanted New Yorker drone.

Mickey wondered where here was and if they meant her exact seat, where she hadn't stopped sweating and typing was becoming difficult. Her hands shook above the keys, and she wondered if they could hear her shallow breathing. She could hear herself breathing. Short, loud intakes of air punctuated by the increased clamminess of her palms. When they'd fired Jordan it had been shocking and sudden, at least to Mickey, but she knew they'd been building a case against her for months.

Mickey's file (because she was sure there was a file) would detail her inability to smile while typing up things she cared nothing about and a lack of knowledge about things that mattered, like which restaurants were good for breakfast dates with PR people, and how to appear less aggressive over Slack. These, Mickey knew, were "soft skills," which she'd worked really hard to perfect but felt were always just beyond her reach, bouncing lightly between Frankie's fingertips and wrestling themselves from hers. Frankie, with her toasted sesame skin and dusty blue eyes, was all the soft skills with none of the hard ones, but that's what made her charming, alluring, and *coachable*.

Mickey, on the other hand, had an innate talent for knowing how to read a room and a good handle on the mechanics of politics and privilege, which made her perpetually angry, weary, and jaded, always simmering at a low boil. Maybe they could see it, though Mickey was sure she hid it well, covering it carefully with layers of platitudes, big smiles, and quick-witted jokes. More likely, they saw that she would never quite fit in, and that someone like Margo, despite her treachery, might. Margo was the evil they knew. The kind that didn't go bump in the night. They'd been in sororities with girls like Margo: someone who slept with other people's boyfriends but wore good headbands. Mickey, on the other hand, brought up the kinds of fears they couldn't name.

The file, because, again, it definitely existed, would also (these were the things they would point to in said firing) outline her difficulty with writing three to four stories a day while simultaneously juggling long-form features that set Twitter alight. They would not note that this was impossible, and that no one, not even Frankie (especially not Frankie), could handle that kind of volume. They would also leave out the many times Nina purposefully buried her stories, making Mickey rewrite them only for them to never see the light of day. Nina would also, and this she would privately delight in, talk about her lack of communication, even though Mickey was often the one who spoke first. It might also, and this was just a guess, mention that she was less than pleasant, which mattered even if it shouldn't.

The shaking, which was persistent and had begun a few weeks after Nina started, was preventing her from filing her story before one. It had started in her pinky, the little finger quivering when Nina "checked in," at all hours of the day, wondering if, when, and how Mickey would meet their story quota, and had since evolved into full-on tremors, her hands hovering frightfully above the keyboard, afraid to move. Mickey was afraid. If it wasn't her production then it was her ideas, treated like half-formed things that needed more shaping, more refining, more weight. Mickey knew that when they fired her, the shaking would be another mark against the record she'd never seen, another note in the imaginary file. She chanced a look in their direction, which was now just Frankie in her over-ear headphones, her head bobbing offbeat.

A wave of nausea signaled that it was time for lunch. Mickey had developed a bad habit of starving herself until lunchtime, chained so tightly to her desk that she couldn't squeeze in a moment for a snack from the well-stocked pantry that sat in the employee kitchen just a few feet from her desk. She was fearful that moving might trigger Nina's Mickey alarm, which would prompt a frantic Slack about a seemingly urgent task that was never all that important. Everything under Nina felt like a continuous game of hurry up and wait.

Mickey silently slid back from her desk, careful not to alert her peers, and ventured to the elevator in search of food. She walked past row after row of six-foot-long desks, past Chelsea, with her mountains of beauty products shrouding her from view; past the social pod, which occupied two long rows and had an almost spartan approach to desk décor; past the design team and finally past the receptionist Donna, who acknowledged Mickey with a nod of her head. Once inside the elevator, Mickey set a timer on her phone for twenty-seven minutes (she subtracted the few minutes it took her to reach the elevator) and tried to pinpoint exactly what kind of food she was in the mood for. She settled on a fast casual spot with lots of outposts in the city, beloved for its seemingly healthy options, big servings, and millennial pink takeout bags.

On her walk, she decided to call Scottie, who at this point (9:17 PST) would be on her way into the office, taking Mickey's calls from behind the wheel of her inky black Tesla—coffee in one hand, phone in the other.

"Hey friend," Scottie sang into the receiver. The sound of Scottie's voice was like a sedative. The two had been best friends since high school, a bond solidified in ninth grade and fortified over time. Even though she had Lex, Mickey was convinced that Scottie was her soulmate.

"Hey girl," Mickey chirped in reply.

"My bad for not texting you back last night. Client dinner."

"Who this time?" Mickey asked.

"No one you'd care about."

"Mhm, sure. Last time you said that it was my man. The one who sings that one song you always play at the gym."

"Last time I checked you were strictly kitty."

"That doesn't mean I'm blind."

A laugh. "Okay, but I promise you don't care about this one. He's some famous jazz musician." A pause. "How long for lunch today?"

"The full thirty. I got two stories up already."

"Look at her go," Scottie said. "Is the timer on?"

Mickey looked down at her phone: 25 minutes. "You know it is."

"So, what's up with this Nina shit? You think they're going to fire you for real?"

"I do," Mickey said. She had caved and texted Scottie in the middle of the night. Mickey moved her small knotless braids from one side to the other and attempted to ignore the pang of anxiety in her chest. "Chelsea pulled me to the side at an event yesterday to tell me one of her friends got offered the job."

Scottie let out a small gasp. "That's shady as fuck." Then, a gagging sound. "I'm sorry, but Chelsea would. I can't stand her."

Mickey laughed. Chelsea was a recurring character on the sitcom that was Mickey's work drama. She played the role of pet, adored by management and their pale-complected peers. Said adoration made Mickey skeptical—she didn't trust Black people who were overly beloved by their white counterparts. Furthermore, she didn't get the hype. Beyond aesthetics (thin, straight hair, a nonthreatening chestnut skin tone) Mickey didn't see the appeal. "Do you think it was sneaky? I feel like she was trying to look out."

"Sure," Scottie said. Then, "Hold on." She paused to rattle off her Starbucks order: a strawberry refresher with lemonade, light ice. "You were saying?"

Mickey looked down at her phone: 24 minutes. She walked faster down Park Avenue South, past the towering buildings that housed music labels and banks and turned onto Twenty-Third Street.

"I just don't know if she's trying to get in my head or give me a heads-up."

"Assume both," Scottie said. "You don't think it's weird she brought you to an event to say that? Y'all basically sit on top of each other."

"Yes and no." Mickey approached Dig Inn and sighed at the line, which was winding dangerously close to the entrance. She checked the time: 23 minutes and 45 seconds. She opened the door and tacked herself onto the end behind a bald man with a well-moisturized head. "Yes, because she could have just asked me to lunch. No because we all think the walls have ears. We don't even talk shit over Slack."

"Well duh. Rule number one, never put anything in writing you don't want someone to be able to pull up later. No receipts, no drama."

"You watch too much *Housewives*."

"I only watch Potomac."

"Still."

"What does Lex think?"

The line inched forward and something like hope bloomed in her chest. She had one more story to file before the end of the day, and if she could get her lunch in time, she'd be on track to do just that. "She's supportive. Telling me I'll be okay either way."

"You will be."

"I mean, yes, but I don't want to have to bust my ass and freelance while I'm looking for something else."

"I hear that's where the money is."

"But the health insurance," Mickey protested. Health insurance was her go-to comeback whenever anyone brought up the dreaded f-word, but it was deeper than that, bigger than that. Without *Wave,* and before that, Hearst, she was just Mickey—and she couldn't be sure that that was enough.

"Lex has health insurance."

"Her job is just as shaky as mine."

"Fair," Scottie replied.

The line inched forward a little more and Mickey spared a glance at the time. At this rate, she might even have time to take a bite away from her desk.

"But look at it this way," Scottie began, ever the optimist. "Worst-case scenario, you get fired and they give you severance like they do everyone else. You'll chill for a few weeks, look for something else, and write those pie-in-the-sky stories you're always talking about in the meantime. Whatever happened to that story you were going to write, the one about coded Black aesthetics in beauty? I thought that was cool."

"It was," Mickey agreed. "But when was I supposed to write that? I don't have the time."

Mickey envisioned a life without *Wave,* endless time at her disposal.

Her throat constricted at the idea, and she briefly wondered if she was allergic to the unknown. Scottie was right, but Mickey didn't want to be everyone else; in fact, she was completely and totally against it.

Nearly everyone had been laid off when their publication had been snapped up by Bevy, the bigger, less established digital site that had become a home for once-cool publications that had lost their way (but more often their funding). Ten years ago, when impossibly thin, raccoon-eyed popstars were spread out on *Wave* covers, blocky script weaving in and out of their tousled hair, Bevy had yet to become a thread of an idea. Then it was just a joke between friends, led by a man who'd founded a sports site before deciding women's media was less crowded and more impressive in his Tinder bio. In the six years since (and millions of investor dollars later), Bevy had collected sites and newsletters past their prime, adding them to the masthead with breakneck speed.

Wave was their first magazine, the first thing Bevy owned that existed on paper and ink. *Wave* was the big get, but that didn't include *Wave*'s staff, who apparently mattered less than the site's URL.

Mickey took a deep breath. "If I lose this, it's going to be impossible not to feel like I failed."

"People switch jobs all the time, especially in media. No one's going to look at you and think you did something wrong because you moved on."

"Yeah, I get it," Mickey responded, even though she couldn't be sure. She was sure people could see the stain of failure all over her, marking her and tainting her, coloring her blue-black. It wasn't supposed to happen this way. In the beginning, she was the shiny new star, a fresh new hire with all the ideas. Everything she said was brilliant. Everything was a story that would change the conversation as they now knew it. Everyone was grateful for her *perspective*. She'd barely gotten started when Bevy snatched them up—a fact she'd learned from a *Business Insider* article moments before they were kicked out of their offices—tossing her entire world into chaos.

The line moved forward by four people and she pulled the phone from her ear to look at the time. She still had a little over twenty minutes. She'd make it. But before she could bring the phone back to her ear to continue talking to Scottie, a Slack message from Nina popped into view.

"Are you at lunch? Need ur next story up in 30 minutes," it read.

Mickey stepped out of the line, hands shaking as she typed.

"Nope! In the bathroom, be right out."

THREE

When a fifteen-minute meeting popped up on Mickey's calendar the following Thursday, she was startled but not surprised. Nina had messaged her immediately before, asking her if she could come in, as if Mickey wasn't on her way already and Nina needed her permission to cut her loose. Mickey nearly said no, but she knew resistance was futile. This was happening, whether she allowed it to or not. Now, Mickey stood just outside the door to "La La Land," a conference room used specifically for letting people go. It was overly large and conspicuously private, the only room with windows that faced only the outside. "Moonlight," coincidentally, was a small, suffocating phone booth designed for one.

She had sensed it coming in the days leading up to the event, but still, she hadn't expected it to happen so soon. Of course, there had been little signs throughout the week, the biggest being the revolving door of well-dressed Black girls that had stomped through the building, past her desk, and into a side room with Nina, where both would disappear for half an hour before reemerging with a beaming Nina thanking them for their time. Mickey, perhaps naively, hoped they were replacing Jordan, but now, it was very, very clear that one of them would be replacing her.

Mickey entered the room and found Nina and Cathy, the head of HR, waiting for her.

"Hi, Mickey, thanks for coming in," Cathy said, her crow's feet wrinkling as her mouth spread into a shape that resembled a smile.

Mickey resisted the urge to turn around, walk to her desk, and start on the day's work, but she met the woman's eyes instead. She could tell that Cathy had been pretty once, when the doughy thickness of her skin had still been bouncy and supple and her lips had been visible, rather than the two thin lines that currently disappeared when she opened her mouth.

"Please, sit," Cathy said, her tone gentle, but insistent. Mickey shivered at the insincerity, realizing they were afraid she would be loud and cause a scene. She briefly considered it, imagined that instead of sitting down like she was told, she would pick up the chair and hurl it across the room, hitting Nina in the head and watching her body crumple to the ground. She would laugh maniacally at the sight, snap photos for memories. Then she would turn to Cathy, who would undoubtedly be mortified, and slap her across the face, tell her to stop gawking and ask in a condescending tone: *Didn't anybody ever tell you it was rude to stare?*

She pulled out the chair instead, gripping the back with unnecessary force and sitting down as gently as her rage could allow.

Nina wouldn't look at her, staring out into middle distance, then the table, before repeating the cycle again. The room was quiet, and Mickey realized that they were waiting for Nina to speak. Nina swallowed and tucked strands of hair behind her ear, her forehead wrinkling from the effort.

"Due to your inability to complete tasks and your performance, we're going to have to let you go," she said, the words tumbling out all at once in an order that seemed unnatural. Mickey felt the words in her gut, alarm marrying devastation and producing an overwhelming shame. It wouldn't occur to her until later that she'd never had a proper performance review. No one had given her the opportunity to improve. But now, she was certain that she hadn't been enough. By the time Nina got up to leave the room, without so much as a glance in her direction, Mickey was on the verge of tears.

Then it was just her and Cathy, who'd begun explaining how everything would work. After the meeting, she would not be allowed to go back to her desk. Instead, her things would be shipped to her home, boxed up by someone (likely Evie) who would make sure she didn't leave a single thing behind. She would get severance and would be able to file for unemployment. Cathy said this part like it was a blessing, like the last act of benevolence was taking care of their former employees. They (meaning the company) wouldn't disclose the reasons for her firing or talk shit about her outside the company's walls, provided she signed an NDA that would stop her from speaking out and writing an article, or, more damningly, a book. They wished her well, with Cathy speaking for the entirety of the "they," and hoped that she would shortly land on her feet.

"Is there anything you'd like to say?" Cathy asked, resting her arms on the table and leaning in slightly to signal that she was all ears. The movement made her stiff shift dress crinkle, and Mickey bristled at the sound. Cathy slid a manila envelope across the table, sealed with papers for Mickey to sign. "We'll send you a copy via email, too."

Then, as if by magic, Cathy produced a box of Kleenex, placing it in front of Mickey with a practiced flick of the wrist.

"Yeah, actually," Mickey began. "What happens if I don't sign?" She was curious, mostly.

"You wouldn't receive severance, and we would part ways," Cathy explained, her mouth hanging open in a half-smile.

"So, the NDA?"

Cathy blinked. "Of course that wouldn't apply."

"Good to know," Mickey said with a click of her tongue, watching carefully for Cathy's reaction. There was none, her aging face remained frozen in place. "I was just checking, because given the circumstances I think people need to know what happened here."

"What happened?" Cathy leaned forward again, suddenly interested.

Mickey leaned in, too. They were slightly too close. It felt conspiratorial. As if they were on the same side, almost. "I'm just confused about how I'm being fired on the grounds of performance if we've never had an evaluation of my performance prior to now," Mickey said, using her most formal voice and speaking slowly. It was the only way of keeping her voice steady, knowing if she spoke faster her voice would get louder and then she would cry. "There were no warnings, or anything leading up to this. It's clear you're trying to clean house and that this is targeted."

Cathy tilted her head to the side. "I'm sorry you feel that way. We truly hoped that it would be a good fit, but unfortunately it didn't work out that way."

"A good fit in what sense? A good culture fit?" Mickey asked, matching Cathy's head tilt and expression.

Cathy reddened. "I didn't say that."

"You didn't have to," Mickey said with a sigh. "You might as well have just said you don't want people of color on the team."

"Of course not," Cathy said, now alarmed. "Letting you go has nothing to do with *that*, it's about performance . . ."

"Then why did Nina say we were moving away from identity?" Mickey asked. "What does that even mean?"

"Well, I'd have to ask Nina," she offered in reply. "I can't speak to the various editorial directions of the different sites, but diversity and inclusion is a global mandate for every publication we own."

"So why didn't you rehire someone after Jordan? Why am I now the only Black person on my team?" Mickey asked. "And why has Nina only hired white people since she got here?"

"That's something we can look into," Cathy said, scribbling a quick message on a notepad.

"I think that would be a good start," Mickey said, feeling emboldened. "But I wouldn't recommend working here to any Black woman or woman of color. Every managing editor in the company is white, and none of them are prioritizing diversity on their teams." Mickey was talking faster now and felt the spit gathering on her tongue and settling in the corners of her mouth. She wondered, briefly, if she looked as enraged as she felt, or if the flash of nervousness in Cathy's eyes was a trick of the light.

"Well, thank you for that feedback, we'll certainly take that into consideration moving forward. I know the person they hired for your position is, uh, African American."

Mickey was livid now. "How was I supposed to even keep my job or improve if they've already replaced me? How is that fair? Can you, or someone, just admit that you planned on firing us from the moment we were acquired?" Mickey tried to keep the desperation out of her voice, but she couldn't tell if it was working. "And recruiting in my group of friends like it wouldn't get back to me? There's only so many Black beauty writers in New York. How was I supposed to do my job well if this is what I'm up against?"

"Well, I'm sorry you had that experience," Cathy allowed, her mouth flipping into a frown. "But it wasn't our intention to hire and fire you. We really wanted this to work out. As for the other claims, hiring is supposed to be confidential, you shouldn't have known about that."

Cathy leaned back into the ergonomic chair, resting her elbows on the curved plastic arms. "I'm sorry that you had to go through that. I could see how that could be stressful for you."

"Well, I did know about it," Mickey said, her voice sounding strange and small. "And it made it really hard for me to do my job."

"And I'm sorry for that," Cathy said, pushing the Kleenex a little closer. Mickey realized then that she had started crying again, her body betraying her will to stay strong. "Really."

"You're not sorry," Mickey replied, snatching a tissue from the flimsy opening. "Because nothing is going to change. And I know that. But I needed someone to at least hear my side."

"Thank you for sharing."

Mickey nodded, shoving the manila envelope into her bag. "How long do I have to sign this?"

"A week."

"I'll have to have my lawyer look over this," Mickey said, even though she didn't have one.

"Of course," Cathy said, with a grim smile and nod. Mickey could feel Cathy's eyes tracing her face, working through the different scenarios to see if she would be a problem. If she would speak up and fight back.

Mickey clutched the bag on her shoulder. She rose from the chair and tossed her work-issued laptop onto the table in front of her, a last act of defiance before leaving the room. This particular conference room was near the HR pod and thus no one glanced in her direction as she walked away, tote bag pulled tight, eyes trained toward the ground. At first, she had been upset when they said they would send her things, but now she couldn't imagine going back to her desk and seeing orbs of pity (or perhaps satisfaction) staring back at her.

Homebodies

Stepping out into the expanse of the city street, Mickey, overcome by the feeling of existing in the middle of the day with absolutely nothing to do, felt giddy and disoriented. She was neither ahead of her work or behind on it. She was devoid of responsibilities and stories to write. It was wholly foreign to someone like her, who had done nothing but strive and ascend since she'd left home. It struck her that she wouldn't be grabbing an afternoon snack with Evie in a few minutes (which was mostly Mickey eating croissants from a French bakery chain while Evie chain-smoked Virginia Slims), and that break to her routine felt the most violent of all.

Mickey walked the short distance to Madison Square Park in a daze, plopping herself on the sunniest bench she could find and letting the sun's rays trick her into thinking she wasn't so far from summer. She didn't know what to do next or who to call. She briefly considered trying her mother, but she knew she was likely somewhere remote without Wi-Fi or a phone. She thought of her father next, who would know exactly what to say—*just get back on the horse*—his voice an echo of the thoughts already playing in her head, but she knew the disappointment would seep through his words of encouragement, his successful daughter now so obviously less so. She couldn't handle that. Not today.

Mickey checked the time. It was a little before noon. She couldn't call Scottie, not when it felt so fresh. It would turn her inside out. She thought of Lex, who would be in a meeting, and decided it was best not to bother her, not until she pulled herself together.

"I could call Elaine," Mickey mumbled, speaking mostly to herself and the pigeon pecking at dirt near her feet. But she didn't move to do anything at all.

The world hummed around her, and she wondered if anyone else felt as lost as she did. If the Black nannies clipping white children into expensive strollers felt as unsure as she did about their next steps, or if the men in blue plaid shirts and smart navy pants also wondered about their own insignificance in between bites of predressed, prechopped salad.

She picked up her phone and FaceTimed Elaine, the phone chirping until it notified her that her friend was busy living her own life. Moments later, the phone vibrated in her hand, and a full, cherubic face popped into view.

"Hey, what's up?" Elaine asked, her face flushed. "Are you okay? You never call me in the middle of the day."

"Are you working out?" Mickey asked, watching Elaine prop the phone up on a surface before folding her body in half and placing her hands on the floor. Then, without warning, she swung one of her legs into the air and began pulsing it up and down, her three-toned leggings flag-like as she pierced the air with her efforts.

"Yeah," Elaine replied breathlessly, switching to jump squats shortly after. "You know, move well, and all that."

Mickey nodded, searching for a way to bring up the news. "How are things at Indoor Intonations?"

Elaine gave a thumbs-up sign before launching her body to the floor, kicking both legs out and jumping back up again. "Whew!" she exclaimed when she finally came up for air. "Technically, I'm working right now. We just rolled out these new leggings," she kicked up her leg for emphasis, "and I need to figure out how to talk about them editorially, so I'm testing."

Elaine jumped up and down rapidly. "See! They don't move!"

Mickey watched carefully. They did in fact, stay in place. "And they have pockets," Elaine said excitedly, shoving her hands into the sides of the leggings and stretching them out to prove her point. "Isn't that great?"

"It is."

"You haven't even asked me when you're going to get a pair," Elaine said with a frown. "What's up with you?"

"They let me go," Mickey said, and she realized she never wanted to say that again. It hurt more somehow, to say the words all together. She felt like she'd failed in more ways than one. Not only had she lost her job, but she'd also missed all the signs leading up to it. She had been convinced that her talent alone would protect her, but that couldn't be further from the truth.

"Are you kidding me? Why the hell would they do that?" Elaine produced a towel from what seemed like thin air and dabbed at her forehead. "I only read *Wave* for your articles." She raised two fingers in a scout's honor salute. "Honestly."

"There's no way they were going to keep all of us on after Nina started, I just didn't expect it to be today, you know. Evie's still there somehow, and she vapes at her desk."

"I'm so sorry this happened," Elaine said, with a frown. "But I'm not surprised. It's how media goes. It's exhausting. That's why I went brand side." As if on cue, she brought a water bottle to her lips with her job's approachable but sleek sans-serif logo emblazoned on the side.

"Yeah, I know," Mickey attempted, her mouth opening and closing as she thought of what to say next. What would she tell Elaine? That she was right? That the unforgiving tumultuousness of media had finally gotten her, too?

If she was being perfectly honest, she hadn't expected it to. She was a hot commodity: lesbian, Black, well-spoken. She never said no to a video appearance or a sponsored Instagram story, even when it was clear that they were using her likeness to mask theirs. Elaine, on the other hand, was everything media had too much of. White, brunette, smiley. Vocal until it mattered. White until someone mentioned it. They were an oddly matched pair, made close by nights spent as interns in the beauty closet, organizing hundreds of samples and breaking down boxes until their fingers ached. They had talked about their dreams while they spritzed expensive perfumes and swatched eyeshadow palettes on the fleshy parts of their hands.

Elaine had wanted to be a beauty director once, lording over a corner of a glossy women's magazine in a midi-skirt and smart heels. Mickey, on the other hand, just wanted to write, dreaming of a cushy staff writer position somewhere that her voice would matter. A place where she would be doted on and fretted over, where other publications would try to poach her once a week. She would always say no, of course, but she would use the leverage to get more money, until she was so rich she could live in a brownstone in Fort Greene with brass finishings and ancient hardwood floors.

"It was bound to happen at some point, right?" Mickey asked, and this sounded so pitiful to her she couldn't help but tear up again.

"Aw, honey. Don't cry. It's okay," Elaine crooned, but Mickey ignored her, the tears running down her face with zeal.

"It's not okay," Mickey replied. "How am I supposed to pay my bills?"

"Wait," Elaine said, placing her hands on the counter and leaning in close to the camera. Her eyes widened in alarm. "Did they not give you severance?"

"They offered, but I have to sign an NDA to get it," Mickey explained with a heaving sigh. "I don't know if I'm going to."

"Why not?" Elaine asked, and Mickey watched as she moved through her house until they ended up in the kitchen, where she was propped up once again.

"So much fucked up shit happened there, I could write a book about it. And I don't want them suing me when I do."

"I mean books are fictional," Elaine explained, disappearing from view. Mickey heard the sound of a fridge opening and closing before she appeared again, iced coffee in hand. "So it's not like they can sue you for making something up. Unless you're trying to write a memoir."

"Oh god no," Mickey said with an eye roll. Every editor, writer, and intern believed they had a New York media memoir brewing just beneath the surface, one that would make their long hours and meager pay worth it. Rarely, if ever, did those come to fruition. Mickey reminded Elaine of this, and her friend who always seemed to have something to say couldn't argue with that truth.

"Well, what do you want to do next?"

Mickey felt her head spin. She hadn't even started to consider where to go from here. "I don't know. I haven't even signed these papers. Should I?"

"Depends," Elaine replied, sipping down her drink. "Do you think you have the energy and time to pump out a story about the things that happened to you without needing therapy? Therapy you can't afford because you'd no longer have health insurance?"

"Okay, fair," Mickey conceded. She briefly thought about her and Lex's recent musings about marriage, if they could speed up the process of claiming each other but decided to say nothing about it. It felt like their private thing, at least for now.

"But if you think you can handle it, and have like six months in your savings, then go for it."

Mickey thought then of her savings account, dusty with disuse and filled with graduation money she received years ago and vowed never to touch. All together she had a little more than three thousand dollars saved, the lion's share scrimped together via an app that rounded up her purchases and dumped them in a place where she could track her progress with pride. "I don't, do you?"

"Of course," Elaine said, disappearing again. This time she came back with a fruit bowl that looked perfect and preprepared. "But I could barely save when I was living in New York." Elaine popped a blueberry into her mouth. "If my parents weren't helping me a little bit with rent, I never would have been able to afford my studio."

Mickey thought back to Elaine's well-lit apartment on the Upper East Side, roomy but dated, and all hers. "Casa Elaine," she'd dubbed it, decking it out with plush, comfy furniture and stream after stream of fairy lights.

"Oh, Casa Elaine!" she replied with a flourish, flicking her hand like she was a flamenco dancer. "I miss that place. But honestly, you can't beat the space in Texas."

Mickey nodded, waiting for the conversation to wind back to the topic at hand.

"Have you thought about using it as a little vacation?" asked Elaine. "Where's your family from again?"

"Maryland," Mickey replied, wondering what she was getting at.

"Yeah, why don't you go there?" She speared a piece of fruit and pressed it between her lips. "If I had nothing but time, I would definitely do that."

Elaine's imaginings of Maryland were coastal, Mickey was sure. Crabs and harbors and bays. Tall brown grass jutting from the water, docks stretching toward the horizon. That was not Mickey's Maryland, not even close. She was from PG County, true suburbia—a land where chain stores abounded and Black people grew old and comfortable. It had its own charm, but Mickey would be the last person to describe it as relaxing. There, she would be forced to contend with the remnants of the life she'd left behind. A life that looked so different she wouldn't know how to find the pieces, much less put them together.

"I just—it just doesn't feel right," Mickey said.

"What do you mean? I'm sure your parents would love to see you. Whenever I go home, my mom is literally thrilled to wait on me hand and foot."

Mickey couldn't relate. She had never known that kind of attentiveness, that level of adoration. Her mother, Sylvia Hayward, was not the type of woman who dedicated her life to anyone else, not even her daughter. She was in search of something bigger and greater, something more than Mickey.

It had been months since they'd last spoken, a brief call from someone's phone in Jamaica. Her mother was dating a new man, a Rasta who claimed to be a close associate of Bob Marley's and had her living off the land. She was a vegetarian now and covered her hair and legs with yard after yard of fabric. That left her father, who was still in the DMV area, but had another family to attend to—a youngish wife named Jamila and a son who everyone swore looked just like Mickey. He wouldn't have the energy, much less the time to cater to her every whim and need. He was too busy playing dad and husband for that.

"I'm sure they'd be happy to see me, too," she said. "But it definitely wouldn't be a vacation."

She briefly flashed to the last time she'd been home, the previous Christmas, a quick trip that seemed to happen in slow motion. There was food and twinkling lights and the faces of the people she loved, but she still felt like she was experiencing it all through a thin pane of glass. No, she much preferred her home with Lex and Mango in Astoria. Even more than that, she preferred employment.

"The way they let me go, it was just wrong."

"It's always wrong. This is media, where layoffs are part of their fiscal strategy." Elaine said this with a little laugh, as if it had been a brilliant observation.

"But everyone wasn't taken advantage of and sidelined for being Black." Mickey wiped at her face and leaned back onto the bench, the sun now assaulting the top of her head and one side of her body. Beads of moisture started to gather in the crook of her elbow and the backs of her knees.

Elaine's eyes popped open in alarm again. "Wait, did they say something racist?"

Mickey combed through her mental catalogue of microaggressions, searching for one shocking enough for Elaine to understand. "Racist in a less obvious way," Mickey began. "Like she wouldn't take Black artists seriously until they collab'd with a white artist or won a big award, or the one time she shot down all my pitches but greenlit something similar when it came out of a white intern's mouth."

"Oh that's fucked up," Elaine said, spearing a blackberry with her fork. "But maybe she's just generally dumb and needs to hear things twice to really get it."

"Or maybe," Mickey felt the temperature of her skin rise, frustration bubbling, attempting to locate her surprise at Elaine's defense of Nina, whom she'd never met, and came up short. "Nevermind."

Mickey covered her face with one hand, ready to hang up and head home, slipping into the fold of people who had somewhere urgent to go before breaking off into the subway, which would be a shell of itself midday.

"I gotta go, let's talk later," Mickey said finally, hovering over the end button with her thumb.

"Did I say something?" Elaine asked, her face knitting into concern.

"Nope, it's fine," Mickey replied, even though it wasn't. "Thanks for hearing me out."

Then, "So the leggings?"

Elaine's mouth stretched into a grin.

FOUR

In the twenty-four hours following her firing, Mickey was damn near upbeat. Verging on giddy. Wave *was holding her back!* she reasoned. *Stealing her shine! Stopping her from achieving her fullest potential, which was limitless and abundant!* She was finally free, able to do what she wanted when she wanted. She was unencumbered by the *voice* of *Wave,* which sounded like a geriatric millennial trying to convince women aged eighteen to twenty-four (the kind of women who referred to themselves as *girls*) that they were, in fact, cool.

For the first time in a long time, she could sound like herself again. She wouldn't have to throw in acronyms where they had no place or add exclamation points (!) when she really wanted the authority of a period. She wouldn't sober up for days yet. For now, she was high on this feeling, and felt a rush of inspiration that made her feel like this should've happened weeks!—months!—ago. She was grateful to Chelsea for the heads-up and happy that Nina had cut her loose (though that bitch would never *ever* be good in Mickey's book).

She texted Scottie her plans for productivity for that day and emailed her closest industry friends, politely dragging *Wave* while also asking them to keep her in mind for future opportunities. They didn't respond within fifteen minutes like Mickey had hoped, but that was okay! They didn't have the time that Mickey had, couldn't be on top of things like she was. They were too busy being bogged down by the corporate structure, which, when Mickey thought about it, was the very thing she'd vowed never to get sucked into. This was the universe's way of course-correcting, reminding her that there was always something *more* waiting for her beyond the confines of the nine to five. She was *free!*

At forty-eight hours, the reality of her circumstances began to set in, and she was reminded by an email from Cathy's assistant that Mickey had yet to sign her NDA. They were fine either way, just wanted to check. There was also a polite-but-firm reminder that this would be her last check on payroll, so she needed to come up with an answer by the end of the week.

At first, Mickey wanted to resist. A last stand. Scottie, ever the pragmatist, reminded her that last stands were only effective when you were still employed, and a paycheck for a few months was better than nothing at all. But still, she had some hope. It had been fucked up the way they let her go. All she needed was one person to see that, to agree that she should give the establishment the finger and expose the entire thing. When she'd posited that to Scottie, her friend had reminded her of the splash and ripple of all movements, that one person taking down the entire company with a single exposé was not only rare but unlikely, even in an alternate universe where Nina had Mickey physically licking her boots and coming to her home at three a.m. to feed her pets. She reminded Mickey of *The Devil Wears Prada* and how, after all these years, people still deified Miranda Priestly despite her being a very shitty boss.

"Worker solidarity in the United States is literally political theater," Scottie had said, and Mickey agreed. But there was still some hope. Just a tiny bit.

She relayed this modern-day vision of David toppling Goliath (she being David, wearing a pair of Margiela Tabi boots) to Lex over oily pork fried rice that night, tossing the idea out while she ripped a duck sauce packet open with her teeth.

"It's just the principle, you know?" she'd said once she concluded, and the look in Lex's eye was one of amusement. It was clear that she was *not* down with the revolution.

"That's exactly what Scottie said," Mickey said, watching Lex bite back a smirk, her plump pink bottom lip disappearing behind her crooked front teeth.

"I didn't say anything."

Mickey stuck her tongue out. "Fuck you."

"It's been a week, so gladly."

Mickey chuckled and spooned more food into her mouth. "She also thinks I should sign the NDA."

"Do you think you should sign?" Lex asked, pausing her eating to regard Mickey carefully.

"I feel like I don't have a choice. I mean, it's not like I have a boyfriend who works in finance who can just hold it down while I take a few months to write an exposé about my time there."

"I'm offended," Lex said with mock indignation, pressing a hand to her chest. "But seriously, I get it." She resumed eating her food, twirling her fork around in her lo mein. "And then there's you being the girl who caused trouble."

"True," Mickey said, and in all that time of plotting and planning she'd forgotten, just for a moment, that it wasn't just *Wave*. It was *Wave* but it was everywhere else, too. If she took on one, she threatened them all. The sudden lump in her throat told her that this was what scared her most of all. The potential of being unemployable, her hard-won career evaporated by a splashy article that would get her followers on Twitter but would do little for getting her another, better role.

Her mind drifted to Tangela Ray, a Black girl who'd pulled a stunt around the time Mickey had been an intern at Hearst. She had been something like a media darling before her abrupt exit from one of the big glossies. There was the meteoric rise up the masthead: beauty director by twenty-seven, the second Black woman to hold the position in the history of the magazine and the youngest to ever do it. She was the kind of Black woman white people loved and Black women had horror stories about.

But everything had changed when Tangela accused one of the top editors of calling her a nigger and no one did anything about it. Defiantly, she remade the homepage in her image, complete with a headline article outing the editor, who was now the editor in chief at the very same publication. The article was up twenty-nine minutes before it, and she, were removed from the company.

Let the rumors tell it, she left kicking and screaming and pulling at her hair, but no one really knew the truth. Tangela was labeled crazy—people still joked about having a Tangela-type of day—and it became a cautionary tale for the Black women she'd left behind. It would be a long time before that magazine let a Black woman rise through the ranks like that again, and it was an unspoken truth that whoever came after her would have it harder than she did. Tangela—the woman, the myth—was never to be seen again. Last Mickey had heard, she'd married white, changed her last name to Sacks, and moved to California, where she now spent her days with a chubby-cheeked toddler named Chase and drove a caviar-colored Range Rover. Tangela had become a footnote, associated with her rage and her pain rather than her brilliance.

"They just want us to sit quietly, eat our food, have our panic attacks and then move on. It's not okay," Mickey said. Her chest opened up and something crawled in. Suddenly she felt small in the vastness of her industry. She remembered her place.

"You're right," Lex agreed. "It's not. But until y'all have a reckoning and everyone comes out at once, you'll be that one. And you saw what they did to Kap."

"I know. And I'm not trying to be the Kap of journalism. These hiring managers and editors will blackball me, I'm sure of it."

"Then I think your mind's already made up. You're bigger than this. And one day you'll be Oprah big," Lex said with a toothy smile. "Then, you can air all your dirty laundry and we'll have so much money they'll be scared to sue."

Mickey smiled and let her mind drift to that faraway place, where she didn't worry about everything that stretched in front of her because the hard things had already been left behind. "Yeah, and I can make you live in the guest house."

"Sure," Lex said with an eye roll. "That would last five minutes before you were begging me to come to bed."

"Six minutes, at least."

FIVE

Do you want me to cancel?" Lex yelled from their bathroom, her voice echoing down their cramped hallway and into the living room. She was in the middle of her skin care routine, a once-simple ritual that now consisted of five products, most of which she'd acquired by way of Mickey, who received so much free skin care she could moisturize everyone in their twenty-five-unit building and still have lots left over for herself.

They'd committed to this dinner with their friends Bunmi and Akira weeks ago, before everything started to come apart at the seams. The two couples had formed something like a four-person supper club, trying out interesting-looking restaurants recommended by the algorithm or name-dropped by coworkers. This was their third dinner since coming up with the idea, and Mickey very much liked them and didn't want to fuck this up.

"You're already getting dressed," Mickey replied from her perch on the couch, an oversized heather gray sectional they'd purchased at West Elm on sale that she painstakingly kept clean with weekly vacuuming and a citrus-scented spray to deter Mango from sinking her claws into the tightly woven fabric and exposing its insides. It was the most money she'd ever spent on any one thing, and she'd be damned if the cat (who she imagined would be deeply offended upon hearing herself referred to as simply "the cat") would undo her hard work.

In the week since her firing, the couch had become her headquarters, with her enthusiasm for work waning the more time went on. She would wake up when Lex did and shuffle barefoot from their bedroom to the living room, where she would wrap herself in a throw blanket and turn on a Pixar movie for the thousandth time. Today, she watched *Ratatouille*. But unlike the rat, she didn't cook, she didn't clean. She only moved to pee and buzz the door for deliveries. Today's lunch—extra-wet lemon pepper wings (flats, fried hard) and crispy crinkle fries—was sitting on the other end of the couch, a graveyard of chicken bones and leftover seasoning.

When she wasn't staring blankly at the television, she was scrolling mindlessly on her phone, watching everyone live their very-much-employed lives. A gaggle of beauty editors were currently on a press trip in Paris, taking plandids in front of heavy, ancient doors and meticulously documenting their days. She tingled with jealousy. Her group chats were alive with activity, and this made her stomach hurt, a constant reminder that she was quickly fading from relevance and no one cared enough to stop it.

Her industry chat had never really commented on her being replaced, which, aside from stinging, had planted a seed of suspicion that they'd all been in on it. She did eventually say something when she'd been laid off, and everyone promised to keep an eye out, though from her vantage point it felt that no one could be bothered to look. When Simone, a senior beauty editor at Condé, proposed they all do drinks soon, Mickey had simply not replied. When Jannah, an influeditor whose Instagram had become #sponcon, asked if anyone wanted to go out that weekend, Mickey demurred and pretended she had something to do. She was extricating herself slowly, text by text, even though the thing she wanted more than anything else was to be back in the fold. She did all this from a supine position, head slightly elevated by throw pillows, so it was easier to move from side to side. This was how Lex found her when she got home: disheveled and wearing the same clothes from the day before, even though she'd promised to be dressed and showered when she walked through the door. Dinner was at seven. It was six fifteen.

"I can get *un*dressed though," Lex said, emerging from the bathroom, skin slick with products. She was glowing. "Bunmi and Akira

53

cancel all the time. Do I need to wear sunscreen at night, or can I stop at the moisturizer part?"

"No baby, we'll go," Mickey insisted. This would be good for her, she reasoned. "And no sun, no sunscreen."

"But you told me that on cloudy days I still needed to."

"Yes."

"But then no sun, no sunscreen doesn't make that much sense."

Mickey rolled her eyes and worked through how she'd explain to Lex that just because the sun was *hidden* on cloudy days, it didn't mean it wasn't there. "How do I put this," she began, but Lex had already moved on, positioning herself in front of their floor-length mirror—a silver one from IKEA that everyone owned.

"Are you sure you're up to it?" Lex asked, pulling at her T-shirt so it hung just-so and adjusting the gold chains circling her neck. She always wore three necklaces: a nameplate, her long-dead maternal grandmother's wedding ring, and the tiniest *M*. "I've been home for twenty minutes and you haven't moved."

Mickey watched Lex watching herself. She looked good, her hair freshly cut, conditioned, and oiled. She wore a pair of brown pants that had been fitted perfectly to her body, crafted by a Lower East Side tailor who had a knack for making clothes. She'd paired it with sneakers and a cream-colored T-shirt that made Jesus look like a superstar, his image framed out with gothic lettering. Atop her head, she wore a dark green fitted cap, repping a team she didn't support. Mickey could smell her from across the room, a musky, spicy, vanilla-y scent with a hint of coffee and incense. Her wrists were adorned with gold bracelets and a vintage Timex she'd lifted from her mother's house. It belonged to her mother's brother, who according to family lore, met a Puerto Rican girl while he was in Panama and was never heard from again.

Mickey briefly thought about fucking her, pulling down the biker shorts she'd been wearing for two days in a row over her hips and offering herself up like she used to when they first started dating and sex was exciting. But the thought of removing her clothes now seemed like too much work. And what next? She would, hair askew, open her legs? It was daunting, humiliating.

In the beginning, before she was exhausted, Lex would press her slim fingers deep inside, pushing Mickey's face against mirrors, sinks, and into the never-washed pillows on her extra-long twin bed. There was something chemical about the attraction when they met—two years out of college and unsure of what came next.

They met, as many couples do, at a party. Mickey had come across the flyer on Instagram, Lex was friends with the DJ. Their eyes locked across the room, and it felt like a reintroduction. As if they'd been looking for each other a lifetime. It wasn't long before they were dancing, gyrating in the crush of Black bodies to Konshens, waists winding to the dancehall beat. Hips pressed against pelvis, hands holding hips, Lex's hands skimming her waistline. Gently, Lex guided her movements, and Mickey remembered feeling like she'd follow this woman to the ends of the earth. Then, Lex's very presence would turn Mickey on, sending chills down her spine and wetness between her legs.

Now, Mickey's brain was foggy with resentment and all she could think about was the fact that she'd need to look just as good as Lex to avoid embarrassing them both. She ran a hand through her braids and was grateful she didn't have to brush her hair into submission.

"I'm sure," Mickey replied, standing up. She gave Lex another once-over and disappeared into their bedroom to get dressed. Mickey sifted through her closet and found herself frustrated by the pressure to perform. Why hadn't Lex canceled without her saying anything? Why did Mickey have to be the one to make the call?

Lex appeared as she was sliding her hips into a knit skirt. "How long do you think?" she asked, and Mickey felt the irritation pricking at the backs of her knees.

"I'll be ready in fifteen."

"Can you make it ten?"

"Seriously?"

"It's just, these reservations were hard to get. You've been saying you wanted to go."

"That was before. Can you help me?" Mickey changed into an orange number that required two people and a shallow breathing technique to zip up. Lex held together the fabric with her hands and used her teeth to shimmy the zipper up her back. Mickey could feel the heat of her breath and the panting sighs as she struggled. It pissed Mickey off to hear her breathing like that, like it required so much effort to get the dress up. It fit; she knew it did. Lex stopped at the middle of her back and came up for air.

"I can't do it," she declared, and Mickey was nearly moved to tears. "Forget it, just get it off."

They did a little dance to wiggle Mickey out of the dress while she looked around for alternatives. If she didn't want to go before, now she was sure of it.

Bunmi and Akira were ten minutes late and Mickey and Lex were fifteen minutes later than that. It had been Mickey's fault. She changed four times before settling on a too-short dress that rode up every few steps and an oversized leather trench with matching over-the-knee boots. It required no assistance. Bunmi and Akira met them out front, looking every bit the coordinated couple, wearing rich shades of emerald green that dazzled against their dark skin.

They had three years to Lex and Mickey's five, and the difference was palpable. Mickey could still sense the electricity between them, some invisible current ensuring they never stood more than six feet apart. They were always touching, as if they couldn't stand to be disconnected by petty things like space, time, people. There was a newness that had long since evaporated between Mickey and Lex, a shiny veneer that had yet to dull with age.

For Mickey, the fresh feeling of new love had been replaced with routine. They fucked on the same days and in the same places, fought at the same time of year about the same things. It was safe and cyclical and Mickey was beginning to wonder if eventually she'd get dizzy riding the same ride again and again, if the vertigo had already begun to set in.

But she couldn't let them see, so instead she plastered on the biggest smile she could muster and started a giddy vibration as soon as her heeled foot emerged from the car. She waved enthusiastically and pulled Akira into a hug with one hand and pressed her face to Bunmi with the other. Even their scents were in conversation.

"It feels like it's been forever," she said once she unhanded them both, her voice verging on a whine.

"It has been," Akira replied.

Lex pulled Bunmi in for a quick embrace and planted a kiss on Akira's cheek.

"Beautiful, as always," Lex remarked. Almost immediately, a pang of jealousy shot through her system, reminding Mickey that she was capable of feeling something other than frustration and overwhelm.

Dinner was at a Mediterranean spot with stellar views of the Brooklyn Bridge; dim, warm-toned lighting, and delicate chairs with small seats that photographed well but made Mickey's butt hurt. It felt cozy and expensive, the vibe she was aiming for in her home but never quite achieved.

The group shared serving after serving of house-made flatbread, which they dragged through pools of hummus and labneh spiked with floral honey from the Catskills. The couples sat beside each other, giving Mickey ample opportunity to observe their friends. Bunmi's hand was always caressing Akira—her fingers danced across the back of her neck, the small of her back, the tops of her arms—much to the delight of Akira, who would send her longing looks of adoration before rejoining the group conversation. Their world, insular and loving, was always just a brief touch away. As if inspired, Lex leaned over and pressed a lip to Mickey's shoulder, exposed now that her jacket sat on the back of her chair. "You look beautiful, babe," she whispered, and Mickey waited for the spark, the quiver, but there was nothing but indignation. She'd said it to Akira first.

As the night went on, Mickey remembered why she liked going out with them. They were unafraid to order everything on the menu, plus Bunmi had freakishly good taste in wine, which meant that the conversation flowed easily, moving from the very public ousting of a celebrity best friend (and the stunning makeup she wore during her explanation video) to *Love and Basketball* being a queer movie (a Mickey take that was hard to convince everyone of) to why studs ain't shit. On that topic, like every other topic, Mickey had lots to say.

"Y'all are the worst," Mickey declared, popping a French fry in her mouth followed by a bite of roasted chicken.

"Hey now," Bunmi cut in, leaning on her forearms and reaching across the table to steal one of Mickey's fries. "Y'all love us, and you know it." She looked up into Mickey's face and winked.

Mickey did her best not to blush and Akira, tuned in to the entire exchange, looked from Mickey to Bunmi and grinned. "See, that's why we don't fuck with y'all!" she exclaimed. Her voice was sweet even when she was scolding. Akira was from Houston and had this drawl that made everything sound appealing. So much so that Mickey wished she narrated audiobooks or announced stops on the subway. "Always trying to flirt and get your way," Akira said as she nudged Bunmi's shoulder playfully and helped herself to a fry from Mickey's plate.

Mickey pushed her plate toward the center of the table to give them better access and fixed her eyes on Bunmi. "So you do that all the time, huh?" she asked. She was two glasses in to a juicy, Napa Valley red and her gaze was molten and brown. She'd been told over the years, by hookups, by friends, by the first woman she loved, that she had sensual eyes, but she'd never felt in command of their effect. Couldn't tell whether she looked sexy or like she had a bit of a staring problem. Now she hoped her eyes were bewitching and might compel Bunmi to tell the truth.

"Do what?" Bunmi asked, leaning back in her seat and spreading her knees wide. Her arm followed, draping herself across Akira's shoulder and the back of her tiny seat.

"Flirt with girls to get what you want."

"I think that—" Lex began, and Mickey's head pivoted sharply in her direction.

"You, be quiet," she said, pointing at her with the tip of her butter knife. "I already know how you are with the girls in your office, ma'am."

Lex threw up her hands in mock offense. "Me? I don't do anything. I just mind my business, go to work, and come home to my woman." Her arms encircled Mickey's waist and she pulled her tight, kissing the side of her neck and then her cheek.

"Yeah, yeah, yeah," Mickey said with a reluctant smile. "Y'all still not shit."

"At all," Akira chimed in before taking a languid sip of a crisp white.

"You femmes keep dating us though," Bunmi said and her mouth stretched into a smile, revealing her bright white teeth. They sat perfectly behind her purple-brown lips, which were the same color as the rest of her skin. She was smooth in every sense of the word.

"Unfortunately. But we must, at some point, as a community discuss the heteronormativity and how it's so *so* toxic."

"Sure. But on a practical level, y'all like that," Bunmi replied.

"How you figure?" Mickey asked. "You think we like the incredibly small dating pool, the mind games and the general shenanigans?"

Bunmi chortled. "What pretty boi broke your heart before Lex?" she asked. "I want to meet her."

Mickey held Bunmi's gaze as she drank the last bit of her wine, careful not to let the sediment pass her lips. It was the last glass of the bottle. Mickey placed her wineglass on the table and signaled the waiter to bring them one more. Lex moved it to the left of Mickey's elbow. Mickey tended to get overzealous with her movements when drunk, known to send a glass, plate, or fork tumbling to the floor.

Mickey sent a brief smile in Lex's direction. "Thanks," she said in a low tone, and Lex nodded, giving her knee a quick squeeze under the table. They took care of each other, anyone could see that.

Akira wiggled her eyebrows. "I gotta hear this." Akira's eyes danced in curiosity. "I can't imagine a young Mickey, sad about some girl."

"Oh, I was very much sad about some girl," Mickey replied, her mind drifting. It had been so long since she'd thought of Tee. At one time, Tee had been her general state of mind. As a teenager, Tee was the first thing on her mind when she woke up and the last thing she thought of when she went to sleep. And then Tee would invade her dreams in various shapes and forms: taunting her, loving her, leaving her behind. The last time they'd spoken, Mickey was six months out from meeting Lex, living with roommates off Tompkins Ave. and trying to figure out if this writing thing was for her. Mickey missed that version of herself, the one who was on the precipice of something rather than on the other side of it. She wanted to shout for her, reach out and tell her not to do it. To leave that job at *Wave* alone. No matter what they promised, no matter how good it sounded. *But Lex*, she thought, glancing over at her partner to make sure she was still there, *Lex she would choose all over again*.

"What was she like?" Akira asked.

"Like they all are. Addicting. Flakey. Sure about you one day, confused the next," shouted Mickey. The waiter poured a modest amount into her glass and set the bottle down at the table. Mickey offered a thank you and picked up her glass, tipping it back and gulping it down.

"Babe," Lex warned, her voice low. She kissed Mickey's shoulder again to camouflage her concern.

"What?" Mickey asked a little too loudly, and she saw the brief alarm in Bunmi and Akira's eyes, the fear that the night was about to take a turn.

"You're yelling," she whispered.

"Sorry," Mickey muttered at the lowest volume possible—which was perhaps not immediately perceptible to the human ear—the embarrassment burning alongside the feelings of inadequacy that had been consuming her every waking moment. And now, with Tee's name knocking around in her brain, the abandonment, too. "But yeah, she was cute of course, but a fuckboi."

"How long did y'all date for?" Bunmi asked.

Here's where it got tricky—things had never been made official. There was a time when it felt like they were getting close to something besides friendship, but that had been flighty, nebulous, always shifting. It was easier for them to exist in a gray space, at least for Tee, allowing her plausible deniability while Mickey was forced to suffer years (and years) of confusion. "It's complicated."

Upon reflection, Mickey found herself questioning if it had ever been anything at all.

"Oh, so it was like a situationship," Bunmi declared, nodding her understanding.

"Sorta kinda," Mickey said. "She was my best friend."

"Whew," Akira said with a headshake that reminded her of her auntie's. Knowing, conspiratorial, and pitying. "That'll do it. Friend breakups are the worst. And y'all was messing around, too? That's a bad mix."

"The worst," Mickey affirmed.

"Do y'all speak ever?" Akira asked.

"Never," Mickey replied. That was by design. To see her now would be too painful a reminder of her former self—one that was needlessly self-conscious and desperate to be liked. It was addicting, the feeling of being seen and loved by Tee.

"Probably for the best," Akira said.

"Definitely."

The rest of the evening passed but Mickey never quite came back to the table, caught somewhere in the in-between.

SIX

There weeks into unemployment (and one severance payment later—in the end, she had caved and signed the NDA), Mickey had developed a new anxiety: Lex coming home from work. Around 5:45, Mickey's chest would get tight and her toes would start to tingle, as she jumped up off the couch to start hiding the evidence of her very-not-productive day. She would begin with her lunch, which consisted of either something heavy and greasy from a nearby restaurant (today it was halal food from a highly rated restaurant on UberEats) or an assortment of snacks she found in their kitchen, whose wrappers were now scattered across the coffee table and floor. These would be frantically tossed in the trash before Lex walked through the door, though Mickey was worried all the while that she'd leave evidence—a sauce packet, a wrapper—behind, the crinkle of plastic giving her up.

Then, she would move on to changing her clothes, which were often a repeat of the day before: biker shorts, an oversized holey T-shirt, and crew socks that she scrunched down at the ankles. Lex wouldn't comment on a T-shirt worn two days in a row, but she might tilt her head in quiet judgment at a third, so Mickey was careful to repeat herself only once. If it was the second day, she'd throw on a new shirt or change her underwear, smear some deodorant onto her armpits and brush her teeth. Hygiene had become an every other day activity. She wasn't leaving the house, she reasoned, so there wasn't much for her to wash off.

Homebodies

Finally, she'd light some Nag Champa, and drag it through the apartment in careful circles, hoping it would mask anything she couldn't remember to conceal. Though there was nothing she could do about the heaviness that clung to her, which wrapped itself around her like a film.

She couldn't identify the source of this heaviness, but it had turned up not long after their dinner with Bunmi and Akira and had refused to leave. It called her a failure and asked her why she even bothered, berated her for not calling her parents and ignoring her friends' calls, and questioned why she'd thought she was ever good enough in the first place. It slowed her movements and rounded her shoulders, but she'd never had good posture anyway. It sent her thoughts into an endless, oppressive loop, making her refresh her Instagram feed every ten minutes to see if anyone had lived a little more life than she had that day (nine times out of ten, they had), and it even drove her to stalk Nina on Twitter, absorbing everything from her musings about *This Is Us* to half-baked reviews of runway shows to retweets of *Wave* covers and articles.

She was stalking everyone these days, and the heaviness told her it was because there was nothing in her own life worth paying attention to. Chelsea had been on that Paris trip and was now headed on another, this time to LA with Dewwy, a direct-to-consumer brand that only sold two products: a colorless highlighter that made the skin look sort of wet in a good way and a lip balm that they kept calling a gloss. Jordan was now freelancing, working from Mexico City and traveling on the weekends, her stories a constant reminder that the only one refusing to get out and do something was herself.

She tried to hide it all from Lex, who would come through the door at six, sometimes seven, toss her keys into a tray by the door, and immediately start on dinner while Mickey halfheartedly asked about her day and attempted to clean around her, meticulously scrubbing one spot to seem helpful. It felt wrong to pile another thing on her plate.

To make matters worse, Lex had begun attempting to encourage Mickey, sending her little positive texts throughout the day and reinforcing the affirmations when she got home. Today, it was a meditation on Mickey's brilliance and how great of a writer she was. Lex would hold Mickey's face with both hands, running the pads of her thumbs across both cheeks and looking into her eyes, as if attempting to access her soul. She'd speak in a low, sure voice, but Mickey didn't believe her. Didn't know how to tell her that despite Lex's best efforts and nicest words, the heaviness wouldn't budge, and Mickey had no more interest in trying to find a job than she did in taking a shower, even though she pretended to desperately want both.

Lex had also begun asking the same questions whenever she walked in the door.

1. *How's my baby?* This question was not, in and of itself, offensive, but because the answer was either neutral or negative, it made Mickey disappointed in herself just to respond, and she wished Lex wouldn't ask at all. She had never really been *good* before, would not describe the conditions in which one crams in three stories a day before heading to a nighttime event and then staying up all night trying to get ahead of the next day's work a *good* place to be, but at least then there was an identifiable source for Mickey's unhappiness, a burden she shared with just about everyone else in her industry. Sad to be there, loath to leave.

2. *What did we do today?* This question felt a bit wicked, if only because Lex found Mickey in the same position every day when she arrived home from work. What kind of question was that?

3. *Have you started thinking about what you want to do next?* This was a new one. Had cropped up yesterday after someone at Lex's company had asked her if Mickey had found anything yet and would she consider coming over to do some copywriting for them. Now, armed with an actual *opportunity* Lex felt free to press with gentle force.

Mickey wanted to reach out and slap her with the back side of her hand for rushing her, let the quiet rage rip from her chest, but she was pretending, so instead she let her eyes get all misty and tried to put on her most grateful voice.

"Wow, copywriting," she said. "Tell your coworker thank you, I'll definitely apply."

"You hate it."

"I didn't say that."

"You didn't have to. You look completely uninterested."

"I don't do brand copy. I write stories."

"But it could just be something for right now, while you figure shit out."

"Isn't that what unemployment's for?" Mickey asked, even though she hadn't bothered to file. Mickey had gotten ten weeks of severance out of *Wave,* an impressive number given that she had only been there for a year. It felt like a significant stretch of time, but three weeks had flown right by, and Mickey had nothing to show for it.

Mickey knew Lex couldn't relate. After all, Lex had been working since she was sixteen, her first job at the Old Navy on Jamaica Avenue, where she folded boxy dresses into neat rectangles and helped women who looked like her mother into dressing rooms. After that job, which lasted her all through high school, she'd worked at the Nordstrom in Garden City throughout college, folding boxes and processing web orders. And when she needed more money, she'd took a second job at Victoria's Secret to make up the difference.

Lex was industrious because she didn't know how to be anything but. She'd clocked in at Old Navy the day after her father died because her mother had gone to her job at the hospital, too. She'd picked up an extra shift the day her brother got locked up and another when he got out. Life happened, but the work didn't stop. All Mickey wanted to do was rest. Maybe disappear.

Lex leaned in and kissed Mickey on the forehead. "I think you'll get something soon. You're too talented not to."

She wondered if Lex would continue spoon-feeding her compliments like a serotonin-depleted baby. "Thanks."

Mickey had thought she was too talented to get fired in the first place. Getting the job at *Wave* had been a big deal, and even though Mickey played at humility and humbleness, she'd expected it. After an article she wrote titled "What Are Cannabis Beauty Brands Doing to Help Incarcerated POC?" went viral on Twitter, she knew the job offers would start rolling in, rescuing her from the beauty closet and whisking her away to the promised land of a staff position. And they did. Suddenly she was saying no to publications who'd ghosted her months before and followed on social by fancy editors who'd never given her a second thought. In the end, she'd chosen *Wave* because it seemed like the most willing to let her continue, unbounded, the most likely to let her soar. But that had been a mistake.

"Are you sure you're good though? We can talk about it if you want," Lex said. Mickey shook her head. It was easier to sidestep conversations that required her to express herself. She feared if she opened herself up to her emotions, she might never find her way out.

"Can we not?"

Lex kissed her again. "Sure. But I got you if you do."

Mickey nodded, but felt nothing where the gooey, melted feeling should've been. In its place was an emptiness so vast and deep she wondered if it had been there all along.

Five years was a long time to love someone, made longer by a mother who wanted her daughter to follow a predetermined path, one that included a husband and a baby and no Mickey. But the busyness of the life they'd built—one where Elda was not a person but a voice in a phone or a name in a text message or occasionally an item carried home by her daughter—had allowed Mickey to pretend that things were much better than they were.

But now that was gone. And there was only the truth of their dynamic in its place. Mickey could see that they had spent much of their relationship mothering each other, filling in the holes that the women who birthed them had left behind. Had held each other up when it seemed like their worlds—for better or worse—were falling apart. Lex's words rang in her head. *I got you.* But she knew Lex didn't understand what it meant for the work to be all there was, for her worthiness and her words to be one and the same. There wasn't enough pasta or forehead kisses or lazy mornings in bed to make up for not being seen by the person she had believed to be her reflection.

SEVEN

Three weeks and one day into unemployment, Elaine called. It wasn't the first or the second call, but the third that urged Mickey to pick up. Despite tracking her cohort's every movement, she had no interest in interacting with them, afraid they might see that she was coming apart at the seams.

Today was also the day Mickey had decided to turn things around. She could feel Lex's disappointment encroaching from the night before. Though Lex would never have expressed something like that outright, Mickey felt it in her careful approach, the way she handled Mickey like she might break, the panic mixed with pity. Mickey never wanted to see it again.

So, today, she committed herself to trying. She woke up when Lex did and hopped in the shower, scrubbing every crevice twice. She used three soaps and shaved her legs. Exfoliated with a scrub that made her dimpled legs feel clean and raw. She moisturized with a lotion and a body butter, polishing her skin to a sheen. She shaved everything, starting with her armpits and working her way down. She kissed Lex before she left, a proper wet smooch that left them both grinning. She even ate breakfast, a real one, at their small dining room table and drank two glasses of water. Afterward, she washed the dish, swirling soapy water in the bowl and drying it carefully with a striped, cotton cloth. She picked up a book, one she'd been meaning to read and read, until she could no longer focus on the words. She allowed herself to check her phone once every half hour and didn't turn on the TV until noon. She felt so accomplished she rewarded herself with a small pizza, topped with extra cheese, bacon, and pepperoni. She threw in some mozzarella sticks as an added treat. She didn't start to look for jobs (one step at a time), but she was sure she could get there. Would get there.

And then the phone rang. Once, twice, three times, until Mickey felt obligated to answer.

"Hey girl, what's up?" Mickey asked, feigning cheerfulness. She was grateful that it was a phone call rather than a FaceTime—disguising her voice was easier than concealing the effects of her high-sodium, seden- tary lifestyle, which could not be erased with a half day of self-care. It had turned her cheeks puffy and skin dull, and her under-eyes had be- come a concerning shade of purply blue from the lack of sleep. Mickey had developed a habit of lying awake for hours at a time while Lex snored peacefully beside her, scrolling, scrolling, scrolling until her eyes hurt.

"Did you see the email? I texted you like four times," Elaine said. There were so many texts. Texts from the group chat, which pinged incessantly, texts from Scottie and Jasmine (she did her best to answer those), texts from Lex, the four from Elaine. Text after text after text. It was too daunting to get to them all, and then she'd get embarrassed by how much time had gone by without responding.

"Sorry, I'll look now."

"Okay," Elaine replied and Mickey could hear the impatience in her voice.

Mickey pulled the receiver from her ear and put Elaine on speaker. She was sure it was some random merger or another magazine folding, which would trigger a game of "Is This Person Still Employed?," where they checked the social media of the affected parties, waiting for the big reveal. It had been entertaining once, when she was still on the other side, but Elaine had always derived a secret glee from watching the in- dustry burn now that she was no longer tasked with attempting to put out the fire. What Mickey didn't expect was the forwarded email glow- ing up at her, its contents almost too much to process at once.

"How did you get this?"

"I have my ways," Elaine, now whispering, explained. "Sorry, I'm at this boutique yoga-Pilates-HIIT workout thing and they want us to take a few minutes of silence before entering the class with our energy. I'm hiding in the bathroom."

Mickey didn't reply, her eyes scanning the email twice more. It was the announcement of her replacement, Gabrielle: a facsimile of herself, only cooler, thinner, and better dressed. There was a lot of effusive, congratulatory language and a link to her Instagram, which featured very few photos of her face and lots of photos of her surroundings: the edge of a newspaper editorial framed with smoked glass tumblers, a reddening sky dotted with orangey clouds, the man she loved. She was so cool it made Mickey sick. The most recent photo announced her new job: Mickey's job. She zoomed in on the photo: a vintage *Wave* issue cast haphazardly on a desk with her nametag glinting under the bright fluorescent light. The caption: *some personal news, update in bio.* Mickey scrolled up to the top of her profile. The copy was simple, but perfect, and Mickey resisted the urge to amend her own.

> I'm boring in real life
> beauty @wavemag
> brooklyn, ny

Of course she lived in Brooklyn. Mickey kept scrolling through her profile until she was at her very first photo, dated only two years prior. Mickey wished she'd had the sense to curate her life, archiving all the embarrassing photos of her as a teenager—photos of her at her prom, stiff-armed and duck-lipped, photos of a red velvet cupcake at Sprinkles, which at some point had felt noteworthy enough to make the feed.

She examined Gabrielle closer. They had lots in common: a viral article, knotless braids that touched the tip of their tailbones, similar amounts of experience, skin the color of pecan shells.

"You still there?"

Mickey had forgotten Elaine was on the phone. "Do you know her?"

"Not really," Elaine said, full volume restored. "She was mostly freelance before this, but she's written some good shit."

"Hopefully she's happy," Mickey said, scrolling through the comments on her most recent post and wondering if they would've gotten along in real life. If there could've been room enough for the both of them. There were a few comments from people she knew, other Black girls in the industry who sent their notes of congratulations with flurries of emojis. But one comment stopped her in her tracks.

"Finally!!!!" Nina wrote, and Mickey wondered how long they'd been working up to this. Had it been the moment Nina started? Or was it the first time Mickey turned a story in late? The second time she wasn't available at nine p.m.? Or maybe it was that day in the conference room, when Mickey had decided she could no longer be quiet about the fact that every cover since Nina arrived featured a barely relevant white woman whose name she could never place. Perhaps it was the time she pushed back against covering the big gold hoops in one of those white women's ears as the beginnings of a breakout new trend. Perhaps, perhaps, perhaps. Mickey was sure it wasn't the days she'd done everything right because she couldn't be certain anymore that any of those days had happened at all.

"Did you see that Nina commented?" Elaine asked, and Mickey wanted to throw her phone through the window. She wanted to jam the shards into Nina's soft-looking, perfumed wrists and ask her when she'd started interviewing someone else for her job. If she had ever given Mickey a real chance. She closed her eyes and pressed her head deeper into the couch instead.

"I did."

"It's fucked up."

"It's always been fucked up," Mickey replied.

"You okay?"

"What do you think?"

"Fair." Mickey heard some shuffling before Elaine's voice reemerged. "Heading into class, but I'll call you soon, okay? Stay strong, you got this."

Mickey wanted to rage, shout into the ether that trying to be strong is what got her here in the first place—damn near catatonic and unable to articulate her feelings.

This would send her spiraling, and obsessing, she knew. By the end of the day, she would have devoured the contents of Gabrielle's life, ending with her boyfriend's sister's ex-girlfriend, who somehow also followed Nina. She wanted to tell Elaine to fuck off, blame her for yet another rabbit hole to lose herself in, but instead she thanked Elaine for the heads-up and wished her a good rest of class.

Once they hung up, Mickey called Lex. She didn't answer, so Mickey kept calling until she did. Instead of greeting Mickey like she normally did (hey babe, what's up?), she sounded panicked. Only then did Mickey realize that she had called Lex fifteen times, so it must've seemed like an emergency. But this *was* an emergency, of sorts. Gabrielle being hired meant that Mickey was ousted for good. She'd been officially replaced.

"You good?" Lex asked. Mickey heard the ding of an elevator and then the rush of outside. Somewhere, a siren blared and a bus shuttled along, loud and slow. Mickey almost missed it. As much as she complained about the daily commute, its absence left a sort of emptiness that French fries at noon and a day without plans couldn't fix.

"The new girl started."

"Damn."

"Yeah."

"You okay?"

"You know I'm not."

A sigh on Lex's end. "I do. You need me to come home?"

Mickey thought about the pizza on the way and panicked. "No, don't worry about it."

"You sure?"

"I'm sure."

"Let me know if you change your mind."

"I will."

"You know her?"

"No."

"That's good, right?"

"Nothing about this is good." Mickey had gone days without feeling much but this pierced through the heaviness and shot straight to her center, radiating throughout her entire being and pulsating.

For so long, Mickey had measured herself against an institution, one that had devoured her, but it had still given her purpose and a place. Now, she was reeling from the idea of having to stand on her own.

"This is just—"

"It's a lot, I know."

"It's hard not to spiral out."

"I get it," Lex replied, and Mickey knew with absolute certainty that she didn't.

"Do you?"

"I know that you're having a hard time. I see it."

"*Wave* just felt like my launching pad, like it was going to push me in the direction I was supposed to go."

"That could still be the case. You wrote some great stories while you were there. Remember the one about the co-opting of trans beauty aesthetics by cis women? You interviewed that entire collective. You didn't stop talking about that for weeks."

"Yeah, but nobody really cared about that one. It came out the same week as the college admissions thing, so maybe five people read it."

"You don't do this for everybody. Right?" Lex said, and Mickey couldn't help but feel like she was on the precipice of disappointing Lex.

"Yeah, but—" The words died in her mouth. Better to quit while she was ahead. "That was so early out. Lily was still in charge. I haven't written anything interesting in months."

"So why don't you start now? You have the entire day to do what you want. You were always saying you needed time. *If you just had the time you'd write all the shit Nina rejected and pitch them to other places.* Remember?"

Mickey remembered. She hated Lex for bringing it up, but she had to admit she was right. A novelty, given that Mickey hated to concede anything, especially to Lex. The conversation devolved into what they would eat for dinner, the drama in their building, and tentative weekend plans. They hung up with rushed *I love you*s as Lex headed back to work and Mickey hung up feeling emptier than she had before.

EIGHT

After four weeks, the pinging stopped. The constant buzz of Mickey's industry group chat, which was part bulletin board (they kept track of hirings and firings as well as speculations of both), part blog (see: stream of consciousness meditations on the wastefulness of PR mailer packaging), and part calendar sync, where everyone tried to figure out who would be where and when, had suddenly ground to halt.

At first, she didn't notice, since she barely skimmed over the messages anyway. But after a full twenty-four hours of silence, she began to get impatient—x-ing out of the app and restarting her phone—and then panicked, worried that she was finally being iced out. After all, there was always someone (or something) to gossip about.

Mickey beat herself up for skipping after-work drinks and snubbing asks for reads of half-formed articles and pitches. Mickey checked everyone's socials, only to find that everyone was very much alive, posting like they always did and not trapped in a manhole in Midtown. Eventually it dawned on her that they might have started a separate group chat without her. Or worse, one with Gabrielle. One where she wouldn't stain them with her failing, even though she'd done nothing but lurk for weeks. She was sure they could sense her uselessness, her lack of productivity and joblessness something contagious to avoid.

Mickey couldn't tell Elaine about the sudden cut-off in communication. She had long left the group chats behind in favor of the occasional link up on the rare occasion she was in New York, when she would become insufferable and recount every bar she'd fucked in and every restaurant she had a good meal.

She couldn't tell Scottie about the group chat—she would say Mickey was bugging. Lex was off the table, too. Mickey knew it would only prove Lex's point: that she was intentionally sliding deeper into the spiral rather than climbing out of it, so she decided to work overtime to conceal her brain's endless churning. She put on a new shirt and laid her edges flat. She pretended she was working on a piece. But there was no story, just a blank document and her thoughts, a carousel of character-assassinating phrases that if spoken aloud would have had Mickey committed.

Two days later, the group chat sprung back to life with a link. It came through by way of Chelsea, who Mickey had forgotten was even in there to begin with. She rarely spoke, save for the occasional self-aggrandizing message about a recent story that she'd written or edited. This message was more of the same.

"They have me doing a bit of editing for *Wave* now," it read.

Mickey almost closed the thread, rolling her eyes, but the title caught her eye. She recognized the story immediately, an opinion piece about the gentrification of hood nail art. She recalled when she'd first pitched it. It hadn't been her first meeting with Nina at the helm, but it was the first time she'd felt hopeful and sure.

It had been a pitch meeting like any other. Writers and editors gathered around the oversized black conference table in the biggest conference room they had: "A Star Is Born." This one had an impressive view of the Credit Suisse building and, when you pressed your face up against the glass, a decent snapshot of the entirety of Park Avenue South.

Mickey chose a seat that faced inward, so she wouldn't be distracted by the goings on behind her. She was focused and energized. She'd slept five hours the night before and showed up in her most fashionable outfit, something that screamed cool-but-serious-writer-with-lots-of-brilliant-ideas: black leather trousers and a cropped black T-shirt, pulled together with a black tweed blazer from ASOS that looked vaguely Chanel. Lex had helped her pick it out.

In her hands, Mickey clutched a black Moleskine, her pen tucked expertly into the band holding it closed. She was prepared! She could do this! Even though many of the faces sitting across from her were Nina-hires and she was from the before times, she was sure that this pitch meeting would be the one. This time, Mickey was sure she'd cracked the code, that this would be the cluster of ideas to finally break through Nina's frosty exterior. These pitches were good, she was sure of it. She could feel the weight of her ideas in her bones: the sturdiness, the structure. She could write any of the three in her sleep. All Nina had to do was listen, and hopefully say yes.

Nina was three months into her tenure at that point, and Mickey had so far gotten nowhere. Only her most basic pitches were greenlighted—ones where she reviewed her favorite lip gloss or waxed poetic about the sports bra that changed her life. But this one was different.

The meeting opened, like always, with a short speech from Nina, whose brown bob had begun growing out and was now tucked into a navy blue mohair sweater. Mickey had to admit that, despite being torturous, Nina was quite pretty. There was something about the slight upturn of her ski-slope nose and the ratio between that nose and her mouth that gave her an elegant look. Nina crossed her arms to signal that she was done speaking, her orange-red nails bright against the pullover.

"So, who wants to go first?" she asked.

Mickey, optimistic and eager, raised her hand. "I'll go."

Nina nodded, her eyes already beginning to glaze over, and picked up her phone. "One sec." She quickly tapped out a message before setting it to the side, giving Mickey a closed mouth smile when she looked up. "Go ahead."

Mickey had prepared three story ideas she believed to be stellar, stories that grew out of her everyday conversations with friends, observations with threads, and late-night scrolls on Black Twitter.

The first, she'd dubbed "All the Cool Girls Have Diamonds in Their Teeth," which documented the resurgence of tooth gems, a trend that took off in the early nineties and had since come back round again. One of Scottie's clients had one and it had sparked a day-long text exchange about whether Scottie should get one and on which tooth (they settled on tooth eleven, which could be seen when she smiled but wouldn't always be visible when she talked). It felt like the perfect story for *Wave*, nostalgic but trendy, and in line with what Mickey cared about: Black women. The Black girls had diamonds in their teeth, so Mickey wanted to talk about that.

The second pitch: body moisturizer recommendations from strippers, who Mickey was convinced were the softest women alive. She'd come to this realization after a night out at Stadium in DC, her hands rhythmically slapping the backside of a brown-skinned girl named Sunshine. Her skin felt like silk against hers.

And then, finally: a piece about hood nail art, which would be part history of the airbrushed, brightly colored, zebra-striped, bejeweled, bedazzled, talon-length aesthetic that populated Mickey's childhood, and part opinion piece about how white women were now wearing the look as if they'd invented it themselves. When she first started in media, Mickey had been careful not to get nails that were too long or too loud for fear of seeming ghetto, but now everyone—including a few of the writers at *Wave*—were sporting long nails in every imaginable shape and design.

"The nail idea is interesting," said Nina, and Mickey felt her adrenaline transform into excitement. "But I think everything can't be labeled cultural appropriation these days. Long nails *actually* started with the Chinese thousands of years ago and have been adopted by different groups over time. How can we say with certainty who really came up with what?"

Mickey felt the synapses of her brain trying to connect and create a coherent response. She was sure there would be some pushback, had practiced a response in the mirror, but responding in real time was different. Her hands began to shake, and she set them in her lap, hoping no one around her noticed. She cleared her throat to speak: "I was thinking it's more so about the nail art style rather than the idea of long nails more generally, which *is* very specific to Black women."

"Got it," Nina said with that tight-lipped smile. "Thanks, Mickey. Anyone else?"

Homebodies

* * *

But now here it was: edited, filed, and posted, attributed to someone random freelancer. She copied the link and sent it to Lex.

She captioned it, "WTF?!"

Her text went unanswered for a few minutes and in that time, Mickey ran through a few scenarios, a number of which involved her pulling up to the *Wave* office and burning the whole thing to the ground. She wanted to say something, *anything*, but publicly talking shit about the company (and its employees) was a direct violation of her NDA. She thought of her next severance check, which was due in a few days, and realized she couldn't risk it. She took to Twitter, noticing that Nina had reposted it, co-signing it with a few exclamation points of approval. She considered drafting a tweet, something scaring, something explosive and revelatory, but thought better of it. There had been something in the contract about not disparaging the employees and this felt firmly over the line.

Mickey, aware of her powerlessness, refreshed Twitter again. The likes were climbing, the comments piling up. People were engaging, interacting. Mickey knew that feeling. It was pure dopamine, all that real-time validation. The certainty that your work—and by extension you—was worthy and good. That had been stolen from her, just when she needed it most.

She found the nearest pillow and let out a guttural scream.

She was still seething when Lex walked through the door, her shirt wet from the heat. It was beginning to warm and transform into Mickey's favorite time of year—the soft heat of June—but she had barely noticed, her outside adventures limited to whatever Lex dragged her to. All the weather felt the same inside the apartment, but the light was warmer and brighter. Peeled through their curtains a little longer. Summers in New York were unmatched. Heat waves chased gloomy days until July, when everyone stripped down to their thinnest clothing and climbed up onto the nearest rooftop or crowded onto a neighbor's back patio to move their bodies in the heat.

The days were still filled with work in over-air-conditioned offices, but the nights held endless possibilities. Mickey came alive and Lex transformed right alongside her. They'd fallen in love in the summer, so the sweat always reminded them of the early days. A time when they'd seen each other most clearly and were unburdened by baggage and insecurities and shortcomings. All they knew is that they loved each other and would move heaven and earth to make sure things would stay that way.

"Hey babe," Lex said, removing her clothing in quick succession—first her T-shirt, then her bra—and crossed the room, bare-chested, to drop a kiss on Mickey's forehead. She wriggled out of her pants, too, and balled them up, tossing them to one side of the couch before dropping her head in Mickey's lap.

"How was work?" Mickey asked, tangling her fingers in Lex's curls. They were Magic Marker–thick and silky, springing from her scalp in a perfect S-shape. Mickey's hair was far kinkier, and she wondered what it might be like to truly wash and go. She moved from the top of her head to the back, running her hands over the close-cropped hair of Lex's freshly shorn undercut. It was in the process of growing back, and Mickey liked when it was like this, soft and short. Her hands migrated to Lex's neck next, and she watched carefully as her eyes fluttered closed, a sigh escaping her lips. She took Lex in, her eyes skimming the length of her body. Her nipples were the same dusky pink as her lips, and Mickey felt a faint stirring of desire.

"That feels nice."

Then, Lex popped one eye open and looked up at Mickey. "Them stealing your pitch is wild as fuck. They really violated. I'm sorry, baby."

"Yeah, I'm upset."

"Are they allowed to do that?"

"Yup," Mickey said with a nod, her anger transforming into defeat. She picked up her phone and looked at the article again. "Look at how many comments there are."

She navigated to the tweet promoting the piece. "Look how many retweets. I knew it made sense. I knew it was good. It just feels so wrong that it wasn't me." Then the crying started, her cheeks wet and chest vibrating with all the emotion she'd been holding close.

Lex reached for Mickey's hand and threaded their fingers together before pressing their joined hands to her lips. Mickey sidled up. "We can pull up on them if you want."

"Can we?" Mickey asked with a laugh, thick with snot. "That would be nice."

Lex laughed. "Why is it that violence is the only thing that satisfies you?" Lex asked, hoping for that smile. "How come you can't be satisfied with a strongly worded letter?"

And just like that, a seed.

NINE

Mickey hadn't planned to release said letter outright. Of course, no one would believe her later when she would promise that it had been an act of catharsis, something done on very few hours of sleep when she was hoping for something (anything!) to make her cyclical thoughts stop. But that's how it happened. Hand over heart.

Okay, fine. There had been a bit more planning than that. She knew during her final read-through that it had been good. That maybe one day someone, *somewhere* would read it, even if it was just a pimpled teen at the Genius bar who couldn't resist peeking at the contents of her melted-but-recoverable hard drive. But she couldn't imagine that she would release it on her own. This part was true. But Lex sparked something, a whisper of an idea that later turned into a roar.

Following her conversation with Lex, Mickey had become feverish with inspiration, her fingers flying nearly as fast as her mind flung sentences. There was so much clarity in her rage, and she channeled all of it into a manifesto of sorts, which was part retrospective on her time at *Wave* and part instruction manual to make sure it never happened again. She dedicated it to Gabrielle because of course she did, and wrote and wrote and rewrote until she felt like she was speaking in her voice and her voice alone. She undid the pretense and stripped her anger down to the studs, while still keeping a level of decorum because Mickey was nothing if not professional. And then the letter was complete, the paragraphs glowing up at her like it was a living, breathing thing.

Somewhere inside of this heightened state, which lasted upward of ten hours and stretched into the wee hours of the morning, she had agreed to dinner at Elda McPherson's home. This was unusual, both the invitation and the acceptance, because the last time anything like this had happened, Lex and Mickey were still pretending to be friends, an act Mickey had put on as a courtesy to her girlfriend, who at the time was still living at home. It was hard to ignore Lex's empty hand, knowing it should be filled with hers, or to ignore the errant sauce at the side of her mouth, waiting to be wiped or licked. But Mickey had done it, endured.

For the first two years of their relationship, Lex was out of the closet everywhere but in Elda's house, and Mickey went along with it, desperate to be liked by Lex's family. She would turn up at events as a "friend"— birthdays, christenings, Elda's retirement party—always standing off to the side, careful not to command too much of Lex's attention. For a while, it felt like they were on the same side. Stealthily infiltrating this conservative, Caribbean family like a band of gay spies.

Mickey figured with enough niceties she could prove her worth, force them to fall in love with her, so that when the time came to tell the truth, they would embrace her, identity notwithstanding. Prior to Lex fully coming out (though more accurately she was outed by a childhood friend who she still saw at cookouts and birthdays), Elda had referred to Mickey by name or, affectionately, as "that nice, sweet-faced girl," but once she'd gleaned the true nature of their relationship, everything shifted and Mickey was never called "nice" or "sweet-faced" again.

"My mom wants me to come for Sunday dinner," Lex said, but to Mickey it had sounded like a blur of words. She could've said just about anything, and Mickey would have agreed. "You too."

"Sounds good, babe," Mickey replied, head buried in her laptop. It wasn't until the next day that Mickey realized what she'd done.

"Are you sure you want me to come?" Mickey asked from their bed, a last-ditch effort to stay home.

Lex gave her a look, the kind that said, "Hey, I'm trying here," and started to rub her fingers back and forth across her forehead. Lex did this when she was anxious, particularly when she was anxious about her mother. Mickey took the hint and rose to change her clothes.

It was settled, they were going. *This was a step*, Mickey thought, as she shimmied her hips into jeans and pulled a puff-sleeved shirt over her head. *It'll be fine*, she told herself, as she pushed her feet into a pair of Converse. She took a few deep breaths as she bent over to tie up the laces. *You're okay*. Before she could think about it any further, the Uber was downstairs and Lex was yelling from their hallway, telling her it was time to go.

"Did you have to wear earrings?"

Lex, who was looking out the window, turned her head to look Mickey in the eye. "What?" Her knee was shaking, bouncing in time with whatever song was playing on the radio. Mickey vaguely recognized the upbeat tune, which sometimes played at their local Key Food.

"The earrings," Mickey said. "Were they necessary?"

Lex flicked the chunky gold hoops in her ears and smoothed a hand over her slicked-down bun. Her edges had been swooped and swirled to frame her heart-shaped face and mascara coated her too-long lashes, turning them comically long and spindly. It reminded Mickey of spider legs. "I just don't want to hear her today, that's all."

Mickey surveyed the entirety of Lex's outfit. She was wearing a smocked top, one that showed off her small breasts and hugged her waist. Mickey had not seen this one in years, had believed it had been abandoned to a Goodwill bin. But here it was, contrasting beautifully with the gold in her ears.

Mickey rolled her eyes. "I don't get why you can't just be yourself."

"The same reason you've been avoiding your dad since you stopped working at *Wave*."

The blow was unexpected, knocking the wind out of Mickey's chest. Shame flooded her senses, as if Lex had cocked back and hit her with her strong little hands. "Whoa, where did that come from? I'm just saying I like how you normally look."

82

"What?" Lex asked. "Okay. Sorry, that was uncalled for." She reached for Mickey's hand before continuing, but it didn't make Mickey feel any better. She held it anyway. "But I'm just saying, our parents have certain expectations, and we do what we can to meet them. For you, that's being the perfect daughter that everyone gets to brag about. For me, it's earrings. If I don't wear any she'll ask why and then accuse me of trying to be a boy."

"You're not though."

"It doesn't matter."

"There's a difference though."

"Is there?" Lex asked. She went back to looking out the window.

"I think so," Mickey began, but her brain was too foggy to articulate why. They sat in silence and Mickey's mind drifted back to the letter. She thought of adjusting tenses and fixing commas. She had emailed a copy to herself, so she could read it on her phone during the long ride and found excitement in the words on the screen.

It soothed Mickey to see that after weeks struggling to pull a text together, she'd written something this coherent, a piece she could stand behind. It was honest, bold, true. It almost erased the shame of what Lex had said. *Almost.* But now there was another thought to add to the heaviness, another painful thing to tell herself when she lay awake at night. *You're not as valuable as you once were to him, and now you're even less so. Good thing he has another kid, another chance. You failed, failed, failed.* Mickey read the letter again and tried to banish the thoughts from her mind.

She looked over at Lex, who was biting down on the side of her finger. The journey from Astoria to Canarsie was a long one, a half hour on a good day with no traffic, but it was five o'clock on a Sunday and it seemed like everyone had a reason to be on the road. Mickey instantly felt self-conscious, vaguely aware that she was the reason for Lex's feelings of anxiety. Lex visited her mother at least once a month without Mickey, and she never acted like this. The black Toyota inched a few feet forward then jolted them to a stop. Mickey's stomach lurched and she looked over at Lex expectantly. She hadn't flinched.

"So what time is dinner?" Mickey asked.

Lex rolled down the window a bit and inhaled deeply. The warm air comingled with the AC circulating in the car, turning it into a lukewarm box. "Whenever we get there."

"Why did she invite me?"

Lex shrugged, but there was something unnatural about the way her shoulders crept toward her ears. Like she was trying to convince them both. Mickey noted it and did her best to ignore it.

"Maybe she's trying," said Lex.

"Maybe," Mickey replied, though she doubted it.

Elda had done everything but physically put her body between them to separate the two. Moving in together had been a drama. Lex backed out twice, both times thanks to Elda's theatrics, causing them to lose an oversized first-floor brownstone apartment in Prospect Lefferts Gardens. It had crown molding, a separate kitchen, and a nonworking fireplace that Mickey wanted to fill with clusters of large white candles. There was a thick wooden staircase that led to the upstairs unit, occupied by a writer who was famous in New York but nowhere else. Mickey had imagined their bitter rivalry, one that would sustain her innate need for deliciously petty drama. She would've had to sell her body to afford it, but she was willing. It cut deep when they lost it after Lex pulled out at the very last minute.

Now, Bunmi and Akira lived in PLG, in a brownstone apartment on a tree-lined street just like the one Mickey had fallen in love with, and there was a small part of her that wondered if they were living her dream life. Mickey banished the thought as soon as it flitted across her mind. It was too late to move, too late to shake things up, but Mickey couldn't stop herself from imagining what might've been. She loved their one-bedroom in Astoria, which she had fussed over and made theirs, but still. The thought lingered the rest of the drive, and when they finally pulled up to Elda McPherson's home, Mickey couldn't shake the urge to hop out of the car and run like a feral animal in the opposite direction. The last time she was here, she hadn't even gone inside. Lex had insisted on stopping by on their way to Jones Beach to pick up a beach umbrella and told Mickey she could stay in the car, so she'd done exactly that.

Canarsie was quiet and tree-lined in its own way, populated with families that looked like Lex's: first generation American, homeowners, solidly middle class. She stared up at the red-brick house, framed by two identical houses on either side. The main difference was Elda's awning was a translucent bronze made of plexiglass with gold trim, which Mickey had always found ugly. It had seemed modest to Mickey the first time she visited, but after a late-night Zillow-hole she realized that Elda owning this piece of real-estate was kind of a big deal. In her hometown, hulking houses were the norm, their colonial façades a bad facsimile of the brick mansions just a few minutes away in DC. Despite outstripping Canarsie homes by thousands of feet, they were far less expensive, a mixed signal of wealth.

Mickey gave Lex a once-over as they exited the car and tried not to be disappointed in what she saw.

"Are you sure you're good?" Mickey asked. "I want to make sure before we go in there."

"Yeah," Lex said. "Are you?" She started up the stairs without waiting for a response, and Mickey had no choice but to follow.

When they arrived, Elda was in the kitchen. Mickey could smell the fried fish from the moment they approached the door, but now inside, the meal took shape. There was the subtle spice of rice and peas, which, simmered for hours in coconut milk, had the *smoothest* flavor; the gamy richness of curry goat; and the unmistakable scent of hibiscus. *She's boiling the sorrel*, Mickey thought. Elda had perfected the ratio of hibiscus to ginger to sugar—it was sweet but acidic and the ginger burned on the way down.

Mickey instinctively put a hand to her mouth in case she drooled. Elda typically kept sorrel on hand, but curry goat was a rarity, as was fried fish. Mickey wondered if Sunday-night dinners had gotten more elaborate, if this was what she'd been missing. She looked around. Not much had changed. The walls were still yellow and crucifixes and tiny Jesuses on the cross still hung above every doorway, a constant reminder and justification for why Mickey wasn't welcome here. She toed off her shoes at the door and flexed her bare feet, self-conscious.

"Come in here," Elda yelled, and Mickey knew better than to follow. She was speaking to her daughter, and her daughter alone. For a brief moment, Mickey worried that Lex had brought her here unannounced, and that her mother would die from the shock.

But a bedroom door opened and Tamera, Lex's oldest sibling, appeared soon after, her son Jaden on her hip. Motherhood had aged Tamera significantly, but she was still a beauty. Her deep brown skin had a golden undertone that made it clear she wasn't American, that her ancestors were a more interesting combination than black and white. Her hair, which when undone nearly touched her waist, was wrapped into a tight bun secured on the top of her head with a silky, pale-pink scrunchie, which complemented her seafoam-green scrubs. The scrunchie had been a gift from Mickey, another free thing she'd gotten and passed along to someone else. Tamera was in the medical field like her mother, a home health aide with the hope that, someday, she'd work her way up to being a nurse.

Jaden had gotten big. Nearly one but not walking, he had grown from a tiny, mewling thing to a person with features, a road map for what he might look like in ten, twenty, thirty years. Mickey's stomach hurt just looking at him. It triggered a deep ache that, a year later, still hadn't subsided. His growth was a reminder that she remained an outsider to what she'd come to consider her family. She only saw the McPhersons if there was an essential Lex-related event, like a birthday—and that had been nearly a year ago. It dawned on her that today was important, though she didn't know why.

"Hey girl," Tamera said as she floated into the living room, pulling Mickey into a hug. It hurt to be this close to her, but she held on anyway, letting the familiar scent of Victoria's Secret perfume and Newports flood her senses. She was sure that Tamera was one of the last people wearing Love Spell, but it suited her, smelled how it intended: alluring and sexy but still young. Mickey had adopted Tamera as a big sister in her head, and after the falling out it hurt that Tamera hadn't bothered to send a text or keep the relationship up. She let Mickey go and suddenly Jaden was in her arms.

"Hold him fa me?" she said, and though it sounded like a question it was really more of a command. Tamera disappeared outside and suddenly Mickey's arms were heavy with the weight of this baby, his soft little warm body an awkward fit. All she could think about was her little brother Boo, who, though five years old, she saw as direct competition for her father's love. She rarely thought of the tiniest member of her immediate family, his existence completely severed from hers. Their lives couldn't be more different. When he had been learning how to walk, she had been cleaning up beauty closets in a cloud-piercing skyscraper alongside Elaine. When he was starting to learn how to use the potty, she had been spending too many nights a week at Le Bain.

When she did see Boo—usually around a holiday—she barely interacted with him. Just a few words, which was often limited to how many questions he knew how to answer. Mostly, it was awkward. She didn't know how to be a sister. Or how to share a parent. Growing up as an only child made sure of that.

But here was Jaden in his little two-piece set, looking up at her quizzically with his big brown eyes like she was a stranger. Even though she'd held his mother's hands when she found out he was coming, had prayed for his safe arrival even though she had never prayed for herself. Mickey hiked him up on her hip, mimicking his mother's hold. She wandered into the kitchen, wielding the baby like a protective spell.

The cool-toned fluorescent lighting flickered and Mickey noticed the once white fridge, which hummed constantly, had been replaced with a hulking stainless-steel one that didn't make a sound. The galley kitchen was small, barely enough room for two people to move around comfortably, let alone three. Elda and Lex were hovering near the stove and speaking in hushed tones. It was clear she had interrupted something with her arrival. Upon seeing his grandmother, the baby squealed and threatened to jump from Mickey's arms. Elda and Lex turned, almost in unison, at the sound.

Seeing Elda was both nostalgic and destabilizing. She wanted to hug her and then remembered they no longer did that. Mickey was now an outsider, an interloper who had corrupted and stolen her daughter, whisking her away from Canarsie to Queens. Elda had grown more fleshy and plump in retirement, the lime-colored top and jeans she wore stretching around her new form. Her hair was a little grayer than before, streaks of silver at her temples and at the crown of her head. It was pulled back into a tightly wound bun, similar to Lex.

"Tam—" Elda began to say, but upon seeing Mickey the words died in her mouth. She pursed her lips and regarded Mickey coolly, putting a hand on her hip.

"Hello, Mickey, how are you?" she asked, her accented voice staccato and prim. It was clear she wanted to make Mickey uncomfortable, to confirm her intrusion.

Mickey felt the beginnings of rage in her chest, roiling like a weak wave. It was an old feeling, this anger, one she'd learned to tame and tuck and channel. Especially with Elda, who insisted on making her feel insignificant and small. She had had enough of that lately. But she wouldn't let Elda see. Instead, she closed her hand tighter around the baby's leg—though not hard enough to hurt—and smiled with no teeth.

"I'm well, thank you," she replied, but Elda had already moved on, stirring something in a big metal pot that met her at waist level. Mickey locked eyes with Lex, who looked lighter, happier somehow, and she was disturbed by the dissonance with her own emotional state. Hadn't she heard Elda's tone? But there was the hint of a smile playing on Lex's features, as if it was a win that they were talking at all.

"Where's Tamera?" Elda asked without looking up, and it took a moment for Mickey to register that she was speaking to her directly.

"She went outside."

Elda sucked her teeth and wiped her hands on a dishcloth hanging from the handle of the stove. "Them damn cigarettes. I tell her every day to leave them alone." She reached for the baby, and Mickey felt the electricity when their hands brushed, the softness of her wrinkled flesh, the scratch of her pearly pink fingernails. Then the emptiness of Jaden's weight as he was transferred from her to Elda. It reminded Mickey how easy it was for the soft things to be taken away from her life.

"Can somebody say grace?" Elda asked. This was a performance. Elda always ended up saying it, but she looked to Lex's brother Junior anyway, who, after their father's passing, had become the de facto man of the house. There was always an empty seat at the head of the table left open for Elroy McPherson Sr., as if one day he would emerge from his grave in Kingston and wander into the house just in time to bless the food. Mickey had never met Lex's father, who passed away from cancer after years of pretending it didn't exist. She didn't know much about him, except that he was strong and formidable but soft with his daughters, especially Lex: his youngest, his baby.

Lex always said she looked like her father, but Mickey didn't see it. To her, she was Elda Jr., copy-paste. Mickey hated how much they looked alike. Staring at Elda was like looking into the face of someone she loved and realizing they didn't love her back. Every time Elda swept past Mickey's face with her eyes—Lex's eyes—it was like Mickey didn't exist. It crushed her, always.

They were gathered around the table: Lex, Elda, Tamera, Tamera's boyfriend Chris (who also happened to be Jaden's father), Junior, and Jaden (who sat up proper in his highchair that had been pulled up to the plastic-covered table). Mickey somehow ended up across the table from Lex and she hated how far apart they were, resented that Lex had allowed it to happen when she knew how hard this night would be.

"Okay, I'll do it, since none of my children would like to thank the Lord for his grace and mercy," she said and her children bit back smiles.

A strange feeling came over Mickey and she decided to open her mouth. "I'll do it."

Lex stared at her in alarm, and if she could kick Mickey underneath the table without accidentally hitting someone else, she was sure she would. Elda's eyes met Mickey's and her gaze was piercing, but Mickey could see she'd piqued her interest, if only slightly. "Go ahead."

Everyone joined hands and bowed their heads. Mickey could feel the callouses in Junior's palm. He worked construction these days and despite wearing a clean shirt, seemed to be covered in a thin layer of grime. She tried to remember a prayer from childhood, a quick one, but all that came out was "Thank you, Lord, for this food, and to Mrs. McPherson for preparing it. Amen." They were still holding hands when Mickey looked up, and it was clear that her sentence of thanks was insufficiently short.

"Amen," said the group.

"Short, sweet. I like it," said Junior. He squeezed their still clasped hands.

Elda made a little huffing sound and looked to Lex, then Mickey. "Okay, let's eat."

Everyone served themselves, spooning food from the plates, platters, and casserole bowls decorated with pastoral patterns—steaming and filled to the brim. Mickey piled a little of everything onto her plate: cabbage, rice and peas, fried fish, curry goat, ackee, and a little oxtail. She went back a second time for extra gravy. It took her a second to realize that these were all of Lex's favorite foods, and her spark of suspicion only grew. Conversation buzzed around her—Tamera was going on about her current ward, Ms. Rowe, an eighty-seven-year-old who lived on the Upper West Side and collected glass dolphin figurines—but Mickey, embarrassed, stayed silent.

Halfway through the meal, Elda called for everyone's attention by clinking her fork against a plastic cup. "Attention everybody, attention." All eyes snapped to the family's matriarch. Elda stood and clasped her hands in front of her body. "Well, I can't say how happy I am to have *all* my children with me on this blessed Sunday evening." She put a hand on Lex's shoulder and squeezed.

"Love you, Mommy." Lex beamed up at her mother, and the look they shared was so sweet and earnest, Mickey thought she might throw up.

"I love you, too, darling." She smoothed a hand over Lex's head before continuing. "And I wish I could get my Lennox to come and visit me anytime just because, but I'm happy she could be with us to celebrate this very special occasion."

Elda's eyes skated past Mickey's face when she said this, but Mickey didn't need eye contact to know that Elda was referencing her. Mickey looked over at Lex, tried to use the heat of her stare to get her to look back, but all eyes were on Elda. Then Lex. The whole table was smiling at her girlfriend, and it dawned on Mickey that whatever this announcement was, she was likely the last to know. Mickey worried this would be another one of Elda's stunts, a ploy to get Lex to move back home.

The first time, Elda had begged Lex to stay at home until she retired from the hospital, even though they'd already had the apartment lined up. The second time (after they'd already lost the apartment), Elda was less resistant, still under the impression that Lex was moving in with a friend. Elda agreed, but just weeks after the retirement party and days after finding out about them, suddenly Elda had precancerous cells. Mickey had to be sympathetic, but she'd wanted to call bullshit. What were the odds?

Now, Mickey thought again about the apartment in PLG and the resentment only grew. Then, she thought of the letter, which had become a sort of talisman in the short time since its completion and ran through its contents in her head. It was the only thing anchoring her, stopping her from rolling her eyes at whatever Elda's important announcement would be.

"Tamera, go and get the sorrel from the fridge for me, please."

"Yes, Mummy," she said, pausing her feeding of Jaden, whose mouth was dripping cabbage juice.

In her absence, Elda continued. "Lennox has received a big promotion at work. And before her twenty-eighth birthday. She's going to be the, what was it?"

Lex looked to Mickey, her eyes skitting nervously, and then at the table. "Head of content."

"Yes! Head of content at her job. We are just so proud of you, Lennox, and wanted to do something special to celebrate."

Mickey's face burned in shame. Why hadn't Lex told her? Or had she, and in her feverish state, been too self-absorbed to realize? But still, she could have warned her on the way over here that all this was for her? Why was Mickey only finding out now? Like this?

"So I cooked all your favorite foods and made your daddy's favorite drink." At this, Lex immediately looked emotional, her face crunching up. Mickey knew if Elda continued with the father stuff, Lex would start crying. Mickey was completely overwhelmed now, her puffy sleeves digging into her arms and her face suddenly hot. She scanned the room, looking for something, anything to anchor her, but Lex refused to look her in the eye. Lex's head dipped down, and she stared into her plate, before asking her mother about her latest post-retirement passion project, firmly avoiding Mickey's gaze.

So, she knows what she did, Mickey thought. Tamera emerged with a cake topped with candles even though it wasn't Lex's birthday. *Was it*

Lex's birthday? It couldn't be Lex's birthday. Mickey felt panic flood once more and she fumbled for her phone in her pocket. The group chat was on fire, but she couldn't look at that now. She needed to focus on the date. Today was June 15, and Lex's birthday was in mid-August. Mickey let out a small sigh, but it didn't solve the conundrum of candles, which sat atop a white sheet cake that said "Congratulations Lex" in loopy red writing.

Elda produced an iPad from seemingly out of nowhere and started taking pictures of Lex. Jaden cooed excitedly at the candles swaying this way and that, entranced by the flickering flames. Mickey was in a sort of trance, too, but for different reasons. She just couldn't believe this was happening right now, that this was her life. She needed to get out of here, but her feet kept her firmly rooted in place.

"A cake?" Lex said, feigning irritation. She loved this. Mickey could see it from the way her mouth upturned on the sides. She was *thrilled.* "Y'all didn't have to do all that."

Her mouth puckered tight, and she blew out the candles to syncopated applause, produced by little dimpled hands. "Yay!" said Jaden, and it occurred to Mickey that that was the first intelligible thing he'd said all night. This was why she stayed away from babies. They never had anything interesting to say.

"We do though, my little sister is about to make millions of dollars," Tamera said, doing a little dance as she reentered with the glass pitcher of sorrel and a half-full bottle of Wray and Nephew. She poured the sorrel into a cup, followed by two shots worth of overproof rum.

"Drink up," she instructed, pushing the cup toward her sister before making drinks for the entire table. Mickey worried how quickly the alcohol would course through her veins. She tried to eat in the meantime, hoping she could line her stomach enough to soak up some of the drink.

"Not millions, not at all."

"Lex, could you let me hold a mil? I'll get it back to you," Junior said, and the two shared a grin. "Nah, but I'm happy for you though. Little sis killing shit." He took a deep sip from his cup and Mickey wondered if he was even allowed to do that on parole.

"Y'all are doing too much," Lex said with a laugh, indicating that they were doing just enough. "I'm not going to make a bunch more money, but I did get a decent raise and a huge title change. Thank you, Mommy and Tamera, for doing all this."

"Don't thank Tamera," Elda said playfully. "She didn't want to get up this morning to wash the goat or grate the coconut for the rice and peas."

Jaden babbled as if in protest and everyone turned their attention to the baby, who seemed to require thanks, too. "My bad, Jay," said Lex. "Thank you, too."

Lex raised her glass in cheers. "Thank you to everybody. I really appreciate it." Her eyes flicked to the empty seat at the head of the table before taking a sip.

What the fuck is going on? Mickey felt like she entered a fever dream of sorts and there was no way to wake up.

Elda sat back down. "Now that you're making more money you need to start saving and investing."

"Yeah, yeah, Ma. But I'm not investing in Sister Stacey's new store or whatever link you sent me. I'm going to put it in a bank like a normal person."

"I'm not saying that," Elda said. "It would be smart, Lex. It's a very good idea, but look here, I'm not trying to tell you what to do. All I'm saying is . . ." She trailed off and her voice dropped slightly, from table volume to a more intimate decibel level. Mickey pretended to eat so she could eavesdrop properly, a skill she'd perfected while at *Wave.*

"I just don't want you taking care of somebody else's daughter," said Elda. "Everybody needs to be pulling their weight. It seems to me like she's taking advantage. You and her is not married and you are not her husband. Remember, you are a girl child. Somebody should be taking care of you. You understand? She wanted you to stop save up your money fi live with her and now look at where we are. Everything mash up and you want me to do what? Sit back and clap? You tell me mummy be supportive but what is it that you want me to support? You living with someone who can't get up and do fi themselves?" She kissed her teeth. "Cho! I won't be quiet about it anymore."

Mickey watched Lex's face twist in frustration. For a second there, she thought Lex would defend her honor, push back from the table, grab Mickey's hand, and lead them out the yellow-brown door. But instead,

Lex's shoulders drooped and she ran a finger absentmindedly over the gold dangling from her ears.

"I know, Mummy. But it's not like that. It's only been a few weeks and she's looking."

"You not hearing me."

"I do."

Mickey was tingling all over and her hands started to shake. Junior, mouth full, looked over at her. "You aight?" he asked.

Mickey knew she wasn't doing a good job of eavesdropping, had made it too hot. So, she left the two to their private conversation and piled more food on her plate. Stuffing herself did nothing for the empty feeling expanding inside her, which would soon translate to tears if she wasn't careful. She hadn't known she could feel both present and detached. Mickey thought about the letter, but that was no longer enough. It didn't bring her back to center, didn't make her feel good or worthy or whole.

Maybe because nobody's read it, Mickey thought. The realization brought with it a steady resolve, and Mickey felt like she'd finally found a solution for her misery.

"Excuse me," she said to the table, and for a brief moment, Lex looked worried that she might finally speak her piece. Mickey let it hang for a small torturous moment but focused her eyes on Elda, who was unafraid to return Mickey's gaze. "Bathroom still in the same place?"

"Mhm," Elda replied before swinging her head back toward her daughter.

Mickey navigated down the hall and to the left, opening the door to the small guest bathroom. Everything was blue, from the tile work on the walls and floors, to the toilet and the tub. She sat on the toilet and pulled up the letter, scanning it through and thinking about what to do with it.

Where do people post manifestos these days? Mickey tried to think quickly, so Lex's family didn't think she'd fallen in the toilet. She screenshotted the Google doc, creating five neat photos that, pieced together, bared the contents of her frustration. Drafting the accompanying tweet had been easy, too easy, so by the time Mickey had peed and washed her hands, all that was left to do was press send. She eyed the bright

94

blue button, daring her to send it out into the world. *Fuck it*, she thought. Her thumb shakily moved toward the phone screen.

Then, a sharp knock startled Mickey, her phone slipping from her grasp and nearly falling into the toilet. She fumbled, catching it just in time.

"You almost done in there?" It was Tamera.

"Yeah, I'll be out in a second!" Mickey replied.

She shoved the phone into her pocket and opened the door, fixing her mouth into a smile. Mickey made her way back to the table and sat down, hands shaking, her fingers clutched firmly around her phone.

Mickey looked for Lex's eyes but found Elda's instead—cold and unfeeling. Maybe mildly curious. She was studying Mickey and all her contours, but Mickey couldn't bring herself to look her in the eye. She felt like a coward, knowing that for all the hell she gave Lex, she'd never stood up to Elda either. Mickey's hand gripped her phone tighter and she swore she could feel it pulsing in her palm. Calling her, taunting her. She thought of the letter, its glowing possibility, and the lump in her stomach—a tangle of nerves and disappointment and shame—lurched.

Mickey shifted awkwardly in her chair, the seat covered in a thick plastic, and forced another bite of food.

TEN

"Are you really not going to say anything?" Mickey asked, plates of food carefully balanced on her knees. They had sat in silence for the first ten minutes of the car ride, the nothingness threatening to consume them. Lex was back to staring out of the window, but her energy was different. The anxiousness had been replaced with a light giddiness that Mickey in no way shared.

Lex leaned forward to address the driver. "Excuse me, can you turn up the music just a little bit?" She sat back in the seat and spread her legs wide, splaying her knees open. It was as if she was coming back to herself, a little at a time. Mickey crossed her arms. So, Lex thought she was going to get loud and give their driver a show? Mickey was so frustrated she could barely speak.

"Well?"

"I didn't want to upset you," Lex admitted and Mickey wondered when she'd become so pathetic. That is, if Lex was even telling the truth.

"You thought telling me you got promoted would upset me? Why?"

"You're going through a lot right now, and I just didn't want to make things about me. You've barely left the house in the past month, and you *just* started showering every day. Why would I tell you right now?"

Mickey didn't quite buy it. "But what made you think that not telling me before we went to your mom's house was a good idea? You had me in there blind. I must've looked like an idiot when she announced your promotion and I'm supposed to react like everybody else."

"I didn't know she was going to do that. The cake and announcement and all that was a surprise."

"But you knew it was for your promotion."

Lex nodded that she did.

"I just don't get it. And then she says that weird shit about you not taking care of other people's children. What the hell was that about?"

Lex's eyes popped open in alarm. "I didn't think you heard that. I'll give you that. She crossed the line."

"You didn't rush to defend me."

"What did you want me to say? You wanted me to curse my mom out in the middle of dinner?"

"Honestly, yes," Mickey said. "At what point will she go far enough for you to say something? I wouldn't let my father bring up the fact that I was paying rent for those months when Davis was waiting for the investor money to come in."

Lex looked wounded. "You told him about that?"

"Of course not. I wouldn't—that's the point. But clearly you had no issue telling her I'm unemployed."

"She asked how you were," Lex said, hands up as if there was nothing she could do.

"Then lie. You know she doesn't like me or approve of us, but you're still giving her the ammo to talk shit. Make it make sense."

"I didn't say anything, really. Just that you were looking for a new job." Lex crossed her arms in frustration. The conversation was going nowhere, fast.

"I just don't get you. Do you have no sympathy for what it feels like for me to sit across from someone who acts like I don't exist and pretend I'm having a grand old time?"

"I know I shouldn't have sprung this on you, but not once since we've gotten in the car have you said that you're happy for me or excited about what this could mean for us. This is a big deal. You haven't said congratulations or even acknowledged that tonight went good. There wasn't any fighting and my mom didn't say any slick shit. Why can't you see that as a win?"

Mickey knew that somewhere in there Lex had a point, but she wasn't about to make any concessions. "If it was that big of a deal then you would've told me in the privacy of our home. I wouldn't have found out like this. And the fact that you think tonight was good says a lot."

"Wow."

"What?"

"Nothing."

Mickey rolled her eyes. "Okay."

"You can never be satisfied. For just one night, it wasn't about you, and yet here we are."

"I'm having a hard time trying to understand how you've managed to flip this on me. It wouldn't have been about me had you not sprung this on me at your mom's in the first place. Like the past three years haven't been me, trying to be sensitive to you, about her."

Lex swallowed hard and went back to looking out the window. Mickey's chest seized at the sight.

"Fine," she said, and the tone of finality carried them home. The sound of their silence was deafening, tension rising with each passing minute. The driver maneuvered the car like a hellion, weaving through lanes like he'd rather be anywhere but stuck in a car with these two. They passed LaGuardia and Mickey was granted a prime view of the skyline, the buildings lit up and stately in the dark. At some point he turned the radio up and the sound of Summer Walker coursed through the car, and the yearning, dreamy quality of her voice lulled her into a more subdued state. *They would get past this*, Mickey thought, trying to convince herself it was true. They always did.

When Mickey entered their apartment, she cursed herself for not leaving the ACs on while they were gone, electricity bill be damned. Fuck Con Ed. Their living room was suffocating, the heat all-encompassing and stuffy. Lex bounded in behind her, kicking off her shoes and tossing her keys into the tray in their entry, which landed with a clink. She brushed past Mickey and disappeared into the bathroom, shutting the door with a heavy thump.

Homebodies

Mickey wanted to strip at the door but instead she carefully placed the plates in the fridge, saggy with everything from dinner plus a little lasagna Elda had baked the day before. *Cheap ass plates.* Mickey was angry but she told herself she just needed a minute, a shower, and maybe a glass of wine. She stood in front of the cool of the fridge, the white light framing out the dark. It chilled her skin, hardening her nipples and raising the hairs on her arms. It felt good. She felt it cooling her head, making her a little more rational. She remembered the letter, and her group chat, and the unanswered text from Scottie. The voicemail from her dad asking her to give him a call. Now that she was home, everything melted back. She listened for Lex's movements. The sink was running and the bathroom cabinet opened and shut.

Mickey checked the time. It was a little after nine, not too late to salvage the night. If Lex got her shit together and apologized they could be made up by eleven, midnight if Mickey had to say sorry, too. She didn't care what time they made it right, only one of them needed to be up the next morning for work. Or maybe the *head of content* could waltz in whenever she pleased.

Of *course* she was happy for Lex, but it was hard to watch everyone around her progress while she tried to locate the broken pieces of herself, let alone put them back together. Even Mickey could admit that if Lex had told her prior, she probably wouldn't have made it to Elda's. She might've shriveled up and combusted right then and there, never to be heard from again.

Now that Mickey had begun to come down from the adrenaline rush of the past few hours, exhaustion began to set in. She reevaluated the thing sitting in her drafts and wondered if she was really ballsy enough to do it. If she could step out and really say those things aloud. Lex's touch pulled her back, her arms around Mickey's middle and her head pressed against her back. Mickey hadn't heard the door open, lost in her own reverie.

"I don't want to fight with you."

Mickey shut their fridge and they were submerged in near darkness, the only light coming from a single orb that always stayed on when they left the house. Mickey spun around to face Lex and allowed herself to be held, though she couldn't fall further into her arms. She was hurt that

Lex had barely acknowledged everything she had been through, everything *they* had been through as a couple, as a family.

Sure, their relationship wasn't the most exciting, didn't dazzle like Bunmi and Akira's, but the stability was why Mickey stayed, why Mickey continued to show up and love her, year after year after year. She knew the feeling would pass. It always did. Everything would be okay in the morning, Lex's curls fanning out across the pillow and their legs wrapped around each other, Lex smiling sleepily at Mickey, like seeing her was a pleasant but expected surprise. She let herself melt, just a tiny bit, allowed herself to be soothed by the sense of security that lay just beyond this moment. She couldn't give in to it too much because *fuck* Lex for the stunt she pulled. But tomorrow it would be *Wow, Lex really holds me down. Really takes care of me. Really makes sure I'm good.*

But what if Lex is tired of that, of me? As if in response, Lex's arms tightened around her waist and she pressed her face to Mickey's shoulder, tickling the skin there by rubbing her button nose back and forth.

"You forgive me?" she asked, opening her mouth to press a kiss on Mickey's soft, fragrant skin. Mickey had showered before dinner, moisturized, *and* put on perfume for the occasion—a ubiquitous scent that smelled of mandarin, bergamot, jasmine, and myrrh. It always made Lex want to devour her. If she played her cards right, Mickey wasn't totally opposed.

"You have to apologize for me to do that."

"Okay, I'm sorry," Lex whispered against her flesh in a voice deeper than normal and Mickey felt the hum of desire rising in her skin. They loved to make up by fucking, some of their best, most spontaneous sex happened that way. The kind of sex they had when they first fell in love, and it reminded her that she could still feel that way, even after all these years.

"I need a better apology than that."

"How do you want me to show you?"

Mickey hopped up on their countertop and opened her legs.

Afterward, they lay in bed, showered and in their nightclothes. Lex held on to Mickey's waist fiercely, resting her chin on her shoulder.

They were moments from sleep when it occurred to Mickey to ask a question.

"Lex," she began.

"Yes, babe?"

"Do you feel like you're taking care of someone's child?"

A beat passed, then two, and Mickey experienced the unique betrayal of someone you love dearly doing the exact opposite of what you expected them to. Mickey felt like she was freefalling. It didn't even matter what Lex said next. But eventually, it came.

"Why are you asking me that?" she asked. "Of course not, I like taking care of you. You're my baby."

Mickey didn't want to feel like anybody's ward, let alone Lex's. It was a sharp reminder that the once-capable Mickey had been reduced to something infantile, someone who needed much more than one person should be reasonably expected to give. However bad Mickey had believed things to be, she now feared it was far worse.

Lex shook her a bit to see if she was awake.

"Yeah?" Mickey replied, voice small.

"Did you hear what I said?"

"I heard you."

"So?"

"So, nothing. You agree with your mom."

Lex groaned and turned onto her back, one hand trapped underneath Mickey's body and the other slapping the mattress in frustration. "Mickey, please."

"How do you want me to feel, Lex? You think it feels good that I've been at my lowest for a couple weeks and you automatically feel like I'm some ward? Like I can't do anything for myself?"

"I've been taking care of you much longer than that." That felt like a blow, a low one, and Mickey wondered how things had suddenly gotten so out of control.

"Oh, please, Lex, and I don't take care of you?"

"Not in the same way. I cook, I clean, I make sure stuff is in order when you come home. Go out of my way to make things a little easier for you. I'm just saying. I do a lot and it can be a lot."

Mickey felt as if someone was playing a cruel trick and she couldn't help but laugh. "So, you just came up with this or you've been thinking about this for a while?"

She turned to face Lex but found she was speaking to her back. The outline of her body didn't reply.

"I didn't think I had to hide what I was going through," Mickey continued, even though she had been hiding, though clearly not well enough.

"It's just different," said Lex, still facing the wall. "I look at you now and I feel like all the light is gone. You're lying about what you do all day—every time I take out the trash it's another box from a random takeout place. You're buying movies on Amazon Prime."

"Now I'm not allowed to watch what I want on TV? Last time I checked, I'm still paying my part of the rent, the checks are still coming through."

"Yeah, and what happens when that stops? What comes after that?"

Mickey wanted to shoot back that she'd be gainfully employed by then, but even she didn't believe that would be true. Instead, she fought the urge to cry.

"Are you even writing?" Lex asked. "You won't let me read what you're working on. Is it even real?"

Mickey thought of the letter. It was very much real. A press of a button away from becoming the property of the world. She could do it now if she wanted. Instead, she tried to smother her urge to scream. She felt the tiredness deep in her bones and realized there was no one around who saw how hard she was treading water. It was exhausting, the pretending, the folding. Making herself small and palatable for people who would never truly see her as real.

Doubling her consciousness had done nothing but create separation in between the folds of her skin. There were so many roles now: Mickey the writer, Mickey the girlfriend, Mickey the New Yorker—all of them parts she'd auditioned for, asked for. She hadn't realized how much she was struggling, how showing up day after day had whittled her down to something thin. But even at her lowest and most ragged, she wouldn't beg.

"You don't have to worry about taking care of me anymore. I got it from here."

Despite not seeing her face, Mickey could tell Lex was rolling her eyes. "What does that mean?"

"I'll do more for myself, make it less difficult for you."

"I didn't say—" A sigh of frustration. Then silence that stretched long enough to make Mickey nervous about what she might say next. She pulled their white duvet closer to her chin and braced herself for impact. "You know what, Mickey? Maybe a break would be nice."

"Don't let me stop you."

"Stop me from what?"

"Doing exactly what you want to do."

There was a rustling and suddenly Lex was out of the bed, her pillow going with her. The silence of Lex's absence was almost too much for Mickey to process, but she forced herself to stay where she was. She thought of the letter and picked up her phone, the screen reflecting blue on her skin.

This was her sun, her orb of possibility in the dark. She opened her browser, then her Twitter drafts, and pressed send, the letter now a missive, existing in space and time. It had its own place in the timeline of history: 10:01 p.m. on a Sunday. Mickey vowed to remember it forever. This, Mickey believed, would change the world. Or at least her little piece of it.

ELEVEN

Mickey woke up to the smell of bacon cooking and the sound of oil sizzling and jumping all over the pan. A Lucky Daye song played softly underneath it all. She inhaled deep and padded into the kitchen, her bare feet hugging the hardwood. Lex was half-naked, dressed in a black sports bra and short-shorts, bright red ones that gripped her thighs. Mango snaked around her ankles and arched her back.

"Good morning."

"Morning," Lex replied, turning her head to take Mickey in. She looked her over and a smile lingered on her lips. Mickey knew Lex was thinking about the night before and the knot in her stomach grew.

"What are you making?"

"Bacon, eggs, pancakes. The usual."

Mickey took a seat at their table and tried to puzzle through the headache ripping through her brain. Maybe it was the lack of sleep—she only got four hours all told. She'd spent the night obsessively refreshing Twitter, but so far her manifesto hadn't made the splash she hoped. By the time she'd finally gone to sleep, only one person had liked the tweet, a guy from her neighborhood in Fort Washington, Maryland, who'd dropped out of college to pursue real estate and now posted an endless stream of millionaire mindset tweets. He knew nothing of trying to take down an establishment. It was out of his depth.

Mickey opened her phone and refreshed again. There were four likes now, and she resisted the urge to do a small jig. This was how it started, right? One was a former Bevy employee, whose username didn't betray her real one. Z-something. *Zakia, Zaniah, Zayna?* Mickey couldn't remember. She was an assistant to one of the big Bevy editors, Celeste Sullivan, who had been working there from the very beginning. She wondered if this Z-girl still worked there, and if she would be sending her letter around the office. If it would make the rounds. The thought both thrilled and terrified her.

"Wait—it's Monday, why are you home?" Mickey asked.

"Juneteenth. Davis said she was being supportive of our people." Lex raised a fist and Mickey lifted hers in reply. "She wants to test out its effects on our productivity, so she gave us a half day to start."

"How benevolent. Aren't there only three Black people at your company?"

"Six if you count the cleaning staff. Her psychic told her there's some kind of reckoning coming, and it would be best for her to get ahead on the D+I wave. Something about being in the Age of Aquarius."

"Psychics predict corporate trends now?"

"Davis's does. We even hired HR."

Mickey's mind immediately went to Cathy and her stomach turned. "Impressive."

"Look, about last night. When I said a break, I didn't mean like a *break* break. Just more help around the house."

"Okay, I can do that," Mickey said. She refreshed her phone. Lucky Daye morphed into Jill Scott and Lex started humming along to "A Long Walk" while she mixed up pancakes in a white ceramic bowl. The bacon went in the oven to stay warm, and Lex poured the batter into the pan, turning the fire down low. Then she picked up her phone. She was quiet for a while, but Mickey was none the wiser. She, too, was in her own little world.

"What's this?" Lex asked, her face still buried in her phone.

"Hmm?" Mickey asked, blissfully unaware. It hadn't occurred to her that Lex had Twitter, too, that she might see the letter. Lex crossed the short distance from the kitchen to the table and showed Mickey her phone. Her tweet stared back at her.

"This," she gestured. "What's this?"

Despite Lex's tone, Mickey felt a rush of euphoria upon seeing her words on someone else's device. Other people could read it. It was working. "You said I haven't been writing. Clearly, I've been writing." Mickey shrugged her shoulders. "Is something wrong?" Her ambivalence only served to anger Lex.

"Mickey, what? You didn't tell me that this is what you were working on. I thought it was an article or something. A short story, even. But this?" Lex looked stunned, her face a portrait of disbelief.

"You gave me the idea, actually." Mickey had just watered the seed.

"Fuck if I did. There's no way I told you to do this."

"You asked me why I couldn't just be satisfied with a strongly worded letter, so I decided to write one." Mickey searched for contrition and found giddiness in its place. Lex was mad, she could see that. But she didn't want to. Mickey looked behind Lex to see suspicious smoke coming from the skillet. She nodded her head toward the kitchen. "The pancakes."

Lex turned and did a quick shuffle to salvage what she could. The bottoms had browned beyond edible. She poured some more and tried again. She looked back at Mickey but made sure to stay close to the fire to avoid a repeat. "You could kill your career with this."

"At least I told the truth. You read it, you know I'm not lying."

"I know, but this isn't some shit you do. As my mother always tells me." She slipped into patois and Mickey bristled at the sound. "There's a million ways to do things, but that doesn't make all of them the right way." As usual, they worked their way back to Elda. The road always led here. She didn't want to hear words of wisdom from the woman who, not even twenty-four hours ago, brazenly disrespected her. An act that had no consequence. Had never had any consequences.

"Didn't someone once say don't look a gift horse in the mouth?" Mickey asked. "And I'm good on Elda's advice, thanks." She rolled her eyes and refreshed her phone. There was a fifth like from her college roommate Cam. Mickey made a mental note to reach out. She'd been meaning to see how she was.

"Is this how it's going to be every time I bring my mother up? She's a person, you know."

"After last night, you should know better. And I don't understand why I'm expected to give all this grace to someone who doesn't treat *me* like a person."

"She's still adjusting. You know how religious she is. To her, this is a sin."

Mickey scowled. "You always say that. Pick a new excuse."

"It's not an excuse if it's the truth."

"Isn't it?" Mickey asked. "Where's the accountability?"

"That's what I'm trying to figure out," Lex said, and then she turned back to the pancakes. There were three now, stacked on a white speckled plate with a raised lip. It was slick but Mickey caught it, and she rolled her eyes.

"I don't understand how every time your mother comes up you throw it back on me."

"I don't, I didn't."

"Don't you? What about last night? I'm always overreacting or making something up or not understanding. She's never wrong."

"She is wrong, sometimes. I tell her that. Maybe not enough, but I do."

"You act like she's this unimpeachable saint or something—"

Lex cut in. "She's done a lot for me. I know it's different with you and your mom, but we're very close. I'm the baby, her baby, so it's just different." Suddenly, Mickey wasn't hungry. She thought about her mother leaving her behind, her father replacing her, her grandparents' acceptance at arm's length. If this is where Lex wanted to go, they could go there.

"Sounds like bullshit to me."

"How so?" Lex's voice was calm but her knuckles, tightly gripping the spatula, told another story. "Look, I know it's not easy for you, I do. I wish things were different."

"And you can't make them different? When are you going to hold yourself accountable? Maybe you should worry about yourself before looking for answers from me. At this point it feels like a choice."

"Yeah, I chose you. I'm here making breakfast, for you, with you. I come home to *you*. I don't go home to her."

"But when I'm around her you act like you barely know me. Can you at least admit to that?"

Instead of replying, Lex fixed their plates and set them on the table, placing Mickey's on the placemat in front of her. Utensils, a cup of orange juice, and a paper towel followed. Eventually, Lex sat down, too. Lex began sawing into her pancake stack, her long elegant fingers slicing her pancakes into bite-sized grids.

She watched Lex eat a bite of pancake and not respond to her question.

Lex looked up.

"Are you going to eat?"

Mickey pushed the plate away from her with her index finger and looked Lex in the eye. "I'm left out on purpose, and you know that. I had to basically blackmail you to move in, and then you backed out, twice! And your mother didn't speak to you for weeks. Or did you forget?"

"She got sick, Mickey. What did you want me to do?"

"She's breathing now, isn't she?" Mickey asked and she felt herself on the precipice of saying something she couldn't take back, but she knew it was now or never. "Getting sick doesn't stop you from being a shitty person. The timing was really convenient though. You try to get up, live your own life, and suddenly she's going through all these things." Mickey was gripping her knife and fork so hard her knuckles felt like they might pop. She watched Lex drop hers onto the placemat in shock.

"Mickey, what? She had cancer."

"Cancer?" Mickey said with a scoff. "Precancerous cells is not cancer."

Lex's face went blank and her voice dropped. "Fuck you, Mickey, for real. That's low. I didn't think you were going to take it there, ever. After you acted all supportive and there for me, tried to act like you were holding it down. Then this is the shit that you pull. Years later? Over a fucking dinner?"

"It's never about the fucking dinner, Lex! Are you that shortsighted that you can't connect the dots?" Mickey was screaming now. She briefly considered tossing her plate to the ground, then remembered she'd have to be the one to clean it up. "You don't see me in the broader context of your life and that's a problem."

Lex took a moment to ruminate, before putting a piece of bacon in her mouth. The silence was deafening and Mickey's anger grew as the seconds ticked by. "I did," Lex said finally. "I really did."

"What is that supposed to mean?"

"What I said."

"Don't dangle that shit in front of me just because I said something you didn't like."

"That's what you think just happened? That you bringing up my mother getting sick and saying that maybe she was . . ." Lex squinted her eyes and searched for the words. "Faking it, is you saying something I didn't like? Nah, that's you taking it way too far. You're freefalling because of your shit and trying to take me down with you. I'm not doing this with you, Mickey. I've always been on your side. Our side." At this, Lex's voice began to quiver, and she let her fork clatter to the table. She cradled her head in her hands. It was silent for a few beats, the apartment suspended in a hushed, still quiet. When Lex looked up, there was something different in her eyes. Mickey didn't know what this look meant, but she knew she was about to find out.

Lex exhaled. "You know what? Maybe we should take a break. A real one."

Mickey had never wanted to leap across a table more than at that moment. She wanted to feel Lex's face under her palm, see her crumple to the ground. She wanted to hurt her. It was the kind of anger that tore through every inch of her body, made her skin hot. The pain chased the anger immediately, and she immediately felt like young Mickey being left behind all over again. Lex was giving up, like everyone else. Doubt and terror pulled at her from every direction, but she would never beg.

"Like I said last night: I'm not stopping you."

"Okay," Lex said. "Good."

TWELVE

It hadn't taken long for Mickey to decide that she should be the one to leave. Leaving felt like the only option when staying meant remaining in a place that, in the blink of an eye, had become foreign, strange, hostile. She'd started packing her things, shoving clothes and shoes into suitcases without taking care to make sure the things she was bringing made sense. She decided she would go home, though home had not been, for a long time, that big house in Maryland where her father lived with a woman who was not her mother and a baby who shared her face but not her mother.

Her father. The thought of showing up at his home with nothing but excuses and a plea for help nearly made her pick up the phone and ask Lex if they could work things out. She couldn't bear his disappointment, not when she already had enough of her own. She didn't want to go home, but the memory of her fight with Lex reminded her why she couldn't stay. She couldn't be somewhere like this, where she was safe only as long as she was productive. That knowledge alone pushed her to pick up the phone.

Grandma Anna picked up on the first ring.

"Hello?" Her voice floated through the receiver and Mickey felt something in her chest open. She instantly felt young. She wanted to confess everything, but she didn't want to give her grandmother reason to think that anything had gone wrong.

"Hi Grandma," Mickey said, attempting to keep her voice steady and strong.

"Who's this?"

"It's me," Mickey said.

"Who's me? It can't be my fancy granddaughter who never calls me." Then a laugh, a warm sound that made everything inside Mickey go liquid. She'd missed that voice. Had not known she was desperate for it until now.

"The very one."

"Well, 'me,' to what do I owe the pleasure?"

"I can't just check on my old lady?" Mickey asked.

"Sure, if you ever did any checking." Mickey's Grandma Anna was a no-bullshit woman. Willing to call anyone on anything with love. Would insult you right before feeding you and building you back up again. To Mickey, she was formidable.

"Yeah yeah."

"So, what you really calling about? And make it quick, *The Young and the Restless* will be on in a minute."

"I'm coming home. Can I stay with you?" She said it as if it was an everyday occurrence, but if Mickey were honest, she was terrified. After leaving PG County, and the greater DC, Maryland, and Virginia area, she vowed never to move back home. Refused to be like most of the kids she grew up with, who would strike out to a new city for a few years (typically New York, LA, Atlanta, or Houston) and then come back to work for the government like their parents did and their parents before them. Most came back within five years. Mickey was on year seven.

"All right, that's fine. I'll see you when you get here. How long you planning to stay?"

"I don't know yet."

"Is everything all right?"

"Of course, can't I just come home to spend time with my family?"

"You've never been the family-oriented type. Not since you was a little girl."

"Well, maybe I'd like to start."

"You don't have to work?" Grandma Anna asked.

Here was the tricky part. Grandma Anna couldn't keep a secret to save her life, and Mickey knew it would spread through the family like wildfire. She didn't need that kind of attention, not yet. Mickey resolved to tell her when she saw her, give her the full rundown in real life.

"I do. I need to use my PTO up though. It's use it or lose it."

"Oh, okay," Grandma Anna said, as if that explained it. "I understand. When you think of coming?"

"I was going to leave in the next few hours."

A sigh. "Well, come on then. I guess I'll see you tonight. I wasn't planning on cooking nothing, but I can see what I have in here to heat up on the stove."

"That's fine, Grandma, I don't need nothing fancy." Just a few minutes in and Mickey found herself mimicking her grandmother's slight twang, her accent by way of South Carolina, and still hanging on after fifty-something years. "Oh, and one thing?"

"Yes?" her grandmother asked, this time in a singsong voice that signaled she was ready to get off the phone. She didn't like to be kept long. Despite being retired from the government for nearly twenty years now, she kept an incredibly busy schedule.

"Don't tell my dad, please." Mickey realized she sounded like she was pleading and attempted to dial it back. "I just want it to be a surprise, that's all."

"All right. Anything else?"

"That's it. See you soon."

"Mhm, see you. Bye-bye."

The line went dead and Mickey was filled with a strange sense of dread. Was she really doing this? Was she actually going to leave? In New York, she at least had the hustle and bustle of the city to keep her motivated (not that she had really left her apartment much over the last few weeks). Back home, things moved at a near-glacial pace, even ordering at the local Starbucks took double the time. People just weren't in a hurry, and the mundaneness was mind-numbing.

But she bought the train ticket anyway. It was due to leave in a few hours, right before Lex got home. Mickey hadn't been back to Maryland for longer than a few days in more than four years, her visits clustered around birthdays and holidays. It had always felt like she had something better, more important, more urgent to do. She would be filled with a rush of nostalgia a few hours after she returned but that would quickly dissipate, the rest of the time filled with Mickey counting down the seconds until she could return to her real life. She rarely stayed longer than forty-eight hours if she could help it, citing her busy schedule at work.

But going back felt like she was working in the opposite direction of her goals. Every missed day was one where she could've been dreaming up her next big idea or studying the city she had adopted as her own. Too many of her neighbors' kids had ended up doing versions of their parents' jobs, stable government work in acronym'ed departments, their paychecks improving year after year. When the government couldn't decide on a budget, the entire block felt it—eight out of ten houses were furloughed, everyone going to work with no pay on the promise that Ms. America would get her shit together. (Somehow, she always did.)

But work wasn't the point. They kept themselves full and whole on the not-work things: the vacations, the side hustles, the kids. Her high school friends had provided a different kind of blueprint, one Mickey wasn't equipped to follow. If there was one piece of advice she'd taken from her mother, it was that she was different from these white kids, and thus could not mimic their laissez-faire attitude toward life, as if things were guaranteed. Could not fathom things like a gap year. Did not have the luxury of going to a small, liberal arts college with limited financial aid. She had to thread a different kind of needle. Work twice as hard because she was Black. Three times because she's a Black woman. Four, because she's gay. Five, because if nothing else, Mickey had something to prove. She left for college and was off to the races, on a rocket that didn't seem capable of slowing down. But it had, making its descent back to Earth soon after Mickey took the job at *Wave*. It felt like the rocket had broken the atmosphere now, burning and splitting and barely holding form. *Maryland?* That signified total engine failure, everything she worked for now flammable material. Things for people to point at as evidence that she had once been good.

But she knew she couldn't stay here, not when Lex was making her out to be some kind of leech. After all Mickey had done to build a life for them, Lex was ungrateful. That much was clear.

Tears stung her eyes as she emptied her underwear drawer. She hadn't prepped anyone for this, had not even gestured at the vague idea of returning, but she was sure they'd be happy to see her. Mickey the golden child, the celebrity, even if no one in her family understood exactly what she did. They told everyone she was a big writer at a prestigious magazine, which was partly true (staff writer at an edgy, admittedly dying publication), and she didn't have the energy to correct them with specifics. Plus, she was verified on Instagram, which, among her cousins, made her unimpeachably cool. Ultimately it didn't matter. She had defined herself by a job that no longer existed.

A meow reminded her that Mango needed to eat. She dumped dry food in her bowl and scratched her behind the ears. Taking care of her had mostly been Lex's responsibility anyway. Mickey was certain she could continue to manage on her own.

She checked her phone. She had to leave in the next half hour to make her train. She did a last-minute walkthrough, trying to figure out if she was missing anything.

She didn't hear the keys in the door.

"Babe?" Lex called out. Mickey's stomach dropped at the sound.

She emerged from the room and met Lex at the door. She had flowers in hand, a double bouquet of white roses that held its shape thanks to a cellophane cone. "What's all this?" Lex asked. "Where are you going?"

"Home," Mickey said. She was sure she looked disheveled, her face puffy from crying, her hair thrown up in a loose bun atop her head, the ends of her braids shooting out at odd angles like little black sticks.

"You are home." Lex looked sad now, now that she realized what Mickey was about to do. That she was serious.

When Mickey didn't reply, Lex tried again. "I got you these."

"They're nice," Mickey responded, but she wasn't moved. It would take more than flowers to stop her from leaving the apartment. She knew Lex would make leaving difficult, which is why she planned for them to miss each other, if only by a few moments. Some part of her had hoped that Lex would come home to see her packing her things into a car and would watch her solemnly from the window with Mango in her lap. But it hadn't played out in real life how she imagined it in her head. This was more complicated and hurt worse.

"Are you really going? Really leaving me?" Lex's voice was uncertain

114

and strange. Mickey's first instinct was to change her mind. She'd always been quick to forgive, allowing Lex's apologies to bring her back, no matter how much resentment sat inside her like a stone. Ignoring it had only made it swell, and now she felt suffocated by its mass. She looked to Lex, whose mouth hung slack in surprise and decided it would be more difficult to stay. It was scarier to keep disappearing into herself, worse to know that Lex had watched and never asked her what she really needed to find her way back home.

A ping from her calendar reminded her that she needed to leave. She pulled out her phone and called a car.

"Only for a little while," Mickey conceded, her face softening. "I think we both need some space."

"Yeah, I thought I'd go spend a few days at a friend's, not that you would pack up your shit."

"I know," Mickey agreed. She hadn't known either.

Mickey looked at her phone. The driver was three minutes away.

"Please," Lex said, a last attempt. "Don't do this to us. To our family."

Mickey set her jaw, the words only serving to strengthen her resolve. If Lex wanted to be a family, she would need to act like it.

She gave Lex a final, withering look, tightened her grip around the handle of her suitcase, and kissed her goodbye.

THIRTEEN

Mickey replayed their fight all the way to DC, thinking about all the things she could've said as she hiked her bag into the seat next to her to deter anyone from getting close. Her phone buzzed in her pocket: a text from Lex asking Mickey to let her know when she made it in. Mickey thought of responding and thought back to their pasta dinner a few weeks ago, back when everything had been near-normal. When they had still been talking about weddings like it was a definite in their future. Mickey still wanted to say yes then, even with all the things weighing them down. She tried to recall that version of herself, the one who could always take on a little more, but instead she found the single-ish girl sitting alone on the Amtrak, Kelela crooning in her ears and a toddler peeking at her from across the aisle.

Everything had spun so suddenly, completely out of control, and here she was on the other side, staring out at her city through a double-paned glass, considering peeling away the thick band of rubber and kicking her way out of the window. But what did she have to go back to? The longer she sat there, the more the circumstances felt melodramatic. People got fired all the time. They didn't all run in response. They didn't all publish open letters to the internet.

As the train whizzed through Newark, she opened her phone to check her tweet. No new likes. The letter had been a flop. Mickey wondered what deity she needed to bargain with to rewind back the previous week, or even a few weeks before that. Mickey tried to dissect the moments leading up to the letter. It had started with seeing her brilliant ideas attached to someone else's name, ideas she'd been told weren't good enough to make the cut. *But they had been celebrated!*

She had needed the world to see her pain, but now she was somehow even worse off. Before, she could've retreated with dignity, but now she'd exposed herself, her rage and frustration on full display. There was nothing worse than a Black girl being angry out loud. It allowed for too many "I told you so's." And her anger wasn't even righteous. It was thinly veiled pity for herself, wrapped in language that made it sound like she was speaking for the collective when she was a party of one. Everyone who knew her would be able to see through that.

With the letter she'd announced to her industry—and all her acquaintances from high school and college—that she'd been wronged, and that she was essentially bowing out. She had canceled herself. How did you even come back from that? And now she was defecting to Maryland. A self-imposed exile. She hadn't even thought to stay and fight. The train slowed to a stop, stranding them between two stations for a moment before pulling off again. Mickey thought of jumping out the window again. Instead, she gripped the arm rests, digging her nails into the textured plastic.

If she could do it all over, she would've left *Wave* first. Applied for other jobs while she still had one. Protected herself better. From Nina and Lex. Said no to dinner with Elda. Gotten to work early. Outwitted Nina and went to HR with her concerns. Maybe Lex had been righteous in her anger, right to question Mickey's motives and reprimand her for screaming her pain out loud. And for what? Once again, no one had heard her. And those that did decided not to respond. It was as if she announced that she was drowning and everyone, in unison, said "Good luck!"

Somewhere between Philadelphia and Wilmington, Mickey had convinced herself that she was wrong, that posting the letter had been the right move. Her group chat was mostly on Instagram, not Twitter. Maybe they hadn't seen it? In a desperate moment of shameless self-promotion, she sent a link to the tweet to the group chat, hoping she would get some, any kind of response.

But by the time they pulled into Wilmington, there were no notifications, and Mickey was dangerously close to slipping her phone into her back pocket and stepping off the train, starting over somewhere where no one knew her name. Instead, she googled the town. Apparently it was Delaware's biggest, busiest city, but from the train platform, it just looked like a mess of trees. Mickey opened the group chat. Not even a reaction or emoji to acknowledge what she'd said. The silence felt like a referendum on Mickey's standing in their group. Mickey crossed her arms over her chest and kicked the seat in front of her like a petulant child. Now her toe hurt, and nothing had been solved.

Once they reached Baltimore, she considered deleting the tweet forever, but something, maybe the last vestiges of her self-esteem, told her to leave it. Instead, she looked at it again, read it for the hundredth time. The sentences felt like lashes breaking the skin. At first it felt like a condemnation of the industry, and now it read like a whiny screed. Mickey closed it and vowed to never read it again. Why had she written this letter? Gabrielle hadn't needed her help to navigate Nina. She had been chosen by that blank-stared bitch without hesitation. It was Mickey who was on the outs.

Even though it was torturous, she needed to see. She opened *Wave*'s website. She had devoted so many paragraphs to Gabrielle without knowing if the girl could write. She clicked on Gabrielle's author page, staring blankly at a pink dot where a little circular photo should be. But there were plenty of articles to read. *She must have no issue with producing,* Mickey thought, and it was painful to know that Gabrielle already seemed better in every way. Sure, the subjects weren't necessarily Mickey's cup of tea, but that didn't matter. She could finish things. Write often. Her hands probably didn't shake. Mickey scrolled. Gabrielle was writing about things like the tension between Instagram filters and self-perception and how to heal your skin through your gut. Her work wasn't Black with a capital *B* like Mickey's, and she wondered if that made her more palatable, too. She wondered why there hadn't been room enough for both of them, and figured maybe she just wasn't very good.

As they passed the Baltimore airport Mickey was certain that her time in the group chat had come to an end. It had been over an hour and a half with no response in the type of group chat where a selfie with a new haircut prompted wave after wave of yassses and heart-eye emojis. The only way they could have missed it collectively was if they had all decided to ignore it. The icing out felt wrong. They were all together in this, right? When Jannah got laid off and decided to go freelance, they had all rushed to alert their editors. By the end of the week, she'd already been set up with three publications. What had been so different? This wasn't even a public forum. What stopped them from supporting her in private? If they didn't announce their support publicly that was fine, there were "politics" or whatever, but this felt uniquely cruel. Mickey tried to access the part of her that still believed in herself. The part that knew for sure that the letter was good, that she hadn't made a mistake in posting it. But she couldn't locate it anymore. Instead, she was crashing, and she didn't know how far or deep she could go.

When they arrived at New Carrollton, Mickey was just plain sad. She was going home, this time with nothing to show for it: she was unemployed, anxious, and uninspired, the perfect trifecta of misery.

When they finally reached DC the air was humid, as expected; the familiar, oppressive heat sinking into Mickey's skin the moment she stepped through Union Station's big arches and into the chaos of passenger pickup. This was the one place people moved with urgency, but it still felt like everyone was traveling in slow motion. A man dropped what looked to be a bus tour pamphlet and the speed at which he picked it up from the ground confirmed for her that Mickey was in the wrong city. But she was here, and she had nowhere else to go. A line had formed for cabs, but Mickey's eyes roamed the crowd searching for her ride. A hulking green pickup truck slowed to a stop, and she stuck her hand into the air.

"Pop!" she called, and too many heads turned.

A large hand raised in reply and Mickey tugged her suitcase behind her, a broken wheel slowing her steps. Richard Hayward Sr. looked the same as he did last time Mickey was home, his close-cropped hair accented with a part on the left-hand side. Sometimes Mickey wondered if he was aging backward. At age sixty-nine her grandfather's penny-colored skin was still somehow smooth and wrinkle-free. But then she would look at his hands, which were thick, doughy, and soft, and remember that he was getting up there in years. Mickey loaded her suitcase into the backseat and took her place at his side.

"Hey Pop," she said, a little out of breath.

"How was your trip?" His deep voice rumbled, and something stirred in her chest.

"It was good."

He nodded once before reaching over to turn up the radio, 102.3 playing an old Kem song Mickey liked to listen to when she cleaned the house. She didn't dare turn it up—Pop was sensitive about anyone touching things in his car. Or doing anything he didn't expect, really.

"Your grandmother told me you got some time off from work."

Mickey found it harder to lie in real life, but the truth was worse. "Mhm. A couple weeks."

"Okay."

He leaned forward and turned the radio up slightly and rolled their windows down. They worked their way through the roundabout and drove onto E Street, folding into the other cars seamlessly. Mickey leaned an arm on the window and stared out. There were people in various states of undress. Some had too many clothes on, and Mickey knew their issues were bigger than the weather. Union Station was close to a shelter, and dozens of people hung close, some setting up tents, others milling around outside. She avoided the eyes of a mother and her baby as they pulled into the tunnel and onto 395.

It wasn't long before they pulled up to the brick house on Leslie Avenue, and Mickey was grateful it looked exactly how she remembered it. She hesitated to call the two-level structure home, but that's what it felt like, with its manicured rosebushes that never bloomed and the small brick fountain that no longer worked. It was one of twelve houses on the street. Grandma Anna kept mental notes of every family that had come and gone over the years, proud that they'd been there over three decades. They were one of only two Black families on the street when they'd moved in all those years ago, and now there were only two white families left.

Their house, with its cherry red door and brick exterior still sat level, somehow, on a hill that called up memories of her childhood, of weekends spent piled up into a bed with too many cousins, preferring to be squished rather than separated. Her heart twisted at the sight of the big Saucer magnolia tree, which all of them had fallen off of at one time or another in attempts to climb and climb. Its leaves hung heavy, the same as they'd been since she was small. For this, Mickey was grateful. She needed something to stay the same, something to hold together, while she herself was falling apart.

Mickey found Grandma Anna at the kitchen table, head bent over her Bible, light streaming in through lace curtains and cloaking her in a column of sun. Something bubbled on the stove and a Shirley Caesar song played on a small white radio, reminding Mickey of summers and Sunday dinners. It was the summer and close enough to Sunday, so perhaps she was right on time.

Grandma Anna looked like she always did, gray hair fuzzy and wild, a cloud around her head. Her walnut-brown skin glistened, a near-copy of Mickey's father's. The reddish-brown of her skin peeked out from beneath a house dress, a floral-print one she had worn since Mickey was a kid. At the sound of her granddaughter and her rolling suitcase, she set her glasses to the side and looked up at her granddaughter with her soft brown eyes.

"Well look who it is," she said, standing. Her slippers scuffled against the floor. "You hungry? You look like you've been eating well." A small smile played on her lips and Mickey held back a smart comment of her own. Her family was always commenting on her body, whether her weight had fluctuated up or down. Her weeks of sitting on the couch had caught up to her, the few extra pounds puffing up her face and swelling her breasts. She pulled at her clothes self-consciously, attempting to hide. But it was no use.

"Uh huh. I have been," Mickey said. She stepped closer to her grandmother, and she conjured a smile of her own. "You going to hug me or you too old to stand up?"

Grandma Anna laughed at that, opening her arms to her granddaughter. Mickey closed the gap between them, angling her head to rest on her shoulder. Despite dwarfing her by a few inches now, Grandma Anna always felt like a giant. Such was her presence in a room. Her hair had gone wispy and gray with age and she was thinner than she once was, but her spirit still hung in every crevice.

This was home.

FOURTEEN

It only took a day for Mickey to realize that her routine in Astoria wouldn't fly in Maryland. The mere sight of Mickey at rest seemed to bother Grandma Anna, who accused her of moping even when she was taking a nap. She wasn't there even twenty-four hours before Grandma Anna handed her a list of to-do's, many of which were time-consuming and far above her pay grade. What did Mickey know about power washing a deck?

But, more than that, Mickey could feel her grandmother *seeing* her. Every question felt like a weighted inquiry, like at any moment she would ask Mickey why she was really there. But she didn't press. She just fed Mickey and then gave her task after task, each one seemingly more random than the next. Even though it annoyed Mickey to track down the number of a distant cousin or cut carrots and celery and onion into tiny bits for broth, it was nice to feel needed. To be useful. She scrubbed countertops, dusted light fixtures, yanked weeds from the ground until her fingers hurt. She walked in the grass barefoot, flexing and curling her toes, the sun toasting her shoulders. After a few days she darkened, her skin a healthy shade of nut brown.

Despite directing her this way and that, Grandma Anna didn't say much else, too busy with her social calendar and her shows, which meant Mickey was often alone with her own thoughts. She wished the stillness would relax her, but instead she was unnerved, the quiet ringing loud in her ears.

She grieved Lex in waves. One minute she was overwhelmed by the idea of the separation, the next she was terrified of staying in it. She broke her vow and reread her letter daily, irritated by the lack of attention. The group chat was still dead, the last text her tweet, which taunted her every time she clicked on the chat. She considered posting to Instagram just for the dopamine hit of likes, but she thought the better of it, nervous that even a selfie against a blank wall would betray that she'd left New York. Even though she craved connection, she avoided telling Jasmine she was back in town, fearful that she would want to meet up and, just like Grandma Anna, see right through her.

Even though she thought about Lex near constantly, she didn't speak much to her either. At first there was the torrent of apologies from Lex, peppered with updates about their shared life: photos of Mango, building gossip, a reminder to send the rent. Mickey responded to the little things, but ignored the big stuff, which felt too complicated to wade through. Despite the change of scenery and routine, she still felt like she was drowning, and she wasn't ready to deal with all the things she left behind. On the third day, something softened. Maybe it was the loneliness, or the sharp break in routine, but despite the alarm bells in her head telling her she wasn't ready, that this wasn't the best idea, she decided to give Lex a call. Lex answered on the third ring.

"Hi" was all she said.

"Hi," Mickey said in reply.

"How are you?" Lex asked next, and Mickey wasn't sure what to say in response. She didn't know how she was. All she knew was that she wasn't mad anymore, not in the same way. She didn't exactly feel much of anything, except for this persistent lump in her throat that wouldn't ease, no matter how much she sipped hot tea or cold water or gulped while staring up at the sky.

"I'm fine," she said. Mickey tucked her legs underneath her body and pulled her oversized sleep shirt over her knees. "How are you?"

"Fine," Lex said, and Mickey could hear the rustling in the background, Mango meowing as Lex shook food into her bowl. "How are things down there?"

Mickey surveyed her surroundings. She'd taken over her grand-parents' front bedroom, a room that once belonged to her father but had since been redecorated, the NWA posters and Backyard Band flyers that once plastered the walls replaced with matching oak frames filled with stock photos of lilies, daffodils, and butterflies. Mickey had only known the room this way, as a place for relatives stopping through, one she filled up on long weekends, summers, and school breaks, squeezed into the queen-sized bed with her cousins, everyone fighting for space, so it felt strange to think of her dad growing up in this room, taking up all this space himself. He still hadn't called, so she could only assume that Grandma Anna had continued to keep her secret.

"It's all right," Mickey said. "The first few days were an adjust-ment," she said with a little laugh, thinking of the way Grandma Anna would shuffle into her room and flick on the lights if she slept even a minute past ten. Then, there was the radio, always tuned to some version of the news, soundtracking Mickey's every move in a low, monotone hum. But otherwise, it was quiet, her grandparents moving around her like she'd been there for years. She wanted to tell Lex she missed her, ask if she could forget the whole thing and come home, but she hesitated. Remembered the dinner at Elda's, then the way she'd secretly felt long before that.

Lex and Mickey talked for a few more minutes, and Mickey won-dered if Lex heard the boredom in her voice, the lack of enthusiasm for the ins and outs of what came before. Their sink was leaking, the couple in 2A who always fought had finally broken up for good, and at work, Davis was in full-on bridezilla mode because her wedding was being featured in *Vogue* magazine. It was easy to let Lex prattle on about the stresses of working in social, lamenting about the struggles of climbing the ladder at Something Else.

Mickey responded to everything with *mmhmm*, but if Lex noticed, she didn't seem to mind, happy to get Mickey talking at all. The call ended with I love yous, and Mickey briefly considered never going home again.

They hung up after Grandma Anna called for her, asking if Mickey could sort through the front hallway closet. She knew this wouldn't be easy. Her grandmother kept everything. In an attempt to make the task more bearable, Mickey pretended she was an archivist, looking for significance in the boxes upon boxes her grandmother stacked high in various closets throughout the house. Maybe there'd be something revelatory in here, a story that would make meaning of the chaos of the past few weeks. A project so big it would swallow her focus, make the confusion worth it.

But there was nothing special, only the expected: obituaries for every church deacon who'd died after being on the sick and shut-in list, a list so long it felt like part of the introduction (Please pray for so and so, and so and so); seemingly meaningless receipts from Giant, Food Lion, and Shoppers; books (both Christian and secular); candy that apparently had no expiration date; and pictures from when they were kids.

The childhood pictures were hard to look at, mostly because Mickey looked exactly the same. She still had the pudgy tummy, which, admittedly, had curved into something vaguely shapely (privately she thought it was sexy, Lex did too), complete with stretch marks she didn't earn. It was Lex who had taught her to love that tummy, had made her laugh so hard that she couldn't suck in. Lex who had kissed every stretchmark and held her stomach close, whispering how she couldn't wait to one day make it big and round with the beginnings of their family. Mickey touched a hand to her middle and tried to bite back the feeling growing in her throat.

It was that very same stomach that now curved out from under her oversized T-shirt and held her iPad in place—the sorting since abandoned. She was watching YouTube videos now and trying to ignore the musty smell that stuck to her clothes. This video was particularly soothing: a young Asian twenty-something blinked back at her while explaining the merits of decluttering, insisting that she was grateful to have so many things to get rid of in the first place, but all Mickey could think about were all the things she and Lex had purchased together. All their clutter. Mickey let the video run for a few minutes before shutting it off. She knew Grandma Anna's wispy, silver head would peek through her door at any minute, telling her to get up and out of bed. She'd been resting long enough, Grandma Anna would say, and if she was going to be staying in her house, she'd have to earn her keep.

Homebodies

* * *

Hours later, Mickey's head bent over a toilet seat, she heard Grandma Anna's shuffling coming closer. "Here," Grandma Anna said, shoving a handwritten list in Mickey's free hand. It was day four, and she was being upgraded to running errands. Mickey suspected her grandmother was tired of seeing her solemn-looking face around her house.

Mickey could barely read her grandmother's handwriting, but she was able to make out *turkey bacon* and *grits*. Her grandparents were getting older, and their grocery lists had changed to go along with it. Gone were the days of Crisco, and pork bacon, and white bread. It had taken some nudging, but they had adapted to wheat bread (though Mickey didn't know if honey wheat even counted) and low-sugar, low-fat foods.

"And can you go soon? I need to start dinner and I barely have anything here," Grandma Anna said, leaning over the toilet to see if Mickey had gotten in every crevice. Mickey could feel the outline of her grandmother's frame on her back. Her sagging breasts brushed Mickey's back. Mickey had found solace in her chest many times before—often after a game of red light, green light, 123 gone wrong, Mickey getting out even when she swore she hadn't moved.

It would be Mickey's first time venturing out, attempting to navigate this old-new world. She would be fine to drive, but she worried about potential run-ins. What if she ran into Jasmine? Or worse, her father.

She fought through the feelings anyway. Her grandparents didn't ask for much. The only condition of Mickey's rent-free occupation of the little brick house was that she do as her grandmother said. There was no use in protesting. Pop wouldn't protect her even if she did. He would laugh at his granddaughter's misfortunes, tiptoeing around her with a wink. Mickey knew it was better to get things done early in the day and get it over with, when the only people puttering around the store would be folks her grandparents' age and the odd adult off work.

Grandma Anna handed over the keys to her 2008 Acura with a whispered "divine order Lord" and a smile. Mickey accepted them, regrettably catching a glimpse of herself in the mirror. It was the first time she'd seen herself in anything other than a sleep shirt in days and she was a little startled by the sight. She wore a wife beater and a pair of sweat shorts, hiked up on her waist and tied tight. Her hair was pulled into a high ponytail, the braids brushing her back. It was time to take them out, but it felt like a herculean task. Cutting and unbraiding would take hours. Instead, she splashed some water on her face, and swiped a gloss onto her lips and stepped outside, the heat warming her instantly. The dusty green Acura sat in the driveway, her chariot. It had been years since Mickey had driven—she hoped she still remembered how to merge.

Somehow, she made it to Safeway intact. The beige building had a low profile, squat and square and located in a strip mall. Back in New York, she and Lex treated grocery shopping like a team sport, racing down the aisles of their local Whole Foods, trying to snatch up organic blueberries and cold brew concentrate and French-cut string beans before they ran out. Now, on her own, Mickey felt overwhelmed by the size and stillness of this supermarket. She wandered aimlessly through the aisles, as if she hadn't grown up yanking things down from those very shelves. She often came here as a child with Grandma Anna, who would let her push the cart while they milled around, weaving through the aisles, accidentally clipping her heels.

Once she got her bearings, Mickey piled a variety of things into her cart: the grits, turkey bacon, and wheat bread they had asked for, plus apple juice, squeezy pouches of applesauce for her little cousins, spinach, bagged salad, raisins, oatmeal, Jell-O (*so* much Jell-O), pears, apples, strawberries, green grapes, red grapes, two liters of Canada Dry ginger ale (never Schweppes), and a quart of Breyers cherry ice cream for her and her grandfather to share. She loaded it all onto the conveyor belt, wishing the self-checkout aisle wasn't temporarily out of order, as she waited anxiously behind a woman she was sure Grandma Anna knew from church.

She kept her head down. She didn't want to talk to this woman, who Mickey was sure was very nice, if not nosy. She didn't feel like standing in the glow of being the golden child, which would require her to smile and perform humility. She knew talking would lead to her asking how Mickey was getting on in New York, and then Mickey would have to lie

128

(which came more easily these days, but frustrated her anyway) and talk about the job she no longer had. Her parents barely understood what she did, except that it was brag-worthy, so it was unlikely that Mickey explaining the ins and outs of her now defunct position in the checkout line would do anything other than make her feel like a fraud.

Ultimately it didn't matter, since all that prestige amounted to her hiding her face behind stacks of magazines while trying to avoid her grandmother's acquaintances. She had done such a good job at camouflaging herself that she barely noticed that it was her turn now, and suddenly she felt exposed under the yellowing fluorescent lights, avoiding eye contact with the girl checking her out. She stared at her phone instead, opening and closing her apps and waiting for her weekly quota of human interaction to come to an end. With coupons and loyalty points, the total came to $79.84. She hovered her phone over the card reader, mentally subtracting this purchase from her recently deposited severance. There were only three payments left, and she hadn't saved much of what she earned, hundreds spent on takeout and unnecessary, late-night purchases. She took a moment to glance up at the person who'd rung her up, knowing if her grandma had been with her, she would have elbowed her for being rude.

Her breath caught in her throat once she realized it was someone she knew.

Tee hadn't changed a bit, save for a few new tattoos—one of which read "202" in thick, shaky gothic lettering—and fifteen extra pounds around her middle. Her locs were longer maybe, but Mickey couldn't tell, every strand twisted into an intricate bun that sat at the nape of her neck. The last time she'd seen her, at a kickback in someone's house nearly six years ago, she had worn them in a braided crown. Mickey's stomach flipped as everything they'd been to each other flooded back in. The messy, half-finished conversations. The friendship. The way it ended: painful, sharp, and then fading into nothingness one day at a time. Her chest ached now with a hurt she hadn't felt in years.

"Hey Tee," Mickey said. Tee had seen her, she was sure of it, head down in her phone, lazily chucking things onto the conveyor belt. Why hadn't she spoken first? It bothered her, just a little.

"Wassup?" she said, her eyes fixed firmly on the mounds of groceries between them. Tee looked like she'd been holding her breath, as if she also hadn't wanted to be seen. The machine spit out a receipt, but Tee didn't move to grab it. The woman behind her had already loaded a cart full of processed food onto the belt and loudly tapped the divider between them.

"My receipt?" Mickey asked. She usually requested that they keep it, putting the perceived environmental burden of wasting paper on someone else, but it was a reason to speak.

"Got you." She reached for it without looking. Her tattooed arm flexed as she pressed it into her hand, her dark brown eyes scanning her face. Mickey didn't know what she was looking for. It's not like she'd changed much either.

She stepped to the end of the cash wrap and started gathering her things, sliding the plastic bags onto her wrists. "Good to see you."

Tee's face did something that resembled a smile. "Likewise."

Mickey practically ran from the supermarket to her grandmother's car, so desperate to drive away that she'd left the empty shopping cart in the middle of the parking lot and didn't look back. She hadn't seen Tee in years, the last time so jarring that she'd blocked it out altogether. It came back to her in full force now, whether she liked it or not.

Even though it had been over five years, the moment felt fresh in her bones, the memory coming back to her in flashes. A kickback in a high school friend's house. Her skin humming with frustration and desire. Tee flirting with Mickey as she always did, the two tucked away in a corner, heads bowed. Even though they hadn't spoken for months at that point, Mickey was immediately intoxicated with her, thrilled just to be seen and acknowledged. And then in true Tee fashion she'd ripped the attention away just as soon as she'd admitted her want, moving on the moment someone thinner with a fatter ass came along. That had been the last straw for Mickey. She'd decided that day that she would no longer come when Tee called. But Tee had made it easy for her: she never did.

Mickey was interrupted by the beep of a car, the Acura veering into a nearby lane. She snatched the steering wheel back and gripped it tight, her chest pumping with adrenaline. She felt her fight-or-flight instincts activate, but all she could do was freeze. She tried to refocus her thoughts but she kept floating back to Tee. After all this time, she still remembered what Tee felt like, how it felt to wriggle beneath her and be steadied by her touch. Tee was her first. It was Tee who had taught her how she liked things, had given her the space and permission to explore. Mickey suddenly felt suffocated in the dinged up 2008 Acura, the car's dusty beige interior too cramped to contain her memories.

Mickey pulled into her grandparents' driveway, careful not to block the vintage Jaguar her grandfather never drove (*just in case he wants to drive*, Grandma Anna would say), and cut the engine. After fifty years together, Mickey figured that's how you made things work. Concessions. Compromise. Consideration. At this point, she wasn't sure she could give that to anyone. Mickey took a second to sit before unclipping her seat belt, popping the trunk to get the groceries out the back.

"You need help?"

She looked up to see her grandfather peering at her through the screen door.

"I got it, Pop," she yelled back, knowing he'd teeter over to her anyway, bad knees hidden beneath pleated, cotton pants. He started his journey down the paved concrete driveway shortly after, shifting from side to side. Mickey knew it was a race then, to collect as many groceries as possible before he got to her. She didn't like when he did too much, and worried about his knees and his back. By the time he reached her, she'd gathered all bags but one, the lightest.

"You don't need to be carrying all that heavy stuff by yourself," he said, looking around for something to grab.

"I got it," she said again, knowing he'd try to take more from her than he needed to. He always did. "Just take this one." She nodded at the lone bag sitting in the trunk, filled only with cherry ice cream for them to share.

He looked in the bag and nodded his approval as he slid the bag on his wrist, turning to make the journey back. Mickey turned, too, careful not to rush the short walk, keeping pace.

"How you feeling today, Pop?"

"I'm all right. Can't complain."

"But if you don't complain to me who you going to complain to?"

"That's what I got your grandma Anna for."

Mickey couldn't suppress her smile. "How long y'all been together again?"

"Fifty-five years this July. Week after next if my mind's still right."

"That's a long time." Mickey thought of what she might look like old and gray, Lex's hand in hers. It had all felt so certain at one time, like an inevitability. And now it felt slippery and tenuous, like the threads of her life had been snipped one by one. An image of Tee's hand in hers flitted across her mind and it sent a chill up her spine. The world felt dizzy at the sudden switch. How easily she'd reverted to her old ways, dreaming about her and Tee at every life stage.

"Yeah, especially with the way she always be farting, stinking up the place."

Mickey smiled but didn't laugh. It had stopped being *ha-ha*-funny twenty retellings ago. She resisted saying *el-oh-el*, which she used with her friends when something was funny in theory but not in real life. They passed under the big magnolia tree that arced over the house, its leathery leaves shading them like an awning.

"How long you planning on staying here?" She knew he didn't mean it like that, but the words were already producing a low, stinging feeling in her chest. It hadn't even been a week. She had just started feeling comfortable and already they wanted her out.

"You been to your daddy's yet?" he asked next. They approached the door.

"No, I'll go by there sometime this week."

He opened the door for them both. "Make sure you do."

"You going to stand in my doorway forever?" Grandma Anna rounded the corner in a seafoam housecoat, the silhouette of her nakedness catching the warm summer light.

"Hi, Grandma."

132

"Hi, baby." She took a few bags from Mickey and pressed a kiss to her cheek before shuffling into the kitchen, her house shoes scuttling across the hardwood floors. "You okay? You look like you seen a ghost." Anna grew more animated with each step, coming alive at the opportunity to inspect her granddaughter's handiwork.

"Pop wants me to go to Dad's house."

"He don't want you to *go* anywhere," she corrected, carefully unpacking the groceries and setting them on the white-tiled countertop, grooved from missing grout. "He just wants you to stop running from whatever it is you think you have to get away from."

"I'm not running—" Mickey began, but the look on her grandmother's face told Mickey she could see through her excuses.

"Look, little girl. We don't have a problem with you staying here, but I'm sure your daddy expected you to stay with him. Now, I still haven't told him that you're over here, but you got a few more days before I do. You've been moping around here all sad-like and you expect me to believe you're here for a little vacation? Now tell me what's really going on."

Her grandmother had a way of peering into her soul, taking her apart piece by piece. Mickey nearly confessed but then Pop appeared, a hush falling between them. His heavy, uneven gait announcing his arrival. "If y'all gon' talk about me, at least be quiet about it." His half-smile was the only indication that he was joking. He placed the bag on the countertop next to Grandma Anna and kissed her on the forehead before retreating to his room.

"I just don't feel comfortable over there and you know that. I feel like there's no space for me to be staying for long periods of time." It was a house where she no longer had a room. It had been awkward, coming home during school breaks, eating Jamila's food, trying to figure out where things had been shuffled around. She swallowed a lump in her throat.

"I understand," Grandma Anna replied. Mickey knew she didn't.

She adjusted her glasses on her face and continued. "The kids'll be over in a minute, your auntie is picking them up from school." Grandma Anna said auntie like *ohn-TEE*, a holdover from the few years she'd spent living "up North," in a one-bedroom apartment in Harlem with her great-aunt Mabel. It was there that she'd perfected her light, high Southern accent, a clipped drawl that made her sound like the kind of woman with a store card she always paid on time.

Mickey started putting the groceries away and braced herself for their arrival. She loved her little cousins Trey and Leah (two and three and a half, respectively) but they required baby voices and running and playing to be satisfied, and Mickey wasn't sure she had anything left to give. At least she had thought to buy the applesauce they liked.

Mickey finished and disappeared into the front bedroom before Grandma Anna could ask her to do anything else. She settled into the room's lone chair and pulled out her phone, swiping away from her group chat with Jasmine and Scottie. Today's topic was *Euphoria*, Scottie was trying to figure out how to copy an eye look. Then, a text from Lex, which drummed up feelings she wasn't ready to wade through. Mickey tried to refocus. She had to work quickly, knowing Grandma Anna would soon appear in the doorway and ask her to grab something that hadn't made the list.

It had been two years since she'd looked through Tee's Instagram. The last girlfriend had been too much for her to witness. Tee really seemed all in that time, and even though Mickey had been three years into loving Lex, it hurt in ways she couldn't name. It prodded at something inside her, something deeper than a high school infatuation gone wrong. It felt personal, for her to be loving somebody like that while Mickey had to learn to love somebody else.

She found Tee's Instagram easily, the name the same as it had always been (TeeTheHoopGawd24) and discovered that time had done little to change either of them. Her grid was filled with high flash, late-night photos, Tee leaning up against cars she didn't own, with bottles she didn't buy and girls she wasn't dating. There were some basketball photos, too, congratulatory shoutouts to her friends who'd made it playing professionally overseas. There were no photos of Tee in her all-black Safeway uniform, only captions suggesting she was up to bigger things. "WE WORKING," said one, where she threw up a vague hand signal next to a celebrity Mickey recognized but couldn't name. "THAT'S ALL ME!" said another. In that one, she held on to a barely clothed blonde with a doll-like body, her deep brown skin shimmering with glitter and highlight.

Homebodies

"Mickayyyy!" A small body launched onto hers, knocking her phone out of her hand.

"Hi, Trey," she said, allowing her body to be crushed by her little cousin's enthusiasm. Trey belonged to her aunt Kizzy, her father's youngest sister. Her full name was Keziah, but nobody called her that. As the de facto baby of the group, she had been the fun auntie growing up, the one who snuck them nips of liquor at family events and took them out to U Street when they turned twenty-one. But now she had kids of her own.

Of all her family members, she probably liked Kizzy the best, and she was almost sure Kizzy felt the same about her. That translated to her kids, who Mickey had a particular affinity for. They could jump on her and pull her hair and throw tantrums, and somehow patience oozed from her pores. It was easy to spend time, to connect. It didn't come so easy with Boo.

Kizzy looked just like Mickey's father. They had the same button noses and thick, wide lips, their foreheads broad and strong. Mickey looked similar, but her head shape and mouth were all her mother's. She remembered hoping she'd grow up to look just like Kizzy, but instead she looked like herself. She was a blend of her parents, part Sylvia, part Richard. Trey, on the other hand, who was now drooling on Mickey's face and getting his navy blue baseball tee wet, had gotten Kizzy's exact looks.

"You're so fluffy," he said, filling his hands with her cheeks. She puffed up her face to amuse him, inflating her cheeks with air until she felt she was ready to pop. He forced her face back to normal and she stuck his hand in her mouth, pretending to gnaw on his chubby fingers until he laughed so hard he was gasping between breaths.

"Yummy yum yum!" she said, her voice high, her chest fighting to expand for full breaths. "Where's your sister Leah?"

Trey sat up as if given an order and crawled off her to the ground, breaking into a clumsy run once his feet met the floor. She knew she was supposed to follow, so she did. He led her, predictably, down the long hallway into the kitchen, where her grandmother was dumping spoonfuls of bacon fat into a pan on the stove. She was still wearing her housedress and bubblegum pink bonnet, her feet stuffed into a pair of expensive shearling slippers the grandkids had pitched in to buy together for Christmas one year. The inner fluff looked worn, and Mickey was happy to see they had been put to good use.

Meanwhile, Leah entertained herself with an iPad, curled up on a chair in the kitchen. She wore headphones that had glittery pink kitten ears, a stark contrast to her otherwise-neutral outfit. She barely noticed Mickey's entrance and when she did finally see her, she simply looked up and waved.

Mickey found it strange. Last time she was here, Leah had been bouncing off the walls, but now this seemingly mature little human had taken her place. Or maybe it was Peppa Pig holding her attention. The kids loved Peppa.

Trey climbed onto the chair, his fat little body wriggling into the seat.

"I want iPad," he whined, and her aunt Kizzy, who was rooting around in her grandparents' oversized Sub-Zero fridge, popped her head out to address her son but glimpsed Mickey instead.

Upon seeing Mickey, she squealed. "Hey Mickey girl!" She temporarily abandoned her food-finding mission to pull her niece into a hug. "It's been what? Six, seven months?"

Mickey smiled wide. "Hi, Kiz."

The "aunt" felt like an unnecessary separator, something that cleaved them in two, and Mickey was happy to see that Kizzy had maintained her youthful outfits. It wasn't unlikely for her and Mickey to own the same pieces, but Kizzy, three sizes smaller, had more options. Today, she wore a silky animal print dress, which showed off her cleavage and hugged tight everywhere else. Mickey was surprised Grandma Anna hadn't commented. Or maybe she had, and Mickey had missed the show.

"Y'all don't got nothing to eat?" Kiz asked.

Grandma Anna huffed at her youngest daughter. "You see me cooking, don't you?" Grandma Anna dumped two handfuls of kale into the pan.

"You eat kale now, Grandma?"

"Yes," Grandma Anna replied. She almost looked offended, as if Mickey had asked her if she knew how to read. "They was talking about it on *Dr. Oz*. Lots of vitamin K. But we've always known about kale.

We just made it different. You eat greens, don't you?" The question was rhetorical and Kizzy knew better than to respond. "Good for bones and helping wounds to heal."

She looked at Mickey when she said that last part, and Mickey wondered if she was walking around with the word *broken* on her forehead. "Well, doesn't it defeat the purpose if you cook it in bacon fat?"

Kizzy giggled. "Now, Mama."

"Both of you hush," Grandma Anna said, but she was smiling, too.

Kizzy looked over at her niece. "Now wait, why *are* you here?" Kizzy asked, her eyebrows raising in curiosity.

"Vacation," Mickey replied. The more she lied, the easier it became.

"I'm surprised they gave you time off from your fancy job," she said with a little wiggle. Leah, who had concluded with her episode, was now smushing her brother's face against the glass-topped table. If there was a point to this assault, Mickey couldn't pinpoint it. "Does my brother know you're here?"

"No," Mickey said, a tiny wave of panic coursing through her chest. "And don't tell him. I'm trying to surprise him."

Kizzy, unfazed by her children's antics but suspicious of Mickey's, returned to the fridge and took out two covered casserole dishes: string beans in one hand, mashed potatoes in the other. "When'd you cook this, Mama?" She opened it up to sniff it. Her lack of reaction signaled it was still good.

Grandma Anna briefly looked over at the glassware. "Maybe two, three days ago, I don't know. Shoot, we don't have a meat. Mickey, can you do me a favor, run back out to Safeway and pick up a rotisserie chicken?"

At the mention of Safeway Mickey's stomach turned. She decided to go to Giant instead.

FIFTEEN

Mickey was in the car a few moments later, grateful she had something to do. A few more minutes and she would've blurted out everything, revealing her real reason for coming home and the pain that came with it. It wasn't easy to hide from Grandma Anna, pretend that things were all right, but with Kizzy, it was near impossible. She had supported Mickey from the outset, was one of the first people to meet Lex. Had given her the courage to come out to her dad, a clumsy confession that was met with a nod of acceptance and not much else. It felt wrong not to update her now, not keep her in the loop.

As she pulled out of the driveway, her phone buzzed to life, a photo of her and Lex blinking back at her. It was an old one, a photo from the weekend they went apple picking upstate the previous fall. She turned the phone over as she peeled onto the main road and immediately felt bad. Seeing Tee had shaken her, and she didn't know how to speak to Lex without calling out Tee's name.

Lex and Mickey had only been dating a few months when the conversation about exes came up, the two of them trading stories over bites of black pepper ravioli from an Italian place in Clinton Hill with an ivy-covered, brick outdoor patio. They took dessert to go, sitting on a grassy hill in Fort Greene Park and feeding each other while watching people enjoying their afternoon. It was the last days of summer and they'd realized they were falling in love.

"So y'all were exes or not?" Lex asked in between bites. Mickey had loved the way the sauce sat at the corners of her mouth. Little white dots speckling her pretty brown skin.

"It was complicated," Mickey said then, even though it seemed stunningly simple now. Now that there had been many years and distance between her and Tee. Now that she loved herself for real. "She sort of saw me before I saw myself. I trusted her vision of me for a long time. It took me a while to realize I didn't need to live and die by that approval. That I could decide who I was for myself."

"Damn," Lex said. "She must've really broke your heart."

Mickey stared out at the shimmering lake, brilliant with sunlight, and watched a duck take off, kicking water as it leapt into the sky. She'd never really called it a heartbreak. There hadn't been a real, full-fledged relationship and no one had ever given her the permission to deem it so. "Yeah," Mickey said. "I guess she did."

It was strange to be seen in that way, by this woman who she'd only just met. But somehow Lex saw her so clearly. She saw Mickey the way she saw herself.

The thought of losing that was crushing. She called Lex back.

"Hi," Mickey said, putting Lex on speaker phone and sitting it in her lap. She pulled up to a red light and leaned back in her seat.

"Hi," Lex said, and there was a buoyancy to her voice, a sharp reminder that for Lex, Mickey made things better, her sadness rooted in them being separated. For Mickey it was much deeper than that. The sound of Lex's voice coming through the phone, blending with the sound of early-evening traffic and filling up the space of the car was surreal. It was confirmation of their separation, the theoretical now concrete. It was disorienting. Mickey had gotten used to being one half of a whole—Lex making up for the spots she missed and the things she lacked—but now all she wanted was to be by herself. Suddenly, the sound of Lex's voice grated in her ears.

"What's up?" Mickey asked.

"I need a reason to call you?" Lex asked, the buoyancy transforming to faint alarm.

Mickey thought on it for a brief moment, moving a sneakered foot from the brake to the gas. *Gentle now,* she told herself. *The pressure of your big toe.* Pop had taught her that. The car jerked forward and she was suddenly faced with the glow of another car's taillights, casting red over her skin.

"No," Mickey said. "I guess you don't. But I thought we were taking space."

"You're not here," Lex said. "Isn't that space enough?"

Lex was trying to make things light, but Mickey found it hard not to lock in to the irritation moving through her, starting in her chest and working its way up her neck and into her cheeks. Lex didn't get it, that much was still clear. What Mickey found relationship-ending Lex deemed a hiccup. This was why Mickey didn't really believe in the essentialism of the nuclear family. It encouraged people to put up with too much.

"Isn't it?" Lex asked. Mickey had been too preoccupied with the corners of her brain and the puzzle of traffic patterns to respond.

"What?" Mickey said. "I mean, I guess." Mickey rolled her windows down, letting her arm hang out as she drove. It was reckless. She had been warned against dangling her limbs out of cars by adults, but the breeze on her skin made her feel alive.

"What's wrong?" Lex asked, and her obliviousness only pushed Mickey further away. "Did something happen?"

Mickey didn't know how to say, *Everything. I saw Tee. She's beautiful still. Scary to me, still. My stomach hurt and then I remembered what it felt like to be loved by her. I buried that version of me to make way for this one. That version of me, that girl, wants out.*

Instead, she replied, "Nothing. Grandma's just on my nerves."

"Then come home," Lex said, her tone serious and sure. "I can take care of you."

It sounded good. Mickey could trust that she would. Lex, in an attempt to right her wrongs, would stop doing all the things that Mickey complained about. But things wouldn't change with Elda. She would just create more separation. Get better at hiding until she had no choice but to drop the mask. Mickey remembered the way she'd crumbled at that dinner table, how Lex had watched, undisturbed.

"Oh, so I won't be a burden? I want to make sure I'm pulling my weight."

"That's low."

Mickey beeped at a car veering into her lane, pressing down longer than she needed to. "Is it? You're the one who accused me of dragging you down with all my shit."

"I apologized for that."

Mickey pouted but her voice remained firm. "Yeah, but you said it."

"I said it because I was angry."

"Maybe, but you meant it," Mickey shot back. She remembered the way that emptiness had catapulted her into their current predicament. How not steeling herself against the casual cruelty of Lex's mother had plunged her further into the deep.

A sigh. "At the time, yes. But I realized that I was just overwhelmed. It was scary seeing you like that. Just day after day. It didn't feel like it would end."

"And what did you do?" Mickey asked. She was disgusted at the thought of her own neediness and even more disturbed that Lex had put her in this position, making her beg for things that had felt guaranteed. "It wasn't even three weeks and you folded. Just like that. What about the three years where I played your best friend, waiting for you to come out of the closet?"

Mickey was screaming now, and she wondered if she looked insane to the cars driving beside her, yelling to a phone no one could see.

"I—"

"Exactly. It's like the moment I needed you, the moment I felt weak—" Mickey's voice wavered and the road swam before her eyes. "You just stopped being there. That's not okay, babe. Not at all. And for you to say that shit with your mom?" Mickey slammed a hand against the steering wheel. "Like what the fuck?" Another slap. "Fuck! I'm just so exhausted. I'm so tired. Of all of it."

"I know, and I'm sorry. I want to do better and for things to be better. Are you crying?" Lex asked, and Mickey felt frustrated by her inability to hide her shallow, breathy sobs. She continued to drive, clicking her signal and merging, pulling the car into Giant's parking lot. She pulled up to a spot far from the entrance and put the car in park before removing the key from the ignition.

"Of course I'm crying," Mickey replied. "I just can't do this. Not anymore."

141

"What are you saying?" Lex asked, and Mickey felt the fear in the car with her, buckling itself into the passenger seat. What was she saying? The part of her brain screaming for normalcy, demanding she do what she'd always done, asked her to be rational about this. To take a step back and think things through. "I'm saying I want to break up," Mickey replied. "For real."

"Are you for real?" Lex asked and upon hearing the sound of Lex's tears, Mickey almost took it back and said that no, she wasn't. "Mickey, baby, please," Lex said, and when Mickey didn't respond, she could hear the frustration seep into her tone. "Five years. And over what? My mom? We've been through so much more than this."

"Yeah, but before I felt like you had me. Or maybe I was stupid. I don't know."

"And you don't think I got you now?" Lex asked. "Seriously?"

Mickey stared at the ceiling and let out a shaky breath. Her phone sat hot in her lap, as Lex waited for a response.

"Mickey," Lex said, her tone lingering between disbelief and sadness. "I'll do whatever I have to, just don't say you're done. Please."

"It's not just your mom," Mickey said. "It's the fact that you don't protect me and you expect me to adjust. To love you more than I love myself. And I can't do that anymore. I've sacrificed too much. I can't do that anymore. Not when I'm going through the worst moment of my life. Everything I thought was going well for me was ripped away, and even then, you're putting me in a position to get kicked when I'm down. I can't do it. I really can't."

"And you don't think I've done the same? I've pushed myself so hard to try and finally I felt like we were going to be okay." Lex exhaled. "I've been trying, too. You see that."

"I see that. I can't keep letting you try. It's just not working for me. You've been trying for years at this point. We've been trying for years."

"Mickey what? We've been good. You've been happy. What happened in a week?"

"It hasn't just been a week Lex. And this is why I'm frustrated. You think we can just brush all this shit under the rug, and I can be happy even though you put me through the most triggering shit of my life and then got mad at me for not being supportive enough. You didn't even consider me. You overcompensate by taking care of me, so I get over the fact that you're not putting in the work where it counts. You want me to be normal and be okay. I can't do that."

"I take care of you because I want to. Not because I have something to prove. Am I not allowed to have my feelings about things? Even when I try it feels like it's not good enough. But I want to keep trying. I don't want to give up." Lex's voice was low and urgent, and Mickey was grateful they weren't in the same room, that she didn't have to see the hurt up close. This was bad enough.

Mickey stared ahead into the parking lot. She watched a mother tug a child toward the car, their feet dragging as they tried to pull their way back into the supermarket. Her tears slowed at the distraction, and when she collected herself, there was a numbness all over. The parts of her that wanted this with Lex were also the parts that ignored the pain in favor of familiarity and comfort.

"Well, you can keep trying, Lex. But I can't. I just need space. Some real space. I need to think. I need to figure some shit out."

"Okay. But are we still together? At least let me have that."

"I can't give you anything right now. I barely have anything for myself."

"So what? You're not my girlfriend anymore? This is just it?"

"I just—" Mickey said. "Let me think."

"Fine, I'll let you think. Can I text you, at least?"

Mickey sighed. "You can text me."

"Can I call you to say good night?"

"Lex."

"Okay." Lex sighed. "Okay. I get it. Space."

"I'll talk to you later."

"Okay," Lex said. "I love you."

"Yeah," Mickey said. "Me too."

Minutes passed but it felt like hours. Mickey watched the supermarket goers, but she saw nothing, noticed nothing, letting the afternoon sun assault her skin through the windshield. She'd forgotten to wear sunscreen. She checked her reflection in the pulldown mirror, which only gave her a good view of her eyes and nose, and noted the puffiness, the added volume in her cheeks. The phone rang and Mickey answered without looking, without thinking.

"Hello?" she asked, attempting to keep her voice steady. Part of her thought, hoped maybe, it was Lex calling to beg once more.

"Bitch, when were you going to tell me you were in town?" Jasmine's voice floated into her ear, and despite the accusatory tone, Mickey smiled almost involuntarily. She was supposed to be sad, but here was Jasmine, and Mickey couldn't stop thinking about the time they got in trouble for leaving empty Oreos on the counter after eating the icing and abandoning the rest.

It had been a long time since they'd been on the phone, just them two. They texted fairly regularly, mostly in the group setting of their text thread with Scottie. But their relationship was still nostalgic for Mickey in so many ways. It grounded her and reminded her of who she'd been. It felt essential to talk to Jasmine when she was worried about losing herself, less so when she was focused solely on how much further she had left to go.

That's where Scottie came in. Their ambition matched perfectly, and Mickey always felt weird talking about work stuff with Jasmine, who, between wrangling a very precocious seven-going-on-seventeeen-year-old and nursing full time, had her hands full of more than listicles and boring beauty launches. But Mickey should have checked in more, she knew.

Over the past few years, Mickey had gotten so wrapped up in her own life and the micro dramas of her industry that her life had reshaped itself to reflect the people who spoke this language. It became one of entrances and exits, of image, of status. Her new friends had become all-consuming, what with their effortless elegance, clothing tailored to fit, the gold in their ears just the right size (medium, chunky, hooped). But mostly importantly, those friends were *real* friends with the people who mattered. Friends that were opening galleries and concept stores, writing poetry and curating galleries in small white rooms. They were doing Friendsgiving by candlelight in Brooklyn apartments occupied by people with day jobs that felt mythical and out of reach.

And Mickey wanted to be in those rooms. To sit around the dinner tables, privy to the drama that would be left out of the memoirs, illuminating what it meant to be Black and creating at a time like this. But where were they now? Now that Mickey was barely making it, and they hadn't noticed. Hadn't called. But stranded in the grocery store parking lot of her hometown, Mickey still yearned for the last-minute invites, dreaming of an alternate summer populated with weeknight dinners in the Meatpacking district and spontaneous excursions to Brooklyn where she could shake her ass at a Bushwick club named after a Haitian saint.

"I've only been back for four days."

"Three days too long," Jasmine said.

"Well, what are you doing tonight?"

"We're actually having a little cookout for Nova. You know her birthday is tomorrow. I would've invited you but, you know, you ain't never here."

Mickey laughed. "I know, I know. I just work a lot. You know that."

"Yeah, you and Scottie both. I work a lot, too."

Mickey acknowledged that she did. While Jasmine was currently an RN, she was also in school to be a nurse anesthetist. When she finished, she would be making more than Mickey and Lex combined. But Mickey, in her mind, had something money couldn't buy: status. Even though it made her queasy to think this way, she knew that she had a job that granted her access to rooms Jasmine never would get into, and that alone made it worth it. Sure, she knew Jasmine worked longer hours, harder hours, that what she did was life or death, but her life was ordinary, and Mickey felt there was nothing she dreaded more. There was nothing glamorous about bed pans and hanging IVs or pushing meds. Even if she didn't feel confident among her industry peers, at the very least she knew she had a leg up on her friends back home. But none of that had saved her, all that clout amounting to this: driving her grandmother's old car and hiding in her hometown, trying to puzzle out how she'd been caught by her childhood best friend.

"How did you even know I was here?" Mickey asked.

"My mama saw you. You know she started working at Safeway part-time when she retired. She works a couple days a week. She likes to talk to people."

Mickey was mortified at the thought and then remembered Tee, whose name tag read her full name, Tiana, and was affixed tightly to her right breast, not that she'd been looking.

"Oh, right. I should've done a better job at bobbing and weaving. I'm trying to be incognito. Surprise my dad."

"Surprise him for what? It's his birthday?"

"No, I thought it might be nice." Upon further scrutiny, she realized how silly she sounded, and worried that Kizzy, Grandma Anna, and Pop thought so, too. "I have a week or two off work so I thought I'd visit." There was that lie again. She hadn't updated Scottie or Jasmine about her current circumstances. They had brushed off the Nina thing like it was any other incident. Another false alarm.

If Jasmine was suspicious, she didn't press. "So can you come?"

Mickey considered the potential for running into her father. She assessed the risk level. It was low. He and Jamila were visiting Jamila's family in Ohio and would be gone for the next few days, Mickey suddenly grateful for Jamila's rural roots. She wasn't ready to see him just yet, worried it would all just come up and then she'd be left with nothing but his judgment. Of her career, of her relationship with Lex. Although her father played at accepting her and her relationship, Mickey had always overcompensated, using her success to shield her against any potential criticism. She hadn't allowed for anything but that.

Mickey gave him so many reasons to be proud, and very few to question her. It didn't matter that she was attracted to women, that she liked the feel of their soft skin against hers. It didn't get in the way of her being her. She still dressed like a girl, whatever that meant, and to the untrained eye, no one would be able to tell she was different. She still looked and acted and excelled like the girl he raised. But now things had changed, and she couldn't bear to see him and face the shame. Whatever pedestal she'd built for herself, fortified by her family's praise, was crumbling beneath her.

"Hello? Can you?" Jasmine asked, sounding a little annoyed now.

"Of course," Mickey assured her. "What time?"

"Five-ish."

"Okay, I'll be there. Does Nova still like Elsa?" She parked, unbuckled, and sank into her seat.

"Oh no," Jasmine said. "She wants an iPhone."

Homebodies

* * *

It felt like years since Mickey had been back to her and Jasmine's neighborhood. She eyed the carved stone structure at the entrance to their planned community, its name etched into the concrete.

Mickey turned onto the main boulevard and started up the hill. She looked over into the passenger seat at Nova's gift, which she'd strapped in with a seat belt to ensure it didn't move. She'd splurged as much as she could, picking out the biggest L.O.L. Surprise doll kit that $40 could buy. It wasn't much, but it had twenty surprises, which Mickey hoped was enough. It wouldn't make up for the many missed birthdays, but maybe it would be a start.

Her street was mostly how she remembered it. All the houses near-identical in style to their neighbor, and the one across the street. The differences were minimal, an extra sunroom jutting out from the side, a slight change in brick, an attractive-colored door. But mostly, they were the same, as were—Mickey would come to learn—the people who lived inside them. Every house sat on a quaint quarter acre, bordered by driveways on either side and dotted with salt-and-pepper men watering their lawns. Every morning the salt-and-pepper men, along with their well-groomed wives, formed a long, shuttle-like line, winding their Tahoes and Suburbans along the roundabouts and onto 210, the brutalist brick of L'Enfant Plaza looming in the distance.

Everyone worked for the government, situated firmly in the middle-middle class, some floating just a hair above if they'd played their cards right. Mickey's family lived in one of the bigger, builder-grade houses, located on the east side of the development on a street called North Star Drive.

It was a testament to Blackness, upward mobility, and a flattening of its origins all at once. The inherent irony of a planned suburban community named by white people for Black people to live in. Their forty acres and a mule had been reduced to a quarter-acre plot outfitted with orange-wood banisters, beige granite countertops, and a half-bathroom off the front hall.

Mickey had arrived here from Columbia Heights, a chubby fourteen-year-old with lofty ambitions: friends and a boyfriend, preferably in that order. There was just one issue—she was painfully awkward in the matters of friend-making and dating, self-conscious of the space she took up in a chair and the way she spilled out of her clothes.

If someone had told her then that one day she would be a fancy journalist in New York City, she wouldn't have been surprised, but if they had called her beautiful, she would've shifted under the weight of their attention, sure they had made a mistake. She didn't consider herself to be much of anything, her baby fat covering all the bits she deemed desirable. Now she had all the confidence but none of the career, and well, wasn't that a cruel twist of fate?

She pulled up to Jasmine's house, where there was an excess of cars lining the street. An elaborate balloon arch decorated the front door. She could see the edge of a big red bouncy castle. Little voices shrieking with glee. *So much for a small thing*, Mickey thought.

She could see her father's home, her home, from here, and she wondered what life might've been like had she continued to live across the street. If she and Jasmine might be closer. If she would have helped to set up the party rather than arriving an hour late with a shiny silver gift bag stuffed with glittery tissue paper in hand.

Mickey rang the doorbell even though the party was clearly taking place outside. The door opened to reveal Jasmine's mother, Sharon, who looked like she hadn't aged a day, her looks preserved in amber. She and her daughter had the same petite features, which made them look both fairy-like and severe. With age, she'd become more mean-looking, though Mickey couldn't think of anyone nicer, or more welcoming. She'd played host to Mickey and Jasmine's many sleepovers over the years, treating Mickey like one of her own, which meant they were praised and punished in equal measure. Mickey remembered when she and Jasmine had snuck out one night during their freshman year in high school, and Miss Sharon had threatened to beat them both.

"Mickey! Hi!" she exclaimed, pulling her into a hug. "Jasmine didn't tell me you were coming 'round this way."

"Hi, Ms. Fitz," Mickey said, taking her in. Her once-long hair was now short, cut into a banged pixie. It suited her. She proffered the bag. "Where should I put this?"

"Oh, we have a little gifting table out back. Come on in."

"I heard you told on me," Mickey said.

Miss Sharon laughed. "I sure did. I was going to say hi, but you ran right out of there."

At the thought of Tee, her heart skipped a small beat. Mickey touched her arm and smiled, following her through the house to the backyard. Their house's layout almost exactly mirrored her own, just flipped. They had remodeled since she last visited, the thin orange-wood planks replaced with a light, wide-planked, wood-looking vinyl floor. Everything was painted white, and the furniture was mostly beige. There were no kiddie things in sight. The only evidence of any small person occupation was the oversized family portrait that hung on the wall, a black-and-white photo of Sharon, Jasmine, and Nova, seated in a step-like formation. Three generations of Fitz women, each a version of the other. Mickey wondered if Nova's father and Jasmine's sometimes boyfriend, Q, would be around. The pair met in high school, and it had kicked off a decade-long saga that had become a regular source of entertainment for their little group.

Her question was answered when she stepped into the backyard, which was teeming with people: Q was on the grill. The scent of roasting meat hit her nose and even though she'd eaten at Grandma Anna's just a few hours ago, she felt her stomach expand to accommodate a little more. She could hear the music when she pulled up, but it sounded like one long alternating bass line.

Now, close to the action, she could make out words and sounds. "Return of the Mack" spilled from the speakers, and people were grooving, singing along and bobbing their heads to the beat. Mickey looked around. This was not a little gathering at all. She recognized a handful of people, most of whom she went to high school with. They looked like stretched out, aged versions of themselves. Mickey did her best to hide from view. She didn't want to catch up and pretend that everything was all right. Not today, not here. She looked around for the birthday girl, decided she wouldn't stay long. She would say her hellos, kiss Nova, and leave. And maybe get a burger and hot dog to go.

Jasmine was holding court, surrounded by a group of women Mickey didn't recognize. She had donned a white linen sundress and chatted while reorganizing the gift table. Mickey shook her head with a smile. Some things never changed.

Mickey thought of the first party she'd attended in their neighborhood. It had been a cookout similar to this, Tee's back-to-school bash, which at the time, was *the* social event of the summer. She hadn't known that then, new to the area, but Jasmine had guided her through it. As always, holding her hand like a younger sibling even though they were almost exactly the same age.

Much like today, there had been people everywhere: clustered in corners, hanging by the grill, baking in the heat, except everyone was fourteen. Tee's father flipping burgers and spearing hot dogs while his wife handed him an uncapped beer and whispered something in his ear. They laughed loudly, his stomach shaking and her mouth opening wide in unchecked glee, and in that moment, Mickey had been sure their love was perfect and pristine. Mickey's parents were nothing like that. They loved each other, sure, but there was no way Sylvia Hayward was getting a man anything that he could get himself. She had wondered at the time what it might feel like to have a mom like that, one that put other people's needs first.

She was self-conscious but secure next to Jasmine, who always knew how to command the attention of everyone in the room. They couldn't walk more than a few feet without being stopped by some boy or girl, wanting a hug or a minute of Jas's time.

"Hey Jas," said one.

"You look so good," nodded another.

No one had said anything at all to Mickey, until Jasmine introduced her, and they'd offer a perfunctory *what's up*, chucking a chin in her direction. She would smile shyly, and they would move on, inching closer and closer to the center of the room.

Even now, Mickey felt a little nervous, wishing she had her friend close. "Jasmine!" Mickey called across the party, making big wide gestures with her arms. She needed an escort. Jasmine met her eyes and waved her over. Mickey did her own come-hither motion in reply, hoping to avoid a group conversation, but it was a few moments before Jasmine was able to break away. Mickey felt exposed. She could feel the eyes on her, wondered what they were seeing. If they remembered who she was. Mickey had only been at Friendly a year before she left for The Conservatory, where they called teachers by their first names, and everyone had money but was good at making it seem like they didn't. As her strange new world had become clearer to her, this one had become hazier, and Mickey had never really found her way back. She had been happy to float somewhere in the in-between, latching on to people who seemed to be going through the same switch, or, like Scottie, had always lived in a world full of white people, had been in private school her entire life, starting with Capitol Hill Day School and working her way up from there. She knew whiteness as intimately as she knew herself.

Unlike Scottie, Mickey came from a world where Blackness was not notable nor commented upon but a shared condition, a shared joy and sometimes a shared despair. Her and Jasmine were supposed to be the same. But life had pulled them in different directions. Mickey had learned to perform her Blackness in a way that made her self-conscious about the way she showed up in a room. Mickey shifted from foot to foot, uncomfortable. It was as if she were fourteen again, waiting for Jasmine to make an introduction.

Mickey scrolled through Instagram mindlessly to seem busy, but was quickly irritated by the app, every photo reminding her that she was stuck at a kid's birthday party instead of laying out at Riis or strolling along Tompkins Ave. She was considering deleting the app, which now served as a symbol of her exile. She x-ed out of it instead. *That's fine*, Mickey thought, even though it was definitely not.

A tap on her waist pulled her from her reverie.

"Is that for me?" Nova's voice had gotten deeper, but it still had a squeak that Mickey found unbearably cute. She was coordinating with Jasmine, wearing a romper version of her mother's white linen dress, but hers was embroidered with her name in loopy blue thread. Her hair was braided into an intricate maze in the front, the back loose, her tight coils shiny and defined, bouncing whenever she moved.

Mickey bent down to meet her at eye level. She didn't have far to travel and ended up in an awkward half-bent squat. "Why, yes, it is."

"Can I see?" she asked, batting her big eyes, her little lashes crushed against her cheeks. She was closing her eyes so tight her eyelids wrinkled. Mickey was sure this little face got her everything she wanted. At the very least, she was impossible for Mickey to resist.

"Sure."

"Yeee!" Nova replied. She was about to reach into the bag when Jasmine appeared, tapping her daughter's hand with a sharp thwack.

"Now you know better, Nova Denise Fitz. Just because it's your birthday doesn't mean you can go around acting up." She took the bag from Mickey. "You need to wait to open it just like your other gifts."

Nova crossed her arms across her chest, her lips forming a pout. "But Mommy, it's my birthday. I'm going to see my presents anyway."

"Little girl. Do as I say." She shooed her and Nova stomped away, her glittery sneakers lighting up with every step. Mickey watched her march of defiance until it ended at the grill, where she was now tugging on her father.

"Ooh, it looks like you're in trouble," Mickey said with a grin.

"As if I care. She's going to run to her daddy and he's going to give her what she wants. Me the bad guy, as usual. But he don't deal with her foolishness every day." Jasmine crossed her thin forearms and the bag dangled from the crook of her elbow, reflecting the light. "What you get her?"

"Some L.O.L. Surprise doll."

"Oh lord, she's gonna be over the moon. Good job, godmommy."

"I couldn't afford the iPhone."

"Yeah, me either," Jasmine said with a laugh. "It's in there though." She gestured in the direction of the table. "A gift from Grandpa John."

Mickey turned her head in surprise. "I didn't know your dad was coming around."

"He doesn't. He just buys her shit."

"Well, that must be nice."

Jasmine did a little kick at the dirt. "Mhm, she thinks so, too."

Mickey watched her visibly shift gears, remaking her face into the picture of composure.

"Anyway, you really got vacation, huh? I can't believe you're using it on little old us. I would think you'd be halfway to Mexico."

Mickey grinned. Mexico did sound nice. "Yeah, I mean, it's been a while. Thought it was time."

"Why now, though? Things okay with you and Lex?"

Mickey tensed at the inquiry. "Yeah, of course. Why?"

"Nothing. Just odd. Y'all are normally attached at the hip."

Mickey hadn't thought to come up with a good cover story for Lex. Had hoped her presence alone would smooth over any inquiries into her sudden return. She figured if she could be honest with anyone it would be Jasmine, who had supported her through just about every phase and misstep without so much as a blink. "I've just been really stressed out, so I wanted to switch it up. I kind of published this manifesto on Twitter and that didn't go so well so now I'm . . . kind of . . . I don't know."

"On Twitter? Girl what? You know I haven't been on that bird app since the Barbz ran me off for saying that Nicki's ponytail was nappy. They threatened to leak my address."

"Damn," Mickey replied. "Never mind."

"You sure?" Jasmine asked. "I want to know what happened."

Mickey was about to continue, but Jasmine's attention was diverted by a wailing child. "Hold on," she said. "I'll be right back. I told Gerald not to get his big self in that bounce house."

Then she disappeared, a blur of white weaving through the crowd, and Mickey scanned the group again, hoping for a more familiar face.

She didn't spot anyone immediately, so she made a beeline for the food table, where burgers and hot dogs and fried fish and baked beans and potato salad and mac and cheese and ribs and grilled chicken sat waiting, suspended in metal baskets and kept warm with little blue flames. She picked up a plate and began to move through the line, taking a bit of everything. She finished making her plate and moved on to the cooler. She was attempting to balance it all, holding her plate slightly above her head as she bent over, using one hand to root around for an extra cold ginger ale.

"You need some help?" The sound of Tee's voice startled her, and

Mickey sat up too quickly, the cooler closing with a loud thump. She turned around to face Tee, wiping her hand discreetly on her shorts. "You look like you're struggling."

"I'm good," Mickey replied. "I got it."

"You sure?" Her mouth lifted into a half-smile. She nodded toward Mickey's hand, wet and empty. "Doesn't seem like you got what you were looking for."

Mickey clucked her tongue. "I changed my mind."

The two fell into silence and Mickey took the opportunity to take her in out of uniform. She still looked good. Too good. She wore an oversized black T-shirt and black mesh shorts, and Mickey couldn't help but glance over at the scar on her right knee, evidence of the accident that had ended Tee's career.

On her feet, Tee wore a pair of Nike Dunks that had long been sold out in Lex's size. Mickey had wanted to surprise Lex with those for her birthday, but they were selling for double, triple the price. A blinding Cuban link chain circled Tee's neck, heavy and diamond-studded, and Mickey wondered how much that cost, how many hours of cashiering she had to do to afford it. Her locs had been released from their bun, and now they curled around her face, big corkscrews that Mickey could get her fingers lost in. They were so long now . . .

Mickey realized she was drifting into fantasy and pulled herself back to the present. She looked around the party as if she had somewhere else to be and tried to locate Jasmine. Hoped that she would come and save her, separating her from Tee before she got too close.

"Why are you here?" Tee asked.

Mickey turned her head to the side and squinted her eyes. "It's my goddaughter's birthday. Why are *you* here?"

Tee shrugged. "I came for Miss Sharon's mac and cheese."

Mickey wrinkled her nose. Mickey didn't touch Miss Sharon's mac and cheese, which she always made with eggs.

"So how you been, superstar?"

Mickey allowed herself a small smile. Tee wasn't even close to correct, but it sounded nice coming from her mouth. Made her feel all warm, especially followed by that grin. "Who, me?" Mickey asked.

"Yeah," Tee said, mouth still stretched wide. "You."

"I'm good," Mickey said with a shrug. "Chilling."

"Oh yeah?" Tee said. "You still stay up in New York?"

"I do."

"You still—" she began, but she was interrupted by Jasmine, speaking in her loudest voice.

"All right y'all, come on. We're about to sing happy birthday to my baby." The party migrated to the center of the backyard, crowding around a six-foot-long table covered in a plastic tablecloth. Mickey took it as an opportunity to move away from Tee, getting as close to Jasmine as she could without standing directly behind the table. Nova stood with both of her parents, basking in the attention of the crowd.

Everyone began to sing, falling into a single harmony, and Mickey struggled to remember the words. How could she forget "Happy Birthday"? She looked away from Nova to scan the crowd and found Tee staring back at her. Oh right, that's how. Something passed between them, and Mickey recalled what it had been like to see Tee for the first time. That same electricity she was feeling now. Mickey had expected it to dim with the passing of years but instead here she was, squirming like she was still fourteen years old, watching her from across the room at a party, waiting to be noticed.

When Mickey had first moved to the neighborhood, she had seen Tee a few times from her bedroom window, but an aerial view hadn't done her justice. Nothing prepared her for seeing Tee up close at her family's back-to-school cookout, taller and broader than she expected. Her small dreads defied gravity, held upright with a cheap, thick rubber band, and her arms, crossed over her chest, were clear evidence of her years playing ball. She spoke like a pastor ministering to her flock, her words tumbling out dramatically before pausing to drink in the nods of the girls who dressed like boys, Nike socks pulled up to their shins and matching black slides on their feet. In the outer rim was a group of starry-eyed girls who obsessed over the basketball girls and dressed like it was too hot for real clothes, all while pretending to be interested in the finer points of the ninth-grade junior varsity basketball lineup.

"Yo! Somebody has to get Lia out of the starting five. Coach

Thompson don't know what she's doing," Tee said, and everyone nodded in agreement.

The girl was magnetic, her laugh traveling from somewhere in her belly and out her mouth, her extra-white teeth gleaming. When she laughed, everyone around her did, too, the energy of the room rolling from the tips of each loc and into the atmosphere, warming them up and bringing them to the edge. Mickey was on the edge, too, sipping a drink too fast to avoid looking thirsty. She remembered the walk back home to Jasmine's that night, feeling giddy and delirious, and drunk. Nothing had happened, but everything had changed.

She was brought back by the Stevie Wonder rendition of "Happy Birthday," and on this one she joined in. Her goddaughter was getting older. Her best friend was so proud. *Mickey* was so proud. The crowd clapped and sang and cheered, then retracted, descending on the table to get a slice of cake. Mickey stood off to the side, and Tee materialized beside her.

"How long you in town for?"

Mickey once again found herself caught off guard.

"I don't know yet. Maybe a week or two."

"How come?"

"Visiting."

Tee nodded, seeming to take things for what it was. "It's been a long time since you visited."

"You're keeping track now?"

A smile. "Nah, but you live down the street." She stepped closer and Mickey could smell her now. Her cologne was musky and masculine, a blend of tobacco, ginger, and vanilla. Mickey fought the urge to inhale. "If you were home, I would know."

Mickey's heart skipped a small beat. "Well, I'm here now."

"It's good to see you."

"That's *my* line." It was Mickey's turn to smile. "It's been what, five years?" A little gesture with her hand.

"A little longer than that I think."

"I didn't think you were counting."

"I'm good with time."

"Ah," Mickey said. "Interesting."

"Is it?"

"A little bit." Mickey felt a sense of impending doom. Or was it a thrill? She pressed on.

"What are you doing after this?" Tee asked. The question caught Mickey by surprise. In all their years of push and pull, Mickey had done most of the pulling. Had made herself accessible, easy to find. Tee rarely had to ask.

"Probably going back to my grandma's house," Mickey said. "You?" She told herself she was being polite.

"You're not staying at your dad's?"

"Not this time."

"You still like ice cream?"

Against her better judgment, Mickey replied, "I do."

SIXTEEN

By the time Mickey slipped out of Jasmine's house and into her grand-mother's car, the sky had settled into a swath of orange, purple, and blue. Tee stood waiting on the sidewalk while Mickey pulled up in front, a glowing blunt between her finger and thumb. While Mickey waited for her to finish, she sat in the car, rolling down the passenger window to let the sticky summer air in. It had been Mickey's idea to stagger their leaving, hoping to avoid questions from Jasmine later on. She quickly checked her phone to find another text from Lex waiting. This one was a picture of Mango staring up at the camera with the caption "Look at your daughter." She clicked her phone closed and fixed her eyes on Tee.

"You smoke now?" Mickey asked, and Tee's mouth spread into a slow, sleepy smile.

"Sometimes."

"Get in."

Tee took a final hit before slipping the joint behind her ear and open-ing the passenger door, adjusting the seat like she'd been there before. Tee liked to sit all the way back, her long, ink-covered arms brushing the back seat headrests when she placed her hands behind her head.

"So, Cold Stone's?" Mickey asked. They hadn't even gotten to the gifts yet and here Mickey was, sneaking off with Tee. She knew it was dumb, but she felt alive. Everything was a little brighter and she was conscious of the minutes ticking by, of Tee's every movement. *Was this how it was before?*

Tee nodded in reply and bit her lip, sending a spark of electricity up through Mickey's fingers and in between her legs.

Mickey started to drive, steering wheel in one hand, her other messing with the dial. She flipped to 102.3 and Cleo Sol peeled through the speakers. Mickey turned the volume all the way up, trusting the deafening sound of the wind and Cleo's crooning to carry them there and back.

Tee rolled up the window, her index finger hooking underneath the lever without moving from her reclined position. "Oh, you fuck with Cleo, too?"

Mickey looked at Tee in surprise. The sunlight was hitting her face just so, illuminating her deep brown skin. "I wouldn't think you listened to music like that."

"I know a little something."

Mickey smiled in spite of herself. "I guess I thought you would only listen to trap or something."

"I guess you don't know me like that," Tee said with a half grin and Mickey couldn't pinpoint why, but it stung. She gripped the steering wheel tighter and thought of Lex. Despite being theoretically single, she still felt tethered. And this felt far outside the bounds of what was okay.

Tee smirked and crossed her arms across her flattened chest, the black T-shirt outlining what Mickey guessed was a black sports bra. Lex wore one, too, but hers was Calvin Klein. Lex preferred the soft, breathable cotton to the restrictions of tight weave, compressive Dri-Fit, which flattened her breasts and made her feel less like a woman. Tee didn't mind.

At a certain time in her life, Mickey had gotten good at understanding all of Tee's movements and idiosyncrasies because she had watched Tee closer than she watched herself. She was rusty, but she could still read: arms back, chin lifted, head bobbing to the beat. She was relaxed. Maybe even happy. Mickey wondered, briefly, if Safeway was her fault. If looking away from Tee had caused her to fall so far away from the sun. She knew the scar above Tee's knee—the one that marked the end of her college career—wasn't on her, she hadn't even been there, so why did she feel so guilty?

They pulled up to the ice cream shop and Mickey let the engine idle. Frank Ocean sang to them about forbidden love.

Tee turned to her and smirked. "Your girlfriend know you here?"

Mickey blinked a few times to slow down her breathing. For years, Mickey had felt alone in her heartbreak—but Tee had been checking up on her, too. And that had to mean something, right? "You've been watching me?"

Tee scrunched up her face. "Ain't nobody stalking you, girl. You be posting shit and I got eyes."

Mickey did in fact post a lot of shit. Her at beauty events (well-lit selfies from below, the sky her background), her and Lex—so many photos of her and Lex: apple picking, at birthday dinners with friends, at Riis, in love. Mickey nodded and pressed her lips into a thin line, the guilt gripping her stomach. "Good to know."

"Aww," Tee said, flashing her brilliant smile. "Don't be like that superstar." It was Tee who misread, but there was that word again, and Mickey felt all tingly inside. "It's not like I didn't miss you," Tee said, meeting Mickey's eyes and holding it there. "Because I did."

Mickey's chest thrummed with anxiety and anticipation. She stepped out of the car and slammed the door shut and Tee followed suit. "Oh, really?"

"Something like that." Tee smiled again and something inside Mickey shifted. Tee used her long arms to push herself away from the car like a soft, bouncy spring and walked toward the glowing interior of the ice cream shop. Mickey watched Tee approach the shop, which was strangely empty for a Thursday evening in the middle of summer. She opened the door and held it open for Mickey to follow, the bells over the door jingling.

Mickey locked the car, hanging back for a moment before following Tee inside.

Once inside, Tee bought a Like It–sized Founder's Favorite (sweet cream ice cream with brownies, pecans, caramel, and fudge) for herself and a kid's cup for Mickey, a scoop of cake batter ice cream drowned in rainbow sprinkles. It was warm out, so they took it to go, driving to an empty lot behind a movie theater and sliding onto the hood of her grandmother's car. It was their old spot, a way to get away from it all, to soak up each other out of view. It was where they had told each other their secrets and made promises that were impossible to keep.

Mickey felt like a kid again, here with Tee, eating the half-melted ice cream with spoons and then with fingers, filling in the past few years with broad strokes.

"I like it enough," Mickey said when Tee asked about New York, careful not to reveal too much about the life she'd constructed there, a curated imagining of everything she'd hoped young adulthood to be. She left out the parts about weekly Y7 classes, knowing Tee would ask and it would be too much to explain. (Tee wouldn't understand why she did hip-hop yoga taught by tan, bony-hipped white women with bouncy brunette ponytails.) She left out most of Lex, too, gesturing vaguely at the length of their relationship (five years in December) and glossing over their rituals (Sunday trips to Greenlight followed by lazy walks through Prospect Park, their Brooklyn-dwelling friends in tow). She explained the work stuff instead, which she tried not to complain about because Tee, apron-less, still smelled to Mickey like the inside of a supermarket—though she masked it well, her body emanating the scent of that expensive cologne. Mickey could sniff out the cedarwood, warm and spicy in her nose.

Tee was evasive in her retelling of the past few years, a series of disappointments bookended with tragedy and the success of people never meant to surpass her. Things were never the same after her injury. She didn't say so, exactly, but Mickey could read in between the lines—the long pauses and breathy exhales that suggested something was up.

But, according to Tee, everything was more or less good. The grocery job was temporary (though it would be a year in just a few weeks), something to do in the meantime, though Tee didn't mention anything about what she hoped would happen next. Her brother lived in Atlanta now, leaving her in that big house with just her parents for company. Tee's friends, most of whom she knew through basketball, had met a variety of fates, some scattered across the country or the world, playing professional or overseas, others in the military, and a few just like her, home and figuring it all out.

It hurt Mickey to see. Tee had been a star, and everyone in the neighborhood knew she would soon be a household name. Mickey thought she'd be the nobody buying Wheaties boxes with Tee's face on it or watching her as a little dot on TV, but here she was: the hero in the flesh, only half of what they'd expected her to be.

It made Tee a little less shiny, and this pained Mickey, too. Tee had once been so bright, but now her light had dulled. Mickey wondered if that's how people would see her now, too.

Mickey didn't know what to say, only that she knew Tee didn't want her pity.

"Your hair got long."

Tee cocked her head to the side and looked at her. It was a face Mickey didn't recognize but it felt like disappointment, like Tee had expected her to dive deeper. It was unusual for Mickey not to press, since she'd always showed up in that way, giving Tee the space to work through her shit. Mickey had been Tee's echo when she was untouchable, but she didn't know where was safe to tread. She'd been gone too long.

"Yeah, it's crazy," Tee replied, shaking her hair loose.

Mickey's pulse quickened. She was unprepared for the fragrant scent that hit her nose as her locs sprung free, a mix of hibiscus and honey with a hint of spice that made her want to lean in close.

Tee pulled a loc straight until it touched her waist. "I just cut them recently, too."

"Wow," Mickey said. She wanted to take one in her hand and thread it through her fingers, but she planted her arms firmly at her side.

Tee pulled a lighter from the depths of her pants pocket and relit the blunt nestled behind her ear. Mickey could smell the sweet grape Swisher wrapper now that she was so close. "I be seeing your dad sometimes at Safeway."

"Oh yeah?" Mickey said, and her stomach did a tiny flip. She would need to start shopping at Giant if she wanted to keep this up much longer.

Tee offered her the quickly burning blunt, its tip weepy with ash. Mickey grabbed it carefully between her forefinger and thumb, letting the smoke hit the back of her throat and burn. She exhaled, smoke coming out of her nose and mouth at odd intervals, which made her cough hard and loud. The next breath hurt.

"You good?" Tee asked, and Mickey nodded, wishing she had some water and a hole to crawl into.

Tee took two hits and blew the smoke out smooth. "Maybe I should just shotgun you instead."

Mickey laughed. "I got it. You don't have to do that."

"You sure?" Tee asked, and Mickey considered it for a moment longer than she should've. They were sitting close now, Tee's thigh brushing hers, and Mickey could feel the heat of her leg through her jeans. Maybe it was because she was high and her mind was drifting and her body was humming, but she wanted to say *yes*. She hadn't been this close to another woman in years, had placed careful distance between her and anyone who wasn't Lex. But now, all she wanted to do was lean in.

"I'm good," Mickey said with a slow nod, and Tee laughed when their eyes met. A full body chuckle that made Mickey laugh, too. "What?"

"Yo, you're so high." Tee brought the blunt to her lips again.

"You think so?" Mickey asked, even though she knew Tee was telling the truth. She could feel it everywhere, like she was sharing her body with something else. Even though her limbs felt heavy, her mind was alive, racing. She was thinking of everything and nothing: about the feeling of the remnants of ice cream fading away on her tongue, the sound of Tee's voice and the way her name sounded in her mouth, if Lex had made anything good for dinner, what her last day on Earth would be like, if aliens were real. Then, she thought of Grandma Anna and her eventual demise, and what would happen if she drove high and killed herself and Tee both. She looked at Tee, who in the dim and dark of the parking lot looked so fucking beautiful Mickey worried she would cry.

"You good?" Tee asked after a moment, and Mickey realized she was staring.

She laughed it off. "Yeah, why?"

"Your eyes are red as hell and you're looking at me like you want to eat me."

"Bro, what?" Mickey asked, sitting up straighter and crossing her legs. "Like cannibalize you? Like eat your arm right here right now?"

Tee barked out a laugh. "Yes, exactly."

"Yo, you're weird as hell," Mickey said with a smile, and she ignored the overwhelming urge to give Tee a hug. She had missed her. This. Mickey lay back on the car instead, making an imprint in the dusty windshield. Tee joined her and they silently stared at the sky.

"Did you really miss me?" Mickey asked.

"I did," Tee said, lacing her fingers together and then pulling them apart.

"Why?"

"Because I could actually talk to you," Tee said, and when their eyes met Mickey swore she felt something pass between them. "And you came back looking all good and shit."

Mickey laughed a big laugh and surveyed herself. Some things had changed. Her face had slimmed with time and she'd grown curvier. She wore better clothes. "Me? I look basic as hell right now."

"Nah, something's different about you. You look real New York."

"What does that even mean?" Mickey asked. She knew she was fishing, but, at this point, she just wanted to hear things that made her feel good. She wasn't used to being seen by anyone other than Lex, and Mickey wasn't even sure if Lex really saw her anymore. Plus, Tee was looking at her from under those dark lashes in a way that cracked Mickey open. Even though Mickey knew not to trust it, it was hard not to feel vulnerable anyway, to want to bare her soul. How *did* she look? *Was* she any different? She didn't feel different. If anything, she'd never felt closer to little Mickey, delirious and intoxicated with Tee by her side.

There were so many memories, so many moments that felt tinged with Tee's presence. So much of Mickey's senior year was spent in Tee's basement, eating her mother Lanita's cooking and watching TV with only a thin cushion to separate them. The proximity taunted her—all she wanted to do was get closer, but it was always Tee who was in control: sometimes she moved the cushion, other times she made sure it stayed firmly between them. After Sylvia left, Tee filled a void, took up so much space Mickey couldn't think about anything else.

It had been complicated, in the end. Mickey in love, Tee unwilling to tell Mickey exactly how she felt. Sometimes Mickey wondered if Tee felt the same way, too, but she couldn't have. The way Mickey's heart had ached for years told her so.

Mickey had always told herself that if she *really* knew how Tee had felt about her, why she had kissed her again and again, then she could finally get the closure she yearned for, would have the clarity to heal the gaps in her heart. But she never got an explanation and had picked up the pieces on her own. She had tried to put all that misplaced love into loving herself, and then Lex came along. But she didn't much like herself right now, and her feelings for Lex shifted with each day apart.

Loving Tee had always come too easily, had been chemical, like she'd felt that way her entire life. Even more, the body remembered. Mickey's traitorous body would always open up for Tee if she would take her.

Mickey stared up at the sky before glancing over at Tee. Mickey was still waiting to hear how she'd changed.

"I don't know," Tee said with a shrug. "Just different. And you smell good."

"Oh really? What do I smell like?" Mickey asked. She nearly leaned into Tee before thinking the better of it, remembering where she was. Who she was, but Tee was quicker than Mickey. She leaned in to sniff and Mickey felt the tip of Tee's nose pressing into the space where her head met her neck and a shiver raced down her spine. She expected Tee to pull away, use better judgment for them both, but instead she felt a tongue, soft and wet, run up the column of her neck. Before Mickey could protest, a hand encircled her throat, firm, but not crushing.

"Tell me to stop," Tee said. Her lips were at Mickey's ear and her hot breath tickled the back of her neck.

"Stop," Mickey said, though she knew it didn't sound forceful or sure.

Tee caught her earlobe in her mouth and bit down. "You sure?"

Mickey's eyes rolled back and she bit her lip. That was her spot. Had always been. Tee had made it so, had taught her how she liked it. She pushed Tee away and slid off the hood of the car, her body's shape a faint outline made of grime. What had just happened? Why hadn't she stopped it? And what would she tell Lex?

Undeterred, Tee swung back around and approached Mickey's side of the car.

"Why are you being like this?" she asked, placing her hands on either side of Mickey's body, pinning her against the side of the car.

Mickey saw that it was a game now, that her playful, then firm resistance made this more exciting of a challenge. If anything, little Mickey was known for not resisting. For replying to every text, answering every call, sometimes throwing herself in Tee's path in the hopes of getting noticed. Even when she was playing it cool, she was sure Tee could sense the desperation rolling off her in waves. But things had changed. She was older now, she had that New York thing, and she was in a better place. She was *in love*.

But something about Tee melted her defenses, even after all this time. And maybe it was because she was high, feeling insecure, and riding high from being called a superstar, *Tee's superstar*, but all Mickey wanted was to press Tee's hand in between her legs to feel what she'd done.

"Being like what?" Mickey asked and Tee pulled back and rolled her eyes.

"You're playing."

"I wasn't aware it was a game."

Tee chuckled. "It's not."

"Then what is it?"

Tee was close again, inches away from her lips. She pressed a kiss to Mickey's jaw. "I told you I missed you."

"Did I ever say I felt the same way?" Mickey asked. She slid from underneath Tee and unlocked the door. "Let me take you home."

"Are you serious right now?" Tee said and a part of Mickey wanted to say no, she wasn't. Telling Tee to stop felt powerful, made her feel big in a space where she'd felt small for so long. Mickey knew all too well what yes looked like, what it meant to bend to Tee's whims. The version of events where she let Tee do what she wanted meant that she would become a different person, fundamentally changed at her core. She wasn't a cheater. She'd said stop, even if it was later than Lex might've liked, and still maintained some semblance of control. Even if she didn't want to. She was still good. Despite everything, she was still good.

"You know I can't do this," Mickey said. She opened the door and sat in the car. For once, Tee followed.

"You love her?" Tee asked in the quiet. Mickey's hands were too shaky to start the car.

"Of course."

SEVENTEEN

Mickey's heart was still racing when she dropped Tee off. The ride home had been silent, Tee scrolling through her Instagram, toggling back and forth between her endless DMs and feed. It was as if Mickey didn't exist, as if Tee hadn't just placed her hands around Mickey's neck.

Mickey examined herself in the rearview mirror. Thankfully, there was no evidence. She knew she should respond to one of Lex's texts—Mickey could see a whole line of them across her phone now. Mickey couldn't shake the unease, and on top of everything else, it felt eerie driving so close to her father's house. She still had her key, could slip in undetected, hang around and be gone before they got home. But it felt invasive somehow, even though her father had always insisted it was still where she belonged. Her hesitation and anxiety signaled that that couldn't be further from the truth. She pulled up until she was hidden behind a bush and unbuckled her seat belt with a sigh.

Being in a car with Tee again had been surreal. She remembered the first time, after one of Tee's high school games. It had been their junior year, the final double header of the season. At that point, Tee and Mickey were still just friends in passing. Mickey no longer went to the same school, had swapped out of their local public high school for an elite private school in DC, so she only saw her old friends in snatches. At basketball games, at house parties, at the grocery store.

Mickey tended to spend her weekends with the kids from her new school (much to Jasmine's irritation), getting drunk in the basement of their million-dollar homes. But that night, she'd decided to go to Tee's game, and somehow, Tee had offered to drive her home. It was shocking to a young Mickey, who, despite rarely talking to her, had maintained a crush so intense it threatened to swallow her whole.

The ride had been quiet, and jerky. It was clear that Tee had just started driving on her own. With every lurch, Mickey wondered if it was a good idea to get in the car with her. But they made it, the sign of their neighborhood glowing in the dark. They turned onto the main road and Tee carefully navigated the twist of the roundabouts, the movement so dramatic that Mickey slid from side to side in the plush leather seats. And then they were on their street, parked in front of what used to be Mr. Herbert's yard. Now it belonged to no one, a rectangular for-sale sign plunged into the grass, a coiffed woman's face smiling sharply back at Mickey. Tee cut the ignition and Mickey wondered why she didn't just drop her in front of the house.

"So why did Jasmine say you had to be dragged to my game?" Tee asked, breaking the silence, and Mickey worried, briefly, that she had somehow stepped into her own personal episode of *Law & Order: SVU*—the pride-soaked basketball star killing her geeky neighbor over her unwillingness to stroke her ego. Mickey silently cursed Jasmine for her offhanded joke and stared in her lap. She looked up at Tee, expecting a taunt, but was surprised to see that Tee had a quirky sort of smile on her face, closed mouthed and young-looking. Mickey could, from just that look, imagine what Tee had looked like at age six: small, adorable, but somehow no less charming.

"It wasn't just your game," Mickey replied, but that was a lie. Despite all the people on the court, Mickey had only really cared about the person sitting next to her.

"Depends on who you ask. Who else put up a double-double and scored eighteen points?" Tee asked, mimicking a shot in the small space, her wrist hanging limp, elbow at a perfect ninety-degree angle. Mickey waited for the sound of the swoosh that never came.

"I'm guessing just you?"

Tee nodded. "Just me."

"I mean, from what I saw you looked like you were doing your thing."

Tee nodded again and they slipped into the sort of silence that Mickey felt desperate to fill. "Congrats on Maryland by the way."

Tee's face flitted between surprise and a bored neutrality. "Thanks, who told you?"

"The streets are talking," Mickey said, but she instantly felt lame. What streets? Who was talking? Her father, for one. He had told her after hearing it straight from Tee's parents, making the mystery embarrassingly basic.

"Oh, so Jasmine said something," Tee said with a laugh and Mickey didn't correct her because it sounded better than the truth. "Yeah, it's cool. Some people said it was too early, but I know what I want."

Something about the word *want* hung weird in the air, and Mickey wished it had a double meaning, meant more than just basketball and next steps.

"You know better than anyone what's right for you," Mickey said, and though she didn't believe it, she hoped it would land in Tee's mind, sticky like a Post-it. A gentle reminder that Mickey had wisdom and was good for something other than a seven minutes in heaven hookup or the occasional laugh.

Tee stared back at her, unimpressed. "I mean, yeah." Her shoulders straightened and Mickey recognized this as confidence, the sure feeling that the universe would bend to your will. "Plus Maryland's dope. I been knowing their coach since I was like twelve. I always knew I would end up there."

Mickey wondered what it might be like to have your steps ordered, a clear path forged thanks to your preternatural talent. She was still trying to figure out if a college would take her with just-okay grades and spotty extracurricular activities. The Conservatory had been harder than she anticipated, a level of academic rigor that no one had explained going in. She was banking on the Conservatory's clout to grease the wheels. The school boasted a 97 percent college placement rate with the other 3 percent taking gap years to figure things out. But here Tee was, shiny and sure, glowing in the staticky quiet of the dark.

"Maybe Jasmine will have to drag me to another game." It felt like a joke now, the beginnings of something between them.

"Yeah, I'll probably be the only freshman starting," Tee said, her small chest puffing up and protruding out. Mickey thought she looked a little like a peacock.

"So you must be really good."

Tee smiled. "I'm pretty good."

Mickey wished she had the confidence to say she was good at things out loud. Sure, she thought it—scrawling sentences in her journal and reading them back to herself with a private pride, but it was her secret thing, something that she would rarely, if ever, say to someone else. She even bit her tongue around Scottie, her Conservatory best friend turned all-the-time best friend. She was afraid people would think she was too full of herself, that she would be setting herself up to fail. But somehow Tee had mastered both discipline and passion, and had, through sheer will, made her dreams come true.

She looked at Tee, who was looking back at her, and wondered what she was thinking. If she saw Mickey for all that she was or just a version of the girl she loved for real. What was that girl's name? Leila? Ayesha? Tiffany? Would Tee rather be with her right now, reaching over to unclip her seat belt and shoving her hands down her pants? Mickey knew how Tee moved. She'd heard the stories. Tee didn't hold back if she was interested.

But this wasn't what this was, as much as Mickey dreamed. This was Tee taking her home, being nice. She'd do well to remember that. But then again, Tee hadn't dropped her straight home. She had pulled up in front of an empty house where no one could see what would happen next, and that gave her hope, and a tingly feeling between her thighs.

Mickey thrummed her fingers against her leg and looked outside. It was mostly still, save for the occasional car pulling into the driveway or person begrudgingly walking their dog. It was late. A little past eleven now, and Mickey was grateful they were peeling into the weekend.

Mickey waited for Tee to do something, say anything, and eventually she opened her mouth. "What happened with your mom?"

Mickey's stomach dropped. She pulled her hair to one side and leaned deeper into the seat, crossing her arms. "Nothing. She moved to New York."

"She didn't take you with her?" Tee asked. "She's a G. My mom would never let me live by myself like that."

"I don't live by myself. I live with my dad." Mickey felt the defensiveness in her voice and tried to soften her tone. She still wanted Tee to like her. She wasn't exactly sure how to make that happen, but she knew it wouldn't be by being rude or cursing her out. Or maybe Tee liked those types of girls.

Tee threw up her hands in surrender. "My bad. My dad can't do shit without my mom except basketball stuff. I would basically be raising myself if she left. I guess that was my way of asking if you're okay." Tee was rambling now, and Mickey couldn't stop herself from smiling at her attempts to smooth things over. She caught herself, then realized Tee was smiling, too. "My parents almost got divorced last year, so I feel you," Tee said next, and Mickey was stunned by the newness of this information. Tee's parents had seemed perfect.

"My parents are not divorced," Mickey said, and this time, it was hard to keep the edge from her voice. She couldn't pinpoint why, but something about the word made her stomach churn, even though it was clear that's where they were headed. "They're just separated. For now."

Mickey had felt the need to clarify and was disturbed by her own willingness to bend her version of the truth. If Tee noticed Mickey's flexibility she didn't acknowledge it, her eyes more preoccupied with searching Mickey's face and then her body.

Mickey hoped she liked what she saw. She'd been trying to hold in her belly the entire way home and was exhausted.

"You'll be aight," Tee said, and Mickey found herself believing it—if not her words exactly, then the force with which they were delivered. She was embarrassed by how strongly she believed in Tee's ability to make the world around her into whatever she required. Mickey wished some of that attitude would rub off on her, that sheer proximity would give her some of Tee's confidence.

Maybe that's why Mickey kissed her. Mickey who had leaned in first, abandoning the 80/20 rule (something she'd learned watching *Hitch* with Jasmine) and pressing their lips together with gentle, but insistent force.

What happened next, however, was all Tee. It was Tee who grabbed Mickey by the shoulders and awkwardly, but forcefully, pulled her into her lap, forcing Mickey to climb across the gear shift like she was leap-frogging sideways. It was Tee who leaned her mother's seat all the way back until they were parallel to the cloth ceiling Tee was too nervous to let down. It was Tee who flipped Mickey onto her back and hooked her already-soaked underwear to the side. It was Tee who made Mickey's neck into a constellation of purple, red, and blue, and then her breasts to match. It was Tee who pushed two fingers inside Mickey before pulling them out to examine her handiwork, pausing when her fingers shone clear and crimson.

"You okay?" Tee asked, their bodies still pressed together. Mickey, sore and breathless, waited for her to continue, hungry for whatever happened next. She'd never gotten this far with anyone, not even herself. A light sheen of sweat had covered them both. Tee leaned up on her forearms and examined her slick fingers. "You're bleeding."

Mickey's stomach roiled at the sight of her blood. "Sorry."

"Did I just?" Tee cocked her head to one side and her eyes glittered in the darkness, their faces a few inches apart. "Are you?"

Mickey closed her eyes, she wanted to disappear. But then Tee's hand was cupping her face and kissing her mouth with a kind of tenderness that made Mickey want to say "I love you," even though, if she really thought about it, Tee was a girl she barely knew.

"You okay?" Tee asked again, and Mickey managed to nod her head before Tee's fingers found their way inside her body again, forcing her mouth open and a cry into the cavern of the car. She clawed at Tee's back through her T-shirt and sports bra, bucked against her and moaned in her ear.

It was embarrassing, to feel so much out loud, but Mickey couldn't help herself: this was a dream come true. In between all-consuming, thought-erasing punctuations of pleasure, Mickey wondered why Tee was so good at this, and how many girls had felt exactly what she did. But she couldn't linger in her head long, Tee made sure of it.

The memory still made Mickey's skin hot. Mickey scolded herself. She was grown now, too grown to be panting about something that happened more than a decade ago. But that didn't explain what had happened just an hour before, how close she had gotten to repeating the past. Gripping the steering wheel, she called Jasmine.

"Can you come outside?" Mickey asked, trying to keep the tone light. "I'm here."

A shadowy figure appeared across the street a few minutes later, looking both ways and shuffling across the road.

"Girl, where have you been?" Jasmine asked once she settled inside. She was laying almost perpendicular in the newly adjusted seat. Even in the dark Mickey could tell that Jasmine was tired, her eyes rimmed with dark circles, her hair tied up into a loose, low bun. "We were singing happy birthday and then poof, you were gone."

"Yeah about that . . ." Mickey pressed her head up against the headrest and stared at the beige, felted ceiling, wishing there was a sunroof so she could sulk with a view. "I was catching up with Tee."

She waited a beat but didn't dare look over to examine Jasmine's face, which she knew was an exaggerated portrait of disbelief. "Bitch, what? What do you mean caught up?"

"We *caught* up," Mickey said, nodding her head toward Jasmine for extra emphasis.

"Please do not tell me you did something dumb." Jasmine shoved the phone charger jutting out from the cigarette lighter port into her phone. It lit up gratefully and illuminated her streams of notifications. "Not over her broke ass."

"I kind of did something dumb," Mickey said, groaning. She wished she hadn't said anything at all, but she needed someone to know, to make it real.

"Girl, she's been working at the grocery store for like a year at this point. She's part-time there and at Foot Locker. Everybody know Tee is washed now, I don't know why you would even waste your time. I really only invited her because I knew she would bring Nova a pair of shoes."

But Tee had paid for the ice cream! Something in Mickey wanted to defend Tee, argue that she'd been going through a rough time. That the grocery job was temporary, and she was just figuring things out. But it was no use. What was she arguing for? Tee's reputation? "I'm just saying I saw her, that's all."

"Well, you look like you did more than that." Jasmine pulled the seat upright and scooted it closer to the dash, fumbling with the levers until it resembled the upright profile of the driver's seat, staring directly at Mickey for the entirety of her slow ascent. "And what about Lex? Y'all are basically married."

"We're not," Mickey said, but that felt like a betrayal, knowing that the only thing missing was paperwork and a big party with their family and friends. Mickey thought again of what their wedding might look like, though it was more painful this time: her in a white dress and Lex in a suit, standing at the head of a crowd of onlookers who loved them together just as much as they did apart. There'd be food, lots of it, served family-style because that's what they were. And someone would make an inappropriate toast, most likely Jasmine, who would recount Mickey's most embarrassing moments with a smile. And she would love every minute of it, grinning wild and covering her face when it went too far, fork in one hand, Lex's hand in the other.

Mickey inhaled until her chest hurt. How could she have been so stupid? How could she have gotten so distracted? Then her mind flicked to that blur next to Lex at the altar, the days and years after, holidays spent separately or with friends, gifts sent along with Lex in place of her presence, kids without lineage. Her stomach turned.

"Damn near. I mean y'all live together already."

"Don't you basically live with Q?" Mickey replied.

"Yeah, when he's not out here in these streets. Did I tell you some little girl came to me as a woman? As if I give a fuck. Plus, we have Nova, so that's different. We have to co-parent, at least."

"She's getting so big," Mickey said, and a wave of affection washed over her as she thought of Nova's gap-toothed smile. Physically, she was a perfect mix of her parents, but personality-wise, she was one hundred percent her mother—precocious and too smart for her own good.

Jasmine smiled wistfully, casting a sidelong look at Mickey. "I know. It feels like I just found out I was pregnant. You were so excited, but girl . . ." She looked down at her stomach and then back at Mickey, her face illuminated by the headlights of a car driving too fast down the road. "I was so scared."

Mickey remembered it differently. She hadn't been the slightest bit happy for her friend, who, like Mickey, was a year away from graduating college and had no resources to bring a child into the world. She remembered looking up into Jasmine's face and wondered why she didn't find shame. Just nervousness and, underneath it all, love. They had already been talking less and less since they'd gone off to their respective colleges: Mickey moving to New York, and Jasmine staying local to go to UMD. Mickey blamed herself for the breakdown in their communication. She was the one who didn't return FaceTimes and forgot to text back.

The pregnancy felt like a permanent splintering of their paths, the moment when she was sure their lives were traveling in different directions. The impending arrival of Nova had felt like the end of her life as she knew it. Tee had a new girlfriend, her dad was busy being someone else's father, and then there was Mickey, trying to figure out where she fit in all of it.

"Don't change the subject," Jasmine said, catching herself. "What happened with you and Tee?"

"It wasn't that deep, basically—"

"Wait." Jasmine cut her off midsentence, unlocking Mickey's phone. "Damn, you left Lex on read . . . so you don't have to tell this story again. . . ."

Scottie answered on the first ring.

"Hi," they said in unison.

Scottie smiled, then rolled her eyes. "Oh, both of y'all. Good. I'm glad you're not just hiding out at Grandma Anna's."

"Wait, you knew this bitch was home?" Jasmine asked, her eyes snapping to Mickey.

"Well yeah, you don't ever check her location?"

Jasmine fixed her mouth into a line. Mickey could sense her irritation at learning the information late. "The only person whose location I have time to check is my baby's. And sometimes Q."

Scottie laughed. "Well, if you looked, you would know. Also, I have a client dinner in twenty and I'm in the back of an Uber so make this fast," Scottie said, slightly breathless. Something thudded to the floor in the background and she suddenly sounded far away, the screen now revealing the roof of a luxury car. "And I'm changing shoes, so y'all are

176

on speaker," a louder thud, "Fuck, ouch, remind my tall ass not to stand up in the back of a compact sedan ever again."

"Who's the client?" Jasmine asked, knowing there wouldn't be an answer. "I'm surprised you're not in a Suburban."

Mickey shot Jasmine a look, to which she mouthed an incredulous "What?"

"We've downgraded car service to be easier on the environment," she explained quickly. "I'm lucky I'm not in a Pool. Re: the client, you probably wouldn't know him, he's a big rapper in Nigeria."

"Makes sense." Jasmine shook her hair out of its bun, her glossy black bundles shaking themselves into place.

Mickey took a deep breath and recapped her impromptu date with Tee. Neither responded immediately and it worried her. They knew her better than anyone aside from Lex, and their disapproval would mean that things had gone horribly wrong.

Over the years they'd settled into something resembling a friend group—Mickey at its center—and they'd seen each other through a lot: Scottie's brief lesbian episode, which ended with the three breaking into said girl's house; Jasmine losing both sets of grandparents; Mickey fully coming out. They'd been through breakups, makeups, pregnancy scares, actual pregnancy, good jobs, shitty jobs, highs, lows, and everything in between. And through it all, Mickey had been the measured one. The one with her head on her shoulders. She didn't make mistakes or do the risky thing. But here she was, detailing an almost tryst with a washed-up flame.

"Wait, so she licked your neck?" Jasmine asked, drawing back from Mickey to assess her best friend. She stared at Mickey like she had reverted to a previous iteration of herself, one that lacked self-control and a girlfriend a few states over.

"You're really tripping," Scottie said, and Mickey's stomach sank. She would never admit this, but she valued Scottie's opinion the most. "What were you thinking?"

"I wasn't," Mickey admitted. She hadn't been considering anything when she was letting Tee sniff her neck and get so close. She wasn't even sure she'd had thoughts, just rough sketches of feelings that felt as familiar to her as the contour of Jasmine's jaw and the sound of Scottie's voice. Mickey took a deep breath as she began realizing what she'd done. She let her head fall against the steering wheel and buried her head in her hands. "I'm so dumb."

"You're not dumb," Jasmine insisted. "You might've done a dumb thing though. Like I said, she's literally working at a sneaker store to keep flexing for Instagram. That's embarrassing. Did you forget who you are?"

Mickey splayed her fingers to peek at Jasmine. "What?"

"Mickey," Scottie began. "You're popping. Losing one little job isn't going to change that."

Jasmine looked at her quizzically and Mickey realized she'd been caught in her flimsy lie. Scottie continued, "Our high school friends talk about you like you're some kind of celebrity."

"You don't get it," Mickey replied, and she felt the shame and embarrassment return twofold.

"I do. You feel like your world changed without your permission. But that doesn't change the fact that I've heard multiple people say they always knew you were going to do big things."

Mickey rolled her eyes. "They don't."

"They do. And Tee knows it, too. That's why she wants to be all up in your face. Because she wants to be next to somebody important," Scottie said.

"Mhm," Jasmine agreed, but her energy had shifted. The excitement had waned, and Mickey could sense the irritation in its place.

"Y'all," Mickey said. "You think it's that deep? We just ran into each other."

"Have you told Lex?" Scottie asked.

The air froze. Mickey swallowed hard. "Not yet."

"Exactly. If it was nothing you would have called her immediately and not us," Scottie declared and Jasmine nodded enthusiastically. "I hate to break this up but I'm pulling up to the restaurant now and I can't be on the phone. It's the type of place where you have to put a sticker over your phone camera. You'd love it," Scottie said and Mickey was grateful for the interruption. The car door slammed shut. "Anyway, love you, see y'all in the group chat. And I hate to say it, but this could've been a voice memo. I thought you were pregnant."

Mickey laughed. "Okay, love you, bye." The sounds of LA disappeared from the call, leaving the sticky silence behind. She waited for Jasmine to speak.

As if on cue, she exhaled loudly. "So, you lost your job? You said you were here to surprise your dad."

Mickey's face contorted and the seeds of embarrassment grew. "I know what I said."

"How long has it been?"

Mickey sighed, the exhaustion settling into her bones. It felt good to be honest with someone else. "I sort of tried to tell you at the party."

"Not hard enough," Jasmine said. Upon seeing Mickey's dejected face, she softened. "Well, I'm sure it was for a fucked-up reason, you're literally the smartest person I know."

Mickey smiled a watery smile. If only she knew. "Thanks, girl."

"I'm serious. You've been like that since I met you."

"When you met me my hair was fried and I was wearing gauchos. I don't know how you saw past that."

"You helped me with my homework."

"True."

"But why come back? Lex waits on you hand and foot. Shit, if Q was treating me like that, I would stay my ass at home."

Anger bloomed in Mickey's chest. "If that was the case I wouldn't be here." It sounded harsher than she intended, the words coming out of her mouth in a frenzy. She instantly felt bad.

"Whoa," Jasmine said, eyeing Mickey carefully. "Where did that come from? Is something going on with y'all?"

Mickey shook her head no and felt the tears sliding down her cheeks. Jasmine grabbed her head and put her face against hers. "It's okay, Key. Whatever it is, it's okay."

"It's just—" Mickey began. But the words caught in her throat. "It's just so much."

"We can talk about it if you want."

Mickey shook her head no and wiped her nose with the back of her hand. "It's okay. I'm just a little overwhelmed. Today was *a lot*."

"You sure?" Jasmine released her face and pressed a kiss to her cheek. "I'll tell Q to put Nova to bed."

"He's still here?" Mickey asked. Her eyes, rimmed red, widened in surprise.

"Yeah, girl," Jasmine said with a laugh. "You know something about him on the grill. It just does something to me."

"I don't want to hear it. I've always said being straight was a disease."

"Trust me, if I could divest from the dick, I would."

Mickey checked the time. It was a little after nine thirty and she knew Grandma Anna would wait up until she made it safely home. "Let me get this car back to Grandma Anna before she starts tripping. You know she waits up."

Jasmine laughed. "Girl, hopefully she doesn't have one of them midnight sermons waiting for you when you get there."

Mickey groaned. "You're going to jinx it."

It felt good to laugh like this, to find their way back through their shared history, picking up where they left off. Jasmine *knew* her. Mickey had forgotten what it felt like to be anchored by this familiarity, so obsessed with the reinvented version of who she'd become.

"Seriously though," Jasmine said, bringing her back. "You good?"

"I'm good."

Mickey pulled Jasmine to her, crushing her thin frame against her breasts until she tapped on her to stop.

"You going to kill me with these big ass titties one day."

Mickey grinned. "You like these bosoms."

Jasmine winked. "You know I do." Her phone lit up with a call, and a photo of Q laying on the beach stared back at them, a half-naked Jasmine perched between his legs. "Girl, let me get in there before he starts acting like he don't know how to work the TV."

"All right," said Mickey. "Kiss Nova for me."

"I will." Jasmine stepped out of the car, her petite body sliding through the opening with ease. She turned back to look Mickey in her face. "Don't ever tell Scottie some shit before you tell me again. Got it?"

Mickey gave her a stiff salute. "Yes, ma'am."

Jasmine, a blur of white, did a little run back to her house, leaving Mickey alone with her father's home. It looked exactly like it always did, a brick façade framed by white windows with too-small shutters that lay flat like open books. Two were missing, swept off before they bought the house and never replaced. A pair of headlights appeared in the distance. It took a moment for Mickey to register that it was her father's car. It pulled into the driveway, parking smoothly next to Jamila's. She could see Boo's car seat jutting out from inside, like he'd bought the car with the baby attached. The car lights switched off and then there were the inner lights of the car, illuminating him and Jamila both. It was brief and she could only see outlines of them from here, but somehow she felt the love. The passenger door opened and her father's head appeared. A brief wave of panic rippled through her, afraid he might see her. She didn't expect for them to be back so soon. But he continued as if no one was watching, unclipping Boo from his car seat and lifting the sleeping boy into his arms. Jamila shut her door and kissed her son, then her husband, before everyone disappeared inside.

Mickey considered, for a moment, following them in and making her presence known. Instead, she turned the key in the ignition and drove in the opposite direction.

EIGHTEEN

Despite Jasmine's warning, Mickey spent much of the following week hanging out with Tee.

One night they rode the Ferris wheel at the Harbor and ate crabs, fingers wet with melted butter and smelling of the sea. Another, they had dinner at a restaurant with passable wings, possibly offensive honky-tonk décor, and a mechanical bull that aggressively tossed riders high into the air before landing in the inflatable pit with a satisfying thump. On a clear afternoon they sat on the edge of a fort wall and talked until the sun dipped into the Potomac, painting the sky a glowing, lapis blue, morphing their shadows into a single moving mass. Physically, they kept their distance, Mickey on one side, Tee on the other (Mickey had made sure of it, and was proud she did). They didn't talk about the night with the ice cream, but they did talk about their ambitions (Tee wanted to coach, eventually; Mickey wanted to work somewhere that would let her speak her mind) and the things that kept them up at night. Tee still dreamt about her accident; Mickey still worried about what her future held.

The night after the park, tucked into her bed, Mickey began flirting with the idea of never going back to New York. It was a passing thought, sparked by the brush of Tee's hand and the full sound of her laugh. She had immediately dismissed it as foolish, but now, in this dark room, it evolved into fantasy. It was dizzying how easy it was, to slot herself into a life she'd once sneered at, with people she admired and pitied in the same breath. How small their lives had seemed. Their hyperlocal concerns and the cyclical nature of time.

For so long, Mickey had seen them as stuck. She believed they had tricked themselves into thinking that stability was synonymous with success. But her world was simple here, populated by a revolving cast of people who had always known her. People she could say *I love you* to and mean it. There was no politics or pretense, and she was free of the anxieties that had come from a world that she'd invented. New York hadn't done much but chew her up and spit her out, depositing her on her grandparents' doorstep shaking and afraid. She was starting to feel more solid now—grounded, open. It was a freedom she'd never known, and it became difficult to remember why she'd stayed away so long and why she wanted to leave in the first place.

Was she allowed to burn it all down? Could she wash it away clean?

There was, however, the matter of Lex. Lex had not stopped texting (there was a voicemail about their upcoming lease that sat unanswered) but Mickey had stopped responding regularly, their conversations taking on an unfamiliar rhythm. It had the predictability of free jazz, guided by Mickey's mood rather than her commitment. *Maybe I just won't sign*, Mickey thought, and her breath caught in her throat. For a brief moment she felt light, like a weight had been lifted from her chest. It was terrifying to think of life on her own, but wasn't she doing that now? Navigating this world without anyone by her side? The thought came again: *I could choose to let Lex go.* Waking up to her own capabilities was terrifying. Despite everything, she'd always felt like Lex was her sure thing. That in choosing Lex she had done the best thing for herself. Life with Lex was a place she could call home without qualifications or apologies. But things had grown complicated, and Mickey had grown up, too. Now choosing Lex didn't quite feel like choosing herself. Mickey was struck by the realization and tried to push it away, but it was out there now, it would never go away.

In the midst of her epiphany, Mickey did the unthinkable: she picked up her phone and looked for a job. New York hadn't made her a writer, she had *always been one*, and could do it from anywhere. The editorial landscape in DC was different. Her options were limited to outlets that did serious journalism, the kind that won Pulitzers and made Mickey sweat with insecurity. It made *Wave* seem trivial in comparison and her writing feel flimsy as a result. She considered speech or grant writing, a path her father had always encouraged as a steady, secure way to live out her dreams. Important people would always need help trying to figure out the right things to say. As she scrolled into the latter pages of the jobs site, she began convincing herself that she could make a life of this, occasionally freelancing on the side. She fell asleep with her computer in her lap, her resume edited and cover letter half-finished, wondering if this was how her life was meant to go. That maybe her journey was a circle, and she was always meant to end up back home.

Sunday dinner was always an event in the Hayward house. Grandma Anna woke up at six to prepare, marinating the pork chops and washing the greens before she went to church, even though people weren't due to come over until five p.m. At 8:09 a.m., she knocked on Mickey's door, rousing her granddaughter from a deep, dreamless sleep.

"Good morning, granddaughter," she said, and Mickey groaned in reply.

"Hello, Grandmother."

"You coming to church with me?"

Mickey cried out, "Grandma, please, no."

"I don't know why you don't want to come. You didn't come last Sunday, and Lord knows you look like you need Jesus."

Mickey opened a single eye to peer at her grandmother. The sun was already shining, cutting through the wood-slatted blinds. Grandma Anna always dressed sharply for church. Today she wore a suit the color of strawberry ice cream, the single button blazer held closed with an intricate pearl. Even though it was warm out, she still wore stockings, flesh-toned ones that turned her cinnamon-brown legs a sickly pale beige. Her hair was swept back into a low bun that would be later concealed by a coordinating, pale pink hat. She looked ready for the Lord, save for her feet, which were still stuffed into her slippers. It would be the last thing she put on.

"You look nice."

"I do my best," Grandma Anna said, striking a little pose. "Want me to take some notes for you? I'm sure pastor's going to say something good."

"Sure, Grandma."

"And when you get up, take a look at the list I left for you in the kitchen. I won't have people coming over to a dirty house."

Mickey resisted rolling her eyes. Grandma Anna kept a spotless home, yet somehow there was always something more to do.

"Yes, ma'am."

"Perfect. I could get used to having you around, granddaughter."

"Don't," Mickey replied. "Isn't this supposed to be my vacation?"

"Ain't no vacation here. This isn't a hotel. You have to earn your keep. You been here what, almost three weeks? You came two Saturdays ago, and now today's Sunday, so yeah, that makes three. If I was a Holiday Inn, you'd be owing me some big money by now. Get up." With that, she closed the door. Mickey could hear her slippered feet shuffling, so loud she couldn't be sure if she was still in front of the door or down the hall.

Mickey pulled a pillow tight over her head and tried to go back to sleep. It was useless, her brain already whirling. Her first thought was of Tee, a sensation both familiar and strange. It had been years since Tee was the first thing on her mind. Mickey pressed a hand to her neck where Tee had placed her tongue. It seemed far away now, and the soft, dry skin made her wonder if that night had really happened after all. Mickey replayed the moment and found herself fixating on her "no." That precious thing. A declaration of her desire. A boundary. What a novelty. Whatever was happening now felt like friendship, or their version of it. There was an undercurrent always, but it was easy enough to ignore. This Tee was different. Gentle, present. Acting like there was no place she'd rather be than watching the sunset or gossiping about their high school friends. She didn't ask questions, like *When are you going to look for something else?* or *Why aren't you writing?* She treated Mickey like she was whole.

She rolled over to pick up her phone and found a text from Tee staring back at her. "Good morning, superstar."

Was this the part when she squealed? Mickey ignored the rising excitement in her chest, swiping the text open and closing out before attending to last night's message from Lex. The lease. Her stomach lurched with uncertainty, and she closed her phone.

Mickey felt the urge to pee, and dragged herself up to the bathroom before venturing into the kitchen to examine the piece of paper her grandmother had left behind. She'd come up with so many things for her to do. The stairs needed sweeping (though Mickey had done that last week), the silverware needed polishing (something she believed only happened on TV), the living room needed dusting, and Mickey needed to bake a cake. Her eyes widened at this. As if she could ever replicate Grandma Anna's famous German chocolate cake. It was a longstanding Hayward tradition. When it was your birthday, you got one of two Grandma Anna cakes: German chocolate or carrot, both made from scratch.

Today they were celebrating Mickey's cousin Jazz. His real name was Jeffrey, but no one called him that. He was turning nineteen the following week, and it immediately made Mickey feel old. She remembered when Jazz was an annoying kid, scaling the walls while pretending to be Spider-Man and running after the older cousins, begging them to take him to the mall. The one time they did it had been a huge mistake, Jazz getting caught in a window display and then trying to smash his way out. Mickey was pretty sure she was still banned from that Forever 21.

But Jazz had grown up, transforming from a short kid with big ears to a handsome young man. He even had a little beard now, his chin and upper lip covered with stubble that gave his face shape. Mickey hated following him on Instagram. He had some problematic ideas about women, furnished by podcasts hosted by men who looked like him. She didn't get what he had to be upset about. Her aunt Isa doted on him—he was her only boy. *Maybe he's looking for his mama*, Mickey thought. She looked closer at the paper, attempting to make out Grandma Anna's barely legible handwriting. Ah, she wanted Mickey to *buy* ingredients for the German chocolate cake. Now that, she could do.

Back from Giant, Mickey decided to start on dusting the many photos that covered her grandparents' formal living room. Grandma Anna

prided herself on showing off all her grandkids, every surface display-
ing her legacy in different-colored frames. Mickey worked through her
task slowly, taking the time to examine the younger versions of her
aunts and uncles. Them as kids, dressed in formal little tweed coats,
the color faded with time. Her aunt Kizzy, a baby, held in her adoring
brother's arms. Richard Hayward Jr., then a bright-faced ten-year-
old, looked down at Kizzy like he loved nothing more, his brown eyes
soft but fierce. She wondered if that was how he had looked at baby
Mickey, if that's how she had made him feel. He had always protected
her, made her feel like the most special girl. *His girl*.

She missed the sound of his booming voice, which would carry
through their cramped Columbia Heights apartment like the scent of
cooked food. "Where's my beautiful baby girl?" he'd ask from the hallway, not caring if the neighbors heard. She'd wait for that voice, dutifully
sitting near the door minutes before he got home from work, popping up
like a puppy when he walked through that door. She'd launch into his
arms at full speed, and he would catch her, briefcase and all.

It dawned on Mickey that her father would likely turn up later that
evening, and a pang of anxiety tore through her chest. She had blocked
out her father after the scene she'd witnessed outside his house, stuffing
down her feelings of abandonment and latching onto the normalcy of
her new routine. She worried that he would be able to sense her lack of
employment just by looking at her, and then she would have to admit
that she had been forcefully removed from the very life they bragged
about to family and friends.

She thought of the letter, and how her chances of returning to the
industry now seemed slim, if not impossible. Mickey swallowed hard
at the thought: everything she wanted was gone. She should have shut
up—waited out her severance and applied for more jobs. Freelanced out
the articles she cared about. Then she wouldn't be a fraud, or a lost girl
playing at womanhood, looking to her grandmother for guidance. She
set down the photo in her hands and picked up the one next to it.

She hadn't seen this one in years, surprised Grandma Anna hadn't
tucked it away in a box with the rest of the photos of her mother. It was
a photo of the three of them: Mickey and her parents. She was about
sixteen, and it was one of the last photos they'd taken as a family.

It was after the volleyball championship, where they'd won by two points against a school who'd beaten them twice before. Mickey was beaming, holding her medal against her chest. Her father was smiling, too, his big hand encircling her shoulder. Her mother, Sylvia, looked a bit bored in her blue top and jeans, her eyes shielded by an oversized pair of red plastic sunglasses. She wondered if she was thinking of splitting yet, if she had known then that she would leave her daughter behind.

Mickey couldn't remember the last time she'd spoken to her mother on the phone. It had been three, maybe four months. After the divorce, Sylvia had devoted herself to self-improvement full-time. These days, she was notoriously hard to get ahold of, often in far-flung parts of the world looking for answers when the truth of the matter was that the answers were right at home. In that apartment in Columbia Heights where she'd lived with Mickey's grandmother. And the house she shared with Mickey's father.

But still, she went looking. Sylvia had been searching for peace almost as long as Mickey had been alive, and Mickey was worried she'd never find it. Even though she didn't totally agree with her mother's methods, she understood her a bit more now that she'd gone searching, too. *Maybe that's where I get it from*, Mickey thought. Mickey would call her, soon; maybe. But the space between them felt too vast, and Mickey didn't know where to start.

Mickey liked to think that being left behind by her mother at sixteen had been the root of her abandonment issues, a core wound, but in truth it had been Mickey's choice. Sylvia was leaving either way, and Mickey had always been free to follow. But Mickey had stayed with her dad after the split, afraid of the woman she called mom.

The logistics of the divorce had been discussed over an awkward feast of shrimp egg rolls, chicken fried rice, and General Tso's chicken from the carryout down the street. *Mickey only had two years left until college and she was already settled in*, argued Richard, *so staying would be best*. Mickey agreed. She was vaguely worried about upsetting her mother, but more concerned about leaving Scottie and Jasmine behind. She was afraid of what it might look like without them, if it was just Mickey and Sylvia relying on each other for support.

Though Sylvia Hayward would never admit to it, Mickey was sure her mother had breathed a sigh of relief. She'd nodded furiously and speared a thick knot of crispy chicken, and Mickey wondered if she was looking away to hide a secret sort of smile. She hadn't understood it then, why she didn't fight.

But now, Mickey saw things a little differently. Her mother's life had already come undone before Mickey was even in the picture. Before mothering Mickey, Sylvia was taking care of her mother, Grandma Ruth, full time. While Sylvia had never been particularly warm, Grandma Ruth had been cold and critical. She was the first person to make Mickey aware that she was fat. She would accuse her of hiding food, even though she could barely see. Afterward, she would squeeze Mickey's extremities with disapproval, unhappy with how much flesh she could hold on to. Her chubby, dark brown fingers would tap at the back of Mickey's little hands, discouraging seconds with a grunt and pulling the food toward herself.

But Grandma Ruth was doting toward Mickey in comparison to the way she treated Sylvia, who could do no right. When she died, Mickey was in fourth grade and Sylvia was taking care of Grandma Ruth full time and had been for years, wheeling her from one doctor's appointment to the next, her face fixed in a perpetual frown. Sometimes Mickey went too, her feet dangling off the edge of an office waiting chair, an old *Essence* magazine spread across her lap. There was a lot of waiting but there was often McDonald's after, which made all the waiting worth it.

After Grandma Ruth died, Mickey learned she'd been sick a long time. It was a taboo subject when she was alive, since her deterioration had stopped Mickey's mother from getting the chance to escape her hometown. Apparently, Sylvia had made it to Philly for three whole months before Grandma Ruth had started losing her eyesight and struggling to walk, her diabetes damaging her nerves.

Soon after, there was Mickey. Sylvia had returned from Philly pregnant, but unaware, caught up in a fling with a boy who she met at a party in New Brunswick. His name was Richard, and he was from the DMV area. She thought she would be home six months at the most, coming home to help her mother before setting off on her next adventure. A girlfriend had moved down to Houston, and she wanted Sylvia to come too. But six months came and went, and at the end of it she was pushing Mickey out at Children's National, a handwringing Richard at her side. He wasn't ready, and neither was she.

This wasn't something they had ever talked about, and Mickey, so young at the time, hadn't considered how her mother might feel. She only felt like they didn't belong to one another, that God had placed them alongside each other as some kind of cruel trick. The one time her mother cracked herself open for Mickey to peer inside, Sylvia had already been one foot out the door.

It was a few weeks after their General Tso feast. Their fate had been decided as a family and Mickey felt good. Things wouldn't change much. Might get lighter, even. Her mother was leaving in the morning, the U-Haul already parked outside. Mickey had already told Jasmine that it wasn't her going, that she wouldn't need to worry. Her mother called for her to help with taping a box, and Mickey tossed her Black-Berry down with a sigh as she walked across the hall to her mother's room, which had already begun emptying out. Mickey was shocked by the wave of emotion she felt, and the sudden emptiness. But she was just sixteen and could do nothing but pretend her feelings weren't threatening to swallow her whole.

"Did I ever tell you about the time I lived in Philly?" Sylvia had asked, pressing the tape into Mickey's hand. Sylvia pushed the box closed on either side and looked up at her daughter expectantly. Mickey stretched tape over the width of the box.

"Sorta?" Mickey said, smoothing the tape flat with a hand. The words "cold weather" were scrawled across it in big, black Sharpie.

Her mother placed the box on the floor and sat on the bed. She motioned for Mickey to sit down. "Yeah. Well, I probably told you a version of it because it's how me and your daddy met, but really, I went up there to try and start doing hair. A girlfriend of mine, your Auntie Dawn, was trying to sing backup with the Roots and get in that whole scene. She was really into the whole neo-soul thing. So, I went, too. Dawn's my girl. I couldn't let her go by herself. So, there we were. Dawn and Sylvie. Sylvie and Dawn. She would go to the house parties and the open mic nights and the studio. Then come home and sleep all day. I would do hair during the days and go to the little local spots and college parties on the weekend. We were chilling. Twenty-two years old, I had the little asymmetrical Salt-N-Pepa bob. I thought I was too fly. You couldn't tell me nothing. Making a little bit of money and having the time of our lives. It was the first time I felt like I was going somewhere."

Mickey didn't understand where the story was headed, or why her mom was bringing this up. She nodded and looked for another box to tape, for anything else to do. They never really spoke like this, and she worried her mother would, at some point, ask her about her own feelings. And that she would have to reveal that she wasn't too sad to see her go.

"Well," Sylvia said, a small smile on her mouth. "Now I'm going somewhere again."

"I know," Mickey replied. Without anything to occupy her hands, Mickey resorted to playing with the string of her sweatpants, The Conservatory's crest emblazoned on the side. She had so many questions. *Where was Grandma Ruth during all this? What made her go back home?* But the words faded the second her mother spoke.

"And someday you might want to go, too, and that's okay. Don't let anybody tell you where you should be, and don't feel guilty about when you need to leave. No matter what the cost. If I could've done things differently, I would've kept going when I felt like I was on the way to something bigger. On to something for myself."

The words sunk in Mickey's chest like a stone. In choosing herself, Sylvia had forced Mickey to choose, too. She wished her mother had waited for a more convenient time to upend her life, had waited until Mickey was more grown. But she couldn't say that. Instead, she said, "I'm glad you're doing something for yourself, Mom."

"Me too, Micks. You can come, too, you know. I know what we decided, but you can always change your mind," Sylvia said, but the look on her face told Mickey it was best if she let her mother go. In the past few days, her mother had seemed to morph before her eyes, to grow into something unwieldy. She was no longer the Sylvia who shuttled her to and from her activities or made sure there was food on the table every night, the one who played nice with their neighbors and hosted Mickey's friend—this Sylvia was restless and full of desire, and Mickey wished her mother could hide her excitement just a little more.

"It's okay," Mickey said. "I'm good here."

"You're my baby," said Sylvia. "Of course you're good."

She pinched the underside of Mickey's arm like Grandma Ruth used to do and handed her another box. "Now take this one downstairs."

A door opened and the sound of Ornette Coleman's unpredictable sax seeped from Pop's room down the hallway, bringing Mickey back to the present. She brought the frame closer to her face and examined her mother. Her expression seemed forced and put on the more she looked, like she was running out the time on an invisible clock. Sylvia had just been excited to get free, and Mickey knew how good freedom could feel. She understood now why someone with everything to lose might still choose to walk away.

She wiped at the tears filling her eyes and moved on to the next frame.

The moment Grandma Anna got back from church the house took on a sense of urgency. Everything Mickey had done thus far was a precursor to the real work: helping her grandmother in the kitchen. She stewed turkey necks for the greens, which smelled up the kitchen with its meaty, tangy aroma, and chopped carrots and onions and celery into fine little pieces. She tossed and dressed a salad she was sure nobody would eat, passing it over for the black-eyed peas, which were currently soaking in a pot of hot water on the stove.

As Mickey made the tiny carrots even tinier, she thought about Lex worrying over their meals, coming up with new takes on classics. Feeding them both had been a labor of love, and she swore to never be ungrateful or complain about Lex's food ever again. If she ever had it again. The thought triggered a wave of panic. It felt like that brief, terrifying moment when you catch yourself falling asleep but are too exhausted to wake up. She thought about calling, but that was quickly dismissed when Trey latched onto her leg and wouldn't let go.

She jiggled her leg. "Trey, you see me cooking, right?"

He nodded and hugged her tight. He was wearing a seersucker playsuit, which matched Leah's dress and Kizzy's top. She washed her hands in the sink and pulled him from her legs into her arms. She kissed him on the cheek, making a raspberry sound, his face buttery soft. He grinned and she dipped him low before setting him right side up. Another shriek. Mickey tried again, but this time her arms hurt. He was getting heavy. Mickey estimated that he'd doubled in size since she saw him six months ago. "Okay, that's it."

He looked up at her and his wide eyes only seemed to grow in size. "One more?" he asked.

"Okay," Mickey said. "Last one."

When Jamila and her father finally arrived with Boo in tow, she was hiding in the bedroom, feeling silly. Her grandmother had shoved her in, and she had to keep up the ruse that she was in fact surprising her father, even though her grandmother seemed to believe her less and less with every passing day.

Mickey could smell the food through the door, her stomach tightening with hunger. She pressed her ear against the door, listening for the sound of her family milling around. She heard Pop's voice followed by the sound of a shrieking child, then her aunt Kizzy and aunt Denise going back and forth. The familiarity touched her somewhere she usually ignored, made her feel like she belonged. The din dropped to a whisper, and Mickey realized they were near ready to say grace (her cue), with the family (minus Mickey) gathering in the kitchen and in the living room, anxiously awaiting the go ahead to migrate to the dining room and eat.

The food was set up on a long wooden buffet. At the end was Grandma Anna's chocolate cake, sitting proudly on a covered glass stand. The youngest cousins were in charge of setting the table, laying out proper glassware for the adults and bright-colored, reusable plastic plates, cups, and bowls for the kids. Mickey had changed into a cream plissé set, which, while cute, was a recipe for disaster. One false move or spill, and her outfit would be kaput.

She heard her father's booming voice followed by Jamila's tinny hellos and Boo's excitable shrieks, their voices intermingling right outside the bedroom door.

"Hi, baby boy!" Grandma Anna said excitedly, and Mickey wondered if her grandmother could feel her irritation through the door. She didn't get excited like that to see Mickey.

As both matriarch and town crier, Grandma Anna had told the family (save for her father and Jamila) of Mickey's grand return, so now everyone was trying to act natural, waiting for the prodigal daughter to emerge. Mickey tried to time it perfectly. Her and Grandma Anna had come up with a plan. When they were gathered to say grace, she would announce that there was a special guest to say the prayer and Mickey would join the circle of joined hands.

Her phone dinged and she looked down to see another message from Tee. They'd been lightly texting over the past few hours, Mickey complaining about cooking and Tee asking if she could come over to get a plate. She had been tempted to say yes.

"And now, we'll have a special guest to say grace." A voice called from the dining room. Mickey was too distracted to notice.

"I SAID, WE HAVE A SPECIAL GUEST TO SAY GRACE." Grandma Anna was yelling now, and Mickey hustled out of the door and into the dining room, sliding into the spot between her aunt Isa and her cousin Connie, whose relation to them was so complicated it exhausted Mickey to explain. She grabbed their hands and began to speak.

"Lord, I'd like to thank you for the food we're about to receive for the nourishment of our bodies . . ." she began, and she watched as her father's eyes popped open to hear the source of the voice. Then, a small smile before he bowed his head again. Mickey continued and when they finished with a choral-sounding Amen, he looked back to his daughter and smiled. He crossed the room to pull her into a one-armed hug, crushing her close to his side. She wrapped her arms around his middle and nestled into his armpit, feeling like a little kid again. He smelled like he always did, fresh deodorant and a little bit of sweat.

"Hi, Daddy."

"Hi, baby." He kissed the top of her forehead and hugged her close.

"Mama," he called out to Grandma Anna, who was helping one of the young kids fix a plate. "You knew she was coming?" he asked, but he winked his right eye, and Mickey groaned. The joke had been on her the whole time. It felt juvenile but she was embarrassed, her face burning with shame.

"Well of course I did, boy, she's been staying at my house." She shooed him away with a hand and went back to the kitchen to fuss over something else.

"So," her father began, his head tilted in suspicion. "How's my writer daughter doing?"

Mickey feared the word *fraud* was scrawled across her forehead and knew the only way she could be rid of it was by telling the truth, but she pushed on. "She's good," Mickey said. "Busy as always."

"Too busy to come by the house."

"I wanted to surprise you," Mickey replied, though it sounded implausible, even to her.

"How long you been waiting to surprise me?"

Mickey winced. "Almost three weeks."

He leaned over to whisper in her ear. "I know you've been here for at least one and a half."

Mickey opened and closed her mouth, wondering who gave her up. "But—"

"Yeah. Ms. Sharon told me when she dropped off some of her mac and cheese. Apparently, you were at Nova's birthday party."

"She's always telling on somebody."

"That she is," he said. "But I ain't think my daughter had no reason to hide." He crossed his arms over his chest. "Something wrong?"

Mickey rolled her eyes. She was irritated now. At being found out. At feeling ill-equipped to be honest, both with him and herself. "Nothing's wrong, Daddy. I just didn't want to be pressured into staying at your house."

"Oh whatever," he said with a dismissive wave of the hand. "Nobody's pressuring you. You just be making stuff up, so you have a reason to argue. You want something to hold against somebody."

"I'm not arguing," Mickey replied and she was resentful at his characterization. As if he'd never done any wrong. She let out a sigh.

"Well, you're avoiding your dad, who has done nothing but love and care for you since you were Boo's size. Even smaller. Did you say hi to your brother?"

Mickey pursed her lips. "Not yet."

He nodded. "Make sure you do." He rubbed a hand across the

bottom of his chin, brushing his palm against the stubble. "I was show-ing your article to one lady in my office—"

"Oh, yeah?" Mickey said, a rush of adoration flowing through her veins. "Which one?"

"That one you wrote about fancy laces?"

Mickey recalled. That one had been pitched specifically to cater to a Nina directive (microtrends!) and had been ridiculously difficult to re-port. Fashion influencers were surprisingly protective about their lacing secrets. "Yeah, what about it?"

"I didn't get it. Why can't people just tie their laces up normally?" he asked. "You know, Boo is learning to tie his shoes now. He can't quite get it, but I think he's close. Right now he's struggling with—"

Mickey didn't interrupt as he prattled on about the finer points of Boo learning basic life skills. She was irritated that a conversation about her success had already turned into a conversation about her brother, who wasn't that interesting if you really thought about it. She nodded throughout, trying not to blurt out what she was thinking in her head: *Shouldn't he be able to do this by now?* She decided to keep that one to herself. As she was escaping to make herself a plate, Jamila materialized, attempting to make small talk with her stepdaughter while she placed a thick piece of fried chicken on her plate.

"Mickey," she began; she reached out to touch Mickey's arm with her free hand. "So nice of you to surprise your dad."

Mickey gave her a once-over and tried to decide if the conversation was worth her time. She knew that Jamila knew, and now she felt that she was being laughed at by everyone involved. She smiled a tight, polite smile. Mickey understood Jamila's appeal, especially to a man like her father, who had spent much of his adulthood tied to a woman who was so flighty and detached. It only made sense that he would run, head-first, in the other direction.

Jamila was overly attentive, hanging on her father's every word. She did her best to integrate herself into every part of Mickey's family, much to her chagrin. She volunteered to take all the cousins to Six Flags and showed up to games. She drove her grandmother to the grocery store and sent birthday cards in the mail. Mickey wondered how long it would take her to just drop the act.

Homebodies

Mickey wanted Jamila to admit she was trying to replace her and her mom. All evidence of Mickey's existence was now sealed up in the basement, carefully labeled and organized by item type. Her old room (upstairs, first door on the right) was now Boo's room, the Tiffany blue paint she'd chosen at thirteen covered with a light, pale gray and trimmed with white. They had hired professionals to do it, something about the blue being hard to cover, and Mickey couldn't help but feel like they meant her, too. It had been awkward, coming home during school breaks, eating Jamila's food; learning that she was having a baby from her father between bites of Frosted Flakes. It was an unceremonious announcement, his way of making the serious less so.

"Jamila's having a baby," he'd said.

Mickey offered silence in response. Eventually, she said something that sounded like, "Okay."

What she wanted to say was that she felt betrayed, and she did say it, to everyone but him. When she returned to school after summer break she wrote furiously. There were essays about it for class assignments, one so good a professor said she should send it somewhere. She went on to submit to the *New York Times* (*We thank you for your effort, but this isn't a good fit for us at this time*) and anywhere that requested Black girls share their pain. There weren't many, but she'd found a few, publishing versions of the same narrative in small pockets of the internet where she could scream loudly and only a few people would hear. She couldn't read them now, embarrassed that she had felt so much out loud, but it had been real. Mickey had fought for her ideas, and she liked to think she was still that girl. The letter had proven that, at least.

"Mickey?" Jamila prodded Mickey on the shoulder, pulling her back to the present.

"Mhm, yeah," Mickey replied.

"It's been so long since you've been home."

"Yup," Mickey said, nodding, filling her mouth with chicken to avoid saying more. "Good to see you."

"How you been?" Jamila asked next. "Your dad said you're on vacation. First time in a while? Maybe ever?"

"I've been good," Mickey said, eyes darting around the kitchen. She was searching for a way out, knowing that they were two sentences away from everything they had in common. "Burnt out. You know."

"Yeah, I get that," Jamila replied, rocking back on her heels. The conversation was dangerously close to its expiration. "Boo's starting school this year, he's getting big."

Had it really been four years? Mickey wondered as she worked out how she would exit, scanning the room for a family member to latch on to. Kizzy was busy trying to convince everyone that she was in fact Pop's favorite, while Leah and Trey entertained themselves with the turkey necks.

"He really is." Mickey widened her eyes for emphasis because he really was getting big and crossed her arms over her chest. "It feels like just yesterday I found out you were pregnant."

She hadn't meant to sound bitter, but the mood shifted between them anyway. Jamila managed a smile and Mickey shrank, her shoulders drooping and back curving into a soft, *S*-shaped hook. She stared at Jamila's stomach and recalled the first time she had seen her glowing and round, her belly containing her father's firstborn son. When she and Lex started dating, and she was at her most bitter, she would joke that Boo had robbed her of keeping the family name going, even though it had never been funny. Mickey fiddled with the hem of her shirt and searched for something else to say.

"I know, right?" Jamila let out an unconvincing laugh. "He made us all a family." She looked over to her son, who sat at the kids' table, clumsily scooping white rice into his mouth with a combination of his fork and hand. "Did you say hi yet? Boo loves his big sist—" Jamila asked.

"I will."

Despite their short conversation, Mickey was rife with anxiety. Being around Jamila reminded her of everything she no longer had access to. It began to feel like the walls were closing in on her, like she needed to claw her way out. For the first time since being back, she wanted to go home, her real one with Mango and Lex, where everything was laid out according to Mickey's exact specifications, down to the all-white washcloths and Belgian linen sheets, and no one made her feel like she didn't belong.

She stepped outside, the balmy summer air hitting her skin. The sun still hung high in the sky and a wind rustled the magnolia tree's leaves. Across the street, one of the neighbors sat on the porch, nursing a glass of iced tea. Mickey raised a hand and waved. She pulled her phone from her pocket and called Lex. Home was just a phone call away. A four-hour drive, three-and-a-half-hour train ride, forty-minute flight. The phone rang and rang and rang until she heard an automated message bleating back at her. Deflated, she hung up. Her phone vibrated in her hand.

Tee.

"You free?"

NINETEEN

Mickey met Tee in the parking lot at the park on Tucker Road. It was something like the perfect midsummer afternoon, the sun making its slow descent and the slight breeze cutting through the heat, which meant that everybody and their neighbor was outside. Middle-aged moms in oversized T-shirts and fanny packs walked the trail in twos, kids swung from every available metal pole on the playground, and people of all shapes and sizes took advantage of the outdoor fitness equipment, doing pull-ups and ladder drills from wooden structures permanently affixed to the ground. The basketball court was overflowing with men and boys who believed themselves to be grown shuffling across the asphalt in pockets of half-court pickup games, sweat flying off their bodies and trash spewing from their mouths.

Tee was there waiting for her, leaning up against the trunk of an inky black Benz. "You came."

Mickey nodded. "I did. You surprised to see me?"

Tee's mouth quirked up in the corner, suppressing a full smile. "Maybe a little bit."

"I'm not dressed for whatever you wanted to do," Mickey said, gesturing at her matching top and pants. It had been a bit fancy for dinner even, but now that Mickey had nowhere to go but the various errands her grandmother sent her on, she would take any excuse to dress up. The airy fabric was made from a high-quality polyester that was thicker than Mickey remembered. Her back was beginning to dampen, beads of sweat coursing down the nape of her neck, forming a single, narrow stream. She didn't know how long she could be in this heat before she was dripping wet.

"That's all right," Tee said, opening the trunk of the car. "I knew you were coming from dinner, so I figured you didn't have clothes."

Mickey wondered which of her parents the car belonged to, the late-model Mercedes too fancy to be something Tee had bought herself. From the trunk emerged a pair of basketball shorts and a T-shirt, and a familiar anxiety resurfaced. Despite Tee softening up, Mickey still outweighed Tee by at least forty-five pounds. The clothes wouldn't fit. It was hard for it not to feel pointed, especially since Mickey was sure Tee's cadre of women *loved* to wear Tee's "oversized" clothes, her T-shirts hanging off their thin bodies all slouchy and cute. This would be a baby tee on Mickey, that is if she could even get her arms through the sleeves.

Mickey accepted the clothing and covertly checked the shirt's tag. A large. Maybe she could squeeze. She worried about the arm openings suffocating the fat on her arms, turning them into sausages. She wanted to protest but thanked Tee instead. "I should be all right." Mickey handed her back the clothes.

"You sure?" Tee asked. "You might get hot."

Mickey considered trying them on and thought better of it. "I should be okay." She looked over at the basketball court. "You're going to play with them?" she asked. Tee kicked off her slides and began lacing up a pair of bright blue basketball shoes.

"Yeah, why not?" Tee looked unafraid, but all Mickey felt was dread.

She shrugged and scrunched up her face. "I don't know, they look rough."

Tee looked at Mickey for a moment and laughed. "Look at you, worried about me." She closed the trunk and locked the car. It beeped in reply. "I'll be aight."

They walked toward the court, shadows kissing and then pulling apart, stretching behind them long and intertwined.

It would be an hour before they spoke to each other directly, before the sun set and the court cleared out, the streetlights humming and glowing with clean, white light. Watching Tee play had been a welcome distraction, clearing her mind, if only momentarily, with the rush of a game. She still played with the easy fluidity Mickey remembered, deftly moving the ball from one end of the court to the other. She kept up with the men, and Mickey was surprised that getting hurt hadn't stopped her, or at least it seemed that way to her untrained eye. It had been six years since Tee got injured, but the video was so gruesome it had been seared into Mickey's memory.

She could still see it if she closed her eyes. There she was, at the 3:45 mark, moving left when she should've gone right and ending up crumpled on the shiny wood floor, hands clasped tightly around her ankle. At 3:47 the camera zoomed in on her face, unable to resist the seduction of Black pain, and it was the first time Mickey saw Tee cry. It was shocking, but somehow Mickey couldn't resist watching it all again, and then a third time. She'd never seen Tee like that: mouth puckered, eyes shut, aching in full view of the world. She told herself that if anyone would emerge without injury, it was Tee, but she couldn't help feeling like she had borne witness to something she wasn't supposed to see, like she'd seen the moment a person lost their God for good.

At the end of the pickup game, Mickey watched as the men returned to their cars, dapping each other up and waving from their SUVs, beeping as they pulled off into the street. And then it was empty, as if they'd never been there at all. Eventually, only Tee and Mickey remained. After all these years, she still felt exposed in Tee's orbit, even though they were the only two people around.

"I see you still sort of got it," Mickey said with a grin, hoisting herself from the ground.

"Sort of?" Tee asked, bouncing the ball between her legs and approaching the basket, hopping up on one leg and tossing it into the hoop. The ball glided through the net and landed in her waiting hands.

"I could do that," Mickey insisted, even though she wasn't very athletic at all. Her capabilities stopped at boutique fitness workout classes.

Basketball required skill and imagination, and Mickey was short on both. Tee smirked and tossed her the ball.

"Okay, go 'head."

Mickey clumsily bounded toward the basket, conscious of the way her lower stomach jiggled when she ran, the way her thighs reverberated when she bounced. It distracted her, which is why she missed badly, the ball bouncing to the far end of the court. Or at least that's what she told herself as she carefully jogged to go pick it up. She returned it to Tee directly, their fingers brushing as she handed it off.

"I thought it was easy," Tee said with a smile, tossing the ball into the net from a few feet away. It slid through like it had no other choice. Tee did something fancy next, a side to side move that ended with a spin and the ball careening toward the basket. She missed that time and Mickey laughed, but Tee wasn't smiling.

"What?" Mickey said when Tee returned with the ball, her face serious.

Tee shrugged and dribbled, passing it through her legs with ease. "Nothing."

Mickey eyed her skeptically. "What, you don't want to miss in front of the girl you're trying to impress?" It sounded less forward in her head. Less like flirting. But the look on Tee's face suggested that Mickey had toed, if not crossed, some invisible line.

Tee stepped closer to Mickey and she instinctively backed up. Tee chuckled. "You scared?"

"Of what?"

"I don't know, that's why I asked you," Tee said, her arms wide and questioning. Mickey wondered, briefly, if it was an invitation, if she was meant to step in.

Mickey didn't know what she was afraid of, so instead she asked, "Do you want to play a game?"

Tee's eyes danced and Mickey worried she'd set them both up. "What kind of game? I know you don't mean basketball."

"The kind where you tell me all your secrets." Mickey's hands opened, reaching for the ball, but Tee stepped back and placed it closer to her chest.

"That doesn't sound like my kind of game," Tee replied.

"It's just questions," Mickey insisted, placing her hands on her hips.

"Aight," Tee said, chucking her chin in Mickey's direction. "You first."

Now that she had gotten Tee to agree, Mickey wasn't sure what to ask. The questions that floated just behind her teeth were inappropriate, thinly veiled markers of jealousy and desire. *Who are you dating? Does she know you're here? Do you still think about me?*

"You ever wanted to say something to the girl who took your spot?" Mickey asked, and she watched the recognition bloom on Tee's face. The last thing to shift were her lips, which twisted into a sort of sneer. Mickey couldn't read it. Was it anger? Disgust?

"How can anybody take my spot? I'm right here," Tee retorted, resuming her easy smile. It scared Mickey how easy it was for her to tuck it back in.

Tee dribbled and made her way to the basket, tossing the ball in with ease. "My turn?" she asked, dribbling the ball back to where Mickey stood.

Mickey nodded and opened her hands. Tee bounce-passed the ball and Mickey let it rotate under her palms, clumsily slamming the ball to the asphalt.

"Why are you really here?" Tee said, stepping toward Mickey and stealing the ball before it hit the ground. It happened so fast Mickey almost missed it.

Mickey was taken aback, but did her best not to show it. "What do you mean? I told you I came to visit my dad." Tee looked up, and when their eyes met, Mickey felt her stomach pool with desire.

"That's a long visit. And you've been avoiding the house. It feels like you're hiding something."

"I think you just want me to be mysterious."

"I know when you're hiding," Tee said, holding the ball in her hand. Their eyes met again and her tone dropped, if only slightly. "And when you're scared."

Mickey resisted Tee's assessment. It lacked accountability. She'd been the one to stuff Mickey with insecurities so deep that loving Lex had felt like an act of resistance. A constant practice of ignoring the voice in her head that told her it was okay for her to be hidden from view. "You don't know me anymore."

"I don't?"

"You don't," Mickey insisted. "We haven't talked in five years and now here you are, acting like you're reading between the lines? I'm good. Like I said, I'm on vacation."

"So what was that on Twitter?"

Mickey's mouth opened and closed but no words came out. She had nothing to say. She hadn't seriously accounted for the friends back home who had seen the letter and said nothing about it. Tee rarely surprised her. So far, she'd managed twice in one night.

Mickey took a deep breath and listened to the cricket symphony soundtracking the night's unexpected turn. "That's two questions."

"You're not playing fair," Tee said. "You posted some wild shit, so you knew I was going to bring it up eventually."

Some wild shit? Mickey rolled her eyes. She sounded just like Lex; she might as well have said it was reckless. Her cheeks burned at being so exposed. She tucked her head down, worried the redness would show up underneath her brown skin, and dribbled the ball. It hit the asphalt with a clunky, hollow sound. "I didn't know you saw that."

Tee acknowledged her words with a nod of her head. "Pass the ball."

Mickey chest passed the round orange orb, and despite the aggression, Tee received it gracefully. "Isn't it your turn to ask?"

"I can't think of anything I want to know."

Tee smirked. "You got me all figured out, huh?"

"Something like that."

"Oh yeah, tell me what you see."

"I try not to do that," Mickey said. "Most times people don't like what I have to say."

Tee shrugged, ever the optimist. Her confidence, as always, seemed unshakable. "Try me."

"You sure?"

"Positive."

"I see someone who, after all these years, with all the time and opportunity, is still trying to figure out what they want. You haven't settled on any one thing, haven't locked into a career or found anything outside of basketball you love. You're trying to find something, anything, that feels like the high of the game, the crowd. But you're still searching, and in the meantime you're just coasting, hoping that nobody sees you for real. You're hiding, you're playing scared because you've given it your all and you know what happens when that doesn't pan out. You're afraid to try again."

Tee's mouth dipped into a frown before she broke out into a patronizing slow clap, cradling the ball to her chest between her elbows. "Wow. You got me figured out, huh, Mickey?"

"I think so."

"Okay," Tee said with a shrug, but Mickey could see the aggression in the twinge of her muscles, the flex of her jaw. "My turn?"

Fuck it, Mickey thought.

"You talk mad shit because you had a fancy ass job and live in New York but clearly you're not happy. I made peace with my shit. I know what's up with me. Where I messed up. It's clear to me that you don't even know about yours. You came back here, for what? To find yourself? To remember how shit used to be? To hide? It's damn sure not to see your family or friends. You probably don't know because you're fucking lost and unhappy and afraid to admit you fucked up your perfect little life. You're running and you don't even know it."

"At least I'm moving. You're out here driving your mom's car and running around acting like you got your shit together, for what? So you can still get bitches? So you can act like you're still that girl? You think people don't see you for who you really are? You're washed, Tee, and everybody knows it. None of this is real. None of it at all." Mickey felt herself choking up at the last bit, like she'd accidentally said a true thing without meaning to.

"If I'm so washed up and you too good to be around me then why you out here with me? Why you not with your girl?" Tee's eyes were trained on hers now, waiting for an answer. Mickey had nothing to say to that.

"What's that?" Tee asked, cupping an ear to the silence. "Speak up, Mickey, I can't hear you."

At the mention of Lex, Mickey stiffened. She hadn't thought of her since Tee started playing, couldn't think of anything but the way Tee's calf muscles flexed when she reared up to take a shot or the way her arms flexed in that Dri-Fit muscle tee.

Tee was mocking her now, and everything in Mickey wanted to lunge and tackle her to the concrete. What came after that, she wasn't sure. Instead, Mickey played as cool as she could, shrugging her shoulders and crossing her arms.

"You invited me here, Tee."

"And you came. You could've said no."

"When have I ever been able to do that?"

"You said no when you left, right?"

"I didn't leave you. I had to keep going. You were in a whole relationship, Tee. It didn't matter what I did. Where I went."

"Nah, Mickey. You tell yourself that so you feel good about leaving all of us behind. But let me tell you this, you're no better than me, baby. You're struggling, too. We all are." Tee bounced the ball and shot it into the hoop. "Yeah, maybe I flex a little bit with my people's shit, but I'm good. I got food in my mouth, clothes on my back. I live with the family that loves me, and I can still play the game. Yeah, maybe not like I thought I would, but I'm okay with that."

"But I'm not okay with that, Tee. That's what you don't understand," Mickey said, her voice rising. "What do you want to hear? That I lost my fucking job? That I published that letter and nobody gave a fuck? That everything is falling apart around me? That I'm drowning? You don't get it. Just getting by isn't good enough for me. I want more. I want it all."

She gestured at everything around them, and then the whole world. "I want the corner office *and* my name on the masthead. I want an ASME *and* a Pulitzer. I want everyone to read my work and to know my name, and it felt like, for a second, that I was getting close. That I was moving in the right direction and now it's just been ripped away. I'm fucking sad and hurt. I'm not okay, okay?"

She was nearly yelling now, tears streaming down her face and blurring her vision. Tee was a watery form, her face unreadable until she got close, so she got closer. Mickey could almost taste her skin. Mickey got lost, just for a moment, in the fantasy, before remembering how she ended up here in the first place. Tee had always been a good distraction.

A perfect smoke screen, obscuring Mickey's wants and needs by taking up all the space in her brain. Everything couldn't be about her. Not anymore. Mickey sighed and wiped her face, and Tee placed her hands on her shoulders and looked into her eyes before pulling her close, her arms wrapping tight around her shoulders.

Mickey wept in Tee's arms, her face pressed against the hollow of her chest. Tee held on tighter, flattening their bodies into one amorphous shape. "Okay," Tee said, so low only Mickey could hear. "Okay."

Mickey couldn't remember the last time Tee held her like this, had forgotten the feel of her skin. They didn't fit like her and Lex, like two puzzle pieces reunited time after time after time, but Mickey still felt safe here, enveloped in this warmth. She didn't care that Tee smelled more like sweat than anything else, or that she was squeezing her a little too tight.

She knew what Tee had said about her running was true. Tee had clocked her, stripped back all the pretenses, and called her by her name. She had held her accountable for the ways she'd excised her family and friends from her life, climbing up the ladder and erasing her tracks as she went. When Tee finally let go, it felt like an eternity had passed, and Mickey felt unmoored in its wake.

"You good?" Tee watched her with a careful intensity she hadn't seen before. It was frightening, almost, to be under such careful scrutiny, and Mickey worried about saying the right thing. But there were no right words, only honest ones.

Mickey wiped her face. "I will be."

Tee nodded. "You will. All that shit," she gestured at the whole wide world, "it don't matter. You gon' to be a superstar regardless. Everybody, even me, can see that. What matters is your people."

"You used to be one of my people," Mickey said. She couldn't resist poking the old wound, tossing out a weak jab. But she was vulnerable and open, and despite there being so many things her mind could spin and spin and spin about, she could only think of one. *Had Tee just accused me of leaving her behind? Had she cared?*

"What you mean, Key? Used to? I still am."

Mickey was torn between elation and frustration. She wanted to toss herself into Tee's arms and punch her in the chest until she crumpled to the ground. *What did that even mean?* Tee hadn't even wished her happy birthday in years. How could Tee belong to her? How could they belong to each other? It was impossible. In the absence of clarity, she clung to what she knew.

"Give me the ball," Mickey said.

"What? I'm supposed to give you the ball because you started crying? Nah, come take it," Tee said.

A smile spread across Mickey's face and she lunged, but she was too late. Tee had anticipated the move, pivoting out of the way and moving the ball just out of her reach.

"Oh, come on now, you could do a little better than that," she teased, dribbling the ball and stepping backward so Mickey had to approach. She lunged again and this time she had better luck, reaching her hand across Tee's body and catching the ball just before it hit the ground. It was inelegant, but it worked.

Tee smiled. "Aight. But can you keep it?" she asked, squatting low and looking into Mickey's eyes as she attempted to dribble. That alone was distracting, those warm brown eyes settling on her with their full attention, determined and focused. Mickey being bad at basketball only made things worse. Mickey attempted to move, dribbling and running at the same time. She nearly made it to the basket before Tee stole it away, redirecting the ball and jumping up to toss it into the basket. When she was finally back on solid ground she was panting.

"So," she said, catching her breath. "Can I ask another question?" She tossed Mickey the ball willingly this time and wiped sweat from her forehead with the hem of her shirt.

Mickey nodded.

"Was it worth it? The letter?" Tee said, and when their eyes met, they stared at each other, damming up the emotions that threatened to break.

Mickey was the first to break eye contact. She passed Tee the ball without taking a shot.

"I don't know."

Mickey still hadn't come to a conclusion. It had felt good in the moment, but that didn't seem enough reason to blow up her life.

Tee blinked at her. "I think it was," she began, and Mickey waited, heart in throat. "Brave. What you did. It was real." Tee looked down at the ground, a smile playing on her lips. "I know you said I don't know you and all that, but I thought it was real." Then she looked up, meeting Mickey's eyes and holding her gaze. "And that's what you want, right? To be real."

Mickey nodded a little too enthusiastically. It was still difficult to look Tee in the eye. "I do, yeah."

"I'ma be honest though, I didn't really understand it," she said with a chuckle. "But I knew it was important and whatever they did was fucked up. *And* it was like six paragraphs. It wouldn't be that long if it didn't matter."

Mickey laughed. "I guess so."

"It was more than what I did."

This was the third time that day that Tee had surprised her, and Mickey had to consider that maybe this woman in front of her was different from the girl she knew. That time spent here, in this place, had allowed Tee to see herself. Mickey had believed that she needed to get away from her hometown, to run to New York and find herself among people who were striving, yearning for something more, but maybe there was value in this, too. "What does that mean?"

"You asked me about the girl who took my spot." Tee dropped her head, her locs framing her broad, defined shoulders. She gave Mickey a sidelong look and dribbled the ball twice before holding it at her hip. "She's playing out in Vegas, three years in. When I got hurt, I could've come back. Did the work, but even when I got back on that court, I was playing scared. I was terrified of getting hurt again. Scared of what that would mean. I never want my mama to look at me like that again, Key. Like the thing I loved had destroyed me. I couldn't go back. Not for real. So I'm not unhappy, no. But I didn't fight like I could've. Not like you did."

"It still kind of feels like I gave up."

"Nah," Tee said, stepping back from the hoop. If there could be a four-point shot in basketball, she'd be standing there. Mickey watched her carefully, the bend in the ankle, the angle of her elbow, the flick of the wrist. Perfect form. The ball soared through the air and Mickey, terrified, held her breath. It coursed through the net with a satisfying hiss.

"You just taking a break, that's all."

TWENTY

You still know where everything is?" Tee asked, flicking on the light in the foyer. Suddenly the Reynolds family home was bathed in bright, warm light, and everything was just as she remembered it. The large staircase greeted them at the door, the oak banister polished to a shine.

Mickey stepped out of her shoes, her feet brushing against the cool hardwood and then the plush rug in the front hall. Mickey couldn't resist peeking through the French doors to the left of the staircase. That was Tee's father's study, a room Mickey had been in no more than twice.

"I think so," Mickey said, walking down the slim hallway to the half-bathroom. "Your parents here?"

Tee wandered into the kitchen, raising her voice so Mickey could hear. "Nah, they're in Ocean City."

Mickey closed the bathroom door behind her. It still smelled like the lavender candles Miss Lanita bought in bulk at Target, which filled the bathroom even when they weren't lit.

Mickey wasn't meant to be here. She had every intention of driving from the basketball court back to Grandma Anna's house, but she was hit with the overwhelming urge to pee. She looked at her phone. It was nearly nine thirty, and she knew it was only a matter of time before texts popped up asking where she was.

Her mind flashed briefly to senior year, the smell of Tee's pillow beneath her head, the feel of her fingers thrumming on the small of Mickey's back, hidden in the S-curve of her spine. Tee's mother, Miss Lanita, had caught them sneaking around a few times, whispering in the dark of her basement, thankfully fully clothed. Eventually she insisted that Mickey just come through the front door.

Mickey wasn't sure if the invite was out of pity due to her own motherlessness or because Miss Lanita believed her to be a good influence on Tee, but it didn't much matter, Mickey was just happy to be invited inside. The occasional dinner turned into Mickey splitting crab meat from bright red shells with fingers and teeth, the four of them sitting out on the porch like a proper family. They were kids then, *mostly* friends then, but Mickey believed the dynamic would hold. Miss Lanita had treated Mickey like her own, given her someplace to belong. Most of their relationship had taken place here, in this house. It's where they'd met for the first time, kissed for the first time, and where Tee broke her heart, hopefully for the last time.

Her last visit was a few months after Tee's accident. Mickey had dropped by under the guise of checking in on Tee, and Miss Lanita greeted her like she always did, loved on her like she always did, but it didn't feel the same. Tee had split her in two by then, and that meant leaving everything, including this woman she'd loved, behind.

The memory tugged at Mickey, a reminder of all Tee had been capable of. Now she was more upset with herself, at letting herself endure, for allowing herself to let even half a wall down. But here she was, peeking over the edge. Mickey washed her hands and opened the bathroom door. She knew better. She needed to get out of here. Mickey glimpsed the entrance to the basement, the door firmly closed. It brought back everything Mickey had worked so hard to forget.

"You good?" Tee asked. Mickey heard the swish of the water, the dishwasher opening and then closing with a squishy, muted click.

"Yeah," Mickey said. "Thanks for letting me use the bathroom."

Tee smirked, as if Mickey had said something silly. "Of course."

They both looked toward the basement door. "You know we remodeled?"

"Really?" Mickey said, with a nod, crossing her arms across her chest. "Nice."

"You want to see? It's pretty much my little area now. Got a bed-room and everything."

"It was pretty much that when we were kids."

"Yeah, but Ma took it to the next level." Tee opened the door, but Mickey remained rooted to the spot. Stepping down there meant returning to a version of herself she'd left behind. That Mickey had trusted Tee with her heart, only to be let down. But she followed Tee anyway, bounding down the sleek, once-carpeted stairs. The layout was mostly the same, but their makeshift entertainment center (which was just a bunch of recliners) had been rotated and redesigned into a living room. It looked like something out of a theoretically nice Airbnb. There was a gray couch with a bench cushion seat, a steel-based coffee table with an oval glass top, and a TV that was too large for the wall, rimmed with color-changing LED lights. Mickey pointed at the pulsing lighting, which shifted from purple to red to blue. "You did this yourself?"

Tee nodded. "Yeah. Cool, right?"

"Yup," Mickey said, even though it was anything but.

There was a little kitchen area now, which was really more of a countertop with a sink and mini-fridge. Mickey, nosy, opened it up. It was stocked with rows of expensive bottled water (both still and sparkling) and sodas in almost every flavor. "Fancy," she commented. Next to the kitchenette was a closet. Their closet.

Mickey, fourteen, had been just as shocked as anyone to be trapped in a closet with Tee. It was dark in there, but Mickey didn't know why she expected anything else. Of course, the closet was dark, most closets were. But all expectations for the night had gone out the window. She couldn't see her own hand unless she held it up close to her face, the only light peeling in from the bottom of a doorway, yellow and imposing. She couldn't see Tee either, who was somewhere on the opposite end, separated by a row of winter coats.

Mickey had been replaying the night's events over and over again, but it was hard to wrap her mind around how she'd gotten here. She knew this was seven minutes in heaven. That they were supposed to kiss and feel each other up (or not and lie about it) and then face a crowd of

213

onlookers with sheepish smiles. In this case, the onlookers were six or seven girls from school, all of whom Mickey recognized, none (except for Jasmine) she knew well. Jasmine had sold this as a movie night, but it had quickly turned into something else, the movie becoming background noise once the pilfered bottles of alcohol snuck from parents' liquor cabinets came out and the lights turned dim.

The vibe shifted in the room, and Mickey didn't know what to make of it. She wanted to look in Jasmine's direction and flash her hand signals of distress when someone suggested Truth or Dare, but she didn't know if she would look dumb gesticulating to herself. She'd gotten through the game by saying truth to everything, but some of the questions were so scandalous, she'd chosen to drink instead: *"Do you play with yourself?"* Sip. *"If you had to fuck anyone here, who would it be?"* A big, long drink.

After just a few questions, she was a little tipsy and Jasmine was too far away to hold her up. The other girls had gone for the dares, as if they needed permission to touch each other in front of everyone else. She'd watched Jasmine lick alcohol out of one girl's belly button and tried not to blush when Tee had to pretend to hump the floor.

Mickey didn't realize that anyone played seven minutes in heaven in real life, so she was surprised when someone suggested it, a girl who she knew dated one of the most popular guys in school. She'd always seen the game as a way to get two characters to hook up in a movie, the lonely shy girl getting trapped in the closet with the hottest guy in school only for him to be swapped out at the last second with his weird, burping friend. But here she was with Tee, and the door was firmly closed.

The way they'd been paired up was strange and complicated, something involving a shot, colored Popsicle sticks, and grabbing things out of a hat. In the end, Tee and Mickey had matching Popsicle sticks and were told to go inside the closet and get it over with. Mickey had turned bright red, and Jasmine leaned over and said they didn't have to do anything if she didn't want to. Mickey did want to go inside the closet with Tee, which is why she didn't say anything then or now, silently waiting for Tee to press her body into hers.

Mickey didn't know when she realized that she was attracted to Tee, just that it was there and it refused to go away. It was irritating, how warm and vigilant she was whenever Tee was around. Everything about Tee was endlessly fascinating—the way the tendons in her hand flexed around the ball, the way her shoulders tightened when she laughed. It forced her to think things she'd rather not. Like what Tee's hands would look like wrapped around her waist and why the skinny girls Tee messed with wouldn't just shrivel up and die. But Tee didn't seem to notice, and for that Mickey was grateful.

"You good?" Tee's voice cut through the silence like soft, buttery bread and Mickey realized she hadn't eaten in hours, the only thing sloshing around her stomach a cocktail of Hennessy and Grey Goose.

"Yeah. Did you start the timer?" Mickey asked.

"Nah."

"You think they're keeping track?"

"Maybe."

"Probably not," Mickey said, laughing a little. Everyone was too drunk or pretending to keep up with who paired off with who, all the sticks having been drawn at once. Mickey thought of Jasmine's matching Popsicle stick, which belonged to a Black ginger named Lo whose skin was toasted and freckled like every other Black ginger she'd seen in her fourteen years of life. She briefly wondered if Jasmine had known this was the plan all along and then if all Black gingers were somehow related.

"Yeah, definitely not," Tee said, and for a second Mickey thought Tee could read her mind. Mickey wished she could just see Tee's face, though she found a surprising boldness in the dark.

"Are you upset you pulled my Popsicle stick?"

"No," Tee said, and the room felt smaller and more suffocating than ever before. "I'm shocked you came in here though."

Mickey's heart skipped a beat. "Why?"

"Because I know you don't like girls."

"I—" Mickey began before closing her mouth again. She was speechless. But she didn't like girls, right? She wasn't even sure she liked Tee— she only knew that no one else had made her feel the things she felt right now. Not even the boy who had felt her up after homecoming, palming her breasts and breathing on her neck. She hadn't felt anything, really, aside from the thrill of being touched by someone other than herself.

Tee hadn't even touched her yet, but Mickey was squirming at the possibility of being held by those hands. She could feel Tee coming closer now, she'd felt the air shift.

"So," Tee said, and Mickey realized she was only a few feet away. "What you tryna do?"

Mickey resisted the urge to reach for her and pull her close, afraid that if she moved she'd jinx the whole thing.

"I don't know," Mickey said. "What do you wanna do?" The words sounded strange coming out of her mouth, so she apologized even though she had no reason to. "Sorry."

"What are you saying sorry for?" She could feel Tee's breath now, close enough that it started feeling like her own. It smelled like Jolly Ranchers, overly sweet, masking the scent of saliva and late-evening breath. Mickey wanted to kiss her, but she didn't know how to go first, still confused as to why this girl, with her glowing skin and pretty eyes, would want to be this close to her in the first place.

"I don't know."

"Do you want to do this?" Tee said, and Mickey was too stuck on what Tee meant by the word *this* to reply. "You going to let me kiss you or not?"

Mickey giggled and clapped a hand over her mouth, worried she'd done something wrong.

But Tee, undisturbed, continued, running a hand over Mickey's face, cupping her cherubic cheek. She couldn't help but think of the way her father grabbed her face, how his hand swallowed her cheek when he called her his little girl, but she shook that thought away. She didn't feel so little now, with Tee's hands on her waist, seconds away from kissing Tee on her soft mouth. Tee pulled Mickey close with a swift tug, and for a moment she felt light, like she'd flown through the air, even though Tee had only pulled her a short way. All she could think about was what she should be doing with her hands.

Tee planted her lips on her neck and Mickey shuddered. Then Tee kissed her neck before making her way to her mouth, sucking and biting like she had something to prove, like she wanted to leave a mark. Mickey felt the slickness of Tee's spit coating her shoulder and she vowed to never wash that spot again, making silent promises in between the tiny sounds she hoped sounded sexy. Tee gathered Mickey's bottom lip in between her teeth and sucked it into her mouth before releasing it with a soft pop and kissing Mickey properly on the mouth, enveloping her lips.

Mickey had never been kissed like this, so her strategy was to do as little as possible, just enough so Tee would want to do it again. When Tee's tongue darted into her mouth, Mickey held it open like a small cave, moving her own tongue in short bursts and tilting her head. Tee seemed to like that, one hand moving to Mickey's breasts and the other pushing her up against what felt like the handle of a vacuum cleaner. She made a sound then, but it must've sounded like she liked it, because Tee only pushed harder, her kisses more insistent, the handle digging deeper into her back.

Mickey was grateful Tee couldn't see her face, which was contorted into something in between pleasure and pain. This was the kind of thing she dreamed about, although she'd never let herself even think about doing it with Tee. But here she was, and all she wanted to do was tell Jasmine that she might be in love.

Mickey was finding it hard to keep up. Every time she thought she got the hang of something, Tee flipped the script, roaming around her body like she was running out of time. As it turns out, they were. A phone chimed somewhere outside the closet, signaling the end of the game. Tee kissed her quickly on the mouth before opening the door, and Mickey was suddenly blinded by the brightness of the basement. As her eyes adjusted, she realized that some of the couples hadn't even attempted privacy, hooking up in full view. Slowly, they pulled themselves apart, and Mickey found her way back to Jasmine, whose face was flushed red. The two settled into a puffy, butterscotch recliner meant for one, Jasmine's legs draped over hers.

"So how did it go?" Mickey asked.

Jasmine shrugged. "She was real aggressive." She smoothed a hand over Mickey's once-gelled puff, her baby hairs curling up and puffy in protest. "How were things with Tee?"

"It was good." Mickey tried to be casual, but she knew the blissful smile said everything she wouldn't, and that Jasmine would press her for details once they were back at her house, tucked into bed. "Really good," she said next, even though her back was tender and her neck sore.

Out of the corner of her eye Mickey watched Tee, who was talking to Lo, their heads bent in deep discussion.

"I've heard she's good at what she does," Jasmine said and Mickey tried not to let the jealousy make its way from her stomach to her mouth. She knew Tee got around, that she was one of many, but she hadn't thought about it until now.

"So, you gay now or what?" Jasmine asked with a smirk and Mickey swatted her arm.

"It was like one kiss."

"Oh, just a kiss?" She tilted Mickey's chin to expose a hickey in full bloom. "It didn't look like just a kiss."

"Oh fuck." Mickey clapped a hand over her neck. "My mom is going to lose her mind. Remember that time she gave me a pregnancy test? I hadn't even kissed anybody yet."

Jasmine clucked her tongue, tilting Mickey's head the other way. "She only got you on one side. That's good."

"She said she knew I didn't like girls."

"Well clearly you liked something." A smug smile spread across Jasmine's face. A moment passed and she leaned her head against Mickey's.

Mickey laughed because she did. Her head lolled back against the recliner, and she fixed her eyes on the blank wall, which was projecting an old episode of *The Proud Family* on mute.

"You think she thinks I'm cute?" Mickey asked after a few moments, chancing a glance in Tee's direction. "I just don't know what this all means, you know? Like what if she—"

"Mickey," Jasmine said, grabbing Mickey's arm and sitting up a little straighter. "It was a game. Don't overthink it. You're probably a little tipsy and still in the mood. You know you can't take Tee seriously. She's hooked up with everyone."

Mickey's chest hurt from the shame. She realized she'd been naïve. "You're right. It was just weird because she kissed me even after the buzzer went off."

"Seriously, don't think too deep into it."

Mickey nodded in agreement, but she was already too far gone, envisioning a world where Tee walked her to class every day. She let out a sigh. "Fuck."

Mickey shook herself back to the present. She'd revisited that moment a few times over the years, but this time she felt how clearly her own vulnerability was juxtaposed against Tee's confident way of moving through the world. It was a dangerous combination.

Tee was busy explaining how she had picked out the furniture in the basement, but Mickey was looking for an escape route.

"It looks so good—" Mickey cut in.

Tee stopped midsentence, unable to hide her surprise at being interrupted. "Thank you."

Mickey held up her phone. "Gotta go, Grandma Anna texted me that she wants to go to bed and I need to, and I quote, 'bring my hind parts home.'" It was a lie, but a believable one.

Tee laughed. "You can tell her it's my fault."

"Oh, I will," Mickey said. "Thanks again, for everything."

"Any time."

Back in the car, Mickey remembered the rest. The hookup itself hadn't been a huge issue, only an inciting force, but what came after had become a core memory that would guide the way Mickey saw herself for years to come.

Things had only gotten worse over spring break, freshman year winding down into another too-warm summer. When Mickey discovered Tee's Twitter, she had taken to checking it daily, obsessively analyzing each tweet to see if they could possibly be about her. She'd only meant to read Tee's single-tweet recap of that night ("Tonight was lit"), and the morning after ("I been thinking 'bout you"), but her Twitter had turned into her own personal Tee news update, alerting her if she was happy, sad, or bored. Tee mostly tweeted about basketball or retweeted funny things from the timeline, but sometimes she used her 140 characters to say something vaguely romantic, which would make Mickey's heart beat faster and send her mind reeling. She googled the most sentimental ones, most of them song lyrics, but Mickey let her imagination run wild. At the height of her delusions, she imagined that Tee was composing a secret playlist just for her, with every lyric a secret code that Mickey was meant to decipher.

When Mickey wasn't going through Tee's tweets or daydreaming about the kind of life they might have together, she was waiting for her phone to ping. Tee had punched her number into Mickey's phone at the end of the night and, despite Jasmine's urging to play it cool, Mickey had texted first. It had started out well, with the two of them going back and forth every few minutes, asking questions so personal Mickey was afraid Tee might show someone the answer.

"Are you a virgin?"

"Have you ever been with a boy?"

"Do you like me?"

"What are you wearing right now?"

"What's your biggest fear?"

"Dying."

"Me too."

Mickey's cheeks burned red at the thought of how open she'd been as a teenager. How naïve. She cast a look at her father's house and started down the road. It had been a while since she'd thought about those last days of high school, when she'd finally been woken up from her delusions about who Tee was and what those snatches of vulnerability had amounted to. Did Jasmine remember? She had to.

"Hey girl. Wassup?" Jasmine's raspy voice came through the phone, and Mickey was desperate to jump to the point.

"Do you remember what Tee said after we hooked up in ninth grade?"

"Huh? Girl what?" Jasmine asked, before the sound of Nova whining seeped through the phone. "One second girl. Nova, get your tail in the bathtub. You can watch *Adventure Time* afterward." A sigh. "Sorry about that. I'm here. What are you talking about?"

Mickey put Jasmine on speaker, putting one hand on the steering wheel, the phone in the other. "When we were in ninth grade, in the gym, do you remember what you told me about Tee? What she said?"

Mickey remembered. It was impossible to forget, but she just wanted Jasmine to confirm it, to remind her she wasn't crazy. It was the first game after spring break. Jasmine didn't want to be there—she would much rather be watching Katherine Heigl play a bridesmaid, the two of them tucked under blankets and eating Ledo's pizza—but instead Mickey had insisted they pack themselves into the sweaty high school gym, Jasmine rolling her eyes while Mickey tried to pick out the number 3 in the blur of blue jerseys.

The texts had all but stopped since school started back up. Mickey had been the last one to text and the first one to wave hello their first day back, to which she'd received a distracted wave. She'd been disappointed but remained optimistic—it had only been a few days. She explained this to Jasmine while the team warmed up, and she watched her best friend's eyes widen in concern.

"Wait, that was how many years ago?" Jasmine asked, interrupting her memory. "What made you think of that now?"

"I saw Tee again and we kind of got into it," Mickey admitted.

"Again? Was it not enough when she tried to lick you? The girl is clearly trying to ruin your life."

Mickey thought back to the basketball court. The ice cream at Cold Stone. The way Tee had looked at her. It had felt real. But upon further examination, it felt like a trick of the light. Either way, she needed to make sure that she'd remembered correctly.

"Do you remember or not?"

"Maybe? Sort of?"

"You remember us hooking up?"

"Yeah. And I remember telling you it was a bad idea. Like I'm telling you now. That she flirts with everybody, and she never means anything by it. Hell, she even used to flirt with me."

For a moment, she wondered if Jasmine had been jealous of her and Tee's bond, the way they'd opened up to each other, if she had wanted

221

it for herself. But now she realized she was falling into the same pattern of defending Tee, propping up whatever fucked up little thing they had in an attempt to make it real. Jasmine had warned her once. Mickey should've listened.

"That's not surprising," Mickey said. "But thanks girl, call you later?"

"Sounds good. And don't forget that—"

Mickey hung up before Jasmine could get it all out. She rolled down the window and tossed her phone onto the passenger seat, gripping the steering wheel as tight as she could. How dare Tee act like she saw her? Like she hadn't always been an experiment or something to check off a box? Jasmine had said so herself. She screeched to a stop at a red light and felt her heart racing, and she suddenly felt like she was back in that gym, waiting for Jasmine to explain her hesitation with bated breath.

Mickey tapped her foot on the bleacher in front of her and stared at the ground. She thought of their steady stream of messages. Had she shared too much? "You think it's weird?" She looked up into Jasmine's bright face. "Why?"

"I wasn't going to say anything because I assumed y'all wasn't talking in the first place, but she said something to Lo that night about checking you off her list."

Mickey's stomach did a flip. "What?" The newfound pang in her chest made it difficult for her to breathe. "What do you mean? You weren't going to tell me?"

"I didn't think y'all were going to talk after the party. I thought you'd just move on and say it was a drunk thing." Jasmine leaned back against the stone wall and kicked up her feet. "Wait, do you like her for real or something?"

Mickey shifted away from Jasmine and crossed her arms. "No. It's just texting."

Jasmine pursed her lips and looked at Mickey with an unmistakable skepticism that made Mickey feel like a liar. "I told you not to take her serious."

"What makes you think that I'm taking her serious?"

"Prove to me that you're not. We're sitting in this musty ass gym, on a Friday, for what?"

"I just didn't want to miss anything," Mickey said, even though it no longer felt true. She refocused on the game and found number 3. Tee looked beautiful when she played, Mickey thought, admiring the way she deftly moved the ball from one end of the court to the other. Tee went up for the shot. It seemed too far away for the ball to make it into the hoop, but a satisfying swish proved Mickey wrong and drew their side of the crowd to their feet. The gym exploded with noise and a nearby teammate clapped Tee on the shoulder. Tee nodded and readied herself for the next play, eager to get back to work.

Mickey couldn't contain her smile or the pride swelling in her chest. Jasmine placed a hand on her knee. "Yeah, we're gonna have to snap you out of this shit. Are you about to cry, bro? Have you never seen her play before?"

Mickey slapped Jasmine's thigh with a thwack. "I'm not going to cry, it's just impressive."

"You need to be impressed with somebody else. She literally said she's never been with a big girl and just wanted to see what it was like."

All these years later, she could still feel the lump in her throat, felt like she wanted to jump out of her skin. It didn't make it better that when Tee started to come around more consistently, shortly after Sylvia left, Mickey had lost a little weight. She'd paced around her neighborhood for hours after school, trying to distract herself from the emptiness her mother had left behind. She'd do anything to occupy her mind, to keep from feeling all her emotions.

But then Tee had come back and filled that spot like it was hers to keep. Mickey should have run then, should have listened to the little voice in her head that played Jasmine's words on repeat, but it was everything she had ever wanted, and she would sacrifice everything just to have Tee for an hour to herself. So she'd stayed, even through the ups and downs, and the eventual heartbreak. Mickey gripped the steering wheel tighter, frustration throbbing at her temples, her palms wet against the leather of the wheel. She turned around and headed back in the direction she came.

It was Nova that answered the door.

"Auntie Mickey!" she said with a smile so wide Mickey worried her face would split in two. She clutched an American Girl Doll in one hand—a butterscotch-colored facsimile of its mother, puff balls and all—and a cell phone in the other.

Mickey kneeled a little. "Hi, Nova." The word *auntie* still sounded strange in relation to her. Mickey felt too young to be an aunt, and the word sounded swollen with responsibility even though it simply amounted to this: occasional house calls and birthday gifts—an honorary signifier applied to too many people in Nova's world to count.

The door swung open wider and then there was Jasmine, wearing a coordinated navy pajama set and a matching bonnet. "Nova, what I tell you about answering the door?"

"But I saw it was Auntie Mickey." She pouted a little, and Jasmine twisted up her face, her impatience palpable.

"I don't care if it's your daddy. Don't open my door again, you hear me?" Jasmine asked. Nova nodded, unmoved, and Mickey was sure Nova would do it again. Her little feet, tucked into fluffy slippers, shuffled across the floor and it wasn't a minute before Mickey heard the sounds of Beyoncé's *Homecoming* album pealing through the house.

Jasmine rolled her eyes. "She's learning how to do that little bunny hop dance." She took in Mickey. "But what's up? The way you just hung up on me, I thought I wasn't going to hear from you for a minute."

Mickey leaned a hand against the doorway. "My bad." She put on her best puppy dog face. "Forgive me?"

Jasmine pushed the door open for Mickey to come inside. "I guess." She walked until she plopped down on the sectional and Mickey followed. She tucked a leg behind her knee and sank into the couch, draping one arm over the back. She looked over at Nova, who had moved on to a YouTube video, but was still dancing and shaking to a silent beat.

"Ma!" Jasmine called. "Can you put Nova to bed?"

Jasmine's mother, her hair pinned and face bare, collected her granddaughter, pulling her into her arms like she was five years younger and couldn't go to bed without being held. Nova, who always seemed so grown (at three years of age she'd proudly declared that she was no longer a baby), folded into her grandmother's body, and rested her head in the crook of her neck. She didn't even complain. Mickey looked to Jasmine, impressed.

"She's so good about bedtime," Mickey commented.

"Yeah, everything's easy with Grandma," she said with a little laugh. A hush settled over the house and although Mickey knew they considered her family, she felt she'd stumbled upon something intimate, intruded upon their nightly routine. The house was a little messier than the day of the cookout, Nova's things dotting every available surface.

Jasmine noticed Mickey's sightline, and as if reading her mind, began to clean up.

"So what's up?" she asked, reuniting a pair of sneakers and tucking them under her arm.

Mickey had nearly forgotten why she came.

"Oh," Mickey said. "You were saying something and I hadn't gotten that far down the road anyway." A lie. She was nearly to Grandma Anna's when she'd turned the car around. "I was rude for hanging up and we didn't get that much one-on-one time at the party anyway."

"Yeah, because you dipped off to hang out with Tee."

Mickey tipped her head to the side, felt defensive at the mention of Tee's name. She wanted to protect herself, craft an excuse that explained her behavior. She could deflect, accuse Jasmine of being too busy to hang out with Mickey anyway. But she knew Jasmine would see right through her, like she always did.

"Yeah, my bad."

"I mean, it's not the first time you left me to chill with her," Jasmine replied. "It's cool."

"It's not even like that."

"Mhm, yeah."

"You left me plenty of times to hang out with Q. Remember IHOP?"

"You were with Scottie," Jasmine replied, but the tone of her voice when she said their friend's name sounded like she was trying to get rid of a bad taste in her mouth.

"You were our ride."

Jasmine waved it away with a hand. "Well, here we are now. Everyone made it home. A bunch of times since then. Because you're here, I'm here. Scottie is probably underneath some nigga." At that, they both laughed.

Mickey looked to Jasmine, eyes sparkling. "You got something to drink?"

They migrated outside and recounted stories of their childhood over glasses of sweet red wine, sometimes laughing so hard they had to catch the red liquid dribbling from their lips. Their conversation pierced the natural soundtrack of summer, crickets and cicadas and the staticky silence. There was the occasional sound of a television, the houses in the neighborhood crammed too close together. Lightning bugs glowed inter-mittently and mosquitos assaulted them in the dark. Jasmine slapped her leg and lit a citronella candle.

It was warm, but neither minded. Jasmine gave her to-the-minute updates about people Mickey no longer knew. Sarena and Odessa—the best friends she'd taken up with after Mickey left their local high school—were both pregnant, though neither knew if they wanted to keep it. Q was out of the house, again, this time because he had skipped a pickup to sit in on Fat Trel's studio session. At that, Mickey had laughed, loud and long, so loud, Jasmine had politely told her to shut the fuck up. Mickey didn't know how they arrived at the topic of Tee, but once she did, they were both good and drunk, and Mickey couldn't stop thinking about leaving Jasmine's house and crawling into Tee's bed. It was only across the street. She wondered what Tee was doing. If she was thinking about Mickey, too.

Talking about Tee turned Mickey's cheeks rosy.

"Girl, are you blushing?" Jasmine asked.

Mickey covered her face. "No!" she insisted. "It's the wine."

"If only Lex could see you giggling like a damn teenager."

At the mention of Lex's name Mickey tensed, remembered she was grieving something, too. She'd largely avoided her feelings surround-ing their breakup, which felt real enough for her to justify whatever was going on with Tee, but not so real that she'd considered everything that went into splitting up their life. She took another sip of her drink. "We're not together right now."

Jasmine choked. "Bitch what? What you mean y'all not together? When did this happen?"

It felt so far away now. "Last week? The week before?"

"You didn't say anything."

"It doesn't feel real."

Jasmine reached for her hand and Mickey let her hold it, even though she didn't think Jasmine understood that it had been her choice, that she had called it off. Or if she did, Mickey didn't understand why she was holding her hand like this, as if they did this sweet, sappy shit.

"I'm good, really," Mickey insisted, and when she met Jasmine's eyes it was clear she didn't believe her.

"If you say so." She rubbed her thumb against the back of Mickey's hand, tapping it twice and then letting it go. "Does Scottie know?"

"I haven't really said anything."

Jasmine threw up her hands. "A miracle!"

Mickey pushed on her shoulder. "Shut up."

"I don't ever hear about shit first. Don't even play."

"Mostly with work shit. I'm boring otherwise."

"Sure," Jasmine said. The look in her eye was skeptical. "So with this Tee shit. Be honest. Y'all fucking?"

Mickey blushed deep. "Of course not."

"Okay, good."

Mickey tapped her foot nervously. "We used to be best friends. You know that. We're just chilling. Catching up."

"I do," Jasmine agreed. "I also know that I spent all of senior year dealing with you crying because she decided she wanted to date Ayesha for real. And you know with Tee it's always a plot, something bigger. She hasn't tried to fuck you since she licked your neck?"

Mickey winced at the thought. She'd been so broken. She didn't think she'd ever recover. But then here she was, testing the boundaries all over again. She hated that she wanted to remember the feel of their bodies pressed together, wanted to lose herself in Tee's warmth. "Nah, she hasn't."

Jasmine made a surprised sound. "Maybe she's changed."

"Maybe she doesn't think I'm all that fuckable anymore."

"See, this is why I don't want you fucking with that girl. You start talking crazy and forgetting who the fuck you are."

"Tell me," Mickey said, mustering a smile. "Tell me who I am, since I'm so great."

"I'm not telling you shit. Because there's no reason you should forget."

She wanted to believe Jasmine, but it didn't feel true. If she was so great, she wouldn't be there. "Yeah, sure."

"You know you're fire and fine and all that shit. I'm just surprised Tee's being loyal."

Mickey tilted her head. "What's you mean loyal?"

"She didn't tell you she was dealing with somebody?"

"Is it official?"

"Be for real, Mickey."

"What?" Mickey asked. Her skin suddenly felt sticky with sweat. The conversation on the court came back in bits. Something real was blossoming between them. She could feel it. "I feel like if it was serious she would say something, that's all."

"I guess she's exactly who she's always been. It's always a game with her, that's why I tell you to leave her ass alone. She's the same as she's always been."

Jasmine hadn't been there. "I'm not saying she's changed. I'm just saying I don't know if she has a girlfriend."

"Bitch what? You haven't been here. How would you even know? Now you want to trust Tee? The same girl who said you were pressed for her even when she was the one telling you she wanted you?" Jasmine clicked her tongue. "Come on now. I would think you were smarter than that."

Mickey bowed her head and took another sip. "I don't think I'm being dumb because we've been getting ice cream and texting here and there. We're cool and I'm grown. I don't know why her having a girlfriend changes that. It's not like we're fucking or kissing, or anything." She didn't mention the dinner or the sunset or the Ferris wheel.

Jasmine rolled her eyes and Mickey doesn't say anything because it was Jasmine who listened to Mickey sob when things hadn't worked out the first time around. "I'm not about to go back and forth with you on this, I just wanted to let you know what was up with Tiana in case you wanted to be dumb." She emphasized the word *dumb*, popping the *m* and drawing it out. "And think she was any different from who she's always been. That girl is all ego. She don't love nobody but herself."

"I hear you."

"You not, but it's okay."

Mickey sighed. "I do."

Silence stretched between them. Mickey was the first to break it.

"Grandma Anna's going to say something if I don't get home." She looked for her shoes in the grass with her toes and tried to remember why she came here in the first place. Attempted to recall what she was looking for. She came up blank.

"I'm surprised she's not calling you now talking about you being fast, even at your big age."

They laughed, and Mickey felt the knot in her stomach unwind.

"I love you," Mickey said. "And I appreciate you. I know you just looking out."

"Yeah, yeah bitch . . . Me too."

An hour later Mickey turned the key in the door, her plissé set clinging to her skin.

"Mickey? That you?" Grandma Anna called out. Mickey peeked her head into the kitchen. Grandma Anna was sitting at the table, bent over her church Bible, which sat in a faux-reptile oxblood casing with handles she carried like a purse. It lay flat, its thin pages creased, silky and fragile from time.

"You know it is," Mickey replied. "Who else would it be?"

"Well, I don't know," Grandma Anna said. "I got a famous person living in my house. Who knows who could be driving up to my house at all hours of the night."

"I'm not famous," Mickey said with a laugh.

"Did you eat?" Grandma asked. "Wherever you was."

"I didn't." Mickey now noticed the emptiness of her stomach, the anxiety she'd been feeling throughout the day replaced with hunger. Her day had taken a turn. Just a few hours ago, she was trying to side-step her little cousins running around her legs.

"Well there's some collards left, and a little meat. Go 'head and warm it up."

Mickey almost protested. She was so exhausted from the day's events, she didn't want to do anything more. Grandma Anna huffed, clocking her granddaughter's resistance, and stood, using the table for

229

support. "Gone sit down." Her slippered feet scuffled across the floor and she began pulling dish after dish from the fridge. "You gotta eat."

Despite her age, Grandma Anna was still quick on her feet, her face a picture of quiet determination. Her brow furrowed, creating a crease in her brow. It was the only wrinkle she had, the rest of her face smooth like poured buttermilk. She was beautiful, and Mickey hoped her face would age the same. "So, where were you?" she asked, dumping leftovers on a plate and placing them in the microwave, covering it all with a damp paper towel. Grandma Anna eyed Mickey expectantly, a hand on her hip.

Mickey felt dizzy at the line of questioning. Instead of responding she picked up her phone. There was a text from Lex and one from Tee, asking her if she made it home. She didn't read the one from Lex—she would get to that later. She texted Tee that she had, and mindlessly opened Instagram. She hadn't realized she was distracted until the microwave beeped and Grandma Anna closed the door with a sharp click.

"You going to make me ask you again?" Grandma Anna asked, setting the plate in front of Mickey and settling back into her chair at the kitchen table, where she'd been eating and praying and gathering since she was a young bride.

"You don't say anything when I'm going to the grocery store." Mickey opened the fridge and closed it again, wanting nothing but something to do with her hands.

"Because you're being of service, to your grandma and the Lord."

"How is me getting you chocolate bars and wheat bread being of service to the Lord?" Mickey pursed her lips to hide her smile.

"Ephesians 6 tells us so," she said, her lips turned up at the corners. She smoothed her hands over the table and turned to the page. "If you're not going to tell me where you were then you have to tell me what's wrong."

Mickey attempted to eat but the food turned wet and soggy in her mouth. "What do you mean?" she asked, cheeks full.

"You look like you're going through it. Sad. Your eyes been looking like that since you showed up here. Tell me, what's going on." She reached over and took Mickey's hand in hers. "My big baby."

Mickey could tell her everything right now, lay all her burdens down. She wouldn't judge her, she knew, but she couldn't make the words come out. She squeezed her grandmother's hand. "I'm okay, Grandma. Just tired."

She forced down a few bites before losing her appetite altogether. She tossed the rest out, ignoring the look in her grandma's eyes. Mickey knew she was watching her, and that she didn't like what she saw.

Mickey disappeared into her bedroom and stepped out of her shoes, slid off her clothes, and tucked herself into bed. She didn't have the energy to shower and scrub herself clean. Not with her mind spinning, conjuring up old memories, dusting up things she'd rather leave behind. She was so lost she didn't hear the buzz of her phone, vibrating on the floor in the heap of her clothes. The vibration was insistent but muffled, but Mickey's mind was in a faraway place. Her phone rang four times more, but by that point she was fast asleep.

TWENTY-ONE

Halloween parties are dangerous things, especially for white people who have been given a theme. It doesn't take their imagination too long to run wild before veering into the inappropriate or fully racist. Such was the case with Teagan Price, one of Bevy's most senior editors. She was one of the organization's first hires, a fact that was frequently pointed out in All Hands about company growth. She was the big boss, though no one was completely sure what she did.

Formally (theoretically), Teagan was the digital director of the company's portfolio, overseeing the direction of editorial. Mostly, she was trotted out like a show pony during events, her beachy blond hair bright with highlights and her thin lips overlined and glossed.

Teagan had connections, which meant she was a shoo-in for Quinn Cantrell's infamous Halloween party. Quinn was a former senior editor at one of the magazines that did journalism with a capital *J*, and securing an invite to his Halloween party meant you'd cleared some invisible red tape. Mickey had never been invited, of course, but she heard rumors that Chelsea had gone twice. It was a glorified watering hole for the cool journalists, held yearly in his West Village townhouse.

Every year there was a different theme. The year prior, it was carnival, and two years before that superheroes. Four years ago, it was "Blast from the Past (early 2000s edition)" in which people were invited to come dressed as their favorite icons.

Homebodies

A few weeks before, the invitation had arrived on heavy, blood-red stationery requesting their presence (Teagan, who had been attending for years, always got a plus one) at the annual fete. Teagan, with her pouty mouth and belly ring, had suggested Britney and Justin, but her new boyfriend, Barrett Yates, was insistent: it was P. Diddy, or nothing else. J. Lo, then, felt like the natural choice for Teagan, lest she go in her own costume and pass up the chance to do the couple thing.

It had only occurred to Teagan when Barrett was smearing her very-dark contouring stick all over his face that the costume might be a little uncouth, but she was too worried about accidentally smearing her bronzer on her jeweled white bandana to say anything.

In the end, there had been no need to worry. The night had been deliriously fun. She'd invited her assistant, Chelsea, to attend, who had dressed up as Kiely from 3LW. Teagan hadn't the slightest clue who that was, but when Chelsea explained that she was also Aqua from Cheetah Girls, Teagan just nodded and smiled at Chelsea, zero recognition in her eyes.

Once they arrived, Teagan knew she had absolutely nailed J. Lo's VMA look, down to the bejeweled belly button and Sean John baby tee. Everyone complimented how good she and Barrett looked together, how *on theme*. Barrett had gone full method, adopting Diddy's tone and inflection, gleaned from a barrage of YouTube videos. He had *committed*, so Teagan felt like she also had to.

So, when the DJ played "I'm Real" and people pointed their phones at her with their flashlights on full beam, it felt like she'd stepped onto a stage and was bound by duty to do her very best "Jenny from the Block." She performed with her clutch as a microphone, dancing and writhing and singing along. She didn't know all the words, but she knew enough to make it believable, and at 2:36, she would cover her mouth and not say the n-word.

But the lights were blinding and she was trying to keep up with the song, and she sometimes sang it all the way through at home. She'd forgotten this time, the word coming out of her mouth with practiced ease. But she hadn't remembered saying it at the time, and the rest of the night was a blast.

But there the video was, on Twitter, four years later, making the rounds thanks to an anonymous account that referred to itself as "Bevy's Basement." Momentum was slow at first, but Tangela Ray, who had emerged from the shadows and made a Twitter to connect with her sizable community of mommy bloggers and YouTube fans, retweeted it. Even though Tangela's therapist had told her to take a big step away from the world of media—and she had—she knew she had no other choice.

After all, Tangela had worked with Teagan back in the day, and to Tangela's knowledge, the word *nigga* was very much in her vocabulary— as was torturing her young assistants, who almost always happened to be Black. Now Tangela had a whole new demographic of fans aside from the Christian, white mommy bloggers: angry Black women who were less than impressed that Teagan was the kind of person Bevy kept on staff and promoted to the very top. The video caught on like wildfire, populating every group chat and timeline. It even made its way to Instagram, reposted and reposted until it made its way to The Shade Room, as well as an industry gossip page with hundreds of thousands of zealous, racism-hating fans—many of them assistants who were, themselves, completely over Bevy's shit.

The video was just the beginning. After thirty-six hours, the account began posting anonymous DMs of the atrocities experienced by Bevy's Black and Brown employees, which ranged from the relatively benign— hair touching, mix-ups, and the like—to offenses that in the right hands could be the basis of a lawsuit. One account detailed being passed up for a promotion because they believed her culture gave her an "ultra-specific lens." Another sent in screenshots of an editor asking her assistant if she thought Cardi B was lying about being Black and asked if she could pull that off, too, before noting that if she had, maybe it would've been easier to get into Stanford.

The account also retweeted one public letter that, up until that point, had only been seen by Mickey's now-defunct group chat, along with the few people who already followed her and cared enough to toss her a like. All in all, it had been on maybe a hundred people's radar for the majority of its lifetime, most of whom sought to distance themselves as far from it as possible.

Bevy's Basement had been one of the one hundred, which had

amassed thousands of followers overnight. By the time Mickey woke up, it was at ten thousand, paltry by social media celebrity standards, but a reach big enough to tap into every corner of their industry. Elaine, no longer directly affiliated with the industry and its goings on, was a little late to the party, and found out four hours later than her New York friends (five, if you counted the time zone change). It made its way to all the industry gossip pages, including La Merdé, which was run by two "insiders" that made it their job to report on the horrors of the industry.

When Mickey got around to checking her phone around noon, her letter had been quote tweeted by Bevy's Basement with a simple caption: "Relatable content. She's the catalyst of this fr. This account wouldn't exist if she hadn't been brave enough to say something first. The only one to call this bullshit out." La Merdé reposted it soon after, racking up tens of thousands of likes.

With that cosign, Mickey's letter exploded, making the rounds from DMs to group chats to inboxes and back again. Those at the top talked about the letter as if it was heresy and those at the bottom—the assistants, the editors, the readers, the bystanders—gobbled it up. By the end of the first day there was even a hashtag (#bevyinblack), encouraging former and current writers to come out of the shadows to tell their stories—which were eerily similar to her own. Mickey's letter was a centerpiece on this mantel of complaints, which detailed (some went so far as to name people directly) the ways Black women have been failed, maligned, sidelined, disbelieved, gaslighted, discriminated against, and just generally disrespected across time.

People called for resignations (none came, except for Teagan, who publicly resigned, before moving to a less visible role in the company), asked for reparations (a few white people sent direct payments to those affected via Cash app and Venmo), and begged Mickey to come out into the spotlight and speak further, to engage in the discourse, perhaps capitalize off the moment and finally claim her crown.

Quietly, the girls in the industry, the ones who had smiled at Mickey at events, split Ubers home, commented on her posts, and asked to get drinks that never materialized, watched, knowing that Mickey would likely never work again. That they would never see her at an event and trade knowing looks over canapés. That they, if they wanted to remain where they were, better separate themselves just in case they started rounding people up once the smoke cleared.

That included Chelsea, who had seen the letter shortly after it was posted. She'd nearly choked while brushing her teeth. She read it again, twice, and let out a small laugh because she couldn't imagine doing something so brazen, so dumb. But somewhere behind all that, there was a sort of admiration and love, a jealousy in knowing that Mickey had done something she could never do. She forwarded the thread around to her industry friends, who also opened up and read the tweet while carefully avoiding the "like" button.

When Mickey finally opened up Elaine's SOS text it was nearly eleven a.m. Grandma Anna had let her sleep in (likely out of pity) and when she had finally dug her phone out from the pile of clothes it was dead. Mickey went into the kitchen to pour herself a cup of coffee, and when she came back, the phone sprung back to life, vibrating almost nonstop.

Mickey lunged to the phone—thinking someone had died, that something horrible had happened—and felt her chest cave in when she opened her texts. Thirty minutes later, she was at least somewhat caught up on what had gone on. The offending Halloween video was on The Shade Room, and Mickey was getting texts from every angle—from random former interns to that random dude from her intro to sociology class. For the first time, Mickey felt her worlds colliding, the niche becoming global.

She needed to sit. She found the nearest chair and plopped herself down, opening her Twitter for the first time in weeks. That had been a mistake. Her notifications were flooded, an endless scroll of orbs, the faces unfamiliar. Her DMs numbered in the hundreds. Proof that someone had heard her. From the looks of it, many someones.

But what did she have to do with this? She'd never even worked with Teagan, much less been invited to that damn Halloween party.

"Mickey, you up?" Grandma Anna called, but Mickey didn't hear. Her mentions were populated with raised fist emojis. Grandma Anna called her again, but this time she pushed into the room.

"You don't hear me calling you?" she asked.

"I didn't," Mickey replied.

Homebodies

Grandma Anna put her hand on her hip. "Get yourself together and go outside and water this grass for me."

Mickey began to protest but Grandma Anna held up a hand. She didn't want to hear it. She spun on her heel and gave Mickey a little salute. "Thank you," she sang.

Mickey felt relieved to have a reason to put her phone down. She would deal with whatever this was later, pulling on a pair of pants she didn't mind messing up and slipping on her shoes at the door.

The sunshine and sticky humidity assaulted Mickey when she walked out of the front door, and she shielded her eyes as she grabbed the hose, stuffing her phone in her pocket. She hated to admit it, but the chores had begun to take on a meditative feel—it was something she could control, a simple-ish task with a clear endpoint. The hose grew in her hands, filling with water and then shooting forcefully from the spout. Mickey concentrated the stream on a particularly dry patch, willing it to grow. The grass tickled her bare feet, the droplets of water splashing back and cooling her toes. It was nearly noon, so the sun was already high in the sky, turning Mickey's bare shoulders an even deeper shade of brown.

She looked up at the cloudless sky, her eyes catching the massive trees that hung out just beyond her grandparents' property line, and she rubbed a hand across her eyes and kept it there, temporarily blinding herself. Her phone buzzed in her pocket, which she ignored, but then it rang again, more insistent this time. She looked at the caller ID before answering. Her phone had been ringing off the hook since the morning, random New York numbers calling every few minutes. Her unread texts (which numbered in the hundreds at this point) were a near-constant reminder that her real life had begun catching up with her, and eventually she would have to respond. She hadn't watched the video just yet, aware that once she dove in she wouldn't be able to stop doomscrolling. Lex had called, too, but she wasn't ready. Not after last night.

She wanted this last little bit of unknowing, this peace. For just a little while more. She didn't know what was happening, but she had a feeling that it would change everything, all over again.

When a photo of Elaine and Mickey illuminated her screen for the fourth time that morning, Mickey gave in and clicked Accept. She had ignored her long enough.

"Hey, what's up?" Mickey asked, laying the hose down and watching it trickle into the grass. She cupped her hand over the screen, attempting to get a better look at her friend. For the first time in a long while, Elaine was sitting still, leaning against rows of fluffy white pillows.

"Girl, where have you been?" Her thin brows were knitted together in alarm.

The ground started to pool with water and Mickey decided her brown spot had had enough to drink. She picked it up and moved to a greener spot. "What do you mean? I'm at my grandparents' in Maryland," Mickey said, feigning ignorance.

"I mean on social. Did you just stop posting? I haven't seen a story from you in weeks."

"Yeah, why, what's up?" Mickey asked. "Are you trying to get me to model again? I already told you I wasn't going to pose in that frumpy little exercise dress." She wanted to avoid all iterations of this conversation, particularly with Elaine, but she would play dumb as long as she could.

"First of all, the Regina is our best seller. It comes in so many colors, you just haven't found the right one."

Mickey rolled her eyes. "But no, you're blowing up on Instagram, Twitter, everything."

Mickey was drowning another patch of grass, but this time she didn't notice. She dropped the hose and settled into a nearby chair.

"Your letter," Elaine said. "It went viral."

A twist in her gut. "What?"

"I thought—"

"I'm trying to avoid it," Mickey said. "It's . . . a lot. When I left New York, it had only gotten like five likes. I don't know how this happened. There's so many DMs."

"I mean, me either," said Elaine. "One minute I was out to dinner with my new beau and the next I was seeing the video all over Twitter. Then I saw your letter and I called you a bunch of times."

"I was asleep."

"I figured. So you haven't seen Twitter?"

"Nope."

"Can you please look?" Elaine pulled her face together in an attempt at puppy dog eyes, but Mickey didn't need much convincing. She had been curious, of course. But all this energy around her work, around this *controversy*, troubled her. It was what she wanted but not how she wanted it. It was too much. Too many eyes, and she couldn't be sure they were the right ones.

"Whoa."

"Yeah."

She looked at the original tweet, which had likes and retweets in the thousands. It was hard to believe what she was seeing.

"This is," Mickey said, slowly, "a lot."

"A lot, a lot," Elaine affirmed.

"What have people been saying?"

"Um, not much really. People are still talking about Teagan and the video. That's been a really big deal. Have you seen it yet?"

"No."

"Ooh," Elaine said, wincing. "Major trigger warning."

"Why?" Mickey asked, though she knew the answer. There were only a few reasons white women got canceled for real. She knew "nigga" was the one thing they couldn't get around, almost certainly a kiss of death. The kind of privilege women like Teagan and Elaine had extended beyond housing loans and school acceptances and pay gaps. It was the ability to do a bit of coke on the weekends and talk about it on Monday morning without anyone looking too closely or batting an eye. It was the freedom to ask if medical marijuana is covered by FSA dollars while Jasmine's cousin caught a charge and a broken rib for smoking under the bleachers after school. It was different. But "nigga" was somewhat of an equalizer, the one thing polite white people couldn't quite wriggle around.

"She was singing a song and," Elaine lowered her voice at this, even though there was no one around, "she said the n-word."

She wanted to remind Elaine that she'd caught her mouthing it once at a concert but refrained.

"Wild," Mickey said, but she couldn't muster the sound of surprise.

She realized the hose had continued to run and a small pond was forming on her grandparents' front lawn. She ran to turn it off, the water sputtering and then disappearing altogether. "Sorry, so what happens next?" Mickey asked. "Has she come out with a notes app apology yet?"

Elaine nodded vigorously. "Very contrite." *Yeah right*, Mickey thought. "It ended with her resigning. I don't think any of us thought she'd actually leave. She's been at Bevy for ages."

Mickey wanted to ask Elaine what she believed to be a fitting punishment, how she believed it should have been handled, but she changed the course of the conversation instead.

"Are people talking about the letter?" She wondered how far-reaching her letter had actually been, if it had bled past the industry and into the mainstream.

"Not really? I mean, media people, for sure. But it's a little insider baseball. At least right now. It's only been a day, not even. Maybe soon. At this point, everyone keeps texting me asking if I know who 'Bevy's Basement' is."

"Why would they ask you?" Mickey asked, unsure about what Elaine had to do with any of this.

"Well," Elaine inhaled deep. "Some people think it's you."

Mickey wasn't prepared for that, the surprise registering on her face. Her mouth went slack and she tilted her head to one side, squinting her eyes. "Why me? I've been minding my business."

"Yeah. I think maybe you've been *too* quiet?"

"So now I'm not allowed to take some time?" There it was again, the pressure to perform.

"Hey," Elaine said, raising her hands to let Mickey know she wasn't the enemy. "I know it would literally never ever be you. I'm not saying that." Her voice dropped again. "But it's like, not you, right?" Elaine asked, her voice trembling. Mickey wondered if this had been why she had called after all. If everything was leading up to this question. She was offended now. Elaine wasn't checking in to see if Mickey was okay, or to apologize to her for brushing off her experience, she was just a missing piece in Elaine's mystery. *Fucking Nancy Drew ass bitch.*

Mickey sighed, her hands flexing and relaxing. She tried to keep the exasperation from her face, but she was sure the exhaustion shone through. "It's not me."

"Oh my god, yeah. That's exactly what I thought. Also, while I have you. I was telling my team all about what happened, and that your letter is blowing up and they wanted to get in early and see if you had any experience with D+I stuff. I know it's only been a day, but you know how these things go. With everyone coming out I don't think it's going to die down soon."

"Mmm," Mickey replied. "Nope." It was a strange question to ask, given that Elaine had met her at the very beginning of her career and witnessed every job since.

"I figured, but they're looking to throw money at someone who can pretty much audit our practices and let us know where we can improve. So, let me know if that's something that piques your interest, and I could put in a good word. I know they'd love to have your voice and perspective in the roo—"

"Oh! Elaine, I'm actually getting a call from my grandma," Mickey said, even though there was no one on the line. Grandma Anna was in her bedroom, taking her early-afternoon nap.

"Oh, okay, you'll let me know though, right?"

"Yeah, definitely, of course." Mickey hoped her voice sounded sunny and bright. "Goodbye."

She turned the hose back on and continued watering the grass, the new circumstances of her reality washing over her. So the calls hadn't been random. She looked through her voicemail box and clicked on the first one she saw from a 917 number. It was a journalist at *The Root*, looking for comment. She clicked on another. *Vice* wanted to know if she had anything to add to the current discourse, as did all the New York titles.

Mickey was overwhelmed by the sudden flood of attention. This had been what she wanted, right? The thing she was looking for when she released the letter into the world. She tried to imagine who could've seen her tweet and reposted it. She knew all five likers and clearly the group chat didn't give a shit. She was spiraling, and the more she thought about the vastness of the internet, all those people reading her words, the more she missed the obscurity. This was what she had asked for, but not like this.

She checked the time. It was a little after ten a.m. in LA. She navigated to Scottie's name and pressed it, waiting for her face to float into view. She got a view of a ceiling instead, and Scottie's deep, sleepy voice.

"What's up? Again, this better not be a voice memo–level issue. It's early as hell and I had a late night."

Mickey cocked an eyebrow. "What kind of late night?"

"The kind that could turn into a li'l morning moment if you hang up my phone."

Mickey clapped a hand over her mouth to stifle a giggle. "Where is he? Can he hear me right now?"

"He's in the bed, and I'm in the bathroom."

"Is he famous?"

"Mind your business."

"Say no more," Mickey said with a smile. "Virgo rising or *Billboard* bae?"

"*Billboard*," Scottie responded and Mickey could hear the laugh in her voice.

"Oh shit. I told you he'd be back."

"Yes, yes, now what's up? He won't be back for long if I don't keep this quick." A toilet flushed and then the faucet started to run. Scottie propped Mickey up on the edge of her sink and Mickey took her in. Scottie was the kind of beautiful that defied time of day. She brushed her teeth for a few seconds before eyeing Mickey expectantly.

"Check Twitter."

Scottie spit foamy white into the sink. "One second."

Scottie's mouth opened and her toothbrush fell from her mouth. "Oh shit, Mickey."

"I know."

"Hold up, I'm reading it now. But from what I'm seeing so far, I already know why you're calling because this is . . . this is a lot."

Mickey bowed her head. "I know."

"This conversation is now billable," Scottie said with a half smirk.

"Yeah, yeah. Add it to the tab."

When Scottie finished Mickey could swear there was a tear in her eyes. "Well, for starters, you can write your ass off. But you knew that."

"A little bit."

"I didn't know it was all this," Scottie said. "I knew it was rough but I didn't know—" Scottie cut herself off. "It's really good. And it's popping off. This is truly the best-case scenario PR-wise. I saw the video but I didn't realize it had anything to do with you. You didn't work with her, right?"

"Fuck no. Imagine her and Nina?"

"Are all these people toxic at your job?"

"Just because you work at an all-Black firm doesn't mean you don't know what it's like. Don't play."

Scottie laughed. "Wakanda forever."

"Bitch, stop," Mickey replied with a smile.

"But what are you going to do about all this?" Scottie asked. "You need to capitalize, and you needed to do so, like, last week."

"It's only been a day."

"Yeah, you're like two hours too late."

"Wait, what do you mean capitalize?" Mickey asked. "You want me to, what? Be the face of the slighted Black girl in the workplace?"

"It's either that or, once they move on from this, hope they don't remember that you tried to publicly drag your last company a few months after they laid you off."

Mickey scrunched up her face and turned off the hose. She settled down into one of the patio chairs and pulled her shirt up, exposing her belly to the sun. "Okay, well, what do you suggest?"

"Before we go any further, I need to inform you of my fee . . ." Scottie began and Mickey laughed.

"Yeah, I pro-rated it in beauty products."

"Speaking of, do you still have that jelly moisturizer that comes in the blue bottle? My skin loves that stuff."

"I can check when I get home."

"When are you doing that?"

Mickey shrugged. "I don't know."

"Well, let me poke around and see what the landscape is looking like, who's saying what. Has anyone reached out?"

"Kind of?" Mickey said. She navigated to her email, that was flooded, too. There was an email from Cathy in HR but Mickey decided she couldn't deal with that now. Whether it was condemning her for starting a sort of digital riot or asking her to say more about what she'd experienced, it didn't matter. It was all the same level of stress. There were media requests from just about every outlet and a few inquiries from agents who wanted to know if she had any plans to write a longer, more significant work. She relayed all this to Scottie, who nodded sagely.

"Yeah, we have to move fast. The news cycle is unpredictable so who knows what could knock this out of the spotlight. At any moment there could be a celebrity pregnancy." She shook her head. "We should've been setting up all this stuff the moment that page retweeted your letter."

Mickey's heart swelled briefly before anxiety settled in its place. A few hours ago, she was fine resting in sleepy obscurity, and now she was suddenly fearful that she might miss out on her moment. Mickey knew enough from her few years of media to understand that her window of opportunity was small and rapidly closing.

It dawned on her what was happening: she'd called them all out, and now, in an attempt to look like the industry was shifting, getting better, instead of dragging her out kicking and screaming like Tangela, they would hire her. Mickey's stomach turned. It was predictable. Once again, she felt used.

"What if I don't want to do all this press and media shit? What if I just want to move on? *Wave* was a dark ass time for me and I'm just starting to feel like maybe I could be okay. Why bring all this back up?"

"Who am I talking to and what have you done with my best friend? Why the hell else would you have posted it on the internet for everyone to see? Clearly you wanted to get noticed. They're going to make you the token either way. Why not control it? Capitalize on it? If we play our cards right, you'll be able to do whatever you want."

"I mean, that was three weeks ago—I had just been fired and I was not in a great place, and right now . . ." The sun hung directly on top of Mickey's head. She shielded her face with a hand and thought of Tee, the way ice cream gathered at the corner of her lips and the way she huffed when she was annoyed. "All I want to do is disappear."

"All right, drama queen. Give me your email login and go disappear. You have twelve hours, and then I'm on that ass."

"Is this how you treat your clients?" Mickey asked.

"Oh no baby, when they pay me I'm very nice," Scottie said with a laugh. "But this is definitely how I treat my about-to-be-famous best friend."

Ever the dramatist, Scottie hung up the phone with a flourish, and then it was just Mickey, unsure of what lay on the other side.

TWENTY-TWO

When Mickey pulled up to Tee's house, she was already standing outside waiting, hands on her hips, her mouth stretched into a smile. For a moment, just a brief one, it felt like coming home, pulling into the driveway to greet her girlfriend rather than one of her oldest friends. Mickey knew she should be, like Scottie said, "focusing on the letter and next steps," so she tried to still the beating of her heart, which was thrumming beneath her thin linen shirt with the kind of insistency that suggested love. So much time had passed since she'd felt Tee pressed close, and yet seeing Tee still sent shivers up her skin. They had been playing at platonic, but there was still something charged between them. A hum of electricity like the kicking in of a backup generator.

Mickey hoped she looked better than she felt. Her hair was pulled back into a low bun, her braids twisted around each other to form a tight, neat chignon. She even wore her favorite shorts, a pair of vintage men's Levi's that she cut right at the middle of the thigh. They were the powdery blue of a dusky summer sky and the ends had frayed naturally, giving them a worn-in look.

She told Tee she needed to talk, and Tee had immediately texted back.

"Come by," it read. It wasn't long before Mickey was in the car.

Mickey still wasn't used to this level of communication from Tee, who had conditioned Mickey to her unavailability. It was her inability to attain and possess Tee that kept her hooked, but now it felt like she could reach out and touch her whenever she liked. She turned off the ignition and peered up at her father's house. She hadn't seen him since dinner at her grandmother's, despite promising she'd drop by for dinner with the four of them. She wondered if now might be the right time, now that she had something to show him other than all the ways she'd failed. She could explain it from the beginning, make it seem like it was all planned out from the start.

But she didn't even know if she wanted this. To throw herself back into the fold and criticize the industry that had raised her, hoping that it would deliver her right side up, her ultimate ask that they bring her back with less hours and more pay. But then again, she had been fired, so who was she to ask for more? Who was she to demand change?

She stepped out of the car and Tee pulled her into a side hug. "You good?"

"Yeah," Mickey replied. "Just a lot going on."

Mickey's phone vibrated in her palm. The group chat hadn't sprung back to life, but people started reaching out individually, praising her for her bravery. It was such bullshit. They had seen it in the beginning and said nothing, Mickey knew that much. Lex had called her twice again since she'd gotten in the car, probably to say "I told you so," and that she especially didn't want to hear. That would make things too real, the final piece of her fantasy falling away. She wanted to hold on to this as long as she could.

"You hungry?" Tee asked, looking down at Mickey, her eyes brimming with concern.

She wasn't used to Tee looking at her like that, her eyes soft and searching. It was unnerving. Mickey resisted the urge to cover herself, worried she was seeing more than she was meant to.

She needed to pivot. To make things light. "You paying?" Mickey asked, her glossed lips spreading into a smile.

"I got you."

They decided to go into the city, the two tucked into a table at a restaurant off U Street that also doubled as a bookstore. It was the kind of place that felt unique until you remembered there were four other locations, along with a fifth in the middle of Maryland that everyone always forgot about. But Mickey was grateful to see that it was still standing, since so many other long-standing cultural institutions, like their once-frequented Pizza Hut, was not. Since she'd left, U Street had been made over in a different image. The DTLR where she and Scottie had once witnessed two mothers fighting over a single pair of galaxy Foamposites had become a gourmet burger spot and then a boutique fitness studio. She said so to Tee while they waited for their table to open up. Mickey was grateful, then, to have someone who had witnessed and remembered what came before, knowing eventually that everyone, including them, would forget. Or at the very least stop talking about it, the sadness of displacement washed down with handcrafted cocktails and grass-fed sliders on bread so buttery it would glide past the lump in your throat.

"I'm waiting on you to tell me wassup," Tee said, spearing a piece of blackened salmon with her fork. The restaurant was buzzing with activity. Twenty-somethings in earth tones and muted, vaguely diasporic patterns peppered the restaurant, trading conversation over chili-flavored shrimp, crispy brussels sprouts, and fried chicken on brioche buns. The waiters seemed to be spinning between tables, flitting from one place to another with ease.

"Remember the letter?" Mickey asked. It occurred to her that they were on what looked to be a proper date, and now, after everything that had transpired, Mickey felt self-conscious of how things might appear. She wasn't famous, especially outside the insular world of media, but what if someone saw? What if one of these people were among the thousands of profiles that had liked her tweet?

"Yeah. What about it?" Tee asked.

"It kind of went viral."

"For real? I been off Twitter. Just too much bullshit."

Mickey wanted to press, but she waved it away. "It's kind of a lot to explain, but this white lady got in trouble for singing the n-word at a Halloween party—"

"Oh shit, I saw that on The Shade Room," Tee said. "You send that in? You know her?"

"It wasn't me. But yeah, we used to work at the same company. Long story short, the person who exposed her also exposed all this other shit about the company and all the ways it had treated Black employees. Everyone was anonymous, but then she also retweeted my letter and then *that* blew up. So now all these people want to interview me about being Black at work and I don't know, I'm just a little overwhelmed."

Tee stared back at her, eyes lit up as if Mickey had done something impressive and worthwhile. "What did I say?" Tee said.

Mickey smiled. "I don't think it's that deep."

"Why not?" Tee asked. "It's a big deal."

"You think so?" Mickey replied, but coming out of Tee's mouth, she believed it.

"For sure," Tee replied. "We have to celebrate." She motioned for the waiter and moments later she appeared.

"What can I do for y'all?" she asked.

"A round of shots," said Tee. "For the superstar."

Mickey knew she was in trouble the moment she stumbled down to Tee's basement, her legs wobbly as she made her way down the stairs. One shot had turned into three, and now here they were—Mickey, a lightweight, too drunk to drive herself home, had let Tee take the wheel. She wasn't too drunk, however, to forget the danger of being this close to Tee. The alcohol stripped her inhibitions away, and the questions that once felt forbidden now threatened to spill from her lips.

"It's so weird being down here again," Mickey said, attempting to balance on the arm of the couch but toppling over.

"Is it?" Tee replied, peeling off her top shirt to reveal a ribbed tank underneath, rooting around for the remote. She flopped onto the couch, spreading her body wide. One arm leaned back against the couch, nearly touching Mickey, who curled up on the end.

"Yeah. I spent so much time here and then one day," she made a little gesture with her hands, "poof. No more."

Tee laughed. "You're drunk." She turned on a movie they'd seen many times.

"Maybe a little, but I mean it. It was so sad, me and you."

Tee glanced in Mickey's direction, her expression unreadable. Even sober Mickey wouldn't have known what to do with that look. She attempted to readjust herself on the couch but ended up clumsily falling onto Tee. She reached out for Tee's forearm to settle herself and ended up touching her thigh. Tee stared at her hand and then Mickey apologized.

"You're good," Tee said, chuckling, her eyes lingering on her face too long. "It don't bother me." She bit her lip and Mickey pulled her hand back like she'd been burned. She blushed deep and tilted her head to one side.

"So, what now?" Mickey asked, her hand warm. The sizzling was part of the air now. Tee's eyes danced in the dim light of the basement, still staring. Mickey wondered what she looked like, how her reflection appeared in those eyes. She leaned closer to find out. Tee didn't back up, but she did look away, smiling into her lap. Mickey's chin hovered over Tee's shoulder and Mickey wondered when she'd gotten so shy.

"Can I ask you something?" Mickey asked, her speech a little slurred.

"Sure."

"This is going to sound dumb," Mickey warned. "But do you remember when we played seven minutes in heaven?"

"Sort of," Tee said.

"Did you tell people that you had only hooked up with me because you wanted to mess with a big girl?"

"Mickey, what?"

"I'm serious."

"When was that? Ten years ago? I was probably talking shit trying to show off. I said a lot of stuff back then."

"But I need to know if you said it about me."

"Why does it matter so much?"

Mickey frowned a little. "Because I liked you. And I thought you liked me, too. That whole thing really fucked me up." She eyed Tee. "Seriously. It made me feel like everything that we had was a game. It never felt real."

Mickey hadn't known she could say that to anyone, much less Tee. She'd never allowed herself to really approach the emotions that came with loving Tee, who had, behind her back, made their relationship seem like a fluke.

But when Tee had come back, eyes shining and sincere, Mickey believed that Tee had changed her mind. That finally, she was worthy of the attention.

"It was real," Tee said, staring in her lap. "It was very real for me."

"So why then?" Mickey asked. "Why all the back and forth? How come it was never—" Mickey stopped herself there. She couldn't go back there. Wouldn't try to make something nonsensical logical. She'd run through the scenarios a dozen times in her head, trying to understand why Tee wanted her, but not enough to claim her. Why Mickey always went back, over and over and over again.

Why have I settled for people and places who haven't chosen me? The thought sent a shockwave through Mickey's body and she couldn't tell if it was the alcohol or the suddenness of everything clicking into place, but she began to cry.

Tee scooted closer. She reached to grab Mickey's hand and stopped herself. "I don't know why. You just got too close. I didn't know exactly what I wanted, just that I needed to get in school and play." Tee sighed, and the words hung in the air. Then she laughed, a small sound. "And I liked that I could have you and still have everybody else."

Mickey sniffled. She wanted to be frustrated, to push Tee away and storm out. But there was a hollowness instead. Tee had simply confirmed the worst of her fears, that she hadn't been enough on her own. "That's fucked up."

Tee caught an errant tear sliding down Mickey's cheek, brushing it away with her thumb. Mickey's whole body went warm and she tried not to lean into Tee's palm. "I know. But if I could do it different, I would've. Especially if I knew it was going to make you feel like this."

Tee was closer than she needed to be. So close that Mickey could almost brush her without extending her hand. The lingering scent of smoke mixed with a musky, woodsy scent.

She's wearing cologne, Mickey thought, *for me,* and a tiny wave of panic washed over her, which was quickly calmed by the liquor and the part of her brain that cared about nothing, the part that only wanted Tee in between her legs.

"I was dumb then, Key. I didn't know what I had in front of me. I know you've been in your situation for a really long time, and I'm not trying to change it or blow up your life, but if I had you now," Tee dropped her head and her tone, her eyes meeting Mickey's, "I would show you different."

The air went still in the room and Mickey realized she had stopped breathing. How much stranger could her life get?

"You want to smoke?" Mickey asked, cutting through the silence. Mickey could almost feel it now, the textured edges of their desire. For the first time, Mickey didn't wonder if it was mutual. After loving Lex, she could tell. She saw the longing in Tee's eyes, the way she took in all of Mickey when they spoke. As if on cue, Tee backed up and slid to one side of the couch.

"Yeah, okay," she replied.

It wasn't long before Tee produced a small, sealed jar of weed and a tray to roll up. She dumped out a small nugget and started to break it down, pulling apart the sticky flower with her fingers. Mickey watched the way her hands moved, practiced. It was elegant almost, the way she scraped the Backwood clean and sprinkled in the weed. The way her tongue swept across the tobacco leaf, pink meeting brown in one swift lick. She pressed it closed, twisted it between her fingers, and ran a lighter across its entirety. Then she lit the tip and sucked deep, the end glowing orange in the dim. Tee took another hit and passed it to Mickey, who held it suspended in front of her lips. "Your mom lets you smoke down here?"

Tee shrugged. "She don't really say nothing, but I don't hide it."

Satisfied they wouldn't incur Miss Lanita's wrath, Mickey inhaled, the smoke pressing sharply against the back of her throat. Every time she smoked, she forgot she wasn't very good at it until she was here, fighting her body to avoid coughing up a lung. She only wheezed a little, and Tee laughed before lightly patting her on the back, her hand drawing small circles before settling in her own lap. She was close again and Mickey was running out of reasons to pull away.

"You good?" she asked.

Mickey nodded before handing the blunt off. "So, when did you even start smoking?"

Tee took a hit. "Not too long after I got hurt, to help with the pain."

Mickey wanted to remind Tee that she'd once left a party because people were smoking inside, terrified of what the secondhand smoke might do to her healthy lungs, but she didn't want the specifics of how and why she'd traded her dreams for this basement, terrified she might find her own road map within the answer.

"Makes sense," she said instead. Tee didn't reply, taking another hit and staring blankly at the television. They sat in silence for a little while more.

"Why wasn't it different before?" Mickey asked, picking up the conversation as if it had never been interrupted. Tee regarded her carefully before passing her the blunt. Mickey took it from her fingers, the tobacco leaf warm, and inhaled.

Tee shrugged. "I was young. Just chasing whoever seemed like the best look."

It was as if Tee stabbed her in the center, and now her gooey insides were seeping out. "And I wasn't a good look."

"It's not like that," Tee insisted. "I didn't mean."

"Yeah, you did," Mickey said, her tone final. She handed Tee the blunt. "And that's fine, but it's almost like we were never anything at all. Like I never meant anything to you." Her voice dropped, the last part coming out like a hiss. She could feel the emotion gathering in the back of her throat, but she didn't want to cry. Not now, not here.

"You meant a lot to me Mickey. I just didn't know. I still don't know what to say."

"Did you ever, you know?" Mickey said, knowing her next question might shatter any illusion she had of what they'd been. "Love me?" The answer terrified her, but she couldn't look away. Not until she knew.

"I've always loved you. Not always like you loved me. But, it was there."

And there it was. Mickey felt a whisper of elation, but more than anything, she was reminded of the pain that came from lopsided love. Loving Tee had felt desperate and clawing, like she couldn't come up for air unless she was by her side. For Tee, it had been something else entirely, something easier to manage.

"I'm glad you're here," Tee said next and Mickey didn't know what to do with that information, not with the word *love* knocking around her brain. It had sounded sensual in Tee's mouth, full and smooth. She loved her?

Mickey rolled her eyes. "Don't get used to it."

"I could though." Oh, she loved her.

"Whatever."

"I'm serious."

"You're not," Mickey said, testing her. "Knowing you, you're messing with some IG model-looking girl, and this is just a case of high confessions."

Tee opened her mouth and closed it again. The fact that she didn't protest signaled that there had been some truth in all that. Maybe Jasmine had been right, but Mickey couldn't be totally sure. She would always wonder what she'd wanted to say, what truth she'd tucked away and hidden inside. Tee stretched the blunt toward her. "You good?"

Mickey thought about it for a moment. "I'm too high to take another hit but I could do a baby one."

"Like a shotgun?"

If you want to get close to my face Tiana, just say so, is what Mickey wanted to say. But instead, she said, "Yeah I guess."

Tee laughed softly and looked Mickey in the eye. "You sure?" she asked.

It wasn't a question. Mickey tilted her chin up toward her.

"Come here," Tee said. Then she took a shallow sip of the blunt and held the smoke in her mouth. Mickey leaned in so close that their lips just grazed each other, and Tee exhaled with perfect aim. Mickey pulled back and opened her eyes, shocked when the smoke came from her own mouth in a neat little stream.

"Oh wow, it actually worked," she said, but she only got the first bit out before Tee's mouth was on hers, swallowing the rest of the sentence up and her lips along with it. The kiss was quick but insistent, and Mickey moved against her, threading her fingers through her locs, which hung loose and long, and pulled her close.

Tee made a sound of wanting and Mickey felt her body go rigid. The sound confirmed that this was actually happening, that they'd finally crossed that line.

"Fuck," Mickey said, her voice high and tight with surprise.

"Fuck," Tee replied. "Can I?"

The way she was looking made Mickey's body tingle, those warm brown eyes staring out from beneath her thick, dark lashes, lips parted with just a hint of teeth. Mickey wanted to taste her again, to part her mouth with her tongue and then her thighs. Tee reached out for Mickey and she came willingly, pressing her cheek into her hand.

Tee kissed her softly on the mouth and then the neck, and shoulder, her lips just barely grazing Mickey's skin. Something electric ran down Mickey's spine and twisted around her thighs. She lay back on the couch, hair fanning out like a crown, and waited for Tee to approach. It was almost cat-like, the way Tee hovered over her, parting Mickey's legs with her knees and placing herself between them. Her hands settled on Mickey's waist and she tugged her close, her hips meeting the curve of Mickey's ass with a soft thump. Legs wrapped, Mickey crossed her ankles and held on. Tee held her waist and pulled her into her lap. For a second, the world started to spin and Mickey remembered how much alcohol was sloshing around in her body. She winced—another sudden movement and it might all come up, but she couldn't stop herself now. She placed her hands on Tee's shoulders to steady herself and ground her hips into Tee's, making up the rhythm as she went along.

Tee groaned and attached herself to Mickey's neck, kissing and licking before moving on to her chest. She pulled Mickey's shirt up and her bra down, freeing her heavy breasts with a quick move. Then her nipples were in Tee's mouth and Mickey was crying out—half in pleasure, half in fear.

Tee sucked them slowly, alternating between the two, her free hand circling and teasing whichever one wasn't in her mouth. Like she was trying to remember the feel of Mickey's skin, like she hadn't been the first to do it this way. Like she hadn't taught Mickey how she liked it. Like she hadn't ruined her for everyone else. Mickey continued to buck and grind and pull at Tee's hair until Tee was moaning, too.

"I missed you," Tee said when she finally came up for air.

"Me too," Mickey said, and even though it was true it felt like a lie. She had missed Tee in the way that one misses something they once loved, something they'd forgotten about and healed from. But it didn't matter then. She would say anything if it meant getting Tee inside her. Tee wound Mickey's long braids around her wrist and pulled, stretching

Mickey's neck toward the sky. Her scalp was bright with the tension, and she moaned louder than she meant to.

Mickey lifted her hips to press herself closer, her breasts smothering Tee's face. She wondered, briefly, if it was a cruel way to die. Tee didn't seem to mind, moaning while she gripped Mickey's thighs, their hips meeting. Tee grabbed at the waistband of Mickey's sweatpants and tugged them down, pulling her underwear to the side. The cold air licked at Mickey's skin, cooling her, if only slightly.

"You sure?" Tee asked, her fingers hovering. Teasingly, Tee ran those fingers up and down, wetness coating her index and middle. Lightning shot up Mickey's legs and spine. "She seems sure," Tee said, plunging her fingers into Mickey's mouth. Mickey tasted herself on Tee's fingers, licking them clean. Tee's eyes got darker with want and she pulled Mickey close, pressing their mouths together hungrily, like she'd been waiting to do this for a long time.

"You taste so fucking good," Tee said into the cavern of Mickey's mouth, her voice syrupy and deep.

Mickey shuddered in her lap, her thighs gripping Tee's waist tighter. All she wanted—needed—was for Tee to be back inside. Tee resumed her teasing, her fingers hovering, pressing at Mickey's entrance, wetting her fingers again.

With the right angle, Mickey could plunge her inside. Mickey groaned and wound her hips, but Tee was quicker, Mickey landing, wet, in her lap instead. As always, it was a game. Mickey lifted herself from Tee's lap and pulled her on top of her, yanking at the hem of her shirt. Tee obliged, pulling it off slowly and smoothly, so smooth Mickey found herself wanting to ask how long she'd been practicing that move. But she was pinned beneath Tee before she could think on it too long, their mouths moving together. It was both desperate and painfully slow, Mickey wishing Tee would get it over with, filling her up with her fingers and her strap and her tongue.

Mickey pulled at the sports bra, but Tee stopped her, guiding her hand toward her pants. She used both hands to peel off Tee's basketball shorts, sliding them off her waist and down her thick thighs until they were a puddle at their feet. Mickey toed off her pants, the gray and blue stacked on top of each other in a revealing heap.

"Tell me what you want," Tee commanded, her arms on either side of Mickey's head. The weight of Tee's body pressed her deeper into the couch, crushing and warm.

"You," Mickey said plainly.

"And how do you want me?" Tee asked. "Inside? With my fingers or my tongue?"

The thrill of the question only made Mickey want her more. She wasn't used to talking this much during sex. She had a routine. There was nothing planned about her spreading her legs for a not-quite-ex who named her for exactly what she was.

She realized she was drifting when Tee tugged on a nipple with her teeth, pulling her firmly back into the present. "You all right?" she asked, sitting up a little and tilting her head to one side. Mickey nodded and took a moment to drink Tee in—her dark skin, the dip of her waist, the tone of her shoulder. Everything shimmered. She'd always been so beautiful. Mickey reached up and brought Tee back to her mouth.

"Everything," she said in between kisses. "Just you, I want you."

The emotion in her throat surprised her. She hadn't expected to voice her desire so clearly, to say the unthinkable out loud. She wanted Tee, she wanted this.

Tee hissed in desire. "Don't tell me that."

Mickey pulled Tee's face to her and kissed her chin, then her jaw, and neck. She made her way back to her lips. When they pulled away, Tee brushed Mickey's bottom lip with her thumb and her eyes shone with an emotion Mickey hadn't seen before. Tee's hands, delicate and strong, pulled Mickey's body closer with practiced ease. Finally, she plunged her fingers inside Mickey and she inhaled sharply, like it was the first time.

"Tiana, fuck."

"Say it again." Tee plunged deeper, hooking her fingers inside and pulling Mickey closer. Her free hand held her steady, ensuring Mickey didn't run.

Mickey repeated herself and Tee sped up, thrusting until Mickey tightened around her fingers, pulling her deeper with every pulse. Mickey's body vibrated with pleasure and she collapsed backward onto the couch, panting and sighing and blissful. Tee removed her fingers and Mickey felt like she'd lost a part of her, wishing it would return.

But she didn't stop. Tee swapped her fingers for her tongue and lapped everything up. Mickey was delirious, feeling the wetness of Tee's mouth and knowing that it was covered with her, that it would get all over her chin and nose. Their eyes locked and suddenly, Mickey felt shy. She wriggled her hips from Tee in an attempt to get free but was swiftly corrected, Tee holding her firmly in place.

"Don't run," she instructed. "Not from me."

Mickey nodded and lay still. Slid closer. Tee licked and sucked until Mickey was shuddering again and begging her not to stop. The third time she came, on top that time, she remembered why she'd crawled back to worship at Tee's altar every time. When it was Mickey's turn, she was clumsy, fumbling with Tee's black Calvin Klein briefs, her hands shaking as she slid them down. She dropped to her knees and pulled Tee's hips toward her face. Tee let out a noise of surprise.

"Oh shit," she whispered, and Mickey looked up to flash her a brilliant smile. She was less drunk now but no less determined. She kissed at Tee's inner thighs first, dragging her mouth against her warm fragrant skin before opening her legs and pressing her tongue at its center. Tee let out a whimper and a sigh of ecstasy, and Mickey felt charged up from the power of having her this open, this vulnerable. She flicked and swirled her tongue, listening, waiting for those sighs. Tee's hands found their way to Mickey's head and pressed gently, then more insistently, Mickey quickening her pace to bring her closer to the brink. Before long she was shaking and twisting, but Mickey held her legs still, pressing her tongue deeper, speeding up the wiggle of her tongue. Tee bucked and cried out her name.

Mickey's mouth was too full to reply.

TWENTY-THREE

Mickey woke up to the sound of her phone buzzing, vibrating and alive somewhere across the room. The room was dimly lit, a single salt lamp softly illuminating the room with a tinge of pink. It was too dark to see anything but outlines. She looked over to see Tee, back bare, head splayed across the pillow. It took a second to register what had happened. What they'd done. She peered down at her own nakedness and tried to think where her clothes were. Mickey sat up silently, peeling the thin sheet from her body. First, she needed to find her phone.

It was hidden beneath a heap of clothes and a harness, still fully assembled. By the time she'd grabbed it, it had finally stopped vibrating and Mickey was able to see her missed call. It was Scottie, who had called three times already. Mickey went on a scavenger hunt for her clothing, which was scattered all around the room. By the time she found her way to the basement's living room she was wearing her shirt with nothing underneath. Her bra was missing, and her underwear, too. She sat on the couch, bare-assed, and called Scottie back.

"Hi, what's up?" Mickey tried to turn the volume down so she wouldn't wake Tee.

"Where the hell have you been? I called you three times."

Mickey made a show of yawning. "I was asleep."

"Where are you? Why aren't you FaceTiming me?" She looked down at her phone. Scottie was initiating a video call. She knew ignoring it would only lead to more questions. She clicked the green answer button and Scottie's face popped into view. "That doesn't look like Grandma's house," she said, tilting her head at the sight of Mickey's face.

"I went out," Mickey said, hoping Scottie would leave it but knowing she would not.

"Out where? With who?"

Mickey hid her face in her hands.

"Oh Jesus. What? Were you with Tee?"

Mickey nodded and Scottie rolled her eyes.

"Mickey, come on. Why would you do that?" Her voice peeled into a sound that verged on a whine.

"I know, I know." Mickey slipped out the basement door and stood on the little brick patio outside. It was empty aside from a single chair and table with an ashtray. She had stumbled upon Tee's smoking spot, and despite everything, Mickey felt a rush at uncovering another private part of Tee. Mickey smoothed a hand over her hair and sat down.

"I'm not supposed to be worrying about you, you're supposed to be worrying about me. I'm the one who's out here living single and—" Mickey watched the recognition flicker across Scottie's face. "Did y'all?"

Mickey covered her face with a hand.

"Mickey! You can't just do shit because you're caught up in the moment. This is your *life*."

"I'm aware, Scottie."

"Are you? Because this is some reckless shit. What about Lex?"

"We're taking a break."

"And when were you going to tell me this?"

"I wasn't," Mickey admitted. "I thought I would come here, go back home, and things would be back to normal. That me and Lex would just work on our shit and be fine. I didn't think any of this would happen."

"Are you going to tell her?"

"I don't know. I sort of feel like I have to."

Scottie cut in. "You do. You absolutely do. But should you? That's the better question."

"Explain."

"You went through this whole Twitter thing, lost your mind, and hooked up with an ex on a drunken night. You could claim temporary insanity. Some things you need to keep close to the chest, especially if you think y'all will get back together." Mickey hadn't thought that far ahead yet. She could still feel the ache between her legs. Her and Tee had been wrapped up in each other the entire night. "Does anyone else know?" Scottie asked.

"Just you." *And I wasn't even going to do that*, she thought.

"Good."

"You called me three times though, what's up?"

"Oh right. Before you distracted me with that piece of news," her eyes narrowed, "I got you booked for *The Early Show*."

Mickey nearly fainted from the shock. "You did what?"

"A thank you would suffice."

"I mean, thank you? But also, what am I even going to go on there and say?"

"They want to do a segment about mental health and being Black in the workplace. I pitched you to talk about the letter and being an advocate for mental health and they went for it."

"But didn't I say I wasn't sure?" Mickey closed her eyes. "I don't know where I want to take all this."

"Didn't I say I was giving you twelve hours? This is going to be good, just trust."

"Fine, fine." Mickey felt the beginnings of excitement. *The Early Show* was huge. Everyone, including her father, tuned in. Then her stomach turned—her father, she would need to warn him. "When do they need me?"

"Two days. In studio. They tape in the city."

Mickey's eyes widened. "*Two days?* That's soon."

"I mean clearly you need something to peel you away from whatever mess you've gotten yourself into down there. Now *this* is worth a three-way phone call."

Mickey panicked. "No! Please. We don't have to talk to Jasmine about this—she'll kill me. And I didn't even want to tell you," Mickey said. Scottie stuck her tongue out in protest and Mickey laughed.

"I'll be there. Two days."

"Call time is six a.m. I'll loop you in on the emails."

"How am I going to do this by myself?" Mickey asked, her voice verging on a whine.

"You won't," Scottie explained. "I'll be in New York tomorrow."

"I want to be excited, but I'm pissed."

"You won't be pissed when you're giving a TED Talk in a year and publishing a book in two."

"You really think I could do all that?" Mickey asked.

"Oh yeah," Scottie assured. "And that's if you don't cooperate. If you're on board, girl, we'll take over the whole world."

When Mickey walked through the door to her grandparents' house, deep purple hickeys on her neck and her hair shooting every which way, she wasn't expecting to find Grandma Anna still puttering around in her slippers, getting ready for church. Upon seeing her granddaughter, her eyes lit up. Mickey stepped back and eyed her carefully, her joy suspicious.

"What?" Mickey asked.

"I'm just so excited my granddaughter is going to accompany me to church."

"Grandma, no," Mickey whined, though she knew it was no use. Grandma Anna hushed her with a raised hand.

"I don't want to hear it. You come up in my house at nine in the morning you're going to church. And hurry up. I don't want to miss praise and worship."

Mickey had packed a skirt, just in case. It gripped her in all the wrong places and skated just past her knees, but it would do, and she threw on a high-neck shirt despite the heat. She hadn't expected to ever wear these clothes, had spent the past two Sundays listening to her grandmother's morning routine as she got ready for church while she lay still in bed, feigning sleep. Her slippered feet shuffling across the hardwood, the brewing of coffee, the hiss and puff of the iron, and finally, the double-click of the door shutting behind her. But today, she wasn't given a choice.

"You look like you need Him" was all her grandmother said. And then she smiled.

Homebodies

* * *

Mickey leaned her head against the honey wood of the pew, her head pulsing and contracting every few seconds. She couldn't drink like she used to, and her body reminded her of it. She attempted to close her eyes, but the church's din was deafening, dialed up to level 10. They were finally on to the morning announcements, after what seemed like hours of speaking before the service was ready to start.

When they first walked into the church, her grandmother had toted her around like a prize, reminding everyone that she was her granddaughter, *yes* the writer one, *yes* the one from New York, who came all the way home just to visit with her. They all smiled and brushed Mickey's arms with their soft, wrinkly hands, smiling and kissing her on the cheeks. She wondered if her grandmother's friends watched *The Early Show*, if they would have a different opinion on her next week.

Now slumped in the pews, her skirt digging into her waist, Mickey was surprised by how many people she recognized. How tall the drummer she once had a crush on had grown, the one who, during a fateful week at vacation Bible school, Mickey was convinced she had fallen in love with. Her grandmother still teased her about that.

Mickey felt a little slap on the side of her hip and sat up straight.

"You are not a child," her grandmother said, and Mickey realized that in here, she still felt like one.

Now everyone was bowing their heads in prayer and Mickey hung her head and shut her eyes. She tried to listen to the words, make them play in the right order in her mind, but instead she was thinking about Tee, and the way she'd felt on the inside. Her stomach flipped at the blasphemy, of sexual-fantasy-turned-feeling in church, then she thought of Lex and felt even sicker. Mickey must have fake-prayed too long because her grandmother's finger poked at her side. When her eyes opened, the choir was fixing to sing, shaking off the morning like pigeons puffing up their chests. Their robes, white with red sashes around their necks, swayed side to side when they stood. And then they opened their mouths.

Cornerstone Baptist's choir was decent but loud. Together, they shook the church and moved people to tears. But only one soloist could really sing. She had the kind of voice that made your lip quiver and face shrink up in awe. Mickey had known Joyce as a kid. Mickey did the math—she had to be at least thirty-six now, but she looked the same as when Mickey had left. Everyone seemed to be frozen in amber, aging slowly but consistently, maybe that's what happened when you did the same thing day after day, year after year. Every once in a while a blessing or a tragedy would change them, but it was mostly: Sundays spent singing the same hymns, asking to be made whole, clean, and good, week after week.

Joyce launched into the beginning notes of "Blessed Assurance," and by the time she got to the words *glory divine,* Mickey felt the tears in the back of her throat. She wanted to cry for a lot of reasons, chief among them her inability to see what would happen next. Loss of control was scary. This was even scarier, because she had taken control, done the risky thing, allowed herself to feel, and now things felt even messier than before. Despite the attention her letter received, Mickey's career still felt flimsy. Things with Lex were likely beyond repair, and all she felt was numb.

Then there was Tee, who, despite Mickey's best efforts, was finding her way into her heart again. Opening her up. She remembered the night before. The way she'd begged for more, telling Tee she loved her. Tee asking her to stay. And then there was the letter, and leaving. Mickey cried harder. *What was wrong with her?*

Her grandmother discreetly slid her a Kleenex and rubbed her back.

"You could've at least waited until the pastor started preaching," she whispered, before letting out a girlish giggle so low only Mickey could hear. Mickey laughed, too, her body shaking silently as the full choir joined in.

Her hand itched for her phone. She wanted to see if anything new had happened in the half hour since she'd last checked. Scottie had handled the media but there were still the people DMing her about how her bravery had inspired them, how proud they were of her for speaking out. Mickey hadn't responded. She wasn't sure what she could say.

For her sanity, and to spare herself the lecture of being distracted during the Lord's time, Mickey had left her phone in the car. She brushed away the urge to run to the parking lot to retrieve it, but she faced front and let the warm sound encase her, winding its way into her spirit and fluttering in her chest. She loved the singing, the de facto sound of worship.

The choir launched into an up-tempo song, their hands clapping and feet stomping in time. Mickey's foot tapped reflexively and she hummed along even though she barely knew the words. She could feel the energy rising in the place, and with it, the congregation coming alive. A little piece of Mickey gave way and she let the words wash over her. It was hard to keep it at bay. She checked the program. They were a few lines away from the sermon, and hours away from the end.

The next hour was a blur of sound and movement. The choir got carried away more than once and the pastor, a short man with a big smile and crisp suit, did, too. One woman started speaking in tongues, her head arched toward the rafters, mouth wide. At that, Grandma Anna nudged Mickey and said, "I wish Dorinda would just cut it out. She can't be feeling the holy ghost every time."

Mickey smiled and her mind drifted. One minute she'd be thinking about Tee and the next what awaited her back in New York. Then she'd think about Lex, and that's when the crying would begin. They'd built a life but it had crumbled under the weight of her sadness and inability to show up. And now Mickey had let someone else have her, had yearned, and begged, and pleaded. She felt dirty, and hoped that being here would make her over, make her clean again.

Then she thought of the upcoming TV spot in less than forty-eight hours and was filled with dread. How could she talk about the letter on live television when she was still questioning herself? How could she speak on mental health when her own felt shaky and subject to change? Her grandmother's hand grasped hers and she leaned in close.

"You gonna be all right Mickey," she said. "Whatever you're crying about, He's going to make it right. But I'm gonna need you to stop boohooing like you're pregnant by somebody's husband. People are going to jump to conclusions and lord knows they don't never know what they talking 'bout."

Mickey laughed through the tears and squeezed her grandmother's hand in return. She wished she were younger so she could lay in her lap, her head nestled across her thighs while her grandmother played in her hair, tracing lines across her scalp until she fell asleep. Instead, she leaned her head on her grandmother's shoulder and tried to pay attention to what was happening in front of her. Somehow, Mickey had picked a longer-than-usual Sunday service, one that included a dance routine by the congregation's preteens and a song by the youngest kids.

By the time they got to the sermon, Mickey was ready to leave, but she half-listened anyway. As soon as the pastor opened his mouth, she waited for something offensive to slip. The shaming was part of the process. You had to be reminded that you were a sinner, imperfect but *made perfect* in God's image. But Mickey was a different type of sinner, the kind whose redemption required her to change so fundamentally that she would no longer recognize herself. And Mickey had never felt closer to God than when she was wrapped up in a woman's arms.

But she'd always admired preaching as an exercise in public speaking, the ability to tell a story from beginning to end, using a text—the same text—to pull out something new each time. Today was about redemption because, of course it was. When the pastor started listing things one could be redeemed from, she was grateful he didn't say homosexuality—the formality of the word always made her giggle. Sermons always had the uncanny ability of saying exactly what you needed to hear, even if you didn't want to hear it.

After, when the pastor had sweated everything he had into an embroidered towel and everyone had done their shouting and Amens, Mickey felt lighter, almost, like something had been lifted from inside her and could be left where she sat. She wondered then if that's what kept people coming back—the release. When she stood, she felt her grandmother's hand on her arm, steadying herself.

It was the first time she'd done that, used Mickey for physical support, and she realized then that things did change, that the passage of time had the power to mold, bend, and renew.

TWENTY-FOUR

It was that very realization that led Mickey floating back to Tee, even though she'd only left her house mere hours ago. She didn't know what she would say, exactly, just that maybe, she could be open to talking about where this left them. She wanted to ask more about the love thing, if there was room for that to grow. She had loved her all this time! Mickey tried not to get ahead of herself but still found herself jumping in headfirst, the thrill of it causing her to shake all over. On the drive over she considered options. Maybe she could go to New York and then come back. Or they could just text and see where things went. Or, or, or.

The air was sticky and thick—so swampy that when Mickey parked Grandma Anna's car in front of Tee's house and stepped out, she couldn't tell where she stopped and the humidity began. She checked the time. It was almost six thirty p.m., so she figured Tee would be home from her shift. Beads of sweat dripped down the back of her neck as she pulled her braids up and out of the way, twisting them into a bun atop her head. There was a car Mickey didn't recognize in front of hers, idling. The taillights glowed yellow-white and red. Mickey got closer and glimpsed Tee in the driver's seat, changing out of her black Safeway polo.

Mickey approached the driver's side, ready to tell Tee that she'd made a choice, that she didn't want Tee to let her go this time. But as she got closer, she realized Tee wasn't alone. Her brain had barely registered the girl sitting next to her, but now she saw her with perfect clarity.

She was beautiful in the way that Mickey was not: her waist impossibly tiny, her thirty-inch weave cascading down her back in perfect waves. Her makeup was matte and expertly applied. Mickey froze, but it was clear they had already seen her. She only had a few seconds to decide what to do. She could make a scene, ask Tee how it felt to kiss another *bitch* with the taste of Mickey on her mouth. Or she could play the unaffected neighbor, a role she'd assumed so many times. She knew how to smile in a girl's face and make sure she was none the wiser, aiding and abetting Tee in her schemes. Mickey couldn't believe she thought this time things would be different. As usual, Jasmine had been right all along.

A window rolled down and the bass-heavy sounds of Gunna flooded their street. Mickey lifted a hand in acknowledgment, an awkward move she'd copied from her father and her grandparents, something she liked to think of as the neighborly salute. From her vantage point, Mickey was able to see the girl up close. She noticed her long lashes first, fluffy voluminous things that were too long to be natural. There were few natural things about her. Her mouth was overplumped and overglossed, her cheekbones unnaturally high. But Mickey was sure she looked good in Instagram photos, that at certain angles she was stunning, and that she knew the best ones.

"Mickey," Tee said, assuming that easy, unaffected smile. "Wassup? You good?"

"Yeah." She checked the time. "Just coming to say goodbye." The word caught in her throat. She hadn't expected to leave things here. Not like this. "I'm heading out tomorrow, maybe even tonight." She threw the last bit out as a bit of a test, eager to see if Tee would react. There wasn't much, except the tiny twitch of her mouth. Otherwise, she didn't show it, her face unaffected and smooth. "Oh cool." Tee leaned back in that easy way and threw her arm behind the headrest, her chin tilted toward the sky. "My bad, let me introduce you to my girl."

Mickey waved. "Hi."

The girl smiled and revealed a row of too-perfect, bleached white teeth. "Hey," she said, and her voice had that sultry rasp that automatically drew you in. Mickey couldn't decide if she was jealous or attracted. She wanted to hate this girl and her big lips, but she had spent so many years hating the women she saw as her replacement. Now she knew they were both members of the same fucked-up team.

"Gia, this is Mickey. We used to be like best friends back in the day."

"Oh cool, you hoop?" Gia asked, and Mickey clocked the skepticism in her gaze and pulled on her skirt.

"Nope, just neighbors. Friends by proximity." Even though the word *friend* was technically accurate, it pained her to say it.

"How long you been in town?" Gia asked, and her eyes briefly cut to Tee. She was looking for any inconsistencies, anything in their story that didn't quite add up.

Tee cut in before Mickey could respond. "Yeah, it's crazy that you're leaving before we even really got a chance to hang out. You know I be so busy working and shit." She turned to Gia. "Her dad lives right there." She gestured toward the house next door.

Mickey held her jaw shut to mask her surprise, or her lack thereof. The hurt came later, a short burst of pain in her chest that shocked her entire system. Instead, she offered her biggest smile. "Definitely. Hopefully I'll be back soon."

Tee bobbed her head. "Cool, cool. You still up in New York? I'm trying to take Gia there one of these days. Go on a li'l weekend getaway." Tee smiled when she said that, using her free hand to grip Gia's thigh, her fingers lingering a little too long. Mickey couldn't help but stare, even though she felt the weight of Gia's gaze on her face. Mickey smiled harder to offset the pain. "We came back from Miami, what was it, babe, two months ago?"

Gia grinned and paused to look at Tee. "Yeah. For Sweet Heat."

Mickey let her lips curl in, but only slightly. She adjusted her voice up a notch, the one she used when talking to friends and coworkers. A nonthreatening, sweet-sounding lilt. "Oh cool! So fun. I've always wanted to go. Whenever you guys come up, just let me know, I have all the good restaurant recommendations."

"You ever been to Times Square?" Gia asked and Mickey tried to keep the amusement out of her expression.

Mickey nodded.

"We'll have to link for sure, show us around," Tee said and Mickey wished she would just look at her, so she could get a sense of what she was thinking, why she was performing like this.

"That would be cool," Mickey said, even though it was anything but. "We can double date." She hoped Gia didn't hear the shake in her voice. "Definitely let me know. Do you even have my number still? It's been so long."

Gia's shoulders relaxed, but only slightly.

"I think I might have you on IG?"

"Okay, cool, just DM me."

"Got you."

Mickey flashed them a final, brilliant smile before stepping back from the car.

"Good to see you, Key," Tee said. "Oh, hold up, I have something I borrowed from your dad, I can grab it quick. Just come in the house."

Mickey tilted her head, and the slight widening of Tee's eyes indicated she wanted Mickey to play along. But she was tired of taking instructions. She didn't want to hear any explanations. There was nothing that justified this. She would no longer accept being half-hidden, shown off when it was convenient.

"Oh, I'm sure you can just drop it off for him whenever you're free!" Mickey said in a tone so enthusiastic, you could hear the exclamation points in her voice. She turned her attention to Gia, who now used an ultra-long, square shaped nail to scoop out weed from a thin plastic bag. "Good to meet you, too, Gia."

Gia smiled. "Nice to meet you," then, a beat. "Sorry I'm so bad with names . . ."

"Mickey," she replied with a tight, toothless grin. "Happens to me all the time."

Tee's grip loosened on Gia's thigh as she shifted off the brake. "Don't be a stranger next time you're in town."

"I won't," Mickey replied, raising a hand in goodbye. The car pulled off and Mickey felt raw and open in a way that made her want to cry. No matter how good she got, it was exhausting to play pretend.

It hurt even worse the second time. She was grown, she knew who Tee was, and she still fell for it. How stupid she was to believe that Tee could change. That she was special. Now, she knew neither to be true.

TWENTY-FIVE

Sometimes heartbreak makes you bold. At least it had that effect on Mickey, who, after weeks of avoiding her father's house, decided to walk right up to its once-red door and knock. When no one came, she rang the doorbell once, then twice. She was relieved to see her father's close-cropped head on the other side.

"Well, look who it is," he said, opening the door wide. "Where's your key?" he asked, pulling her into a hug and dropping a kiss on the top of her head.

"I don't know," she lied, wrapping her arms quickly around his middle.

She wanted to tell her father everything, starting from the beginning, but stepping back into her childhood home, she couldn't help but feel like she was sixteen again, vying for the attention of a heartbroken man.

She was deterred by Boo, who sat on the stairs, trying—and failing—to put on his shoes.

"Hi, Boo," she said, tentatively.

"Hi, Mickey!" he said, with his gap-toothed smile. Mickey studied his face. He looked just like their father—the sloped nose, dark eyes, broad forehead, identical grin. She'd missed watching him grow from this small, swaddled bundle that terrified her into this self-contained person who could call her by name. "I'm going to the park, look at my new shoes!"

He stuck his foot out at an awkward angle to display a pair of gray New Balances. He'd gotten them on, but the laces were hanging limply at the sides. Mickey crouched down in front of him. "Want me to tie your shoes?"

"No, thank you," he replied with a grin. "I'm a big boy, I can do it."

"He's been practicing," her father said. "One second, his chicken nuggets are in the microwave. Watch your brother for me."

She watched her father's back retreat to the kitchen before turning back to Boo. Mickey watched him fumble for the next few seconds and resisted the urge to stick her hand between his and finish the job. She watched as his face contorted into quiet determination, his brow furrowed, mouth slightly open, his little fingers gripping both laces at the same time.

"I can tell you the little story that helped me," Mickey offered, and when Boo looked up at her, it was like she was seeing him for the first time. They had the same eyes, dark brown, almond-shaped things. Pop's eyes. Her dad's eyes. Her eyes. It had never occurred to her that being a sibling meant seeing parts of yourself, often unexpectedly, in somebody else.

He giggled and nodded vigorously. "Okay."

"Is it okay if I do one?" Mickey asked and wondered when she'd become this patient.

"Yup!" he replied, sticking his foot in her face.

She sniffed his sneakered foot, bringing her nose almost to the sole. "Ew, stinky feet!" she shrieked and he scream-laughed and wiggled his feet, daring her to get close again. She smiled and pressed his foot gently to the stair.

Her father reemerged with dinosaur-shaped nuggets in a small plastic bowl, but Mickey hadn't noticed his entrance. When she did, she found him staring back at them, his eyes crinkled at the edges as he watched his two children interact. Mickey ignored the intensity of his gaze and continued, determined to teach.

"Okay, so first, you make a little x, like this." She looped the lace through and pulled tight. She checked Boo's face. "That feel okay?"

He nodded for her to continue. "Then you make loops, like bunny ears. They'll look like this," she explained, creating two exaggerated loops. Then, she began her little rhyme. "Bunny ears, bunny ears, playing by a tree, crisscrossed the tree, trying to catch me. Bunny ears, bunny ears, jumped into the hole, popped out the other side, beautiful and bold." When she was done, it looked a little clumsy, but it would do.

Her father rubbed the top of Boo's head before rubbing hers, further frizzing up her braids. "My kids," he said with a smile. He dropped a kiss on the top of Mickey's head.

"We going to the park, right, Daddy?" Boo asked, twisting his laces back and forth between his slim fingers. He was making them dance now, tying them a distant memory. Her father nodded. "Is Mickey coming to the park?" he asked next, looking up at them both.

Her father looked to her. "Is she coming to the park?"

Mickey considered her options and nodded. "I can come to the park."

Boo shot up with a triumphant "yay!" and did a little dance that Mickey had seen on Instagram. It required stiff arms and moving his body from side to side, threading and alternating as he moved to an imaginary beat. "You're going to play with me, right?"

Mickey nodded that she would.

"Where's Jamila?" Mickey asked.

"At her parents' place," he replied. "It's Boo and Daddy Day."

"Y'all have a day?"

"Oh, don't start that. You did, too."

"It didn't have a name."

"Sure it did, we just never told you," he said with a grin, the kind that made her heart ache.

Boo swung from the monkey bars upside down, his small feet an-chored through a bright yellow hoop. "Look at me, Mickey!" he said. "Look!"

His body hung and his hands stretched down toward the wood chips covering the ground.

"I'm looking!" Mickey called back. She leaned back on the bench, a metal structure that had been painted a shade of deep green. The park was near empty, the only other family a young mother with her daughter who couldn't be older than three. Her father sat to her right, scrolling through his phone.

"What are you doing?" she asked.

"Working," came the reply. Then a yawn. He ran a hand through his salt-and-pepper beard and scratched at the skin underneath. He looked at his daughter and Mickey could see the exhaustion in his eyes. "How much longer you going to be here?"

"Until tomorrow."

"You didn't tell me you were leaving."

"I didn't know until yesterday."

"Work told you to come back?"

Mickey thought about what to say next. He'd set up the lie for her, all she had to do was say yes, they needed her for an interview later in the week. Tell him that she'd send the article when it came out. But she was tired of hiding, of playing this part. "Actually, no. I have to go on TV."

"Oh," he said, looking up from his phone to regard his daughter, eyebrows raising and scrunching his forehead into three meaty rolls. "What channel? We'll tune in."

"*The Early Show.*"

"Wow," her dad said, genuinely impressed, and it was the most emotion she'd seen from him in years. Her father had never been a particularly expressive man, but Mickey felt he'd gotten more detached over the years—pulling back from her the more she lived out loud. He never said anything about her relationship with Lex or made her feel like she was wrong for loving the way she did, but there were little, subtle cues that signaled he didn't totally approve. His lack of interest in her life beyond work was one. "That's big. You think you'll get to meet Melinda and Ed in real life?"

Mickey laughed a little. "Yeah, probably."

"Aw that's what's up. I like Melinda," he replied, a smile playing on his lips. "What's it for? Are you going to talk about one of your articles?"

"Sort of," Mickey replied.

"Mickey!" Boo screamed. "Watch me again!" This time he was moving deftly from bar to bar, the rounded metal fitting neatly in his little hands. Mickey watched as he flipped himself upside down again before dismounting with a flourish, his hands above his head. He took an exaggerated bow and Mickey made a show of clapping enthusiastically.

"You should put him in gymnastics," Mickey commented.

Her father scrunched up his nose at the thought. "Seems like more of a girl thing to me."

"Lots of guys do gymnastics."

He nodded. "That's true. I don't want to make him short though." A pause. "Remember Jerome? Felicia's son?"

"Yeah."

"He did gymnastics. Never got taller than five-four."

Mickey shook her head. "Miss Felicia is five-one."

"Still. Stunts your growth."

"Where did you hear that?"

"I just know," he said, and the matter-of-factness in his voice reminded her why sometimes, even when she did her best to listen to herself, it was his clear baritone she heard instead.

"So, I'm going to be talking about my work but not really one of my articles," she said.

"Oh yeah?" he asked, crossing his foot at the ankle and settling back on the bench. He did this when he was intrigued. "Tell me about it."

Her father often took this position when Mickey was younger and would come home rattling on about all the things she learned at school. He was less concerned with the mundanity of adolescence but seemed to be fascinated with the way Mickey's mind worked—the questions she asked and the books she read. He would push big classical texts into her hands and ask her for her thoughts, curious about her take on things decided long before she was born. When she said something new, or interesting, he would lean back and run a hand over his chin, like he was doing now. Then he would offer his own, often competing, analysis, which Mickey would then absorb as her own.

Once she got to college, their debates got more combative, Mickey absorbing the information and synthesizing it like a sentient sponge. She left for Rutgers and reinvented the old Mickey, building herself into something she no longer recognized but might admire on the street.

Someone her father might find a worthy adversary. She became militant. Radicalized. Told him his ideas about Black masculinity were staid and passé. He laughed at that one and asked her to cite her sources. She pointed him to her heroes—June Jordan, Toni Cade Bambara, bell hooks. It consumed her, her face so deep in critical race theory she psychoanalyzed and pathologized everything from the food in the dining hall to the way white women did their hair. All of it was racist, all of it was unfair. She devoured bell hooks and obsessed over the oppositional gaze, convinced that Black women alone would save the world. She fell asleep with Toni Morrison's words flashing behind her eyelids, and then woke up and read Audre Lorde and realized she'd spent a long time hiding. Everything was a system, a complex maze meant to be puzzled out. Everything was a tool incapable of dismantling the master's house.

"I wrote a letter on the internet about the injustices in the workplace I experienced as a Black woman and it kind of went viral. They want to have me on to talk about it."

Her dad nodded. "And what kind of injustices have you faced?"

The question alone rattled her. How could she explain her trembling hands to her father, who often reminded her that their grandfather had to fight to be an electrician in the fifties and sixties? But she did her best, detailing the way her ideas had been dismissed and buried. How her words were the only things she had and the way they had been twisted to become the property of someone else. When she finished, he wiped his brow and stared ahead at his son.

"Five minutes, Boo!" he called out, and Boo pouted in reply. "Trey," he warned, and Boo stiffened at hearing his more formal name. Richard Hayward III, who was sometimes Trey and often Boo, knew that Trey was the middle ground between a stern talking-to and a spanking. It was best that he tighten up. Mickey only had the one name, and thus less of a warning.

"Are you going to say anything?" she asked.

"Why didn't you tell me you lost your job?" he asked. "You been applying?"

"Not yet."

"So you've been writing blog posts in the meantime?" he asked, his tone became firm, verged on disappointed.

"It wasn't a blog post." Telling her dad it was on Twitter would only make it worse.

He cut his eyes at her and pursed his lips. "What was it then? Because it sure as hell doesn't sound like a job."

"Is that all you care about? Me working? Did you not hear what I just said?"

"Aw come on, Mickey. We all have anxiety." He put the word *anxiety* in scare quotes and screwed up his face in disbelief. "You don't think I'm tired? Or anxious? Whatever you want to call it. We're Black, Mickey. Welcome to America."

"So just because I'm Black I can't have anxiety at work? Or I'm just supposed to suck it up and act like it's not happening?"

"Yes," her father intoned. "Your generation is too soft. You go to work, you go home. As long as your boss isn't being outright racist or discriminating against you, you keep your head down and get it done."

"It's more subtle than that. That's what I'm going to explain."

"I hope you don't get on TV and say what you're saying to me."

"That's exactly what I'm going to do," Mickey replied.

He shook his head. "You're going on this show, unemployed, to talk about why they need to change things at work. We'll see if they hire you after that. And I'm not giving you money to shack up with anybody, either. Boy or girl."

"So there it is," Mickey said, folding her arms across her chest. She fixed her mouth and leaned back, crossing her ankle across her knee. Her pose mirrored his, though she didn't notice. "You have a problem with me and Lex."

"I don't have a problem. I think Lennox is a nice girl."

"But you just called us shacking up. We've been together for five years. Longer than you knew Jamila before you knocked her up."

Her father's eyes, her eyes, shone with aggression. "Watch your mouth. I know you think you're grown but you better remember who you're talking to. That's your brother's mother. And you are my child."

Mickey shook with anger and frustration knowing she could say no more without crossing some invisible line.

"I'm gonna go," she said, and her father didn't stop her. She approached Boo, who had moved on to the slide, kissed both his cheeks, and walked back to the car.

TWENTY-SIX

Mickey's face was still wet with tears when she approached her grandmother's house. There was a strange car in the driveway, a silver four-door sedan with a New Jersey license plate. She wiped her face before opening the door, knowing her grandmother likely had company and would force Mickey to socialize and perform.

Mickey still felt hollow and numb. First Tee, then her father. Everyone she had opened herself up to had disappointed her, and she realized that coming home had been a bad idea. That she should have just trusted her gut and stayed in New York.

She wanted to kick herself for believing Tee could be different, had any capacity for change. Of *course* she had a girlfriend. Of *course* they had been together for months. Of *course* Mickey would only ever be the girl Tee wanted in the dark. As if on cue, her phone came to life and Tee's name stared back at her. She declined the call and opened the door to the house.

The house's smells greeted her; a potpourri blend her grandmother purchased at TJ Maxx filled the air alongside the scent of a fresh laundry-reminiscent reed diffuser Mickey had gifted her last Christmas. Something was cooking on the stove. It smelled like venison, the gamy meat brewing in a thick brown gravy that Mickey's grandmother always paired with collard greens and rice. It was one of Mickey's favorite meals. She kicked off her shoes and was about to ask her grandmother what the special occasion was when a familiar laugh rang out from inside the kitchen. Mickey held her breath.

When she entered the kitchen to see Lex staring back at her, it was as if she was staring at a ghost. Her phone slipped out of her hand and clattered to the ground. She didn't know if this was an answered prayer or a test from the universe, but a rush of emotion consumed her, weakening her knees. She didn't trust herself to walk toward Lex, so instead she stood still.

Lex seemed out of place among her family's things, in what Mickey had come to see as her new home. Lex had been to her grandmother's house before, but never alone, never like this. Grandma Anna was smiling beatifically at Lex, who had slipped into patois. Mickey had come in at the tail end of her storytelling, Lex telling her grandmother about the time her own grandmother had walked in to find Lex, then five years old, covered in a tub of Vaseline. She had been *too slippery to beat*. Lex had initially told that story to Mickey to illustrate how she would *not* be raising their theoretical kids (children that, prior to six weeks ago, seemed like a sure thing), but Lex was laughing now, her charisma making the traumatic seem comical.

"Hi," Mickey said, and both heads turned.

"Hey," Lex said, softening a bit, and Mickey wasn't quite sure of her approach. Their cadence had been disrupted, and Mickey could feel the chasm that had grown between them. Mickey felt panicked at the space and the fact that Lex had shown up here in the first place. Her mind immediately rushed to the worst places. Had someone passed away? Why hadn't Mickey just answered her phone when she called? She sent Lex a panicked look, widening her eyes in alarm, hoping Grandma Anna didn't see, but Lex missed every cue, continuing to woo her grandmother with her easy charm.

One thing Mickey liked about Lex was her ability to handle herself, and her uncanny approval rating among parents. Even the most conservative, uninterested person couldn't resist her charm. It warmed her to see Grandma Anna engaging and smiling back. There was a playful push of a shoulder and then the cackling laugh that Mickey had only ever really heard around family. She saw her life stretch before her in a flash of images, the two of them working hard to figure it out, miraculously bringing their families together along with their own wards. Was that an option? Could they pull it off? Is that what Mickey even wanted?

Mickey needed to touch her. To see if she felt the old hum of desire in her skin, but then thought better of it. Lex's family had put her off from affection of any kind, especially around elders.

"You're here," Mickey said, though it sounded like a question.

Lex nodded. "Yeah. Scottie didn't tell you? I came to pick you up."

Of course Scottie hadn't said anything. It all clicked into place. Lex had come to make sure Mickey didn't back out, and Scottie had hoped that pushing the two together would force them to reconcile.

"Oh, really? And what if I don't want to go?" Mickey asked, crossing her arms.

"Oh, you're going. I want my house and my husband back," Grandma Anna said.

"Grandma! That's gross."

"I'm just saying. You been here for weeks, you can't cook, you complain about cleaning, and you act like a power washer is going to hurt you."

"You wanted me to get on a ladder with that thing and clean the gutters!"

"I've done it," Grandma Anna said. "I have done it. And the Lord kept me."

Lex put a hand over her mouth to stifle a laugh. "Amen," she squeaked.

Grandma Anna looked at Mickey and winked. "At least she's God-fearing."

"You knew that," Mickey replied. "You've met her at least five times."

"Hush up, girl, you know my memory isn't what it used to be."

"Mhm," Mickey said with a skeptical eye. "But somehow you don't forget to tell me what to do every morning."

"That's different. And don't talk back to me. I don't care what you say and if you're going to be on TV, I will still take my slipper off and tear you up."

Mickey widened her eyes and turned toward Lex. "You told her?"

Lex shrugged. "What did you want me to do? Lie? She was going to see at some point."

"I like to be able to tell my business when I'm ready."

Grandma Anna interjected. "Cut all that out, Mickey. Now nobody really believed you was here on a vacation. Don't blame the girl for telling me what was really going on. I *asked*." She stood and began shuffling around, fussing over every steaming dish before opening the fridge and starting the cycle all over again. "Now y'all sit down to the table to eat. Food will be ready any minute."

It was nearly midnight by the time they got out of the house. There were three rounds of goodbyes and insisting that they couldn't stay the night to get them out the door. It was strange to see Grandma Anna treat Lex as if she were one of her own. At previous family gatherings, Lex had just been background noise, present but off to the side, playing with the little ones or joking around with her cousins. It was the first time she'd interacted with Grandma Anna one-on-one and, for a moment, Mickey wanted nothing more than the two of them, here, visiting often and entrenched in the community Mickey had grown up with. But then there was Tee, who had made a home in her heart and promises she clearly couldn't keep. She wished she could snap back and close herself up again unharmed, but she felt split in two.

Lex lifted Mickey's suitcase into the car, tossing it into the trunk with a plop. Mickey was already buckled into the front seat, her phone charging in the built-in port, a car-version of her iPhone taking over the entirety of the screen. She hadn't lifted a finger. In fact, when she mentioned grabbing her stuff, Lex told her to sit down. Mickey had nearly forgotten what it was like to be taken care of, to go through life with an expectation of assistance. A partner and helpmate in all things. She'd missed it, missed Lex, but she would trade all that, including Lex, if it meant never feeling that heaviness again.

"You good to drive?" Mickey asked, gesturing at the clock on the dashboard.

"It's the best time, no traffic," Lex said with a grin, shoving the keys into the ignition and setting off down the road.

But the air in the car still felt different, damp with the reality of the way they'd left off. Mickey hadn't forgotten, even though Lex seemed to be doing her best to make things smooth, beaming and smirking in Mickey's direction as if she'd been waiting for this exact moment her entire life. Mickey felt guilty that she didn't feel the same. She was still thinking about Tee's unanswered call and the conversation with her dad. The minutiae of the life she'd created here and all the people in it.

She looked to Lex, whose curly hair had been pulled up to expose the shaved underside. It was freshly cut, presumably for this, and Mickey wished she would've been able to put a little more effort into being presentable. Her face was still slightly puffy from crying, and she had thrown on a random outfit, the first thing that fit.

The car ride was silent for the first half hour, the two flying down 95 with nothing but the ambient sound of lo-fi R&B soundtracking their journey. It was the easy silence of a life lived alongside each other, comfortable and unhurried. Mickey relaxed into the cloth seats and let herself sink into the silence. Her mind drifted to Tee and there was another pang. This time, so deep, she worried it would swallow her up. She instinctively reached for Lex's hand before feeling bad that she was using Lex to comfort her about someone else. *I had fallen for someone else.* It was the first time she'd admitted that, and the reality sent a shiver up her spine. Suddenly, she wished Lex's hand was Tee's hand, that Tee would hold it close and make it all better like she'd promised.

Her hand stopped just short of her thigh and Lex, glimpsing Mickey's hand out of the corner of her eye, grabbed it before she could completely withdraw. She laced her fingers through Mickey's and there was an instant calming effect, their hands fitting together like they were never meant to be separated. *Why did I think I could give this up for good?* she wondered while she held Lex's hand close, stroking the back of her hand absentmindedly. Lex looked over, her eyes flitting from the road to the outlines of Mickey's face and then back again.

"You're so beautiful," she whispered, and Mickey could tell she meant it. She wondered if Lex could smell Tee on her skin, if she would taste Tee when they kissed.

"Thanks," Mickey said. "You look good, too."

"I really missed you," Lex said. "And I get why you left. I really do. I shouldn't have made you feel bad for being depressed. I should've been supportive and understanding of the situation. It was three weeks, and I was already pushing you. I regret that, really I do."

Had the apology come three weeks earlier, Mickey might've never left at all. But there was more to it now. Mickey knew more about herself, too.

"Thank you for apologizing. I appreciate it. But—"

"I just, I just want us to work on stuff and try to figure it out. I know it won't come together all at once, but it's been five years and I don't think we should, wait, you were going to say something. What were you going to say?" Lex was talking fast, her words coming in a blur.

"Nothing," Mickey said. "Go 'head."

"No, you go," Lex said. "I want to hear you."

Mickey shook her head. "It's nothing."

"Okay. Well, I also wanted to apologize for how I handled everything with the letter. Scottie told me how huge this could be and of course it is because you're brilliant. I looked at Twitter and I can't stop reading how many people really connected with your work. I've always known how talented you are, and I should have said that then."

The authenticity in Lex's voice made Mickey want to scream. She was so sincere, so thoughtful, so *adoring*, but all Mickey could think about was why they were in this situation in the first place. Lex had filled so many roles for so long, and in her absence, Mickey realized she had expected Lex to be her everything. There was no world in which this was sustainable. She knew that now. It was unrealistic, and dangerous. Another part of her, a smaller part she tried to suppress, knew that she needed to figure out the size and shape of the hole in her heart alone, without trying to fill it up with someone else.

"I appreciate that, too."

Lex looked over. "What's wrong? You seem off."

"Off how?"

"I don't know." Lex shrugged. "Different. I guess I thought you'd be more excited to see me."

"It's not that I'm not excited," explained Mickey. "It's just a lot to process. I didn't think I was going to see you today, much less leave."

"Well, when were you planning on coming back?"

Mickey hesitated to provide an answer and the pause prompted a look of alarm in Lex's eyes. "You were thinking of staying."

"I didn't say that."

"You didn't have to."

"I didn't have a plan or anything," Mickey insisted. "I didn't know what I was going to do."

"But it was a thought."

"A thought, yes."

Mickey's phone vibrated and Tee's name popped up on the navigation screen, a single letter *T* glaring back at them. Lex looked at the screen and then at Mickey before looking at the screen again.

"Who's that?" she asked. Mickey didn't answer immediately. She didn't trust herself to lie with any dexterity, not when her stomach felt as if it was going to drop out of her body. She'd been caught. Well, almost. There was nothing solid or concrete yet—no admissions had been made, but Mickey felt the air shift. There were only so many Tees.

"Uh, it's Tee."

"*Tee,* Tee?"

"Yeah."

"What's she doing texting you at one a.m.?"

"We've spoken a few times since I've been home. I ran into her at the grocery store."

Lex nodded and Mickey could sense the suspicion, the unasked questions.

"Why?" Mickey asked, hoping to get in front of it. There was nothing to hide, really. They had been on a break, hadn't they? Or at least that's what she told the knots in her stomach threatening to turn her inside out. The guilt was immense. The shame was, too.

Tee's name pinged again.

"What does she want?" Lex asked, her hands gripping the steering wheel tight. "Open her text."

"It's not that serious," Mickey insisted, turning her phone facedown. Lex pressed on Tee's name and Siri, with her stiff, robotic voice began to read aloud.

"*Message from T.* Mickey please. I can explain everything. Please tell me you didn't leave. I can come to wherever you are. Can we talk? *Would you like to reply?"*

Siri was a fucking snitch.

Mickey leaned her head against the window and braced herself for Lex's wrath. She was rarely angry, but when she was it was a sight to behold. Her entire being would become energized, her voice loud and reedy. The tears were sure to follow. All that emotion had to go somewhere. Lex tended to alternate between crying and cussing. Sometimes both at the same time. But it didn't come.

"So," Lex said, her voice eerily calm. "What is she talking about? What did she do?"

"Nothing," Mickey replied. "Nothing. We're not even speaking anymore."

"But something did happen."

"I don't want to talk about it. Not right now. I can't get into it, Lex. Just . . ." A sigh. "Please."

"Okay." Lex took a deep breath. "Okay."

Mickey nodded. "Okay, good."

Mickey looked over and she wished she hadn't. The hurt she saw there—the folding of her brow, the quiver of her lip, the confusion in her eyes—would haunt Mickey for the rest of her life. She wanted to apologize, to explain, but the words wouldn't come.

In the distance, the signs guiding them home glowed green. Mickey stared out at the stretch of highway, only darkness ahead of them.

TWENTY-SEVEN

When Mickey woke up the next morning, Lex was gone. There was a note on the bedside table that simply read *I love you*, with a glass of water on top. They had gotten home at four a.m., and the rest of the ride home had been awkward, bordering on painful, all the unsaid things stretching between them like a flimsy rubber band.

It wasn't until Mickey opened her eyes that she realized she was back home in Astoria. She found herself listening for the sound of Grandma Anna's shuffling feet, but it had been replaced by the metallic clunk of the train and the staccato beeps of passing cars. She stretched wide, her hands feeling around the bed, waiting to bump into a calf, ankle, or arm, but there were only sheets sliding beneath her and a folded piece of paper, propped up like a little tent.

Then, she remembered, and her chest ached. Things had gotten complicated when they got home, and with her interview less than a day away, she had to pretend that everything had been all right. Lex had tried to sleep next to her but woke in the middle of the night, shaking Mickey awake. *She had to go*, she said. *To clear her head*. Mickey didn't know what she would get up to do at five o'clock in the morning, but she didn't protest. She had let her go—she needed to figure things out, too. Back in their home, the realization of what Mickey had done set in. She had risked this, complicated this. Guilt crept in, threatening to swallow her up.

In preparation for *The Early Show*, Lex had made an appointment for Mickey to get her braids touched up and her nails done. But first, Scottie. Mickey picked up her phone to see a text from her best friend-turned-publicist glowing back at her.

"On the train now, I'll be there in thirty! Let's talk outfits," it read. Mickey pressed a palm to her face, she hadn't realized the time. She dragged herself out of bed and threw on an oversized dress, and then headed to the bathroom to splash water on her face, staring back at her reflection until she felt like a distortion of herself. She clearly looked like she'd been crying for days, which she had, her face slightly swollen and plump.

Scottie arrived at her door almost exactly on time, lattes in both hands. LA had been good to her, deepening her bronze skin and lightening her hair. Mickey wondered if it was hard to look this effortless, Scottie's nude two-piece set pleated and flowing in all the right places.

Scottie pulled Mickey close the moment she opened the door, nearly dumping coffee all over Mickey's dress. They rarely hugged, so Mickey stiffened in her arms, unsure of what to do with the boniness of Scottie's frame.

"Girl," Scottie whined. "Hug me back."

Mickey closed her arms around Scottie and squeezed tight. "Sorry, we just don't hug."

"Today we do. It's been a lot."

Mickey could agree that it had been, but she didn't trust herself to speak. Seeing Scottie had loosened all the wound-up bits, and now they threatened to spill forth. And they needed to decide on an outfit.

Once in the apartment, Scottie slammed the coffees down on the kitchen counter and made a beeline for the bedroom, throwing open Mickey's closet and drawers with a critical eye.

"Cute dress," Scottie said, holding up a brown plissé dress with a mock neck.

"Really?" Mickey asked, frowning. "I feel like brown washes me out. I want something a little more chill."

"I feel like brown makes you pop," Scottie insisted, before tucking it back inside the color-coded closet. "But fine. It's your day. What are you thinking?"

Mickey shrugged. "I dunno. A T-shirt maybe?"

Scottie rolled her eyes. "What about this?" she asked, holding up a red dress with floral detailing and a cap sleeve.

Mickey scrunched up her nose. "Eh, it feels like a *Sound of Music* vibe."

"Okay, fair," says Scottie. "But I think it's giving breezy, effortless summer vibes." Scottie released Mickey and looked her over. "Not the move for *The Early Show*, but I'm a fan."

The two made eye contact and broke into matching grins. Neither had quite gotten used to being separated by thousands of miles. "I missed you, too. How was the flight?"

Scottie let out a groan. "Girl, somehow I always end up on a red eye so I'm exhausted."

"Well, I appreciate you making the trek for little old me."

"Of course. There was no way I was going miss my best friend becoming a superstar."

Mickey's mouth went dry at the word *superstar*, which now felt coded for Tee. Tee had been texting her nonstop, but Mickey couldn't bring herself to respond. It was surreal to feel chased by her, to be the one on the receiving end. She always wished the tables would turn, and now she wasn't sure she wanted that at all.

"It's just a TV spot."

"Bitch," Scottie said, her eyes rolling. "Don't be silly. This is '*The*' *Early Show*. Millions and millions and *millions* of viewers. It's going to change your life. You just don't know it yet." Then a smile, a genuine one. "I'm so proud of you."

Mickey beamed, because she knew Scottie meant it, even though she wasn't sure if she could be proud of herself just yet. "Thanks," Mickey said, the smile falling inch by inch from her face. "It just doesn't feel like there's much to be proud of."

"Last time I checked I'm here because you're going on THE EARLY SHOW tomorrow. How many times do I have to say that? How many *people* can say that?"

"Yeah, but I had to lose myself to get here. And I still don't have a job."

"Trust me, after tomorrow, everyone will be fighting to give you one.

Plus, transformation requires sacrifice," Scottie said, and Mickey was sure that last one had come from one of the yoga classes Scottie was always going to. "Oh, I forgot to mention—they want you to read the letter on air."

"Wait, what?" The air went staticky and Mickey wondered when Scottie had been planning on telling her that she needed to bare her soul—loud and bold—on national TV. She'd pored over the letter many times before, but reading it aloud, live on air, that was beyond comprehension. "Oh, you're going to spring it on me just like that?"

Scottie dismissed Mickey with a wave of her hand. "You'll do fine. I've read it, I think it'll roll off the tongue." Scottie brought her coffee to her lips and stared at Mickey over the lip of the cup, waiting.

Mickey laughed. "Fuck you. You knew what you were doing."

Scottie raised a hand in protest, her pale palm facing Mickey. "I promise I saw the email when I landed."

Mickey ran a hand over her braids, twirling one between her fingers. "So what? I'm supposed to just read it?" Mickey inhaled sharply. "That's a lot."

Scottie waved her concern away. "We can practice." Scottie's face looked expectant, and Mickey cocked her head to one side.

"Right now?"

"When else?"

Mickey cried out, "I don't wanna." She pulled up the note on her phone anyway, amazed how these few paragraphs had completely upended her life. They stared back at her, and she felt a rush of pride. This wasn't just a celebrity roundup or a trend report—this was her, Mickey, describing her world as she saw it.

But the longer she looked at the text, the more it seemed to morph into something terrifying, unwieldy. Millions of people would hear her words, and then they would quickly stop being her own. She would be memeable: her voice could be interpolated to become the hook of a Drake song or a cringey reaction gif and there wouldn't be much she could do about it. She opened her mouth to read the first line, but nothing came out.

Scottie was staring at her expectantly. "I can't do it," Mickey said, her voice defeated.

"Oh," Scottie replied, pressing a hand to her chest and pouting her lips. "You're so cute. Start at the beginning. The first sentence even."

"Okay," Mickey said. She took a deep breath. There was no safer space than this, here at home with her best friend.

"To The New Me,

"I hope that when you read this, you are not sitting at the desk where I once spilled an entire cup of tea and no one rushed to help me clean it." Mickey took another breath, then dove right back in.

"I say this not because there's still a stain (I did a very good job cleaning it up) but because I spent what felt like a lifetime screaming into the void of a place where it seemed like no one had ears. A place where my needs were ignored in favor of using me as a prop, trotted out as proof that we were not, in fact, working in a white echo chamber, that there were at least a few dots on the page. A fly in the buttermilk. A brown crayon in the box. In reality it was barely a year, something I'm sure you'll realize once you settle in.

"They will make it seem like I never fit, like my exit was inevitable. And maybe it was. That's the thing with being Black, right? We never know if it's us or the skin suit they see, the one that clings so tightly to our bodies that it turns everything inside black, too. They think that until they see us bleed, shocked, if only slightly, that it's the same purple-red."

Scottie snapped her fingers like they were at a poetry slam and made a motion for Mickey to continue. Mickey laughed a little and rolled her eyes before scanning the note to find her place.

"I hope they give you a new desk, not the one that belonged to me or the other Black girl who was there one day and gone the next. I hope they give you something of your own. I hope you aren't compared, constantly, to a white woman who does less with more and constantly tells you you're coming up short, despite trying, every day, to do your best.

"I hope they don't ask about your hair, touching it wordlessly in their minds. Curious when you change it, horrified when they don't recognize you at first glance.

"I hope they don't turn you into a scapegoat, forcing you from the ivory tower with a swift kick and a couple grand to keep you silent.

Because they will try to silence you, in the end. They will, like Zora promised, kill you and pretend that you liked it because they'll rob you of your ability to speak.

"It'll be tempting to shut up. I almost did. Well, I did, and now I'm not because you, Gabrielle," Mickey winced at the name, "I'll cut that," and Scottie nodded.

"You inspired me—if only because I couldn't let you go out like that. I couldn't let another one of us go into that wilderness with nothing but good clothes and a smile.

"Or maybe I'm being naïve, and you don't need my help. Maybe you already know. Maybe you had someone to tell you how to send a thank-you note and type an email with enough exclamation points to make white women comfortable. Maybe you had someone to tell you to ask for more money (I hope you asked for more money). Maybe you know how to smile. I hope so, because I never could quite make both corners of my mouth lift at the exact same time. I always struggled to hold my rage tight in my belly and suck in my stomach. Never mind the smiling.

"It won't be easy, although I'm sure you now know that nothing, not even stepping into a role that promises freedom, is easy in this industry. That the only easy thing is, unfortunately, to bow out. But there are good things, too, moments when you'll feel the full heat of the sun, the full weight of attention. I hope you have more moments like those than I did, that when you read this you're still be ignorant to the way they chew us Black girls up, gnawing thoughtfully, picking our limbs from between their teeth. Using our look as templates for their own.

"Don't let them hide it. Plant the evidence like seeds for us to find. We'll know because we've always had to read between the lines to survive.

"In Solidarity, Mickey Hayward."

When Mickey was done, she felt that old rage bubbling inside her, a faithful friend. But something else met her there, too. A certainty that she had done the right thing. She ventured to look Scottie in the eyes, and she swore they were a little misty.

Homebodies

"Fuck," Scottie said.

"Yeah," Mickey replied.

Mickey stood on the street until Scottie's car turned the corner and she became a dot in a sea of traffic headed to the city. She meant to turn around and go back to her apartment, but her legs carried her to a nearby park instead. It was teeming with people intoxicated with the warmth of a perfect summer day: 83 degrees and sunny, with the hint of a breeze. A group of teenaged boys were messing around on skateboards, kickflipping and failing, the sharp thwacks hitting the concrete like a drum. Kids ran from their parents, steps ahead of their strollers and scooters, their bodies tearing through the air like they were fighting gravity. Groups of twenty-somethings languished on blankets and sheets, sipping wine, smoking weed, playing music loud. Families gathered. Then there were the couples, leaning close, holding hands, closer than the heat should allow. Mickey remembered when she had that, when the world watched her, and she didn't care who saw.

She found a nearby, half-shaded bench and sat down. She knew she should have been back at her apartment prepping, but the sun felt too good on her skin. She wondered what people thought when they saw her now, how they would see her on their television sets. Black girl, long braids, thick thighs, alone. Would they think her dress was frumpy or oversized and cool? Would they want to be her friend? Would they get that she was a writer, a real one? Someone who got paid to whip up snappy paragraphs and go to events? Would they think she was just okay at her job? Would she be believed?

Could they tell she liked women? All women, but especially the ones who dressed like boys but were all the soft things underneath? Did they know she'd gone viral? Changed her little bit of the world? Did they know, though Mickey was sure they couldn't possibly tell, that she was terrified of loving the people who loved her for real? That she feared one day, everyone would appear from behind some thick, heavy curtain and say *gotcha!* all at once? That she had done all this loving for free, and they'd all just been pretending to love her back? Did they think she was a fraud? Or, and this scared her the most, would they perceive her at all? Or was she just another face in the crowd?

For now, at least, she was just another Black girl on a park bench, soaking up the nice weather, looking for love or perhaps filled with it, fated to fade into the background, forgotten when the sun went down.

TWENTY-EIGHT

Miriam's braiding shop was an hour away on the train, but it was worth the trip. The shop, which had white MDF paneling for walls and a small TV on a stand that played episodes of *Supernatural* on a seemingly endless loop, was located on a busy street in Brooklyn, down the street from a Jamaican bakery that made dense, hard dough bread.

When Mickey emerged from its confines, her hair was slicked and swooped and fresh, her scalp glistening in the sun. Afterward, Mickey felt like she was floating, *she could really do this*. She practically danced her way to the subway, her steps light as she trotted down the stairs and into the throngs of people commuting to and from work. It was midafternoon and Mickey couldn't tell if people were coming or going. She fished her MetroCard out of her wallet and swiped, pushing herself through the turnstile and deeper into the station. She waited on the platform for the train, pushing her earbuds back into her ear. She was a few minutes into her podcast when she felt a tapping on her shoulder.

The beginnings of a panic attack coursed through her body as she whirled around to see who was demanding her attention. She was relieved to find that it was just a girl, one who reminded Mickey of herself. She, too, had knotless braids that licked at her tailbone. She looked vaguely familiar, but Mickey couldn't place her. Did they follow each other on Instagram?

"Sorry," the girl began. "I saw you and I just had to say hi."

Mickey pulled out an earbud. "Hi. Good to see you."

"You probably don't remember me."

"Can you remind me of your name?"

"I'm Zariah."

Mickey smiled to mask her embarrassment of not remembering. She knitted her brows together and tried again. It wasn't ringing a bell.

"I was an assistant at Bevy and we'd DMed a little bit when I was still in college. I reached out to ask you about your experience."

"Oh yeah, I remember," Mickey lied. "How'd that work out?"

Zariah shrugged, her shoulders bobbing up to her ears and back down. "It went. I mean, I was grateful for the experience, don't get me wrong, but I thought it would be different."

"I get that. It's never what we expect."

There was a beat of silence and Mickey waited for her to leave so she could go back to her episode.

"I saw your letter on Twitter," Zariah said. Mickey fought for a smile, but she was sure it looked more like a grimace. She knew lots of people had seen her tweet, but she hadn't expected a public spotting by a near stranger. It was embarrassing, almost, to be recognized in this way. Zariah stepped closer and Mickey resisted the instinct to step back. "It kind of changed my life."

Mickey smiled, and her embarrassment faded into something softer. Then, excitement. A real-life person, a Black one, had read it. And it had meant something. Yes, she'd scrolled through the DMs, but this was different. This was real life.

"Wow, thank you. I'm really glad it spoke to you."

"It did," Zariah confirmed, her mouth widening. "I had an epiphany basically."

Mickey tilted her head to one side. "Really?"

"Yeah. I started working at one of the Bevy titles a little while after I interned, and it was the same shit you went through. I thought I'd have to put up with it forever. Well, until a few weeks ago. I quit."

A shock reverberated through Mickey's chest and then her stomach flipped. She wanted to ask questions, but she didn't trust herself not to say something shocking. "Wow," she replied instead. "Good for you. So, you were there when everything went down?"

"I was—at my little cubicle in the basement," Zariah said, and Mickey swore she saw a mischievous twinkle in her eye. Then, Zariah smiled, the kind of smile you put on when you're stupidly sure you made the right decision.

Mickey found it disturbing. How could she be so sure? She hoped it wasn't Mickey's letter that did it for her, it was too much responsibility for her to bear. *Is this,* Mickey wondered, *what it was like to give it up to God?* Maybe the girl had both: God and Mickey.

"I feel really good about it," said Zariah, as if responding directly to Mickey's thoughts.

"What are you doing now?"

"I don't know, but it feels good, you know? I just don't want to keep operating under these post-capitalist conditions and seeking validation from a space that will never actually see me. Those places aren't for us. Even if they include us, they'll never make it completely comfortable for us. But what am I saying? You get it. You got out."

"I get it, I do," Mickey said, even though now she felt like a parrot. Like a fraud. Mickey wanted to say that she was forced out, but she didn't bother correcting her. She didn't want to be yet another "never meet your heroes" story, though she was sure Zariah would say something along those lines anyway. She didn't have any gems to drop or additional nuggets of wisdom to offer. Just a few smiles and affirming nods. Internally, she was losing it. They hadn't even pushed Zariah out; she'd just been inspired to action. Now Mickey understood why they banned books.

"You spoke up for us and I really fucked with that. It changed my whole perspective. Anyway, what are you up to now? It would be cool if you started something of your own."

Mickey nodded. "For sure. Right now, I'm just writing my own thing." A lie. A big one.

"I love that." The N train pulled into the station and Zariah rocked back on her heels. "Is this you?"

"Yeah, it is."

"Oh, me too."

The two women stepped onto the train and Mickey wondered if they looked like friends. Zariah plopped down on an available bench and Mickey sat beside her.

"Even after being in New York for two years, I still don't think I'm used to the subway."

Mickey laughed. "Where are you from?"

Zariah smiled. "Guess. Everyone says I have an accent."

Mickey hadn't heard one. "I need a hint."

"Girlaaaa, you 'bout to meet me down Gallery or what?"

Mickey's eyes widened slightly and a smile, a real one, consumed her face. "You're from home?"

Zariah nodded with a smile, thrilled her performance had translated.

"What high school did you go to?"

"McNamara."

"Oh nice," Mickey replied. Zariah felt almost like a mirror now, and for a moment Mickey wondered if she was losing her mind and making her up.

"Do you go back a lot?"

Zariah snorted. "Girl, no. I've been back twice since I moved up here."

"How come?"

"Running around," her hand did a motion that suggested a lot was going on. "I don't have the time. Plus, there's nothing there for me. Just all the people I went to high school with doing the same shit they were doing five years ago."

"Whew, a word."

"It's wild."

"So, where'd you go to college?"

"Bowie."

"Oh, so you stayed local."

"Yeah, it was nice. I lived on campus though. I could not have done that commuting shit."

"Oh god no."

"Did you like it?"

"I did." Zariah nodded in an old church lady kind of way. "I did. It was a good experience. I couldn't wait to move here though."

"Do you think you'll stay?"

"I hope so," Zariah said with a shrug of her shoulders. "I just know my mental health isn't worth the stuff I was going through."

"That bad?" Mickey asked. This gave Mickey a glimmer of hope. If it had been truly egregious, then maybe Mickey had just given her the push she needed.

"Not the worst. Just overworked and underpaid. Dealing with the slick racist shit. You know, the usual."

So, it hadn't been that bad, or particularly racist. Mickey's stomach turned again.

"I just want to write," Zariah continued. "Things that make Black women feel seen. That's all I care about. And I felt like I couldn't do that anymore."

"I get that. That's all I want to do, too."

"Shit, you're doing it."

"Barely," Mickey said, and her breath caught at the slip.

"Girl, what? Your tweet is still the topic of discussion in the group chat. Mine at least."

Fucking group chats. Mickey almost laughed out loud at her trajectory. She'd gone from being cast out to being the topic at hand, her words quoted and analyzed and *discussed*. It was all she'd ever wanted, but now she felt herself yearning for more connection. More engagement. Writing that felt alive and real.

"I just feel like you're going to change the world," Zariah said. "You changed mine."

Mickey didn't know she could blush that hard, that she could feel it from the top of her head to her toes. Her? Change the world? She'd like to think she could do something like that. But didn't everyone? They pulled slowly into another station and Zariah popped up.

"This is me," she said.

So soon? Mickey wanted to say. Instead, she replied, "Okay, well, it was good to meet you." Another smile. "Again."

"Good to see you."

"Yeah. I look forward to reading your work."

"And I look forward to reading yours."

Mickey gave her a small wave and watched her disappear into the crowd. The doors closed and the automated announcer droned on about the next stop. As the train pulled off into the tunnel, she felt grateful just to be alone. She put her earbud back in, restarted her podcast, and texted Scottie a few additional outfit ideas for tomorrow.

Mickey couldn't shake the thought of Zariah for the rest of the ride. She found herself wondering about her 401K and if she had any savings, if she had something lined up in the meantime. Or if she was just existing off vibes and manifestation—had she helped or hurt her? Mickey couldn't be sure. That's what fucked with her.

Zariah seemed happy, she seemed free. But it had only been a week. There was still time to regret her decision. Still time for this to be the inciting incident that propelled the rest of Zariah's life into a series of shoulda-coulda-woulda's. She'd go from brilliant and employed to struggling—a bright light snuffed out. And by one of her own.

She tried to call up the image of Zariah at work, attempting to place her in the employee kitchen, in the bathroom, in the hall. She cycled through every scenario until she dialed into one that was right. She imagined Zariah's name in her inbox, asking for . . . oh *shit*. Teagan's Net-a-Porter order had once got mixed up in Mickey's mountain of packages and Zariah had emailed, politely asking for it back. She searched through her phone for her photos and found the original screenshot of the likers, she had wanted to commemorate the post the morning after. And there she was. Zariah's handle—Zariahonfiya—stared back at her. It dawned on Mickey that she was the only Bevy person who had liked her post.

Fuck, Mickey said, her mouth turning downward, impressed. After everything, Zariah would be all right.

The train doors opened at the next stop, and Mickey briefly looked up from her scrolling to survey the newcomers, just in case someone crazy stepped on and she needed to switch seats.

The clump of locs caught her eye first, then the cut of a jaw. Mickey's stomach dropped and flipped. Next to the jaw was a girl whose hair was long and fake. Mickey stared at her lap before trying to watch them from the corner of her eye. She saw the hands of the darker one. She knew those hands, had kissed those fingertips, had licked them clean. They were intertwined with someone else's. The girl. Mickey soon realized they weren't watching, that the magnetic pull she'd imagined between her and Tee only existed when there was no one else in the room. She didn't see her in a room full of people, or even a half-empty train car. Mickey stared back at their hands and wondered how long she'd been with this girl, if there had been overlap between the two. If they'd shared Tee days or hours apart. Her stomach twisted and she thought of Lex, the way she'd placed everything on the line for something half-formed. She dared to look up, and when she did, she realized it was someone else. It wasn't Tee at all.

TWENTY-NINE

The studio lights were brighter than Mickey anticipated. She didn't know what to expect from a set, but it was high octane, everything in bright, oversaturated technicolor. She worried about her outfit. Hoped she'd made the right choice. Scottie insisted that only the top half mattered, but Mickey had wanted to pick out something that looked cohesive from head to toe. On top, she wore a T-shirt that said Diversity & Illusion (a not-so-subtle nod to Elaine, who hadn't texted her since their FaceTime) and a flouncy black skirt to match. Her braids were pulled back from her face, and she wore a striking red lip, carefully applied by a makeup artist who had also read the letter. She told Mickey she was proud to beat her face, and that lit her up from the inside out.

"You ready?" Scottie asked, materializing by her side.

"I think so? Is it normal to be this nervous?"

"If you weren't, I'd be surprised."

Mickey inhaled deep. "How long?" She asked.

"Two minutes."

"Can I have my phone?"

Scottie handed Mickey her phone, which was lit up with notifications. First, a text from Lex. It read: "I always said you'd be Oprah big. This is your Oprah moment." Mickey smiled at that, the familiar feelings of love and adoration panging in her chest. Despite everything, there was still so much love.

Then, a text from her father with a picture of the back of Boo and Jamila's heads. They were tuned in to *The Early Show*. "We're so proud!" it said. Mickey felt the tears coming on, threatening to ruin her makeup. She dabbed at her eyes. It didn't fix everything, but it was a start.

Finally, a single question mark from Tee. As if beckoning Mickey to answer. At that, Mickey closed her phone.

"You ready?" Scottie asked, squeezing Mickey's shoulder once, then twice.

Another deep breath. "As ready as I can be."

"Girl, you got this. Remember, you're the most brilliant woman I know."

She squeezed one of Scottie's hands and stepped up to the wings. A woman wearing all black and a headset spoke quickly, explaining what would happen next.

Mickey Hayward.

Suddenly, it was her turn.

She tried to go over what she planned to say in her head. Scottie had coached her through it. To hit the talking points. Media—broken but fixable. Mickey—strong and capable of doing that. The job offers would roll in, Scottie said. She'd have her pick. Or she could start something of her own. Apparently newsletters were going to be the next big thing.

But she also considered blowing it all up, pulling a *Tangela* and attempting to burn everything to the ground and herself down with it, using her rage to force a real change. She looked at her phone and reread the letter, and something clicked. She knew what she would say now. Knew exactly what to do.

The lights came on, illuminating her skin. She caught a glimpse of herself in the monitor, her face beaming back at her. There it was. There she was. Her light, her sun.

Acknowledgments

This was the book I had to write before I wrote anything else. A story I needed to tell. And I'm so grateful that I had a community of people to get me there.

There's so many thank you's:

Danielle Bukowski, brilliant. Perfect. One of one. An agent above all agents. You keep me sane and aware and excited about everything to come. Thank you for navigating these waters with me. To Sterling Lord Literistic, I'm grateful to be counted among your ranks.

Danny Hertz and Gotham Group, for envisioning worlds for *Homebodies* beyond the pages of this book.

Emma Kupor. This is ours. I'm grateful for your insight, your perspective, and wisdom. You believed in this at every step, even when I wasn't sure I was saying what needed to be said. Thank you for reading between the lines.

To HarperCollins and HarperCollins UK—Melanie and Manpreet—for falling in love with the book and making sure everyone else did too. The support has been beautiful to say the least.

Natalie Hallak. You saw me early, and often. Thank you for reading (and rereading) and supporting this book every step of the way. I'm eternally grateful to you for holding the door open.

To the Stuyvesant Writing Workshop crew, thank you for seeing Mickey. For loving her like I do and holding her close.

Acknowledgments

Nicole Dennis-Benn, your support and belief in this work is immeasurable. You told me this was not a short story but a novel, and (unsurprisingly) you were right. You saw into this world and this character when it was five workshop pages, with just a supermarket and two girls seeing each other for the first time in a long time in a checkout line.

Sara Burnett, Dana Lotito-Jones—thank you for reading close. For investing in me and this work. For cheering me on every step of the way.

Allison Corralejo, to sum up what you've meant to me and this novel—words are insufficient. Thank you, for the one a.m. rereads, the crazy plot pitches, the psychoanalyzations of the characters' identities for hours on end, the podcast-length voice notes, the belief, the support. Just everything, everything, everything.

Madison Mikell, for reading as many times as I asked, and assuring me that nothing was lost along the way. Thank you for being one of my people and holding space for all that I am.

Madison Utendahl, for being a model human being and the epitome of grace. Thank you for affirming me every step of this journey and speaking life into my goals and dreams. Because of you I know it's not if, but when.

Maya Singleton, for helping me understand Tee's world. Without you, I wouldn't know what a double-double is, or if the words sounded right on the page. I'm your biggest fan.

Carrie Carrollo, you affirmed my dream when it was a whisper. When it was the thing I was too afraid to say out loud. For listening to every whisper since. Being your goalmate changed my life.

Chayla Lewis, thank you for being my mirror and showing me parts of myself I couldn't see on my own. Your impact on me is incalculable. I love you always and in all ways.

To Lacey Herbert—my first call and best decision—and Chamel McBride—my confidante and sister-friend—without the two of you I wouldn't know friendship. Thank you for seeing me through this life and anchoring me. I know that with the two of you next to me, I'll always find my way back to myself, I can always come home.

To Chubbz, my brother in all things. You were excited for me before I was excited for me. I love to grow alongside you, because sometimes you see me before I see myself.

Acknowledgments

To my family—aunts, uncles, cousins, play-cousins—the way you love me and accept me and cheer for me means more to me than you'll ever know.

Uncle Kenny, you knew who I could be from early. Thank you for taking me (and my dreams) seriously from time.

Uncle Bryan, I know if you could have read this, you would have been so proud.

Uncle Timmy, for your unending and unwavering support across oceans and seas.

Auntie Chandra and Auntie Debbie for mothering me every summer, holiday, and long weekend. I've always felt like yours, too.

And my cousin-siblings—Halimah, Azizah, Mohsen, Samiah, Kaylah—for making it easy for me to be myself. You've never asked me to be anyone else.

To Kadidra McCloud, for talking me up and calming me down. Life is better with you in it.

To Tasmin Hurst, who will read this one day and know that life really started for me when I met you.

To Sharif Denton, for seeing the best in me, and thinking I'm pretty cool. Big compliment coming from you. I love you.

To Nace Denton-Hurst, for being my first best friend, the other half of TembeNace, my sister, and an endless source of support. I only ever want to make you proud.

To Grandma Da, Grandma Sarah, and Daddy Vic—my cornerstones, my building blocks. You three have loved me from the day I was born and nurtured me every day since. I love y'all.

To Stacey Denton and Tazewell Hurst III (also known as Mom and Dad), I am because you are. Two halves to make a hyphenated whole. Thank you for raising me to believe that I could do anything and that my words hold weight and have meaning. For putting books in my hands and encouraging me to write.

Connay, home is wherever you are. Thank you for this life, our life. It's more beautiful than anything I could've ever imagined.

And to the girls who look and love like me, I hope you see yourself on every page. This is for y'all. For us.

About the Author

TEMBE DENTON-HURST (known on the internet as @tembae) is a book-obsessed beauty and culture writer and author. Currently, she works as a staff writer at *New York* magazine's The Strategist, where she covers beauty, lifestyle, and books. When she's not writing, Tembe can be found on her couch in Queens, where she lives with her partner and their two cats, Stella and Dakota. *Homebodies* is her debut novel.